♦ ♦ ♦ ◇ ♦ ♦ ♦

HARMONY

HARMONY

C. F. BENTLEY

DAW BOOKS, INC.

DONALD A. WOLLHEIM, FOUNDER

375 Hudson Street, New York, NY 10014

ELIZABETH R. WOLLHEIM

SHEILA E. GILBERT

PUBLISHERS

http://www.dawbooks.com

First Printing, August 2008
1 2 3 4 5 6 7 8 9

DAW TRADEMARK REGISTERED
U.S. PAT. AND TM. OFF. AND FOREIGN COUNTRIES
—MARCA REGISTRADA
HECHO EN U.S.A.

PRINTED IN THE U.S.A

For Father Richard Toll
who helped me find one path to Harmony.

ACKNOWLEDGMENTS

Tackling a book as big and complex as "Harmony" involves more people than I know how to count. Many thanks to Deborah Dixon, the best brainstorm partner there is and to beta readers Lea Day and Jessica Groeller. I owe a group hug to the people of Joys Of Research list group for their invaluable help. If I've misinterpreted your suggestions and facts, please forgive. Shelia Gilbert, the best editor in the business, and Carol McCleary of the Wilshire Literary Agency showed me ways to make this book possible. And much love goes to my husband and the rest of the family for putting up with my moods, my need to immerse myself in this world to the exclusion of all else, and my neglect of simple housekeeping. You reminded me to eat, sleep, and breathe when I forgot. You make me a better person and a better writer.

Then there are all those who have taken me by the hand and led me through the convoluted paths of faith and perception. You know who you are. That's more than I can say for myself sometimes.

CHAPTER ONE

SWIRLING, TURNING, DIVING deep and deeper. Sissy let her mind follow the guts of the nav unit where it wanted to take her. There! That's where she needed to place the final chip.

A yawning vacancy beckoned her to fill it with the black crystal grown in a matrix of Badger Metal.

Not yet, she told the opening. *I can't let you come alive until I get this last chip in place.*

Sissy du Maigrie pu Chauncey hummed as she picked up the precious, fine-as-a-hair piece of silicon with Badger Metal tweezers. "Two more pieces to the puzzle and I can go home."

She bent over her workbench in concentration, allowing her dark hair to swish forward and form a shield between herself and the rest of the world. Then she hummed a little louder, completing the barrier.

Badger Metal, a ceramic-metal alloy in a crystalline lattice, gave her tools the tensile strength necessary to hold steady the sliver of microscopic computer circuits as she rotated the navigational guidance system to the proper place. She adjusted the note in the back of her throat, seeking a harmonic vibration between herself, the unit, and the chip. When all was ready and sympathetic, she deftly dropped the chip into place. It nestled snugly in its proper location, precisely between two upright crystals.

Robots could make most of a spaceship. But only she and a very few others could assemble the tiny pieces of the interstellar guidance system. Someone had described the process to her in big words she didn't understand. She just did what felt right. No exotic magnification. Just her and the nav unit.

Her ability made her one of the highest paid workers in the factory. The money she brought home meant that her extended family could all live together in two connected flats, as the Goddess Harmony ordained.

Sissy sat back and breathed deeply. A fine sheen of perspiration coated her face and back. The large workroom seemed brighter and noisier, jangling her nerves.

The dinner bell gonged. A raucous note that didn't harmonize with the chips, or with her.

Quittin' time. She sensed only a few workers clearing off their workbenches and heading out. Management, meaning Lord Chauncey, didn't appreciate workers who left unfinished items overnight.

Sissy would have stayed even if management tried to push her out. She had to get the black crystal column in place and the housing fastened around it before she could go home. The High Council needed this last system to complete their upgrade of the military fleet.

She shuddered at the idea of alien invaders and predators pressing against the Harmonic Empire from every direction, threatening their sovereignty as well as their culture, religion, and prosperity.

If she had built the nav system on the Lost Colony's ship, they wouldn't have gotten lost in hyperspace.

"You done yet, Sissy?" her older brother Stevie da Jaimey pa Chauncey called. He was responsible for making certain the components were packaged and cushioned properly by other workers and getting them to the shipping bay on time. He couldn't go home until she finished.

His caste mark, a brown X on his left cheek, the same color as his hair, stood out in stark contrast with his pale skin. Day shift Worker caste rarely saw the sunlight except in high summer.

"One more minute," she called back and plucked the black crystal from its nest of cushioning material with a special padded tool. This final and crucial piece of the nav system anchored a ship to a homing beacon so it couldn't get lost in hyperspace.

Scientists in a secret lab grew the black crystals very slowly with liquid Badger Metal thoroughly mixed in the growing solution. Temple caste supervised every step of the process with special rituals and chimes in the crystal nurseries, a different note in each room to guide the crystal formation to its final purpose.

She found a note within the crystal and matched it with her voice. All in harmony for the final insertion.

Gently she tapped a button on the floor with her bare toe. A wheel in her workbench began a slow rotation with the navigational unit fixed firmly in its center. Once around, and she spotted the precise place to anchor the crystal. A micrometer off and the nav system wouldn't lock on to a beacon in hyperspace. Twice around, and she harmonized with the blank spot waiting for the crystal to complete it, to bring it into Harmony with the universe.

Third time around, she inserted the crystal.

The navigational unit slid a micron. She missed.

Hastily she jerked up the fragile column to avoid damage.

Three long heartbeats while she calmed herself. She had to check the crystal before risking another insertion. If the thing had even the tiniest scratch, no wider than a nano, the entire system would fail. The ship it guided could jump through hyperspace to an unknown point, lost, alone, drifting in hostile territory.

Her worst nightmare. To be alone. Lost. Without her family. Her heart ached for the Lost Colony. Gone some five years now and still an open wound in their society.

She pulled over an atomic microscope and inspected the black crystal. The facets gleamed back at her, begging her to look deeper into its core, to join with it and reach out to meld with the universe.

She jerked her vision away from the enticement.

Clean. She'd avoided touching the crystal to a chip.

She let out a long breath. She could lose her job for damaging a crystal.

"Come on, Sissy. I want to get home," Stevie whined. "I'm hungry and Mama promised us roasted goat and yammikins for dinner."

Sissy's mouth watered at the thought of the rare treat. Pop's birthday warranted a celebration of meat.

She cleared her mind and concentrated on completing the unit. The wheel within her workbench turned slowly. A note formed in her mind and her voice. She opened her mouth and let it slide over the nav unit. The proper place for the crystal, the only place for the crystal, appeared in her mind and before her eyes.

The table tilted, sending the navigational unit sliding three degrees to the left.

"Quake!" she shouted.

Even as she rose to run for safety, she took two heartbeats to put the fragile crystal into a protective sleeve, padded with air and gel. Then she tucked the cushioned crystal into the pocket of her brown coveralls.

"Quake!" she shouted again. "A big one."

All around her, late workers jumped to their feet and began running for the nearest exit. Three children, twelve years old, the minimum working age, headed for the central tower.

"Not safe." She grabbed the collars of two of them and pushed them toward the exterior stairs.

Inside the windowed core of the round building, she spotted several supervisors fighting to get to their private stairway, totally ignoring the fate of the people in the open space all around them.

The factory was made almost entirely of transparent bio-plastic windows, with a few clear Badger Metal pillars supporting each floor. Not enough of them. The windows would shatter, threatening the workers closest to them—the ones who needed the most light to perform their chores.

But if the central tower—also made of bio-plastic with little or no precious Badger Metal supporting it—should crack, the entire building would collapse.

They had to hurry.

Tremors vibrated against Sissy's bare feet as she guided the children toward the outer rim of the building. Seven exterior staircases would take them seven stories down to the ground and safety.

Even as she herded the children outward, she felt the building sway.

"Gods above and below, and those all around me, hear my prayer," she invoked the entire host of seven with a chant. "Please let everyone get out safely."

The tremors in her feet struck a clashing chord against the rhythms in her body and mind.

A column sagged. Then another. Fully two thirds of her fellow workers remained inside. Trapped. Workers from the other floors above and below clogged the stairs.

She had to do something.

Her workbench broke in two and slid toward the tower. It clanged against the interior windows. A crack rippled and spread across the bio-plastic, clouding it. The supervisors couldn't view the entire floor of the factory from there anymore.

Automatically, Sissy belted out another note, one that didn't clash with either the groaning building or the planet screaming in distress.

Her feet ceased to tingle for half a heartbeat. She found another note, up a third from the previous one as she dashed toward the tower.

Did the building sigh in relief?

Her imagination was working overtime. She had to get out of here. If she died, the last nav unit would never be complete. The fleet would lack a crucial vessel. Harmony and her empire, everything that was good and right about Sissy's home, would die beneath the flood of change brought by outsiders.

A tremendous crash rocked the building as an upper story succumbed to the quake.

Sissy hummed an entire scale that complemented the notes she'd already sung. Still pouring the harmonies into the air, she knew what she had to do.

Ignoring the shouts and pleas of Stevie and her coworkers, Sissy planted her feet between two tower supports and placed her hands on the cross struts.

"Please," she chanted. "Please, Harmony, find calm. Find peace. Stop your temper tantrum. Please."

Over and over she sang. Over and over she pleaded with the planet to forgive Her people for digging too deep with their mines, for fighting natural weather patterns with satellites. For polluting Her air and water with their waste.

She sang of her love of her home, of the bounteous oceans, the mystery of the dark forests, the grandeur of the open desert. She sang of her family—all seven children, her parents—and their parents and how they all crowded into two joined apartments. How they fought, how they cried, and how they loved each other and protected each other. As Harmony said they should.

She sang of the six colony worlds, making a seven-planet empire and how each fitted a niche in their society.

She sang of the rightness of the seven castes and how each one served Harmony.

She sang to each of the seven gods, Harmony, Empathy, their children Nurture and Unity, balanced by their stepchildren Anger, Greed, and Fear. She sang to them in turn and then all together.

And all the while she sang, she caught the energies gathered by the planet and pushed them down, deep into Harmony. Deeper, broader, find places for them to run to the surface without harm. Find sympathetic vibrations. Find peace. Find harmony.

The energy that escaped she guided upward through far-flung channels. A little bit here, a little bit there. Not too much in any one place.

Darkness crept around Sissy. She drowned out the sounds of destruction with chord after chord of sound that sought harmony in chaos.

The crystal in her pocket vibrated. She found a sympathetic tone, matched, and joined with it. Together, they reached out beyond Sissy's sense of self, beyond Harmony, out into the universe to find the threads that bound everything together. They sought the broken threads and a way to mend them. They found the connections to all life in all the far-flung planets, friendly and alien. Bit by bit they spliced them, stronger than before, until the entire web worked together so that Harmony could heal.

CHAPTER TWO

MAJOR JAKE HANNIGAN MONITORED the schematic on his cockpit screen. He adjusted his wing trajectory a micron to keep in formation.

Bronze Squadron, based at Space Base III halfway between Zephron II and the jump point to this system, drilled endlessly to keep this sector of civilized space free of the marauding Marils.

For over one hundred years individual planets of humans had fended off malicious and unprovoked attacks by the winged aliens. Then a hundred years ago humans had banded together into the Confederated Star Systems, a loose alliance that needed to become tighter and more organized to better fight their enemy.

Drills. He hated drills. Flying in formation for endless hours, then breaking off in precise and predetermined patterns. Real flying, real fighting against the enemy wasn't precise or predetermined. It was messy, chaotic.

And fun.

Right now, Jake could use some fun in his life. The Marillon Empire had retreated after the Confederated Star Systems fleet had whupped their ass at the battle of Platian IV right on the edge of the Harmonic Empire. He hadn't seen any action since. Other than drills. Four effing Terran months of drills.

Not even any music over the comm to break the monotony. He hummed an old tune, tapping his fingers on his controls in a rhythm only he could hear.

Everyone wanted access to Harmony and their lock on Badger Metal. Aloysius Badger had joined the cult of Harmony when it was still based on Earth, then taken the formula with him when the religious fanatics went off to found their own world. Reverse engineering on his prototype just didn't shield spaceships from radiation and the sensory disruption of hyperspace like the real stuff.

The aliens who congregated at Labyrinthe Space Station, otherwise known as First Contact Café, pretended they had good substitutes for Badger Metal. But Jake was sure they were just biding their time, waiting for the CSS, the Marils, and the Harmonites to slaughter each other, and then the other species would step in and take the leftovers.

So far, neither the Marils nor the CSS had broken the Harmonic border, either peacefully or militarily. And neither side was willing to team up with the other just to have a go at Harmony. Nor would either allow the other to breach Harmony's borders to get access to Badger Metal.

Harmony had closed their borders and severed all contact with the rest of the galaxy fifty years ago. Before that, they'd only allowed a few selected merchants to trade in neutral space. The dribble of real Badger Metal they allowed out didn't match the need for it.

Now, with the war claiming vessels right, left, and sideways, everyone was running out of Badger Metal. Wildcat scavengers made fortunes collecting battle debris for scraps of Badger Metal that could be recycled.

The effing vultures sold those scraps to the highest bidder. Even if the money came from the Marils.

Since the last battle, both sides had gone into holding mode. Neither one wanted to continue the war without fresh Badger Metal in their hulls. Neither side was willing to let the other have it.

And Harmony didn't seem to care as long as they were left alone. No one had seen a Harmonite outside their borders in decades. Possibly longer.

And no CSS merchant or agent had entered Harmonite space and returned alive in fifty years.

So every person who wore a CSS uniform was trained to home in on any casually overheard conversation in a bar or marketplace, that mentioned Harmony in any context. The tiniest hint of a rumor coming out of Harmony captured their complete attention.

Jake ceased his rhythmic tapping and edged his fighter three degrees starboard out of formation just to see if the colonel would notice.

"Get back in line, Hannigan!" Colonel Warski barked over the comm.

"Yes, sir. Correcting for drift." Jake adjusted his position. So much for that ploy.

"No time for drifting in combat, Hannigan," Warski continued his rebuke.

"This ain't combat," Jake muttered with his comm off. "Not even close."

Suddenly Jake's screens exploded with data. It looked like a hundred Maril fighters had homed in on the squadron. And behind the fighters loomed a huge battle wagon. The Tactical Tech Team back at base had come up with a new scenario for target practice. And they'd waited until the flyboys were nearly asleep with boredom to spring it on them.

Jake picked his target quickly. On the starboard edge of the formation, he was responsible for making sure none of the bogeys slipped around behind them. Just like in a real battle.

"Sheesh, I hope this is only a simulation," Lieutenant Marti James breathed. The rookie. A good pilot, on the verge of being almost as good as Jake, but untried in true combat.

Jake could almost smell the woman's sweat. He keyed in a private comm line to her. "You know this is simulation because the TTT are all born and raised in gravity. They think in two dimensions. The Maril have wings. They are conceived and born in the air. They think in three dimensions. Their formations have depth. This one is flat."

James breathed a sigh of relief. "Ever seen one of them critters?"

"Yeah, captured one two campaigns ago. His ship was damaged and he had a concussion so we could tow him in before he suicided. Small bodies, very lightly boned. Feathered wings tucked into an extra fold of skin at the back of the arms. Evolved down from real wings. They can still fly in atmosphere, though. Very dexterous hands, talons on the elbow joints that can tear a man in half. The warriors have black wings, hair, and eyes. Iridescent black. It shimmers and shifts colors in the light. Awesome. Beautiful. Terrible."

"Heard about that one. Too bad his ship was so badly damaged we couldn't reconstruct their nav system," James replied.

"Cut the chatter. Close to two thousand klicks and pick your target," Warski overrode Jake's private line.

"Closing," each pilot replied. As one, the entire formation moved closer to the swarm of Marils that were really only data blips on their screens.

Jake kept a wary eye on all of the data, including a real-time screen to the left of the simulation. No sense in letting a real bogey come in out of nowhere while they were occupied with data blips.

Of course the TTT team in the control tower of Space Base III were supposed to be monitoring for that.

He'd known them to slip up before. TTT tended to get caught up in the game of throwing rogue elements into the drills. All in the name of keeping the pilots on their toes.

Jake's screens flashed white, then went black. Flickers of static pinpointed with red continued. He cursed fluently as he shut down.

"Hannigan, get back in formation," Warski growled.

"Propulsion overload," Jake replied as his diagnostic flashed a solution. "Have to reboot the entire system. I'll catch up." This could be a bug programmed into his ship by the TTT. It could be real. Either way, he wasn't going anywhere for the next six heartbeats.

He counted off the time, then powered up. Lights flashed on and off across his screens. Something . . .

"What's that anomaly sneaking out from behind Zephron's major moon?" Jake asked across the system as soon as he had comm. The glare from the minor moon almost masked the new blip on his screen.

Then it winked out.

Real or simulated?

"You're imagining things again, Jake," Warski complained. "Watch that bogey to your starboard."

The anomaly blinked back on.

"You see that, Ron?" he asked his buddy in control back on the station, as he took out an imaginary bogey with simulated pulse weapons.

"See what?" Ron yawned.

"The unauthorized blip that just ducked behind the big moon." The anomaly was gone again. His squadron had moved beyond range for picking it up. Jake still lagged behind with a trajectory to the blip.

"Yeah, I saw it. It disappeared. Not to worry," Ron said.

"Whaddya mean not to worry? Is it part of the simulation or not?"

"Lemme ask."

Jake counted to ten, then ten again while he waited for Ron to interrupt the TTT in their game. He fiddled with his screen resolution as an excuse to remain behind and out of the main action. There it was again.

And gone.

"Not part of the sim as far as I can see," Ron replied. He didn't sound excited or interested. "Must be a glitch in the program. Can't find it now."

"Bronze fifteen to Bronze one," Jake called Warski. "I'm going to investigate an anomaly."

"Stay in formation, Jake. No side trips are authorized. Control can't find your blip. I never saw it. Must be a malfunction in your system."

"But it could be the real thing, Colonel. It's not part of the sim. You're beyond the window to see it. I'm not."

"Control says it doesn't exist. They are in a better position to monitor the entire system than you. I order you to stay in formation."

The blip appeared again. Bigger, closer. More dangerous.

"Bronze fifteen to control. Are you sending out someone to investigate the unidentified blip?" He held his breath. This could be it. The big push the Marils had put together while they seemed to retreat.

His heart raced with excitement.

"Boss man says to watch and wait," Ron said. He sounded just as bored as ever.

Jake twitched nervously.

"I don't think it's a drone," he said on an open channel. "It's not flying a straight, preprogrammed path."

"Stay in formation, Jake. Leave the thinking to those who are trained to do it," Warski ordered.

The anomaly stopped wandering, paused as if assessing the risk, then began a straight and accelerating trajectory aimed directly at SB3.

"Bronze fifteen to Bronze one. I can take it out. I am within range. I can intercept before it takes out the base."

"Base is armed and aware. If that thing truly exists. Which they say it doesn't. Stay in formation, Major."

"At that speed it will be on top of base before their weapons power up. I can take it out, Bronze one."

"Stay in formation. You do not have permission . . ."

"Screw it." Jake discommed and banked his fighter fifteen degrees to starboard and ten below his horizon.

"Hannigan, get back here," Colonel Warski shouted.

Jake shut off all communications. The blue comm light blinked at him accusingly, letting him know that people wanted to talk to him. "Well, I'm done talking to you."

He powered up his weapons for real, watching the energy run up the scale as he closed with the blip. Five thousand klicks away, he switched to real time and overrode automatic targeting systems.

This bogey he'd take out with skill rather than overwhelming it with superior forces. In pitched battle the CSS fleet had only ever won when they outnumbered the Marils three to one. Today he had only himself to pit against the wily predators.

For that, he needed to see things as they happened and not with the nanosecond delay while the computers interpreted.

The black triangular vessel showed as a mere reflection in the dim glow from the sun and moon. No running lights. It flew by sensor. Who knew how good those sensors were?

Pretty damn good, based on combat experience. And pretty fragile. They'd never found enough parts in the wreckage to reconstruct one. Not even in the ship they had towed back to base.

Three thousand klicks and he was just outside his effective target range. The Maril fighter paid him no never mind and kept going. It looked like it would ram the station.

Jake chilled at the thought of thousands of people sucked out of their safe and secure world into vacuum without EVA suits. Little chance of rescue. Thousands of his buddies killed.

He'd already lost his parents and only brother to the Marils the year Jake entered the Academy. They'd been on land, with atmosphere. That hadn't saved them. The bombs had wiped out an entire colony. EVA suits wouldn't have saved them.

He closed to twenty-two hundred klicks and fired his laser cannon. Practically point-blank.

The bogey dodged to port at the last nano. It kept going forward.

Jake adjusted his aim and fired again, this time expecting a jog to starboard.

The bogey ducked under the blast of searing light. The laser revealed the sculpted feather markings on the wings as it passed. Then the vessel nearly disappeared again in the blackness of space.

Damn.

He knew Marils were smart. Bordering on telepathic in avoiding hits. Something to do with the flocking instinct of avians and the need to communicate while staying in formation.

Time to outthink the bogey without thinking.

Jake closed his eyes a nano and let his hands caress the controls, feeling with his entire body how they responded.

When he opened them again, he saw the Maril ship clearly outlined against the lights of SB3, now only fifteen hundred klicks away.

Too close to the station.

If he hit the bogey now, the blast would damage the hull at the launch bays. Any closer, and debris would rupture SB3 in the living section. He had one shot.

"Okay, God. It's you and me. Let's take this guy out. Now."

Before he could think about it, he ducked under the Maril, flipped, and faced its belly.

He fired.

The laser raked the enemy fighter from stem to stern, right through the engine compartment.

Jake jerked his fighter to port and around the station in a tight loop. Debris pinged his tail. He kept going, right back around to his squadron.

A quick sensor check revealed minimal damage to the station. The debris blew outward, just as he planned.

"Major Hannigan, report to base," Colonel Warski overrode Jake's comm lockout. "The old man is going to skin you alive and hang your hide on the launch bay doors."

"I got the bogey while you were minding your ass!" Jake protested.

"You took out one of our own. An operative returning with a captured ship for study. We've never had one with an intact sensor and nav system before, and now you just killed a comrade and our only chance to figure out how these things fly!"

CHAPTER THREE

"**O**VER HERE, MY LAUD." The anonymous worker in a hard hat beckoned to Gregor da Ivan pa Crystal Temple, High Priest of Harmony.

"This had better be good," Gregor grumbled. The eight-point-nine-magnitude quake had ripped Harmony City to shreds. Even the Crystal Temple had not been spared the planet's wrath. Two of the seven great crystal columns that supported the open forecourt had collapsed, bringing the roof down with them.

Marilee du Sharran pu Crystal Temple, the High Priestess, had been trapped beneath. She lay gravely injured in Crystal Temple Hospital. Gregor should be at her side. He needed to be there should she pass so that he could control the political maneuvering to replace Marilee as Harmony's avatar.

He prayed fervently that his partner would recover.

But he was also HP of *all* Harmony. Some emergencies outweighed politics. He made sure the ever-present media hover cam caught him picking through the wreckage on a mission of mercy. If the media wanted to separate from the Professionals and become their own caste, let them earn the right. And Gregor's favor.

His acolyte Guilliam kept the hover cam at a respectful distance, occasionally speaking words of encouragement to the masses at the other end.

The reporter remained at a safe distance.

Thousands lay dead or dying. Large portions of the city crumbled. Fires raged. Broken water mains added rivers to the churning water table. That much moving water turned the land to a slurry of quicksand. The liquifaction had flooded low-lying areas. Riverbanks washed away to the sea.

And all around him, he heard the wails of the injured and the grieving.

The stench of death rose like a poisonous miasma, ready to grab him, too, if he weren't careful.

No caste had been spared. Harmony wreaked havoc on all of her children with equal fury.

"You shouldn't be here, My Laud," Guilliam da Baillie pa Crystal Temple whispered shakily so that the hover cam couldn't hear. He looked back the way they had come. "You need to remain safe. With Laudae Marilee injured, Harmony needs you protected."

"No one is safe anywhere in the city," Gregor grumbled. He shuddered as flashes of prophecy from ancient times flashed across his memory.

> *And the time shall come*
> *When Beloved Harmony*
> *Lashes out in anger.*
> *Out of the ashes of Discord*
> *Will Rise*
> *One who loves us all,*
> *Appeases Harmony,*
> *Brings Chaos,*
> *And restores life.*

Gibberish and nonsense. Prophecies only worked in retrospect, not in forecasting the future.

"Go back if you are that frightened, Guilliam. I am needed here." Gingerly, Gregor picked his way through a field of debris that had once been a major factory with important Spacer contracts. Destruction here meant disastrous delays improving defenses on the frontier. And a disruption of Gregor's plans.

Guilliam heaved a sigh filled with martyrdom and followed reluctantly. "May I remind you, My Laud, that this quake will be seen as a portent. Your leadership will be questioned. You need to call the High Council and maintain your role . . ." He droned on and on.

The only reason Gregor kept him on was because of his blood bond to Lord Chauncey, a member of the High Council. The only intermarriage between castes allowed was Temple to Noble. Both had small numbers and needed to keep the gene pool from becoming inbred. Intermarriage also allowed alliances to strengthen and grow. Not that Temple people needed marriage or alliances among themselves. Dedicated to Harmony, and only Harmony, their relationships remained as fluid as those of the Goddess' plants and animals.

Gregor's assistant also did a good job of organizing the HP's office. Too much work to teach another acolyte how to do that. Too much work finding an adult acolyte with no ambition to raise to the priesthood and take over from Guillian.

The HP stepped gingerly around chunks of support columns and crunched through mounds of broken bio-plastic. The outside walls had shattered outward, taking huge sections of the twelve floors with it.

Proof that no building should be allowed to grow beyond the sacred seven stories.

Strangely, the central supervisory tower remained intact. And so did the seven exterior exit staircases.

The ground beneath his feet rolled. He braced himself against a chunk of building as tall as he to ride out the aftershock. More debris rained down on him. He ducked and covered his vulnerable neck and head with crossed arms.

Guilliam cowered and trembled. "Really, My Laud, this place is too dangerous. It will wait until morning. You have no reason to risk your life for a mere Worker."

"Get out that monitoring equipment we borrowed," Gregor snarled at the toadie. He should have brought a scientist. Someone more fascinated with the quake than the safety of his own delicate butt. Outside the Spacer caste, true scientists were rare. Gregor had little authority to command the presence of a Professional caste scientist without going through multiple layers of bureaucracy. He should change that. Harmony's High Priest needed more authority in case of an emergency.

This was definitely an emergency.

After the shock had spent itself, he asked the Worker who led them, "How many dead here?" If ever he needed proof that Harmony was angry with her people for accepting Marilee, a charlatan priestess, as her avatar, this was it.

By Discord, Marilee was convenient. She never questioned Gregor, never interfered, and managed the trivial details of ritual and protocol meticulously.

"Only seven died in this building, My Laud," the worker said. He had the sharply angled features and long limbs of a higher class. He certainly spoke intelligently. Education had smoothed the rough edges of his accent. The brown X of his caste mark nearly faded into his dark skin. He probably had a noble in his family tree, but the lower caste mark, present at birth, always dominated.

Gregor contained a shudder of dismay. Interbreeding had become too common. It had to stop. Harmony showed her anger today at the many violations of the order set down countless generations ago at the beginning of civilization.

He dared not think of the disruption should a child born to a Worker woman bear the blue diamond mark of his Noble father. Or if a Noble family was disgraced when one of their daughters bore a child with the green triangle of the Professional caste. He touched his own purple circle on his left cheek as verification that his breeding held true. His sensitive fingers just barely registered the slightly smoother texture of his Temple caste mark above his midnight stubble.

The castes had to maintain the divinely ordained structure of civilization. All else was chaos.

"My Laud." Guilliam touched his sleeve. "The graphs indicate we are very near the epicenter of the quake. We can't stay here. The aftershocks could kill you."

"I can see that." Gregor grabbed the sensor from his assistant and stared at the unusual graph in amazement. No wonder Lord Chauncey da Chauncey, who owned this factory, had called him out.

"Only seven dead, you say? Had the Workers all left for the evening?" Something truly strange occurred at this factory if only seven died with this amount of destruction at the epicenter of the quake. And why was the tower still upright and intact?

"No, My Laud. Most of the day shift were still in the building. Swing shift was arriving. The place was more crowded than usual. The seven who died were trampled by their coworkers trying to get down the too narrow staircases."

Gregor gulped. He remembered the horrible trapped feeling within the spacious Crystal Temple with only two hundred people to evacuate. The thought of thousands of Workers, crammed together on those fragile staircases made his lungs freeze.

Guilliam slapped him on the back. "Breathe, sir."

Gregor drew in a large gulp of dust-tainted air and coughed it back out again.

"Show me," he ordered the Worker. "Show me the miracle that might end this nightmare."

The Worker gestured toward the nearest staircase. It hung crookedly, half its bolts shaken loose.

"Is that safe?"

"As safe as any." The Worker shrugged and led the way up.

The railing swayed a little under the man's heavily muscled weight, but held. Perhaps the odd member of his family tree was Military rather than Noble. The Military caste with its red square mark tended toward broad shoulders and put on muscle more readily than the effete nobility. Worker and Military was an almost acceptable cross. Not that any cross was acceptable.

Gregor waited for him to get halfway to the first landing before following. Distribute the weight. Slowly, they picked their way up seven stories. Three times the Worker had to reach back to help Gregor and Guilliam over broken steps. Twice they rode out aftershocks frozen in place.

At last, panting and sweating, they reached the seventh floor. The worker ignited a battery torch and played it around the chaotic space. Workbenches lay on their sides; expensive equipment crushed beneath them. Clear Badger Metal support beams tilted drunkenly.

Dark clouds of dust thickened the gloom.

"Best use a filter, My Laud." The Worker fished two cloth masks out of his pocket and handed them to Gregor and Guilliam. Primitive barriers compared to what the Spacers could produce, but all that the Workers had available.

They covered their mouths and noses. Then Gregor breathed a little easier. He hadn't realized that he had kept his inhales short and shallow.

"What about you?" he asked the Worker.

The man donned his own soiled mask and breathed as deeply as he could. Dust already clogged the layers of woven cloth. He'd been on site a long time. Then he led them deeper through the maze of destruction. His light picked out hints of the delicate computers assembled here. Fortunes in Spacer parts, industrial systems, hospital diagnostics. All ruined.

Another major setback in the planetary economy. As if they needed another on top of the quake damage, after the out-of-season hurricane last month, and the erupting volcano on the Southern Continent the month before.

Gregor envisioned disaster after disaster until the entire planet, the entire empire collapsed beneath Harmony's fury. They needed a proper High Priestess, one who truly had the gift of Harmony, prophetic visions, then perhaps the planet would calm enough for them to recover.

Not likely to happen. Prophecy was a thing of the past, dubious at best, confusing as Discord at worst.

"Sir?" Guilliam gulped. He shoved an alien-looking gadget in Gregor's face. The glowing screen displayed a new graph.

Tight lines shooting to the extreme right and left of center showed a classic quake of high magnitude. Then the lines spread out. Wider on either side of center, but spaced broader, less intense. Abruptly, they shortened in frequency but did not return to the first magnitude.

"What?"

"The manual says that's the epicenter, sir. Somehow, the energy spread out and went deeper. It started out shallow and very destructive, then dissipated." Guilliam's voice shook, muffled by the mask. "I'm out of my depth here, My Laud. You should have brought a scientist. May I fetch one for you?"

"Later. I need you here and now to witness for me."

"*Someone* spread the energy, My Laud." The Worker shone his light on the figure of a slim young woman braced against the tower.

Her head and shoulders drooped in fatigue. She whispered a breathy and poignant tune.

A young man of similar build and dark hair paced around her anxiously.

"Sissy, it's okay little'n. You can let go now." The Worker who had led them here put his light on the floor to free his hands. Then he caught her shoulders. "I've got you now, Sissy. You can let go."

"She can't," the other young man whispered. "I think her hands have bonded with the pillars. I've tried over and over to free her, but she doesn't even know I'm here. And I'm her brother!"

Gregor stepped closer in alarm. The girl seemed so weak, she must be frightfully injured.

She turned and stared at him. Her straight, jaw-length, dark hair swung away from her pale, olive-toned face and slight almond shape of her eyes, revealing a circle of seven caste marks neatly arranged on her *right* cheek. The Temple purple circle at the top was flanked by the Noble blue diamond and the Professional green triangle. The black bar of the Poor and the Worker brown X sat at the bottom flanked by the Military red square and the Spacer yellow star.

Gregor gasped in fright and wonder. No one—absolutely no one— ever bore more than one caste mark. The marks always appeared on the left cheek. They were genetic, fixed in the DNA, symbols of Harmony's order and organization of life. Everyone had their place, their niche to fill to make a complete and harmonious whole.

Except that Harmony was no longer functioning in an orderly and organized manner.

A quick check showed that the young woman's brother bore only the normal brown X of a Worker on the proper cheek.

In the diffuse light the young woman's eyes shone an unnatural silver, like starshine on a moonless night.

"You cannot find what you seek until you stop looking and accept," she whispered.

She swallowed as if the dust-permeated air clogged her throat. Then she turned her gaze upon her brother.

"Stevie, if you follow your ambitions, you will marry late and not for love. You will never find Harmony. Marry your heart's desire now and earn a better ambition," she said aloud with an awesome echoey quality that filled the vast factory chamber with sound that sent fowlbumps up and down Gregor's spine.

She spoke with the authority of Harmony herself.

CHAPTER FOUR

"**EAT, DRINK, AND BE MERRY,** for tomorrow I die!" Major Jake Hannigan lifted his shot of single malt to salute the noisy crowd in Willie's Bar and Grill.

"Ain't that the friggin' truth," the drunk next to Jake slurred.

None of the patrons were pilots. Jake had scouted and chosen a distinctly civilian bar. Still, on a closed space station, everyone knew everyone else's business. These guys just weren't as keen on detail as his comrades.

He sniffed the exotic fragrance of the drink, then savored varied flavors in a sip. He downed the shot, relishing the explosive burn all the way to his stomach that reminded him he still lived. Then he chased the fine liquor with a quaff of dark beer. Liquid bread. The best stout in three parsecs. It slid down his throat with soothing coolness after the fire wrapped in velvet of the scotch.

"Uh, Jake, don't you think you'd better slow down? You face a court-martial in the morning. You'll need a clear head." Willie, the owner and bartender, stayed Jake's hand from taking a second long draught of beer.

"Yeah, his ass is in deep doo doo with the admiral," the man on the other side of Jake began to giggle at his supposed pun.

"Why bother? They're going to fry me, no matter what. Drinks for everyone in the house!" Jake called to the crowd at large.

A cheer with applause surged around him.

"Jake, this is going to cost you a lot of money," Willie warned. He kept his hand on the green flag that signaled a free round to all patrons.

"Can't take it with you." Jake slurred his words and crossed his eyes. "I really screwed up big time, Willie. Ain't no tomorrow for me." No one left to claim his "estate." Sixty-five credits on his thumbprint and another two or three thousand stashed in an Earth bank. His entire family wiped out in one Maril raid on SB8. Close friends and lovers evaporated in space battles. Nothing. No one.

"You said it, buddy," the first drunk agreed, holding up his glass for a refill. "Nobody on this friggin' base can screw up like you can."

Because everyone else on this friggin' base had someone to care about. Jake had nothing left to lose.

The friendly pub on the bright civilian side of the space station looked funny, blurry. Two of everything. Jake swayed and wished he hadn't. His head had trouble keeping up with the movement. The room spun.

God, he was going to hurt in the morning. He didn't care anymore.

"You're pretty." He smiled in adoration at a passing barmaid.

"You're pretty, too, Jake." She pointedly removed his hand from her breast and moved on.

Willie held up the green flag. The room erupted in noise.

Jake's head pounded. Breath whooshed out of him as three guys in suits pushed him aside to get their free drink.

"Rude bastards," Jake muttered. "Pretty bastards." He careened into a tall stool in his effort to find a stable horizon. "Pretty bar stool." He patted it affectionately. With one hand on the stool and the other on the table, he turned to face Willie with a stupid grin on his face.

Willie also held up a red flag.

Uh-oh. That was a call for security. Jake had known this afternoon when he stormed out of Admiral Telvino's office he'd face the music in the morning. One last night of freedom. One last roaring drunk.

No sense in throwing him in the brig. Only so many places to hide on a space station.

He hadn't the will to elude the goons any longer. Another day he might have drawn out the game of cat and mouse for a week or more. Maybe steal a vessel and run away to the fringe. Or the supposed Lost Colony that rumor claimed was making noises about being found again.

There was always a colony getting lost from somewhere. Ghost ships and lost colonies, the stuff of space legends. The stories were almost as fantastic as rumors about Harmony and the loathsome fanatics that ran the place.

"You're pretty." He lurched into a barmaid. The same one as before?

"Hey, Willie, where's the jakes?" he called over the din. Then he giggled at his pun. This wasn't the first time he'd been likened to a public men's room. Usually of the unsavory type.

"We'll take you there, sir," an MP said in a deep somber tone. Both the man and his partner positively bristled with weapons. Jake counted a taser, a pellet pistol, a billy club, and something sharp stuck up their sleeves. His eyes crossed at that point, and he swayed again before he completed the inventory. "Pretty weapons."

He practically fell into the arms of the MPs.

"Gonna hurl," Jake mumbled, clenching his jaw. He puffed his cheeks out and let his eyes flit frantically about the crowded bar.

The MPs each grabbed an elbow and frog-marched him out of the bar, down the evening-dimmed promenade, left into an even darker tunnel and then through the swinging door of the jakes.

Jake landed facedown. He let the cool tile floor absorb some of his discomfort. A tiny morsel of relief washed through him. Maybe he wouldn't throw up after all.

How much had he drunk? More than he intended.

"Crap." He'd relaxed too soon. He almost made it to the urinal before his stomach turned itself inside out.

Some time later the door swished open. "Time to go, Jake," Pamela Marella called to him.

"You are a sight for sore eyes, Pammy. Pretty Pammy." Jake didn't like the way he slurred his words.

"You didn't have to really drink that much, Jake. You were supposed to fake it," Pamela admonished. She stood with her hands on her ample hips.

"Never seen you in civvies before," Jake said, admiring her long jean-clad legs, and how her boobs strained against her knit shirt. She might be pushing fifty, and thirty pounds overweight, but she was still one damned attractive woman. "Pretty tits, Pammy." He reached up to grab them and missed.

"On this base, I'm a civilian. I always wear civilian clothes." She looked puzzled. "And keep your paws off my tits." She slapped his hand away.

"Ah, but you always dress as if your suits are uniforms. You stand so straight you'd put a drill sergeant to shame, pretty Pammy. But you're prettier than any drill sergeant I've met. Smarter, too. Pretty tits."

"I have to be prettier and smarter to survive in this game." She bent over and grabbed his ankles. "We can do this hard, or we can do this easy, Jake. Your choice." She began dragging him out of the restroom.

"Can't make it easy. I'm gonna die tomorrow."

"Actually Major Jake Hannigan just gave up the ghost. He choked on his own vomit. When you wake up in the morning, you will be Jeremiah Devlin."

"But I'll be *Lieutenant Colonel* Jeremiah Devlin. I get a promotion for dying. Should a' thought of that years ago. Will you marry me, Pammy. You're pretty."

Jake had to think hard about his next words as his head bumped over the sill to the dark tunnel outside the jakes. "Isn't Lieutenant Colonel

Jeremiah Devlin the spy I'm supposed to have killed? That Maril fighter was just a mock-up and a drone thrown together by your boys?"

"That's right. Two of my men had fun playing games with it while you chased it. And now you are going to become the man you killed. A man who never existed until this moment." Pamela looked right and left before dragging Jake around the doorway to the left.

"Ouch." He rubbed his shoulder where he bumped against the doorjamb. It didn't hurt as badly as his head did, though.

"If you could walk, I wouldn't have to drag you to my office." Pamela dropped his feet abruptly. They bounced hard against the floor. Jake's spine jolted and his head threatened to explode. Again.

Jake stifled a groan and spewed a load of puke all over Pammy's pretty tits.

"Feel better, Jake?" Pam grunted in disgust and dashed back into the jakes.

Jake knew time passed because he drifted in and out of consciousness several times before Pammy came back, somewhat cleaner and a whole lot wetter. Her nipples puckered beneath her knit shirt.

Jake had sobered enough to realize this wasn't the time to let the alcohol in his system do the talking. "I think I can walk now, if you'll help me up." A good excuse to wrap his arms around the delectable woman. Maybe he'd get to feel those pretty tits.

Pamela knelt and got her shoulder under his, then hoisted him to his feet.

"Strong as well as beautiful."

"I have to be. Only way I can keep a bunch of randy spies in order." Balance settled, she walked Jake through a back corridor, well away from Willie's and the two MPs standing guard at the entrance to the promenade.

"And what am I going to have to spy out for you as my first assignment, pretty Pammy? Gonna let me be the one to find the Lost Colony?"

Pamela rolled her hazel eyes and sighed. She blew a stray wisp of straight brown hair out of her eyes before speaking. "I've already found Harmony's Lost Colony. Came up empty. No formula for Badger Metal there. But we've found someone who swears he can make an insulation out of liquid metal ceramic alloy that can withstand hyperspace better than Badger Metal. If it works, you are to get the process from him any way you can, legal or not. Moral or not. We need that process."

"And if it doesn't work?" Jake's knees buckled and he nearly dragged Pam down with him. As he groped his way back to standing, he used her conveniently lumpy chest as handholds.

She slapped his hands hard and shoved them into his pockets.

"Then your next assignment will be to go to Harmony and steal their formula."

"Easier to invite them to join the CSS." They both laughed at that preposterous idea.

CHAPTER FIVE

GUILLIAM DA BAILLIE PA CRYSTAL Temple shifted his weight anxiously as he faced John da John pa Harmony City Broadcasting, known as Little Johnny. A pest of a Media Professional if there ever was one.

"What aren't you telling the citizens of Harmony about the Worker taken away by ambulance to a Temple hospital," Little Johnny demanded. His hover cam parked itself directly in front of Guilliam's face.

Guilliam had to school every muscle to show calm and confidence. "Temple caste is concerned for all citizens of Harmony. Worker hospitals are full to overflowing, their staffs overwhelmed with casualties of this horrible natural disaster. We merely wish to ease their burden where we can," he said slowly, speaking each syllable clearly and distinctly. He couldn't let on how deeply he wanted to run to the hospital. He had duties and responsibilities to many people there, including Laud Gregor and the injured Laudae Marilee.

"Why aren't Temple hospitals overwhelmed?" Johnny asked, his sly smirk hidden from the hover cam. "And why do you take in only one Worker caste instead of the thousands that need care?"

Time to end this before Guilliam told the reporter what he really wanted him to know, instead of what he should know.

"I am not in charge of sorting who goes where. As divinely ordained, we must keep the castes separate as much as possible. The young woman we transported was clearly identified as in need of specialized care. We were afraid she might be shuffled into a back corner and forgotten. She is in line for having her caste mark Lauded. Any taint from the mingling of castes will be kept to a minimum."

"Why's she in line for being Lauded? She's just a Worker making Spacer components."

Guilliam took a deep breath. "We search constantly for the one prophesied long ago who will renew our Covenant with Harmony and restore balance."

"Shouldn't the Chosen One of legend come from Temple caste," Little Johnny spat. Clearly, he had no belief in Prophecy. A sad condition all over Harmony.

"We do not presume to choose for Harmony. Our Goddess will reveal her Chosen One when and where She chooses. We can only be alert and help those we guess might become special." Guilliam turned abruptly and headed in the direction of Crystal Temple Hospital. He'd have to walk. Laud Gregor had ridden in the ambulance, the only vehicle working in the immediate vicinity.

"Mister Guilliam," Little Johnny said quietly.

Guilliam paused, not willing to turn and face the man and his hover cam again.

"I've turned the hover cam off. What is really going on here?"

Guilliam smiled to himself. "Something of great import. I can't say what yet, because I am not certain myself. You'll be the first to know when I have more facts."

"Promise?"

"My word of honor."

"You're the only Temple caste who has any honor left," Johnny muttered.

"In the meantime find a copy of the Prophecies and read them. All of them."

"I'll be in touch." Little Johnny turned his cam back on and wandered off to the next knot of activity among the ruins.

Guilliam began the long walk across the city, hoping he arrived before things got out of hand again.

✦   ✦   ✦

Jake skimmed through six different technical manuals. If he narrowed his focus to one word at a time, he could almost forget the pain pounding in his head.

The constant thrum of the station's power plant, out of sync with his headache and pulse, intensified his hangover. But Pammy had chosen these secret alcoves for her offices and quarters. No one came down here unless they had to. Her payroll extended to every maintenance tech who serviced the heart of SB3. She paid them extra for discretion and loyalty, almost double the going rate.

Jake sipped at a cup of coffee. Only lukewarm and it still burned his tongue.

None of his standard hangover remedies had worked. He'd drunk liters of water, downed anti-inflamatories, even a precious raw egg in a glass of synthesized tomato juice with a dash of Worcestershire sauce hadn't eased the fire singeing every nerve in his body.

His reader flashed page after page of details about Badger Metal, its properties, its peculiarities, and weaknesses. Lots and lots of pages about the consequences should hull plating fail.

Lots and lots of flashes of light that made him dizzy.

Concentrate, he admonished himself. *Just read the words and forget the rest.*

He scratched where the rough cloth of his anonymous station overalls rasped against his skin. That just turned the itch to flames darting about from one patch of flesh to the next. Pammy had taken away all his comfortable uniforms. He'd have new clothes just before he took off on his mission to Prometheus XII, a boil on the backside of the universe. That planet couldn't hurt him any more than his own stupidity and a bottle of scotch with beer chasers. Far too many beer chasers.

Then he hit the section on theories and forgot the scratchy weave of his loose clothing. Forgot the sledgehammer trying to get out of his skull through his eyes. "Why can't scientists just admit they don't know what the hell Badger Metal is or how to make it?" he grumbled, running his hands along his scalp. Damn, even his hair hurt.

"Because if scientists admit they don't have the answers, then the masses lose their faith in science and revert to superstition and religion," Pamela Marella said from the opposite side of her office where she prepared documentation for Jake's upcoming mission.

"And anyone who puts faith above science has to be as crazy as the Harmonites," Jake added. "They're religious and they have Badger Metal. That does not compute."

"You got that right."

"So how do I figure out if this new product on Prometheus XII works?" He swiveled his chair around so he faced Pammy. And wished he hadn't. His head took several seconds to catch up with the rest of him.

Pammy worked efficiently, not an errant keystroke or mistake. He took a few moments to appreciate her finer points. If only she weren't so bossy, he'd like to get to know her a lot better.

But then, Pammy's bossiness made her the best spymaster in the entire CSS. When she growled, strong alpha males jumped and did her bidding. Like himself.

"You know it works if you shoot it with a full blaster on max setting and it doesn't dissolve into a puddle of space goo," Pammy said, never looking up from her work. "And while you're at it, see if the matrix bath is compatible with crystals."

Jake rolled his eyes. "I'm a pilot. And a damned good one. Not an R&D robot. What do you need crystals for?"

"Another theory in the works. Last report out of Harmony, fifty years ago, said they were working on a crystallized form of Badger Metal that would provide instant communication through hyperspace and act as a homing beacon to get a ship safely out of hyperspace."

Jake whistled softly. "Now that is something worth stealing."

"Worth more than your next three promotions. In fact, if you can bring me a working crystal and the recipe, I'll promote you to admiral, grant you an estate overlooking the ocean on New Earth, and give birth to your sons."

"I'll keep my eyes open." But Jake figured that a crystal with those magical properties was just theory. Even the best scientists in the CSS couldn't come up with one of those. Hell, they couldn't come up with real Badger Metal.

"There's an image of what a BM crystal should look like on page nine hundred fifty-six, manual three. Take a good long look at it. Study every facet, and memorize the color variations." Pammy fiddled with something behind her desk.

"Sure," Jake said dubiously, pulling up the specified page. Before he could do more than blink at the blinding facets, Pammy jammed a long syringe into his thigh, through his station overalls.

"Yeooow!" Jake screeched followed by a lengthy string of curses.

"This is really a painless procedure," Pammy said, holding the syringe firmly in his thigh. She barely blinked at his profanity. Doubtless she'd heard worse. "Painless but necessary. And it will cure your hangover."

✦　　✦　　✦

Sissy roused from her light doze, aware of people crowding around her. The nasty sharp odor of disinfectant and fear belonged only in hospital.

She identified her mother, Maigrie, by the scent of hot cinnamon, fresh from her baking. Her father, Jaimey, smelled of sawdust. Stevie smelled of . . . Stevie. He needed a shower.

Then she realized he hadn't left her side since the beginning of the quake.

How long ago?

How long had she slept?

She needed to finish that nav unit and get it out to the Spacers. With a tremendous effort she heaved herself to her side so she could get out of the bed. Sharp pains ran from her hands up to her shoulders. Her lungs burned. She flopped back against the pillows. Tears pricked her eyes.

She had failed in her duty to complete the nav unit. Another ship might be doomed to drift endlessly, lost in hyperspace.

"Easy." An unknown masculine voice. A strange hand gentled her shoulders.

Then she opened her eyes, expecting to find a nurse or med tech at her left.

Her gaze lighted upon a middle-aged man, older than her father, with wisps of gray at his temples and not much other hair on his head. His soft blue eyes looked troubled. A bright purple circle on his left cheek, and his funereal black shirt and trousers identified him as Temple caste. He should wear green. Temple always wore green unless . . .

The quake. He wore black for the many funerals and grief blessings to come.

She didn't recognize him from the local temple. But then the priests, male and female, changed about every half year. The Crystal Temple didn't like their caste becoming too attached to any neighborhood. Their allegiance belonged to Harmony first and the Temple second. Any other bond was frowned upon. Even marriage, she'd heard whispered.

She held up her hands, both bandaged heavily. Last she remembered she couldn't pull them away from the Badger Metal pillar outside the central tower at the factory.

"Who?" she croaked out. Her throat felt raw. She needed a drink. She needed to get back to work.

"I am Laud Gregor. You were injured in the quake, but we are taking care of you." He held a water tube with a bent straw to her lips.

Sissy sipped greedily, then turned her head to find her mother leaning on the bed railing, peering at her.

"Mama? Why aren't you and Pop and Stevie at work?" Mama could have had an exemption from work after her fourth child. Her services were more valuable caring for her family than taking so many children to care centers while she plied her talent as a baker. Sissy's and Stevie's salaries as skilled workers allowed them to bring grandparents back into the family fold, so the elders—long past working age—could care for the younglings while Mama worked.

Better than shuffling family off to care facilities. Too many accidents happened there to those beyond usefulness.

"I have given your entire family leave to visit you while you are in hospital," Laud Gregor said quietly.

Sissy looked at him sharply. No local priest had that kind of authority.

She took in the careful tailoring of his black clothing and the pendant of
Empathy, their sun and consort to Harmony, around his neck. Diamonds
outlined the sunburst of real gold.

"High Priest Gregor da Ivan pa Crystal Temple from the Crystal
Temple?"

He nodded in acknowledgment.

"What's wrong?" High Priests from the Crystal Temple didn't come
into Worker neighborhoods. Nor did they bother with simple working
families.

"Very soon the nurses will prepare you for surgery. The physicians
need to implant an extra filter in your lungs to get rid of all the dust you
breathed in. They will also try to remove some more layers of the Badger
Metal bonded to your hands," Gregor explained.

A high-tech procedure reserved for the most wealthy and highest
caste.

That wasn't what Sissy wanted to know.

Behind her, Stevie chuckled a bit. "We had to use a laser saw and an
electron microscope to cut you out of that pillar. Good thing I was there.
All the others trained with those tools had gone."

Sissy smiled up at her brother, craning her neck to see him at the head
of the bed. "You are the best, Stevie. Even if you did get educated to be a
supervisor. Thank you for staying with me. I heard you talking to me the
whole time. You kept me from giving up."

"What was you doin' in there, gal? You should'a left with t'others."
Mama clucked her tongue in disapproval.

The High Priest shook his head at Maigrie. A forbidden topic. The one
Sissy needed to talk about most.

"I had a chore to do, Mama. You always taught me to finish my chores.
No matter what."

"You always was a good gal." Pop patted her shoulder.

"I have a special chore for you, Sissy," Laud Gregor said quietly. "A
chore that will require all of your skills."

Sissy tried to will her heart to stop pounding so hard. It didn't obey
her.

Before she could ask what kind of chore, two nurses came to the door,
hands full of gadgets Sissy could not identify. Both nurses bore a priestly
purple circle around their green triangle caste marks.

"We ain't at the factory hospital, is we?" With all the death and injuries
from the quake, why was she scheduled for minor surgery? Weren't the
hospitals overrun with more serious injuries?

"No, my dear, you aren't. We brought you to Crystal Temple Hospital," Laud Gregor said quietly.

"Why?" She did her best to capture his gaze, but he kept looking away from her.

Laud Gregor waved the nurses away. "We'll be ready in a few moments. But we need a bit of privacy first."

The nurses backed off and slid the bio-plastic door closed.

Sissy continued to stare at the High Priest, willing him to speak. Her parents and brother fidgeted nervously.

"I need you fixed properly so you can take special training for your chore."

"What chore?"

"First off, Maigrie and Jaimey, I need to know why you did not report Sissy's unusual caste marks at her birth." Laud Gregor turned a hard gaze upon Mama and Pop. The blue in his eyes paled, looked like frost on a clear winter's morning.

"Didn't know we was supposed to," Mama whispered. She hung her head.

"The physician should have."

"Sissy was birthed at home, just like my other six kids. Workers cain't afford to go to hospital for a simple thing like givin' birth."

"Surely her teachers would have made note."

"Temple schools may have enough teachers and textbooks for everyone. Factory schools don't," Stevie took over the conversation for their parents. He could speak better. "Factory teachers barely have time and energy to deal with the normal paperwork involving sixty or more students apiece. Do you know how much paperwork is involved in reporting an anomaly like Sissy's extra caste marks, My Laud?"

The High Priest opened his eyes wide and shook his head.

"Enough to take a teacher out of the classroom for a month; with no one to replace them. Teachers don't have time to deal with anything but day-to-day lessons."

They all stared at each other in silence for a long moment. For the first time, Sissy got scared. She'd heard stories of what happened to kids born out of caste. Mutants. Loods. If they let her live, they'd make her Poor caste. Lowest caste won out over higher. She'd have to live on the streets, probably starve to death. Or be thrown into an asylum, chained to her bed. They'd never let her finish the nav unit or speak to her family again.

Cold sweat broke out all over her body. She began to shake.

"And when you were tested at the age of twelve for your aptitude?" Gregor broke the silence. He looked long and hard directly into Sissy's eyes.

"Automated testing center for manual dexterity and ability to read and do maths," Sissy said on a quiet breath. Where was all this leading? Why was she in a *Temple* hospital anyway?

"So you have grown up with no one in authority taking note of your ah . . . unusual caste marks?"

Sissy nodded, not daring to take her eyes off the High Priest. If she looked away, she might miss some clue as to what dire consequences she faced.

"How did you hide it from the Workers?"

"Cosmetics," Mama said quietly. "I saved out extra to buy her makeup."

"And the way she wears her hair, cut straight at the jaw," Stevie added. "She looks down a lot, shy-like, lets her hair flop forward to cover her face."

"And what about your prophecies?"

"What?"

"You know, them cute things you say to make people stop and think," Mama said cheerfully.

"That's just Sissy, My Laud. She doesn't mean anything by it," Stevie said. He tried to edge between Gregor and Sissy. The High Priest held his position. Stevie had to back off.

"Doesn't she?" He looked at Stevie squarely. "What about what she said to you earlier? Something about marrying early and being happy so you could earn your ambitions later."

Silence again.

"What did I say?" Sissy tugged anxiously at her brother's arm with her clumsy bandaged fingers.

"Nothing, Sissy." Stevie blushed.

"You told him to marry the love of his life now, and not to wait and marry for advantage later," Gregor intervened. "He needs to earn a better ambition."

"If I marry Anna now, I'll not be considered for supervisor next term." Stevie pounded one fist into the other.

"If you don't marry her now, boy, her dad'll marry her off to Tyker, maintenance supervisor. You willing to watch that happen?" Pop said quietly. "Could be Sissy's right. Maybe you aren't really ready to be supervisor. If you wait, you could go all the way to manager."

Stevie looked at his shoes.

"You told me that I would not find what I sought until I stopped look-ing." Gregor smiled crookedly at Sissy. "What am I looking for?"

Sissy's insides went all quivery and her vision began closing in from the sides. She hated when that happened. People usually got angry when she said what needed saying.

"Don't fight it, Sissy," Stevie whispered. "You hurt worse if you fight it."

She kept her breathing shallow so's she wouldn't cough.

"Your gift of prophecy is important, Sissy. What am I looking for," Gregor repeated.

"You look for the truth, but you won't find it till you admit your truth is not the truth."

CHAPTER SIX

GREGOR LEFT SISSY'S ROOM quickly without explanation. He had to think, and think hard. What was he going to do with that girl?

He found himself staring through the clear wall into the special room where his High Priestess struggled for life. A bland-faced physician joined his vigil.

Laudae Marilee's twin sister Marissa sat on a rolling stool, holding her hand and weeping.

White-clad people bustled urgently about, making almost no noise. Every Professional caste mark in the place had a purple circle around it. They had all passed rigorous tests of intelligence, discretion, and loyalty for the right to serve in Crystal Temple Hospital. Only then had they had their DNA manipulated to "Laud" their Professional caste marks.

They kept the lights subdued, the machines blinking in synchronization, and the sounds harmonious, as life should be.

Only life had spiraled into chaos of late.

"You cannot die, Mari. I will not allow it," Lady Marissa insisted inside the sterile room.

The sight of Marissa's tears disturbed Gregor more than the dire injuries of his HPS, Marilee. Lady Marissa had taken over all of her spouse's land, assets, and political positions upon his death ten years ago rather than pass them on to her children. She'd even had her caste mark changed. The blue diamond of her Noble caste mark that surrounded the purple circle of her birth caste now obliterated her Temple origins.

Lady Marissa embraced power and learned to manipulate it. Her twin sister, the High Priestess, enjoyed the trappings of power and did little else.

Gregor was glad he did not have Marissa beside him at the ritual altar. She'd have taken over Temple like she did Noble, leaving him without a power base to guide Harmony in the proper direction. He knew what Harmony needed.

Marissa knew only what she wanted.

"Marissa," Laudae Marilee said quietly. "Stay with me. I cannot face death alone."

"You can't face life alone. I have always been beside you. You have always done as I say. Now I tell you to live. You have to live," Marissa insisted.

"How . . . how is she?" Laudae Penelope asked, coming up beside Gregor. Tears leaked down her cheeks. No trace of red sullied her lustrous brown eyes. This magnificent woman was one of the very few who looked beautiful crying.

For the first time in her life, she appeared vulnerable and helpless, closer to her true height than the tallness she projected with posture, confidence, and high heels. Another disturbing sign. If Penelope thought of anything beyond her own appearance and grabbing the highest place in ritual protocols, then Marilee's condition must be grave.

"We can work miracles in surgery," Physician Jerem da Neal pa Temple Hospital answered Penelope's question.

"When will you work this miracle?" Gregor asked coldly. He didn't like the word "miracle." It belonged in the same arcane vocabulary as "prophecy."

"Just as soon as we stabilize her blood pressure and heart rate." Physician Jerem kept his eyes on the machines crowded around Marilee's bed.

"In other words, you need divine intervention more than your skills as a surgeon to save her." Gregor refused to panic. Penelope should easily slide into Marilee's place, allowing him to continue guiding the High Council without interference.

Unless she turned to Lady Marissa, her mother's twin, for guidance rather than himself. He could see that happening. Easily.

"You have to save her." Penelope grabbed the lapels of the physician's traditional white coat. "She's my mother. I'm not ready to watch her die."

"My prayers for your grief, Laudae. Some things I can fix. Some things Harmony ordains are beyond me." He kept his eyes on his shoes.

"My mother is High Priestess of Harmony. She wants to live. Harmony has decreed you must help her live." Penelope continued shaking the man.

"Laudae Marilee needs our prayers. Perhaps we should retire to the hospital temple." Gregor eased Penelope's grip on the physician's clothing before her long fingernails ripped the sturdy cloth.

"We shall perform a ritual of healing with a full array of crystals," Penelope said. Her tears evaporated, and she lifted her chin determinedly.

"Good idea. You may preside in my place." Though she had no ear for making the crystals chime in true harmony. "I have duties elsewhere." Gregor hoped she'd be so happy to take the lead that she wouldn't notice what he did.

Time to make new plans.

+   +   +

Guilliam watched from the shadows as Gregor retreated from the death watch and followed silently. Then he returned, gathering up a newly calmed Penelope from the tiny temple alcove on the main floor.

"We need to be there, My Laudae, at her side," he said quietly. She nodded and allowed him to escort her back to her mother.

Within moments he realized Gregor needed to be here as well.

"My Laud." Guilliam grabbed Gregor's elbow and near dragged him out of Sissy's sickroom. "I have made arrangements for Sissy to travel to the retreat center on the Southern Continent as soon as she is able."

"Excellent." Gregor straightened his back and turned a fierce eye on the family of Workers. "Miss Sissy, you need training to control your gift of prophecy."

"But you cain't take me away from my family," Sissy protested.

"I must. A gift such as yours must be carefully nurtured."

Hidden away, Guilliam added silently.

"Is such extreme isolation necessary, My Laud?" he asked when they'd cleared the room and headed toward the opposite end of the hospital where Laudae Marilee drifted in and out of consciousness. Her vital signs grew weaker each time she closed her eyes.

"Of course isolation is required. We can't have the media learning about a new prophet emerging. They'll drag out all the old ones and start looking for portents and signs in everyday life, making Temple look inadequate. They will rally around a Worker, looking for leadership, ignoring their divinely ordained High Council."

"Little Johnny already suspects."

"Because you told him?" Gregor sneered.

"No, My Laud. Because he watched you escort a solitary injured Worker to Temple Hospital when there are thousands in more dire need of our help."

Gregor paused and fumed a moment. "Shut the man down. Transfer him to the Serim Desert or the Southern Continent."

"Won't do any good," Guilliam replied. "His father owns and runs Harmony City Broadcasting. Together, they are the core of the movement to separate media from the Professional caste."

"How can we turn this to our advantage, Guilliam, without actually saying why we have taken Sissy into our custody?"

"Let me think on it. Meanwhile, Laudae Marilee is losing ground." Guilliam didn't want to complete the message. Didn't want to acknowledge the tempest that must rise. "The surgeons don't dare operate until she is stronger. Despite their best efforts she is getting weaker. You should be at her side."

Gregor grumbled. He looked longingly toward the main entrance.

"You have more experience with this sort of thing, Guilliam, coming from the country, working with families in the burial caves . . ."

"I cannot do this for you, My Laud." Guilliam had his own responsibilities in this matter. More than just the HP was affected by the HPS passing.

Oh, the paperwork would be endless.

At the doorway to Marilee's room, Gregor hesitated. His nostrils flared at the unaccustomed odors of sharp antiseptic, acrid fear, and the cloying sweetness of a body shutting down.

Guilliam let the scents transport him back in time to his earliest years. His parents presided over a Funerary Temple next to a series of burial caves to the far west on the Northern Continent. He remembered the solemn processions where he was privileged to swing the aspergillum filled with smoking incense. Once more he shared the sense of unity as families drew together in grief and then celebrated life with a grief blessing. The family who called him Gil. Only one person did that now. The only one who knew anything of his past.

In his mind, Guilliam heard the soft chiming of seven crystals as his mother and father intoned the proper prayers. Their voices blended effortlessly with the notes and chords they drew from the crystals. And then at the culmination, together they rapped a special black crystal. Its sweetness swelled and encompassed all the others. The acoustics of the cave amplified and reverberated the full chorus of notes.

And grief that had been an all-consuming solid barrier shattered into thousands of tiny pieces. The family of the deceased could manage the little pieces, cherish them as memories. One and all they departed the rites healed and ready to go about their lives.

The moment Gregor took his place at the foot of Marilee's bed, ready to catch any last words she might utter—and try to make them profound, though Guilliam doubted Marilee had a wise thought in her entire life— Guilliam slipped away.

He knew better places from which to observe. Secret places.

At the end of the corridor, Guilliam found a door. A metal one too heavy for weak patients to open, solid enough to hold out fire, with a reinforced jamb to withstand quakes. He checked over his shoulder for observers. None. Staff, patients, and families all had more important matters to occupy their attention.

On the stairwell landing on the other side of the door, he found the outline of another door. It had been cleverly concealed beneath layers of paint. Only maintenance staff knew to look for it. And Guilliam.

He pressed around the edges until he felt the wall board give just a little. More pressure made it swing inward a few inches. Within seconds he had slipped through and closed the panel behind him.

Darkness engulfed him. He embraced the warm close feeling, so near to a cave. It smelled dusty and rarely used, like home. He didn't need a light to find his way. He'd done this too many times, first in the burial caves, then within the walls of the various temples he'd served. His other senses opened and guided him. Touching a wall here, smelling a draft there.

A glimmer of light and the susurration of muted voices to his left seemed almost an intrusion upon his quiet communion with the darkness.

Duty compelled him to peek through the gratings into each of the hospital rooms. Time after time he peered in at severely wounded Temple people. He knew most of them, shared the pain of those who could only sit beside them and mourn. He worked with them daily, lived beside them. Most often the injured had only a single companion. Usually a lover. He could foresee a long line of grief blessings and far too few rituals to celebrate healing in the next few days.

At each observation post, he made a note on his little computerized pad of name, position in Temple, and condition, as well as those who watched. He wished he had the time to reach out and offer them comfort.

Laud Gregor had no one to share his burdens. Discord only knew if the HP actually felt anything but frustration at having to seek out a new HPS. Gregor did not make friends easily and took lovers only casually. Guilliam already suspected that Gregor had no intention of elevating Penelope, the logical candidate.

Finally, he found Marilee and those who kept her death watch. At first glance she seemed the same as when he'd left the room scant moments ago. Lady Marissa wept quietly, holding her sister's hand. Penelope paced anxiously, sobbing loudly, dramatically. Gregor stood in a corner, frowning. A study in their typical behavior.

A bubble of tension seemed to isolate them from the rest of the world, muffle the sounds. They moved jerkily, as if in a television drama where the sound and the action no longer matched.

A second look and Guilliam knew something had changed. The monitors beeped. Equipment dripped. A machine wheezed as it breathed for the fallen HPS. All in different rhythms. The tones were wrong. Out of synchronization. Out of Harmony.

And then a buzzer blasted. Three heads jerked upward alertly.

A physician and three nurses ran into the room. Noise and Chaos in their wake. More machines. Shouts, terse commands. Marissa shoved aside. She bristled at the affront to her Nobility.

Penelope grabbed the older woman's shoulders and held her tight, embracing her as if comforting one of her children. Only this close could Guilliam pick out the family resemblance in the shape of nose and cheekbones and texture of dark hair. Penelope's broad shoulders, erect posture, and magnificent bosom dwarfed the fine bones and delicate stature of the older women.

Guilliam knew how much Penelope resembled Marissa in strength of will. And how much Penelope had inherited of Marilee's concern for protocol and ritual, as well as her rather shallow view of the world and politics outside of Temple.

"I'll have your heads, one and all, if you allow my sister to die," Marissa shouted.

Wisely, the medics ignored her.

Penelope kept her from raging forward and throwing aside Professionals and life-saving equipment alike.

Gregor pounded one fist into the other. Then he stomped out of the room.

"Time to go back to work." Guilliam arrived back at Marilee's room just as the physician shook his head and looked at the large clock on the wall.

"Come." Guilliam enfolded Penelope into his arms. She nestled her head into his shoulder, her entire frame shuddering with grief. "You, too, My Lady. There is nothing more we can do here. A private grief blessing is in order."

"I'm not finished with these incompetent fools!" Marissa proclaimed. "I will have justice for the loss of my sister."

"My Lady, can you claim justice from Harmony Herself?"

"If I have to. I will take my sister's place as High Priestess."

"My Lady, that is just the grief speaking. You cannot replace your sister, only mourn her," Guilliam soothed. "Come, I will perform a grief blessing for both of you. Privately. All the people of Harmony and her empire will share in one publicly. Later."

CHAPTER SEVEN

"**P**AINLESS PROCEDURE, MY ASS!**" Jake grumbled. The most demanding itch was on his rear. Every square micron of his skin burned and twitched. Damn, but he needed to scratch.

Good thing his heavy flight suit and gloves prevented him from doing more than rubbing his cheeks occasionally. The demands of piloting a three-man cargo vessel occupied his hands most of the time. But not his mind. This run to Prometheus XII was so routine he could have flown to the jump point in his sleep.

Maybe just this once he'd make use of the sleepy drugs while the computers flew them through hyperspace. The sensory distortions of the space between space didn't usually bother him enough to give up control of his body and mind to medication. He'd never encountered a ghost in hyperspace, even when he wanted to. But right now he desperately needed relief from the constant itching.

He'd almost rather have the hangover, which had miraculously disappeared within seconds of the first shot.

Pammy had promised him he'd barely notice the five syringes of nanobots that worked to darken his skin, broaden his nose, swell his lips and add tissue to his face to make his cheekbones look higher and broader. By the time he and his crew reached Prometheus XII, he'd look like any other Numidian trader. His own mother wouldn't recognize him.

When humans first ventured away from Earth, a tribe of Africans from the upper Nile region wanted their own planet where they could restore an ancient culture and religion. The planet they drew in the lottery offered barely enough resources for them to eke out an existence, let alone rise to the glory of their ancient past. Then four years after they set up housekeeping on New Numidia, a revolution in jump drives—right after they made contact with Labyrinthe Space Station—had changed the space lanes and placed New Numidia right smack dab in the middle of the biggest crossroad in the galaxy.

The Numidians proved themselves worthy of their revered ancestors and bargained the best deal imaginable with spacefaring humanity. They charged huge rents for limited leases and guaranteed that seventy-five percent of all employees in the port, from the lowest janitor to the highest management and the most technical engineer, were all Numidians.

A generation later, merchants from New Numidia were the most respected traders in the galaxy. They drove hard but fair bargains and got the goods where they were supposed to be when they were supposed to be.

The best cover possible for Jake was black skin and Negroid features. He could go anywhere unremarked, from the most exclusive country club to the darkest dive in a back alley.

"You lied to me, Pammy. I itch so bad, I hurt," he muttered again.

"You say something, boss?" D'billio, his copilot asked. Billy had the advantage of being a true Numidian and didn't have to endure three hundred million nanobots running rampant under his skin.

Jake muttered something under his breath. Then he decided to be sociable. Maybe conversation would take his mind off his twitching skin until they reached the jump point and he could trigger an injection of sleepy drugs.

"What made you succumb to Pammy's wiles and go to work for the CSS' spymaster?" he asked.

Billy laughed long and loud in a voice so deep it nearly rattled Jake's bones. "She blackmailed me. Me and my brother D'mikko." He jerked his head to the navigator's seat behind them.

Mickey flashed them both a blazing smile, pearly white teeth shining in his handsome black face.

"What brought you into her service, Jake?" Billy asked.

"She bribed me. Gave me a promotion when Warski was getting ready to bust me back to shavetail lieutenant for insubordination." Jake had to chuckle. "Pammy always gets her way."

"More than that, our asses belong to Pamela Marella now. What she says we do. No questions. No outs." Mickey shook his head in dismay.

"Remember that and you'll go far in her service," Billy added.

More than just Jake's skin itched with that thought. *What have I gotten myself into?* he asked himself. *Probably not the freedom to run hard and fast away from my memories and the loneliness, like I thought.*

"You think this scientist on Prometheus XII really has a substitute for Badger Metal?" Billy asked, probably just to fill the void of silence.

"I hope so," Jake replied. "We need to beef up the fleet before the Marils attack again. I'd rather make our own hull shielding than try to force a break in Harmony's isolation. They *really* don't want contact with outsiders."

"Last thing I read about Harmony, they've been isolated so long they've forgotten they're human," Mickey said.

"Maybe they aren't human anymore. Legend says they transported most of their colonists as embryos. They had some of the best genetic scientists in their crew. Who knows how they manipulated those eggs," Billy said.

"I read the report on the last interview with a Harmonic merchant who left the Empire." Jake shook his head in wonder at the ineptness of the interrogators. "They left so many questions unasked it was pitiful." They knew precious little about the Empire of seven planets that controlled the process for Badger Metal.

If only their lost colony had procured the formula. . . . According to Pammy they hadn't. But they had broken through communications barriers long enough to petition for asylum and eventual membership in the CSS.

One less lost colony to fill the folklore books. One less ghost ship to haunt the space lanes.

"Harmony has their own creation myths, their own religion, totally different from anything from Earth," Jake said, remembering every word of the interview. "They've done enough DNA manipulation to give them all caste marks at birth. The process may have achieved genetic drift. And it's only been seven hundred years."

"Jump point coming up," Mickey interrupted.

"Thank God," Jake added. He keyed the computer to take them into hyperspace. Even before the lights shifted to a new prismatic scale, he hit the injection button at the base of his helmet. He barely noticed the jerk and jolt to his stomach and the loss of gravity as his eyes closed and the itching beneath his skin faded to a dull irritation.

The unquiet in his mind persisted in long involved dreams more real than reality.

✦   ✦   ✦

"I'll not have Marissa as my HPS," Gregor said firmly. "I'll not have her disrupting all that I have accomplished for Harmony."

Marissa had the same training as her twin Marilee. Easy enough to manipulate her caste mark once more, bring it back to a natural Temple purple circle. She'd had the Noble blue diamond added artificially at her marriage.

Gregor shuddered at the thought of having the lady outvote and out-maneuver him on High Council. Would she relinquish her position as a Noble in favor of the presiding position as HPS? No. Knowing Marissa as he did, she'd claim both places and both votes. She'd rule Harmony unquestioned. A true queen rather than the first among equals dictated by the Covenant with Harmony.

Resolutely he marched across the hospital complex. He had only one solution.

"Maigrie, Jaimey, please, I need a word with your daughter alone," he announced from the doorway of Sissy's room.

"I want my family to hear what you have to say," Sissy whispered. Her voice was raw, her breathing shallow. She truly needed the surgery, sooner rather than later.

Gregor bristled a bit. He'd had enough of families tonight. Whatever happened to thinking for oneself?

He forced himself to remember that independence had been bred and manipulated out of Workers. Only Temple and Noble had the spirit and intelligence to make decisions.

Whatever else Sissy might be, she'd been raised to think like a Worker.

"Very well." Gregor looked sharply at Stevie who perched on the stool beside the bed, where Gregor had sat before.

The brother vacated the seat slowly, almost reluctantly. He never released Sissy's hand as he moved.

Gregor assumed his place, imagining it a throne; an invisible altar and authority between him and the Workers.

"Sissy, would you rather stay in Harmony City for your study and training?" he asked without preamble. He didn't have the time for niceties. He had to have everything in place before Marissa could enact her ill-conceived plan to become HPS.

"I don't want no more schooling. I'm happy doing what I do. I make good money. Money my family needs." She dissolved in a fit of coughing that racked her body so fiercely she couldn't breathe. She jerked and convulsed trying to coax air in and dust out.

Stevie immediately bent her forward and rubbed her back. Finally the spasm passed. Sissy lay back against her pillows, spent and weak.

"Just as soon as your fancy physician says, I'll jus' go back to work." Sissy set her chin and frowned.

Gregor wanted to slap the determination out of her. He'd dealt with too many stubborn people of late.

"You have to understand, Sissy, Harmony needs your gift of prophecy, your unique ability to bond with our mother planet and calm her temper tantrums. We need to know how you can do these things."

"You mean you'll put her in some asylum and cut open her brain, just like any other Lood," Stevie snapped. He clenched his fists as if he wanted to punch Gregor.

Gregor blanched. At the man's suggestion as well as the implied violence. "Not at all. I have great plans for Sissy. Harmony needs her whole and healthy. I have important work for her to do that will benefit the empire."

"Like what?" Stevie asked suspiciously.

"Just a few moments ago, our High Priestess, Laudae Marilee passed." Gregor bowed his head and moved his lips in prayer. But his mind worked furiously.

"You can't mean . . . ? That don't make sense," Sissy protested.

"Why else are you in Crystal Temple Hospital, my dear, with the High Priest giving your family permission to miss a day of work." Gregor had to make this seem as if he'd planned it all along. "I'd hoped we had more time, could let you ease into your new life. Events have moved more rapidly than I thought."

"What are you saying, Laud Gregor?" Stevie faced him squarely, his chin set in the same stubborn thrust as his sister's. "Spit it out, plain and simple."

"I mean that you, Sissy, are now the High Priestess of Harmony. As soon as you recover from surgery, we will move you to the Crystal Temple and begin your education. In a few months, when we have mourned the passing of Marilee and you are ready, there will be an ordination. Already, you are bonded to Harmony. When you recite your oaths and receive the blessing of the Host of Seven, you will become Harmony."

"No," Sissy said, shaking her head. "That's too much. I don't know how . . ."

"But you will learn, my dear."

Stevie's eyes opened wide.

Gregor could almost see his mind churning with possibilities. No wonder he'd been slated for extra education and supervisory roles. Somewhere in his gene pool, he'd found the ability to think.

"That's quite an honor, Sissy. You'll never have to work in the factory again," Stevie said. The ambitious one in the family. He didn't look beyond "success" to the broader issues. He had to learn to do that before he'd make a *good* supervisor.

"You can't take me away from my family," Sissy insisted.

Gregor looked puzzled. *They are just Workers. Of little value,* he thought.

"They are more than just Workers. They are my family. Without them, I am nothing."

"Without you, they are nothing. You are more valuable than all of them put together." He had to take back control of this conversation before the girl started reading his mind for real.

Stuff and nonsense. Just like her prophecies. He had to teach her to speak her riddles and innuendos only when he needed her too. Make them vague enough and even Little Johnny could be manipulated into making of them what Gregor wanted made of them.

"They are my family. I will not be your priestess, your tool for manipulating the High Council."

Gregor reared back at that statement, shocked that she had delved so deeply into his motivations.

"Take me from my family and you will have a worthless mutant on your hands."

"I promise that your family will have the right to visit you," Gregor conceded. Small enough price to pay for having the HPS he wanted and controlled. "Whenever they are off work." Gregor stared at the floor, avoiding her direct gaze and her ability to read his face.

That was all she did, read expressions and postures.

"Every Holy Day and legal holiday," she insisted.

"You must preside at Temple on those days." He'd not give in to her fierce bargaining. If he showed any weakness now, he might never recover from it.

"Then let them come to me on Holy Days and holidays."

Gregor paused and thought. Eventually he settled his face into a mask of decision. "Your family may come to the Crystal Temple. Special dispensation. I can arrange seats for them where they may watch you without being forced to mingle with another caste."

"In the mornings I go to Temple. The rest of the day I visit my family." She reached out with her bandaged hand and knocked it against his arm to force him to look at her.

She couldn't suppress the gasp of pain that gesture cost her.

"Very well. You may visit with your family on Holy Days and holidays. They may come to your private quarters." He finally lifted his eyes.

She caught his gaze with her own. "Promise by the life-giving rays of Empathy."

His hand reached for the pendant around his neck at the same time his mouth formed a protest.

"Swear, or I get up and walk out of this hospital right now."

"I so swear," he breathed.

Sissy sank into her pillows. She closed her eyes and sucked in extra oxygen through the clear tube in her nose.

"Change is coming." Her voice sounded strange, deeper in tone, echoing around the room. Multiplied a hundred times by a power she could not control. "I am the harbinger of change. We must prepare for the future and meet it face on. We cannot afford to run and hide from change any longer."

CHAPTER EIGHT

GUILLIAM TAPPED THE STEERING wheel of his little car impatiently. Construction Workers with a huge piece of machinery backed and forthed across the street in front of him, clearing debris.

As he watched, the front shovel of the monster machine slid under a mass of broken wood and stone, crumbled pole lights, and crippled trees in the middle of the street. Ponderously it lifted a couple of tons of destruction and swung around to deposit it all in the box bed of a truck. Then it returned for another load.

At this rate the street might be cleared in two hours. Then the crew would have to move to the next street and the next.

Only half a mile from the Crystal Temple. He could walk faster than this. But he'd have to leave the car. Temple property, signed out to him. In the chaotic aftermath of the quake the car might be stolen or vandalized. He didn't want the responsibility for that. Though if it happened to someone else, the paperwork would stop at his desk.

A niggle of temptation urged him to invoke Temple privilege to allow him to pass. Laud Gregor had no idea how much work would fall on Guilliam's desk in order to shift Sissy du Maigrie from pu Chauncey to pu Crystal Temple. Even more work to shift all her data to change her caste. No precedent for that. No ancient myth to fall back on.

Couldn't Laud Gregor have waited a day, or even a few hours to make this decision; time for Guilliam to calm Lady Marissa and divert her from trying to take over for her sister. And time to prepare Laudae Penelope for the change. That formidable woman fully expected to succeed her mother, as Marilee had succeed her mother, and so on back four or five generations.

At least he'd managed to complete the grief blessing and send both women to their homes with healing tears and fond memories.

As much as Guilliam wanted to get started on the paperwork, he had other responsibilities. He knew he'd end up doing it all. Gregor didn't have the vaguest idea of how much paper it took to run the Temple; how many forms signed in triplicate; the *FILING!*

Worst of all, the task of informing Penelope du Marilee pu Crystal Temple that she would not be elevated to high priestess, fell to Guilliam. He sat back and waited more patiently for the Workers to finish. Anything to delay confronting Penelope.

✦   ✦   ✦

"You can't possibly mean to bring that . . . that freak, that *Lood* into our sacred space!" Laudae Penelope du Marilee pu Crystal Temple screeched at High Priest Gregor.

Gregor cringed and wished he could cover his ears.

Dawn had just crept above the horizon, after a very long night. Birds sang joyously in the bright sunshine. Fresh dew coated the ground and lessened the horror of yesterday's quake. Gregor did not want to deal with Penelope's histrionics yet.

"Your little pet should be taken out to the Serim Desert and left for the scavenger birds to rip out her heart." Penelope threw her arms up in the air and began pacing back and forth, back and forth, in front of his desk.

He let her pound excess energy into each step rather than in screams.

Penelope crossed her arms beneath her bosom, emphasizing her cleavage. Nearly forty, she'd borne any number of children and now reached toward her prime in beauty, poise, and confidence. She supervised detailed religious education for Temple children as well as a less rigorous curriculum for the other castes, and did it with quiet efficiency.

But in matters of politics and protocol she was anything but quiet. She invoked drama with every grand gesture and pregnant pause.

All of her features appeared chiseled from the finest marble, long face, high cheekbones, straight narrow nose, and flawless white skin offset by her auburn hair. She looked the part to fill the vacancy of High Priestess.

She had the maturity that should command respect. But did she have the wisdom? The charisma?

Petite, dark-haired, olive-skinned Sissy, on the other hand, had no great claim to beauty. Just ordinary. Everything about her was ordinary. Except her charm, her smile, and those mutant caste marks.

And her prophecies.

Gregor swallowed the anger that boiled up his throat. He'd gain nothing by allowing his emotions to rule him and giving Penelope control of this interview. He remained seated at his desk deep in the bowels of the Crystal Temple. Outsiders had to wend their way through an intricate maze of corridors and bureaucracy to get to the High Priest of Harmony.

Penelope wasn't an outsider. And neither were the other five priestesses and their senior acolytes who crowded into his office.

"Harmony has spoken," Gregor replied quietly.

"Not to me!" Penelope persisted.

"Then you aren't qualified to be our next HPS." Beneath the cover of the desktop he clenched his fists and fought for control. He'd considered creating a special position for Sissy as prophetess and allowing Penelope to elevate to High Priestess. Together they could take control of the High Council. Together they could dictate every law and action of life on Harmony.

Together they could reclaim the Lost Colony before rebellion sent ripples of chaos throughout the empire.

But could he control Penelope's vote? She wasn't quite as shallow as her mother Marilee. Fashion might occupy a great deal of Penelope's time, but not all of it.

Lady Marissa had ties of blood and friendship to Penelope. Gregor could not allow those ties to shift the weight of authority in High Council.

"You trained me, Gregor. You *promised* me. And my dear departed mother Marilee. Tradition places the responsibility of the HPS in a direct line of descent from Harmony."

"That's a new argument. First I've heard it," he muttered. "I did not inherit this position from my father."

The archivist Ivan—so old people had forgotten his da designation—had given him little except a desire to do something more important than keep records. Someone needed to search records for precedents. Not Gregor. Opportunity passed one by while searching records.

Gregor needed to actively mold Harmony to the path dictated by the Goddess. He made it his business to *know* that path, as much for his own benefit as the need to guide Harmony.

"I don't recall reading inheritance by Temple caste on the Covenant Stones," he said mildly, as if it were of no import.

"Hmmm, no one has publicly read the original Covenant Stones in living memory," Guilliam added.

Penelope either didn't hear them or chose to ignore them. More evidence of her willfulness when he needed compliance.

"Do I need to remind you that my aunt, Lady Marissa, Marilee's twin sister, presides over the High Council until a new HPS is ordained? If she doesn't approve your choice, she will not relinquish her position." Penelope planted her fists on the desk and leaned over so that her eyes were level with his.

"Better the enemy you know than the one you don't," Guilliam whispered into Gregor's ear from his place by the credenza behind the desk. The acolyte kept his back to the throng of Laudaes and their acolytes.

"Miss Sissy's total lack of education, confidence, and imagination I can control," Gregor reminded Guilliam quietly. She'd do everything he said, precisely, without question.

"Harmony has spoken," he said aloud to Penelope and her women. "I interpret her signs and portents, not Lady Marissa. Miss Sissy is our new HPS. She will need assistants. I ask for a volunteer." He broke eye contact with Penelope and looked to the half circle of Laudaes ranked behind her. Five priestesses with only a senior acolyte apiece. Most of the seven assistants assigned to each had been left behind for this volatile meeting.

"None of you will serve the usurper," Penelope whirled to face the Laudaes. No longer *her* Laudaes. Within days they must look to Miss Sissy.

Discord! he needed to find a more sophisticated name for the girl. Something that carried the majesty of High Priestess.

The five Laudaes, all wearing bright green dresses (they should have gone into funereal black) of various styles, all quite fashionable, cringed as they retreated as far as they could. They pressed the few acolytes, in lighter shades of green, all equally fashionable, into the walls. The short ones were in danger of suffocating.

In a blinding flash, Gregor understood that they wore green because the color complimented Penelope's coloring magnificently. Black made her look sallow.

"Would you prefer I command *you* to serve Miss Sissy, to guide and train her through the intricacies of Temple life, to prepare her for ordination?" Gregor asked Penelope. "You are, after all, Education Supervisor."

"You wouldn't dare," Penelope sneered. "My aunt . . ."

"Your aunt is of the Noble caste now. She has no influence in Temple. Her *only* authorized contact with the Temple is through the High Council." Gregor broke out in a cold sweat. He'd spent hours last night, actually early this morning, in the archives making certain no Temple who married a Noble had come back to Temple.

Two erasures. He defied even Lady Marissa to detect his tampering. Harmony required he eliminate all interference from Her path.

"Have you paid attention lately to the reality of politics on Harmony?" Penelope raised one sculpted eyebrow.

"When was the last time we had a High Priestess who spoke with the authority of Harmony?" Gregor countered, forcing his voice and posture to remain calm. One wrong word, or betrayal of his near panic, and all his plans could go tumbling to dust.

Discord would reign.

"Faith and prophecy guide Temple, not politics." He truly believed that. His faith showed him how to manipulate politics to Temple advantage.

"You don't actually believe in 'visions of the future,' do you?" Penelope scoffed. She straightened and relaxed her shoulders.

The Laudaes behind her shuffled their feet and looked to each other, perplexed.

"Have you actually read any of the ancient prophecies?"

Penelope snorted. "Myth and legends. No basis in reality. You can find answers to any question *in the past* but never the future."

"I have heard Harmony speak through Miss Sissy. I recognize the message."

"Do I need to remind you that our late HPS was *my* mother. I should know if she had visions or not." Penelope planted her fists on her hips and glared at him.

Gregor almost laughed. Marilee's only interest in her children was to make certain they didn't bother her, and that their names reflected her glory as High Priestess. Every one of them had been raised entirely in the nursery from the moment of birth.

"And I am most likely your father. We of the Temple have no need of marriage alliances, or familial ties. We are all one family, raised together, educated together. We all know each other intimately. I *know* that Marilee had no visions."

"Neither did the previous HPS, her mother, or her mother before her." Penelope looked smug.

Temple politics had become as inbred as civil politics. This had to stop lest humanity's covenant with Harmony be shattered. He had the means and motivation to bring about change.

Did he have the courage to see it through? Change was anathema to Harmony. The order of society and civilization was set in their DNA and recorded on stone tablets beneath the High Altar of the Crystal Temple.

But Harmony had dictated this change by giving Miss Sissy prophetic visions. And those strange caste marks.

"None of those women should have become High Priestess without the gift of prophecy," he said quietly, with new conviction. "We have deviated from our Covenant with Harmony. Harmony demands a High Priestess who can speak for her. Harmony demands a High Priestess who believes in Her more than in politics. Harmony has given us Miss Sissy. It is our duty to bring her into the Temple," Gregor proclaimed.

Another shuffling among the Laudaes.

"I ask one more time for a volunteer to aid Miss Sissy in her journey. Or must I assign one of you to serve her?"

"You'd demote an ordained priestess to the rank of . . . servant?" Penelope sneered.

"A volunteer would stand beside the new HPS. A respected mentor. A conscript would not fare so well."

The ranks of Laudaes shifted again, uneasily.

"If any one of you even thinks about volunteering, I will make certain you are transferred to the most isolated silent retreat on the Southern Continent and shunned by every member of the Temple caste," Penelope ordered. "You will be alone, unliked, uncared for. You will be cut off from all those you love and hold dear."

Family, Gregor thought. *We are family of a sort*. Sissy had her own family.

And he had to cut her off from them.

Necessary. Like amputating a rotting limb to save a life.

The Laudaes shied away from Penelope's vehemence, ordained priestess and acolyte alike.

Except for one.

Gregor looked hopefully toward the middle-aged woman in the corner. Early fifties, slightly plump but still fit and energetic. He didn't recognize her. She wore the bright emerald green of an ordained priestess. But her caste mark lacked the sparkle peculiar to those born and bred in the Crystal Temple. A country woman, newly come to their ranks.

Every five years or so the rotation of priests and priestesses brought an outsider to the Crystal Temple. A token acknowledgment that the Crystal Temple was subject to the same shuffle of personnel through all of the parishes. This avoided a cult of personality developing around any one member of the caste and also gave Gregor the chance to temporarily banish troublesome members of his staff.

Guilliam had come to him from some farming community. He'd proved too valuable to rotate out.

Penelope would be the next to go. He'd make certain she was cut off from her power base.

Gregor looked to the country woman in expectation. "Step forward, Laudae."

She looked hesitantly toward Penelope, as if she might hurt her.

"What is your name?" Gregor asked mildly.

"Shanet du Maya pu Crystal Temple, my Laud," she said, keeping her eyes on her feet. She came forward one step while sidling as far away from Penelope as she could get.

"Will you work with Miss Sissy?" Gregor asked. He needed her to say it, out loud so there was no question where her loyalty lay.

"Yes, My Laud. I would be honored." At last she looked up. Something close to pride flashed across her eyes.

"Never!" Penelope growled. "You are the lowest worm. None of us will speak to you again."

"No difference. You don't speak to me now. You're all just waiting for me to be rotated out, so you don't have to put up with an outsider."

"Thank you, Laudae Shanet. You will move your things to the secondary suite beside Miss Sissy's. Laudae Penelope will shift to your previous quarters. I will meet with you in the HPS' office in two hours to go over what is necessary to welcome our new High Priestess."

"You will regret this, Gregor," Penelope warned.

Gregor shrugged. "You are all dismissed to your duties. We have a state funeral to prepare for. For *your* mother, Penelope, as you reminded me. We are in mourning. Black clothing is required. I have also scheduled meetings with civil officials to begin rebuilding Harmony City. We have our duties to all of Harmony as well as to the Crystal Temple."

CHAPTER NINE

"**A**RE YOU SURE THIS IS the place?" Jake whispered to Billy. He rubbed his thigh idly with his gloved hand. The slight irritation of clothing and insulated ship suit rasping his skin soothed the lingering itch a little. A very little.

Mickey was back on the ship, keeping pirates and port authorities—was there a difference on Prometheus XII?—from pillaging the cargo of frozen shrimp and caviar as well as the ship itself for spare parts.

"This is the address our guy found in the public directories," Billy said quietly, checking his handheld.

They both stared at the broken pole lamps, the litter, and the gaping maw of the dark side street. Of course this was the one night of the year when all three moons chose to show their black backsides on this haven for thieves, confidence masters, pirates, and refugees from organized crime. A thick cloud cover prevented even starlight from aiding them in their search.

Those clouds sent the humidity soaring on an already hot night. The ship suit strained to keep Jake's body temperature controlled.

"My questions is: why would a topflight scientist capable of producing a substitute for Badger Metal choose to live *here?*" Jake pulled a stylus light from his pocket.

The thin beam reflected the red eyes of an ugly hairless rodent bigger than his boot with bigger teeth and an even bigger attitude.

Jake bared his own teeth and growled at the beast. It scurried away, disappearing into the piles of refuse—organic and non—piled along the walls of the tall buildings.

"Grecko's here because he's using techniques outlawed by any civilized government. Lot of medicos and engineers on Prometheus who have only a nodding acquaintance with ethics. They are doing 'pure' research without constraint of law or concern for the lives of their human guinea pigs." Billy played his own light over the stone walls looking for a doorway. No convenient and comfortable plas-form buildings here. The denizens of Prometheus used native materials for construction.

Jake shuddered inside his insulated and air-conditioned ship suit. He liked living aboard ships and space bases where he had control over the climate and lighting. And the smell. Even the helmet on his suit couldn't keep out the rotting garbage odors in this dead-end street.

"Found it," Jake let his light linger on the tarnished brass numbers above a narrow iron door. He searched further for a bell or intercom or other primitive device to request entrance from the owner.

Blank. Not even a sensor for a key beam from a handheld.

Billy stepped up and banged his fist on the door. "Haven't spent much time dirtside, have you?" he chuckled.

"As little as possible."

"Forgotten the primitive options. Not everyone relies on electronic control. Sensor locks can easily be hacked. Too easily. Iron locks take brute strength to break. Or a key."

"Or a good set of lockpicks." Jake grinned at his companion. He had a set tucked into his back pocket. Pammy had spent hours teaching him how to use them. All the while he'd played along, not certain Pammy was sane in her assumption he'd need them.

Apparently, he might. Along with the CSS illegal and totally forbidden projectile weapon. No blasters allowed on Prometheus XII. They liked their deaths messy and loud.

How primitive could they get? All civilized worlds had outlawed bullets and missiles as soon as they ventured into space. Projectiles didn't just kill an individual. If they penetrated a bulkhead, an entire sector of a ship or space station would lose air and pressure, endangering everyone aboard. Not a pretty way to die.

Almost as ugly and painful as dying from a bullet to the gut.

A shuffling sound behind the door sent Jake fumbling for his weapon. Some things were instinctive even if he hated and feared using the primitive gun.

Billy stayed his hand. They waited several long moments in tense silence. Jake's skin itched more furiously as his shoulders reached for his ears and his hand ached to hold a real blaster.

At last they heard the protest of metal sliding against metal, without the aid of a lubricant. The door opened a crack. Dirty yellow light spilled into the street. Jake could just make out the shape of a human eye peering through the narrow opening.

"Whasss you want?" a man slurred with a voice made raspy by smoke and liquor. Too much smoke and liquor by Jake's estimation.

"We need to talk to you," Jake said. Before the person behind the eye could react, he shoved his shoulder against the iron door. It budged a few microns, then caught on a chain slung across the opening.

"Heh, heh," the raspy voice chuckled, then dissolved into a hacking cough.

"Sir, my friend here is too impatient. He's carrying . . ." Billy paused, looked around anxiously, then dropped his voice to a whisper. "Money. We heard you have something to sell. We have an interest in buying."

"Why dinn't you shay so?" Mumbles and grumbles as the door closed slightly while he fumbled with the chain.

"Need some help in there?" Jake asked. He kept his eyes moving and his hand on his loosened gun. Who knew what was listening? The promise of money in his belt could bring in any and every predator on a planet inhabited only by predators.

"Nah, nah, I ghosht it." A clank and a thunk and the door creaked open another few microns.

Jake leaned forward, ready to force the door open.

Billy held him back. "Remember your manners."

"Manners be damned. It's dangerous standing out here."

"Let me see the color of your money," the raspy voice demanded, less vague, less smoky.

Jake hesitated, hand tightening on his belt.

"Do it," Billy whispered. "Or he'll never let us in. Never let us see the formula."

Heaving a sigh and keeping his eyes warily searching for danger, Jake opened his belt pack with one hand, letting the pouch gape just enough to reveal a thick wad of CSS notes that had little use in the CSS. Physical money, not account transfers activated by thumbprints and retina scans. The CSS only printed the notes for transactions outside their borders.

Worlds like Prometheus preferred the uncivilized, anonymous passage of bills. They could hide a lot of criminal activity behind bills. Only criminals demanded currency.

"Welcome, friends." The door opened just wide enough for Jake and Billy to squeeze through. Their host remained behind the door, using it as a shield against the outside.

"Lieutenant Colonel Jeremiah Devlin, CSS," Jake hissed the moment they were inside and the door closed again. The dirty yellow light came from a weak, unshielded incandescent bulb high up against the ceiling. He could see little beyond a long narrow corridor walled in stone, just like the outside construction.

"Major D'billio." Billy nodded his head and bowed slightly in a greeting typical of his people.

As an afterthought, Jake bowed also, less gracefully.

"Well, you know who I am, or you wouldn't have come here," the little man said. He stood barely as tall as Jake's shoulder. He blinked uneasily behind thick old-fashioned spectacles. "Follow me to the laboratory. I gather you need a demonstration of my invention."

He padded on bare feet the length of the corridor. Like most residents of Prometheus, he wore short pants that cut off about mid-thigh, held up with suspenders and no shirt.

Jake's suit registered the interior temperature a comfortable twenty-four degrees Celsius. Outside, it was easily ten degrees hotter. And this was the dead of night in the depth of winter on Prometheus. He broke out in sweat along his spine and across his brow just thinking about what summer would be like. His suit immediately compensated, recycling the moisture.

"Dr. Marcus Grecko, citizen of Zephron, educated Oxford, England, Earth. Worked for Tri-Chem, Inc. until ten years ago. Then you disappeared, only to surface here last month with reports that you had something of value to sell to the highest bidder," Jake recited.

"Got a delegation of Marils coming in tomorrow. You're lucky you got here when you did," Grecko chuckled.

Only the pirates of Prometheus would dare sell to the avian predators from the Marillon Empire.

"Your asking price seemed low," Billy said. He too loosed his weapon.

"Part of the deal is to take me with you back to Zephron. The Marils are likely to shoot me the moment they take possession of the formula." Grecko opened a series of heavy locks with keys and twists and combinations on the laboratory door.

Jake tried to memorize his actions. The man moved too quickly to follow. He wasn't as drunk as he pretended.

"Then why sell to the Marils?" Jake asked. "Why even talk to them?"

"They picked up my signal to the CSS and made an offer. A spectacular offer."

Grecko pushed the door open slowly, letting lots of bright white light flood the corridor.

Jake blinked several times before his helmet adjusted to the change.

Grecko fairly bounced into the room, easily the width of the house, twice that in length, and two stories high. Arcane machines bubbled and churned and dripped all over the place. Only a narrow twisting path between them allowed Grecko access.

"You might as well stay there. I can't have you touching things and messing up my settings and calibrations," the little man ordered.

Jake eyed all of the huge machines skeptically. Then he edged farther into the room, keeping his hands close to his sides.

"I said stay back," Grecko ordered. Panic tinged his voice.

"What are you hiding?" Jake asked. "I need to see the entire process, start to finish, to make sure the product is genuine, that you haven't substituted real Badger Metal." Which was getting very scarce, and therefore very expensive. Could Grecko have bought even a little bit of it?

He kept moving forward.

Grecko shifted his feet uneasily. He looked all about him with too much haste. Jake couldn't make eye contact with him, no matter how hard he tried.

Billy blocked the door, the only visible exit. They had Grecko cornered. He had to produce.

"But . . . but . . . the process takes days," Grecko said. His eyes twitched.

"You're lying," Jake said, keeping his relentless steps moving toward Grecko. "But I've got days. I've got as much time as you need to come up with the genuine article."

"The port will confiscate your ship if you stay more than one day." Grecko looked a little too satisfied.

"I'll send my men into orbit until I call them back," Jake pressed.

"But . . . but . . . I really need the money to complete the experiment. It's . . . it's not quite finished. But it will work. I know it will. I just need the money."

"No." Jake turned his back on the little man and reversed his steps.

"You can't leave me. Not yet. I'm just microns from completing the process. But if you don't take me and my lab back to Zephron, the Marils . . ."

A black burn hole appeared in the center of his chest, cutting his words short. Blood bubbled from his mouth. Slowly he crumpled, dropping to the floor like a boneless blob.

CHAPTER TEN

GUILLIAM STEELED HIMSELF FOR the onslaught of verbal abuse he expected the moment he walked into Laudae Penelope's office. He should be used to this by now. He'd known Penelope for decades, since he first came to Crystal Temple as a young man and she was just approaching ordination.

But he wasn't ready. He'd never be comfortable with her in a temper.

"Laudae." He bowed respectfully.

"Oh, come in, Gil," she snapped. "Tell me what Gregor is up to now."

"Nothing new." Guilliam marked how Penelope paced a convoluted pattern around her cluttered office. How she shifted one pile of books from chair to shelf, another pile from shelf to chair. She mixed textbooks intended for Temple education with the mostly picture books reserved for Worker caste children. Then she stamped her foot and began all over again with her sorting.

Nervously, she ran her hands through her thick auburn hair, the same color as Gregor's until the HP began to go bald and then gray. She was trying to make order of the chaos of her thoughts with her actions and not succeeding.

"He still plans to bring that Lood here to our Temple," she spat.

"Yes."

"Then I'll just have to get rid of her. Somehow."

Guilliam groaned inwardly at the paperwork that would involve. And he'd just managed to complete the stacks necessary to get Miss Sissy into the Temple. He'd twitched and tweaked the procedure for a Worker to have their caste mark Lauded when they began serving at Temple.

The archivists hadn't questioned a single paragraph when they accepted the thick folder for filing.

"I have a plan, Laudae."

"You always do." She paused in her constant shuffling of things to quirk a smile at him. "No one is listening. You can drop the title."

Guilliam allowed himself a small smile. Remote cameras and microphones were listening. And he knew precisely who sat at the other end of the wires. It wasn't Gregor. He had no idea the listening posts existed.

At least Gil hoped he didn't.

"My Laudae, what if I shift a few acolytes around?"

"Who?" Her eyes gleamed as she caught his idea only half formed. "Laudae Shanet will soon lose her oldest girl to marriage to a Noble. I thought your Bethy might fill that place."

"Bethy?" A moment of panic flashed across her face. She relied heavily on the fifteen-year-old girl.

"Yes. Bethy has experience with the religious curriculum from her time with you. She will be an excellent teacher."

"But her loyalty is to me."

"She can report back to you. You will know everything that happens in Miss Sissy's quarters." And she might learn something about the world beyond the Temple, something Penelope hadn't managed to or taught to her girls.

"Excellent idea, Gil." She touched his hand with affection born of many years of close association.

"I thought you'd like that idea. I'll start the paperwork right now. All will be in place by the time Miss Sissy arrives in a couple of days."

"Thank you, Gil."

"My pleasure, Laudae."

✦   ✦   ✦

Sissy dialed a number on the telephone in her hospital room with care. She'd memorized the number for her family's apartment complex her first day of school. In all those years, she'd only called it a handful of times.

She heard it ring three long and mournful tones before someone picked up.

"Kin y'all call Stevie da Jaimey to the 'phone?" she asked the sort of familiar voice. Two hundred families lived in the building. She knew all of them by sight. But the phone distorted voices just enough to scatter her recognition.

"That you, Sissy?"

"Yes, sir. Who'm I talkin' to?"

"This here's ol' Zeb."

"Old Zeb!" she cried in delight. The man was so old he'd lost his da name. Didn't matter anymore, his folks had passed decades ago. Too old to work, he spent his days in the community room near the front door, monitoring the comings and goings through the building. Better security than the thugs Lord Chauncey paid to patrol his factories.

"How be ya'?" Sissy asked, suddenly so homesick she ached from her toes to her hair.

"Same ol', same ol'," Zeb chuckled. "So's how they treatin' ya' over there in that fancy place?"

"Good, Zeb. Good. They's takin' care of me right fine."

"Well, if'n they don't, you jes holler and I'll come teach'm how," he chuckled.

"Please, Zeb, I need to talk to Stevie. Kin you call him to the phone?"

"Sure thing, Miss Sissy. You just hang on at your end a bit. I'll have to send sum'un upstairs. I cain't climb five flights no more."

"I'll hold." This call would cost someone a fortune. She didn't care. Somehow she'd find a way to pay for the call once she was released. At least she presumed she'd have some kind of salary in her new job.

And then there was the cost of all this hospital care and surgeries. Where'd she get the money to pay for that?

She really needed to hear her family. None of them had come back to the hospital since that first day. Three days she'd gone without them. Three endless and lonely days.

Four times Sissy set down the 'phone to check traffic in the corridor. Then she raced back to press the receiver tight against her ear, desperately afraid she'd missed Stevie. So far no hospital official had come to end her call.

At last Stevie came on the line. "Sissy? Is that really you?"

"Oh, Stevie, I've missed you," she sighed. She let his familiar voice wash over her. Tiny muscles through her body relaxed, leaving her aching and limp.

"Same here, Sissy. Listen, I asked Anna to marry me, just like you said I should, and she said yes!"

"Oh, Stevie, that's wonderful. When you gonna do it?"

"I'm really sorry I didn't tell you first. I should'a told you first, but we didn't know how to get through to you."

A tear crept into Sissy's eyes. "Soon's I get over to t' Temple I'll git you a number to call. And Laud Gregor promised y'all could come visit on Holy Days and holidays."

"We'll be there. But, Sissy, you've got to be more careful how you talk. They're going to expect you to sound educated. Remember to complete each word, just like they told us in school."

"I'll try, Stevie. I'll really try." So much to learn. How'd she fit it all in her brain? "So, tell me, when you and Anna gonna do it?"

Stevie chuckled. "Well we thought maybe since I'm now related to the High Priestess of Harmony that maybe I could ask her to perform the ritual."

"Oh, Stevie, that would be wonderful. But I won't be a priestess for months and months."

"We'll wait. For you, Sissy, we'll wait."

"Okay. Kin I . . . may I speak with Mama?" She could hear several voices clamoring in the background. Surely Stevie hadn't trekked down five flights by himself. At dinnertime, they'd all be there, all gathered round for this special surprise of a 'phone call.

"You behavin' yourself, Sissy?" Mama asked. She sounded breathless and excited despite the sternness of her words.

" 'Course, Mama. I'm brushing my teeth every day and washing my hands."

"Pickin' up after yerself?"

"Not much to pick up, Mama. I'm still in hospital. Still wearing nothin' but nighties. And mighty ugly nighties they be."

"You jes remember your manners, child. Politeness belongs to ever' caste."

"Yes, Mama."

"Your Pop wants to talk to ya." Abruptly Mama handed off the 'phone.

Each of the family came on line in turn, right down to Ashel and Marsh, the two youngest. "Thitthy?" Marsh asked.

Sissy was surprised the boy actually said something. But then he'd always talked more with his biggest sister than anyone.

"H'lo, Marsh. Did you lose another tooth?"

"Yeth."

"Good for you. Pretty soon you'll be a really big boy and go to school."

Silence.

"School ain't scary, Marsh." Not nearly as scary as going to the Crystal Temple and starting a whole new life. Alone. Without her family to come home to at the end of the day. "Ashel will be there to help you the first few days. Then you'll have new friends and new things to do every day."

"Don't want friends. You come home, Sissy?"

"I'll try, Marsh. I'll really, really try. But you and Mama and Pop and Stevie and the others will come see me real soon."

"Pwomise?"

"I promise, Marsh. I promise by Harmony and Empathy that we'll see each other soon." She prayed she wouldn't have to break that promise.

Laud Gregor wouldn't make her break that promise. He just wouldn't.

Would he?

✦ ✦ ✦

"That's a tight-beamed Maril laser, Jake," Billy hissed.

Jake fired his bulky gun in the direction the laser had to have come from. Rapid shots covering a wide swath. The recoil of the gun destroyed his aim. The noise set his ears to ringing. Anger made him reckless. He advanced still firing, praying he caught something, anything that moved.

Billy ducked beneath a counter and mimicked his fire.

Glass beakers shattered. Metal projectiles screeched. One shot after another they destroyed the lab looking for the assassin.

"Get down, Jake!" Billy called.

A single black laser beam singed a hole in his sleeve. The suit's gel armor compensated and closed the hole.

Jake concentrated his fire on the source.

"That's a Maril, dammit, Jake, get down!"

"Not until I get a piece of that damned bird." Two more steps brought Jake to a jumble of discarded equipment. He ripped through the clumps with one hand, keeping random shots firing into the mess. He didn't stop until he hit stone wall and a neat square hole where a chunk of rock was missing.

"Looks like they chiseled through the mortar and removed a single stone to wiggle in," Billy said, coming up behind him.

"Then retreated the same way as soon as the going got tough." Jake changed ammo clips and loosed another series of shots into the hole out of sheer frustration.

Billy returned to Grecko's limp body.

"He still alive?" Jake asked. He needed to hit something. Then get drunk. No way to salvage this operation now.

"Nope. But I found this." Billy pried Grecko's dead fingers away from something inside Grecko's pocket. Then he withdrew a shiny new handheld. "Might be important. He clutched it tight in his death throes."

"Bring it. We've got to get off this boiling rock and back to Pammy with the bad news." Jake's gut sank. He really didn't want to have to tell Pammy that he'd failed on his very first mission for her.

"Worse news is that one of us is going to have to go to Harmony now and get the formula for real Badger Metal," Billy said with a bit of chuckle in his voice. "Won't be me or Mickey. Pammy's magic nanobots won't bleach our pure skin and turn us into Harmonites. They are all mutant Caucasian—to eliminate any Earth-bred prejudices. I'm going to miss you, Jake. No outsider has gotten into Harmony and back out alive in over fifty years."

Jake opened the door to the outside and peeked out. The street looked as black and empty as when they arrived. He opened the door a few more microns to slip out.

A blinding white light flashed on. "Put your weapons down and come out with your hands up. You won't get a second warning," an androgynous voice boomed and echoed off the buildings.

CHAPTER ELEVEN

"**D**O YOU SUPPOSE, BILLY," that those rogue Marils are still hanging around the back door?" Jake asked as he slammed the front door closed on the light and the voices demanding surrender.

"Would you?" Billy eased back down the dim hallway to the lab.

"No, but then I'm not a Maril warrior, born and bred to fight and to suicide if captured. Never known one of those birds to flee anything but overwhelming odds." Jake was right behind Billy, keeping his gun trained on the door. The alien projectile weapon began to feel comfortable in his hand, almost a natural extension of his need to express his anger and frustration. Something about the bang and recoil . . .

"I'd call the guys out front and us two inside overwhelming odds," Billy muttered.

Someone banged heavily on the iron door. The hinges would break before the door did. But those hinges hadn't been in great shape to begin with.

Jake hastened his steps and ran smack dab into Billy. "Get moving." He bumped his partner, still facing the front and possible pursuers. The hinges and the doorjamb had begun to buckle and screech.

"Ah, Jake, do you know how to open those locks?"

"What?" Jake risked a look over his shoulder. A stream of curses erupted unbidden from his mouth.

Billy cringed from the venom in his voice.

"Watch my back," Jake ordered. He holstered his weapon and ripped off his gloves. "Pammy hired me for a reason. Several reasons actually. Not all of them my pretty face."

He let his fingertips caress the first of the locks. Simple electronics. "Let the handheld take care of that one," he muttered and set it to talking to the circuits and codes. "Now this one will take some finesse." He placed his fingers on the keypad and closed his eyes.

The memory of how Grecko's hand had moved replayed in his mind, almost as clear as if he watched a holo. Jake let his fingers mimic the pattern.

The handheld beeped and the keypad clicked. "One more," Jake breathed.

"Hurry it up, Jake," Billy said anxiously. "The door is buckling." He pressed his body closer as if trying for a few extra microns to separate him from the front door.

"Working on it." Jake looked blankly at the old-fashioned keyhole. He'd heard about these things. Pammy had even drilled him. All he needed was a set of picks.

Like he'd known to requisition picks three times the size of standard ones intended for little locks. The tumblers inside had probably rusted their gigantic parts and would require a crowbar to loosen them.

"Hurry it up, Jake." Billy didn't sound happy.

"You know anything about picking a lock?"

"Nope."

"Then what do I do?"

"This." Billy flipped out his gun and fired three times into the lock.

Metal screamed and shattered. The lock hung loose.

"Come on, come on," Jake shoved the heavy lab door.

The front door groaned one more time and crashed to the floor, bringing the jamb and the hinges with it. A dozen figures armed with wide-muzzled, long weapons boiled through the opening.

Jake put his shoulder to the lab door and shoved with all of his might, his fear, and his frustration.

Billy added his own weight.

The door flew open. They tumbled to the ground.

"Close it, close it, close it," Billy jabbered.

Jake slammed the door closed shoved a workbench across the opening, and pinned the door shut.

They sprinted for the back corner, vaulting over benches and broken equipment. Jagged glass cut Jake's bare hand. He hardly registered the injury. Adrenaline pumped through him. His legs churned up the intervening space.

A loud bang. Then the whine of a projectile zinging past his ear. He ducked and rolled the last two meters.

The scraping sound of the bench across the door being shoved aside.

Another bang.

The pile of debris covering the hole hadn't moved since he'd been here a few minutes ago. He flung aside wooden crates, dirty clothes, broken flasks, jagged bars of metal, rotten food. Whatever had outlived its usefulness to Grecko.

"Billy, time to go," he called over his shoulder

No answer.

"Crap!" Jake risked lifting his head to the level of the nearest workbench.

No sign of Billy.

"Billy!" He crawled back the way he'd come.

Another bang. He caught sight of that God-awful huge muzzle sticking through a gap in the doorway.

Jake ducked and nearly banged his head on the toe of Billy's boot.

"Come on, buddy. We got to get outta here."

Billy didn't move.

Jake grabbed the boot and tugged. Still the man didn't move. He looked beyond the half-meter-sized boots to the body and face. A dark hole opened a third eye in the middle of his forehead. "Oh, crap, Billy. What am I going to tell Mickey? Hell, what am I going to tell Pammy?"

More scraping and the sound of angry voices. Three people, a tenor, a bass, and an alto screamed something in the peculiar singsong accent of Prometheus XII.

Jake scooted backward.

"We know you are in there, Grecko. Come out peacefully and we'll only confiscate your formula," the alto called. "We'll let you live in exchange for the formula."

So that was how government on Prometheus XII worked. Pirates, one and all.

"And what will you do to me when you find Grecko killed by a Maril weapon?"

He didn't wait to find out.

He dove through the hole and came up running. Shouts and weapons fire. Someone added a modern, and locally illegal, blaster to the mix.

Jake dodged and pivoted. He faced a maze of narrow streets. "Better to be lost than dead."

Right, left, left again. He came to a broad thoroughfare. Bright lights. Music blaring from every corner speaker. Crowds of laughing and dancing bar-hoppers. A man on stilts juggled balls of fire. A sloe-eyed woman in gaudy skirts and scarves danced to the music of a cacophony of instruments. The crowd laughed and swayed and moved to some other tune out of sync with the lovely woman.

Nightlife on Prometheus XII was one long party.

Keeping close to the buildings and the shadows, Jake worked his way toward a wide intersection. His ship suit didn't blend in very well with the scanty clothing worn by the locals. But there were a few off-worlders opting for the comfort of a suit. Maybe one suit for every twenty locals in brightly patterned shirts and shorts—not always color-coordinated.

Over the top of the nearest bar—all the joints seemed to be bars here— he spotted the familiar outline of the comm tower at the spaceport.

Jake dared a tiny bit of hope that he might get through this alive.

"Everyone, stand where you are!" an authoritative voice bellowed over loudspeakers.

Jake melted into the nearest shadow, keying the chameleon unit to darken his suit and dim the interior lights. With luck he'd look like part of the stone and brick scenery.

He avoided touching his belt—a dead giveaway that he hid valuables there.

But he was still wearing a suit. If anyone looked directly at him, they'd see a man in a suit trying to disappear and not succeeding.

He noted that most of the other suits also went chameleon.

The crowd kept laughing and dancing in the street.

"Put down all weapons and stand where you are!" the voice drowned out the music.

A few in the crowd looked toward the speakers for about a micron before returning to their party.

Jake took a chance and slid farther along the wall.

"Weapons down and stand in place, or we shoot all of you!"

Still no one bothered to obey the law. Pirates one and all.

Jake kept moving. Closer. Ever closer to the comm tower and the safety of his ship. Once off the ground, he knew he could outfly any of the local jockeys. But he had to get to the ship.

He spotted the arched gates to the spaceport. Just beyond them, in full view, sat his merchant vessel with a real cargo masking the latest ob-servation and communications equipment. The heavy iron gates swung shut across the port entry as he watched. Armed guards stepped in front of them.

Jake eased to his left. More armed officials appeared in their tan shorts and shirts with broad-brimmed leather hats set at a jaunty angle. The brim on one side folded up to make way for those long, long weapons with the huge muzzles.

"Mickey, I need some help," Jake whispered into his helmet comm.

"Where's my brother?" came back the panicked voice.

Jake gulped. No sense lying. Mickey wasn't dumb. "Sorry, buddy. He caught a bullet in the last go 'round."

"He's not dead!" Mickey protested.

Jake winced at the volume penetrating his ears and echoing around the inside of his helmet.

"Calm down, Mickey. I know you're hurting, but panic now and we're both dead."

"You killed my brother, Jake Devlin!" As he spoke, the hatch of the ship slid upward and Mickey, wearing gaudy shorts and shirt sprinted down the ramp. No ship suit with its gel armor. No weapons. Just cloth and very vulnerable skin.

"Get back inside, Mickey. It's not safe out here," Jake said. "That's an order."

Mickey must have made a noise off comm. The guards at the gates swung around, weapons at the ready. The officials behind Jake pushed past him. They opened the gates.

"Go back, Mickey," Jake pleaded. "Just get back inside and we'll talk when we're free of this. We'll mourn Billy properly. Together."

Mickey kept coming. He bolted through the gates. Guards and officials followed him.

Jake edged back toward his ship and safety. He pulled his gun. "I hate shooting people in the back," he moaned as he took aim at the nearest guard.

Too late.

Rapid reports of gunfire.

Mickey screamed. He threw up his hands and fell face first into the dirt.

Guards marched forward. One of them kicked at the lifeless body.

Jake swallowed the lump in his throat and bolted for his ship.

He managed to hold back his tears and pain until he lifted to orbit and shot for the nearest jump point.

CHAPTER TWELVE

STRANGE SOUNDS AND ODORS crept into Sissy's awareness. Sleep dragged her back to a land of even stranger dreams.

Exhilaration and fear made her heart pump hard and loud in her ears. Something weird and wonderful and terribly frightening . . . what?

A sparkling purple circle pulsed before her mind's eye. A man with stubble staining his cheeks. Days of pain and confusion all blended into one.

A sharp tug across her chest between her breasts.

Surgery!

Hospital.

Breath came sharp and short in her chest.

"Breathe, Miss Sissy," said a kind male voice beside her right shoulder. "Remember to breathe."

"Who?" she said. At least her mouth formed the words. Her ears caught only the sigh of machines and soft voices in the distance.

No one spoke loudly in the hospital.

"You've had another surgery, Miss Sissy. Filters to help clear your lungs," the voice continued.

Something familiar . . .

She forced her eyes open a crack. They felt as if her Badger Metal tweezers clamped them shut. A dry crust broke free from her lids and she looked up into the gentle smile of a man with a purple caste mark.

Not the scary man she'd dreamed about. His assistant.

"Name?" she croaked.

"You only dreamed I'm here. Here to make your life at Crystal Temple a little easier." He leaned over her.

A quick prick on her cheek, in the center of her caste marks.

Her hand flew to cover them. Never expose them to strangers. Never let anyone know how different she was.

"You'll never need to hide them again, Miss Sissy. Soon you'll sparkle with the best of them. Remember from now on to flaunt your uniqueness. That is what we must learn to value. Now remember to breathe."

She blinked her eyes in puzzlement. When she focused her eyes again, he was gone.

Another blink.

Stevie stood over her.

She raised her arms as high as she could with all the equipment and needles attached to her. He slid into her weak embrace, kissing her cheek.

"Stevie—"

"Don't try to talk yet. The nurses say I can only stay a moment. And you must remember to breathe."

Sissy inhaled as much as she could before the incision in her chest caught and her lungs protested.

"That's my girl." Stevie smiled, but worry creased his eyes and drew lines down his gaunt cheeks. Had he lost weight in the four days since the quake?

At least she thought only four days had passed.

"I've brought you some books. We all chipped in, everyone in the apartment block, even Old Zeb."

Sissy frowned and felt anew the needle prick on her cheek. What had the man been up to?

"You'll need to do a lot of reading to become High Priestess. So we thought we'd give you a head start," Stevie said. He tried to sound lighthearted. But she could tell something nagged at him, made him look tired and haggard.

"I don't like to read," Sissy protested. Speaking came a little easier. Her throat was still dry, though.

"You don't like to read because you haven't had enough practice," Stevie reminded her. "I got you easy books. History and stories about Harmony and Empathy and their battles with Discord. That nice Mr. Guilliam, Laud Gregor's assistant, helped me pick them out. He added a couple from Temple stores as well."

Guilliam. Was that the name of the man who'd just been here?

"Now don't grimace. I'll be back this evening when you are more awake and help you through the first one. It's one they use to teach Temple children."

Another eye blink and Stevie disappeared, too.

Sissy stared at the stack of seven books piled on the visitor's chair, within easy reach.

Tears leaking down her cheeks, she turned her back on them. What had she gotten herself into?

✦   ✦   ✦

"Come on!" Jake coaxed the merchant ship into life. The control panel still showed mostly red systems lights. One by one they switched to green. Ten down, five to go. "Thank you, Mickey for keeping it at idle." A horrible waste of fuel, but essential for a fast getaway.

Oh, God. Mickey.

Both Mickey and Billy dead. Jake choked. His hand fell away from the pilot's screen.

Why bother escaping?

"Warning, unidentified object approaching from one-eighty degrees," the soft androgynous voice of the ship's system alerted him.

Adrenaline shot through him. If he didn't get out of here fast, the pirates would do the same thing to him that they did to Mickey and Billy.

Shoot him dead.

"Can't just sound a proximity alarm?" Jake was not amused by the mild voice.

Sensor readings showed a small wheeled vessel creeping up behind him.

He loosed a blast of burning propulsion gases. Fire and smoke ejected out the ship's hind end, accelerating him forward and upward at two gs. They also burned his pursuers to a crisp. That should put a crimp in the trigger fingers of those pirates.

Serves them right for killing my buddies.

Finally the last of the red lights switched to green. Good thing. He was halfway to orbit. The blue comm light blinked at him furiously. Probably the pirates demanding his return. Jake gave them a halfhearted salute as he whizzed toward them.

"I'm sorry, Billy, Mickey. I can't go back for your bodies." No telling what the pirates would do to them. Rumors had it the Marils ate carrion and relished the ripe bodies of their fallen enemies as a gourmet treat. Could the denizens of Prometheus XII desecrate their fellow humans like that? Or worse?

No time to think about that. He had to get out of here. Now.

"A little higher. Just a little higher." The ship rose rapidly and angled off toward the upper atmosphere.

A klaxon bonged and clanged with enthusiasm. "Warning. Unidentified fighter closing at one hundred fifty degrees."

"Now I get a proximity alarm!" Jake banked starboard and dove as the following fighter flew right over where he'd been. "Damn, they've stolen the latest Stingray 852 from the CSS." He'd only seen a holo image of a prototype. Faster and more maneuverable than anything the Marils had at the battle of Platian IV.

Shit. How was he going to stay ahead of them?

His mind snapped him back to flight school. *Play dumb as long as you can,* he almost heard his tactics prof yell at him. *Let them think you are wallowing in their wake. Then at the last nanosecond slide sideways and upward at twice the speed they expect.*

Jake careened off to starboard again, letting his boxy looking ship tilt and wobble. All the time he climbed at so shallow an angle he might appear level on the enemy boards. He considered ejecting his cargo. A lot of weight to carry in atmosphere. But if he could just get above the drag of gravity, all that squishy shrimp and caviar would give him a lot of mass to absorb a hit from energy weapons.

A team of five Stingrays swooped toward him.

"Warning. Enemy weapons locked. Acquiring target."

"Don't panic, Jake," he told himself. "Hold on just a micron."

"Warning. Enemy weapons have acquired target. Warning. Enemy weapons firin . . ."

Jake trimmed his flight path and slammed to port at three gs. He pulled upward at too steep an angle. He lost speed. Five plasma cannons clipped his ship's belly. The force sent him into a wild spin to port.

He let the ship roll, turning it into a spiral upward.

"Done and done," he crowed, with a rictus grin as acceleration pasted him flat into his chair. He gritted his teeth and forced his hand onto the control screen. Slowly. Too slowly he pulled out of the spin. He picked up speed.

So did the Stingrays.

Another volley of laser weapons singed his port side. "Too close to the engines."

He dodged up and down, side to side, wild combinations of movement, slamming the vessel about without thinking.

The Stingrays matched him move for move.

Damn. They were as good as Marils.

Double damn. Maybe they were Marils, or had Maril tech.

He needed to be better.

He needed a miracle.

He broke free of atmosphere and headed for the jump point. Well, that was a minor miracle. At two gs he was still two hours from safety.

"This isn't a lumbering merchant. It's a state of the art CSS spy ship,"

Jake muttered. "What kinds of surprises did you pack this time, Pammy?" She hadn't taken the time to drill him on the particulars. That was Mickey's job, with Billy to back him up.

Sorry. No more Mickey or Billy.

No time to read the instruction manual. He pressed his hands on the screen at random, hoping a familiar icon would show itself. A massive cannon icon appeared, nearly filling the screen. He ran his thumb over it.

"Are you sure you want to do this?" scrolled across the screen. "Reports will be filed."

"So file a report." He pressed the icon hard.

The ship shuddered from stem to stern then back again.

The Stingrays crept closer.

The screen flashed another warning.

"Oh, just get on with it." Jake slammed his entire hand over the icon.

The ship plunged forward at three gs. Jake's eyeballs dried and flattened, trying to squeeze into his hindbrain. He slid his vision down, fighting the acceleration that brought the jump point closer and closer. An hour away.

Could he survive that long at this acceleration? He'd be wasted and sore by the end. Maybe suffer a broken rib or two.

The cannon on his screen displayed three shots fired. Another portion of the screen showed two Stingrays peeling off and heading home. Sensors picked up a lot of debris.

"Damn, Pammy. That's one fine weapon." But he didn't feel his usual glow of triumph. Mickey's and Billy's bodies were still down on that cursed planet.

"Fuel reserves low. Recommend return to nearest port facility," the ship said in its super-sweet and overly polite way.

"Forget that nonsense." He tapped into emergency reserves, shed speed, and cut life support to minimum. Enough air to breathe. No gravity. No lights. Just him and his regrets.

CHAPTER THIRTEEN

"THIRTY SECONDS TO HYPERSPACE," the ship's voice filled Jake's cockpit. "Hyperspace transit expected to last twelve hours, seventeen minutes, and thirty-five seconds."

That didn't mean much. Real time and hyperspace time rarely coincided. He ran a couple of formulas through his head. Probably five days.

In a souped-up merchant vessel designed to be flown by three.

He had it all to himself now.

Damn.

Double damn.

"Twenty seconds to hyperspace."

He should put his helmet back on. Standard safety protocol when flying alone. Especially if he had to cut air to conserve fuel. Damn. He shouldn't be alone. He couldn't even recover the bodies.

Damn.

He scrubbed his face with both hands, free of gloves. Two days of stubble rasped against his palms.

"Ten seconds to hyperspace."

Grudgingly, Jake lifted his helmet. At the last second he cast it aside. He'd weathered hyperspace before. He knew what to expect.

Well, no one knew what to expect. Hyperspace treated everyone differently. Each trip was different.

"Three, two, one. Hyperspace achieved. Computers on auto. Sleepy drugs available on demand."

The dim cabin lights shifted to the left of the prism. Dust motes that shouldn't have been there swirled and sparkled like tiny insects swarming around a warm body.

Or maybe they were faeries. Jake tried to remember childhood tales of the incredible beings that flitted through life without a care.

Oh, how he wished to put his cares and grief behind him.

The remnants of gravity from acceleration deserted him. But the faeries didn't.

The pinpoints of varicolored light continued to fly in tight spirals inward, then they abruptly reversed their pattern and spread outward, around and around him.

He half heard faint giggles over the hum of cockpit instruments and components fighting to find a path through the realm between realities.

The faeries changed pattern again, split in two, and tightened up. The sparks combined and became tiny flamelets, then they grew bigger and darker, more solid as they clumped together.

Jake rubbed his eyes. Hallucinations. That's all it was. He wasn't seeing a bunch of faeries making two humans.

Images born of stress and grief.

"Nice that you grieve for us," D'billio whispered from the form on his left.

Jake could almost see through him to the spark of life where his heart should be.

Ghosts. He saw ghosts in hyperspace. The most common reaction.

He'd never seen ghosts before. He should. He'd lost family and comrades in battle to the Marils.

Alien enemies hadn't killed his two partners. Other humans had. If the dear citizens of Prometheus XII were still human and hadn't regressed to some baser life-form. Those *things* had killed his friends for no reason. No honor in their deaths.

They had a right to haunt him.

"I am so sorry, Billy. Should have been me taking that bullet." As he spoke, a black hole gaped in Billy's head. Right where the bullet would have gone. Did go.

"And me? Do you grieve for me?" D'mikko sneered. "You always resented that I could navigate and pilot better than you. That Pammy trusted me more than you. Look at you, going it alone without a backward glance."

"Not even wearing your helmet and gloves," Billy added. "What happens if the computers miscalculate and slam you right into a hunk of space debris?" He reached for the autopilot interface.

"Go ahead. Turn it off. Let me die out here, lost, alone, and forgotten. Useless. My life has been pretty useless." He recalled all his drunken brawls, his unauthorized flights to "investigate" something that turned out to be nothing more than a party. And the women. How many women had he bedded and promised "forever," then abandoned and forgotten in the morning? Too many.

All in his quest to run away from grief and loneliness.

He regretted it all. Them all.

"Your time to die has not come yet," Mickey said quietly. "You have a bigger destiny to fill."

"Live, Jake," Billy added. "Live well, and learn."

They faded back to a swarm of dying sparkles.

Jake shook his head, uncertain what had just happened.

"Coming out of hyperspace in two minutes. Two-minute warning. Antidotes to sleepy drugs available upon demand."

Sissy pressed herself deep into the cushions of the long black motorcar—a real car, not a cart pulled by loxen, or a sedan chair carried by Workers. A car she shared only with Mr. Guilliam, who sat across from her with his back to the driver, and Laudae Shanet beside her. They wore their formal robes—deep green for her and pale green for him. But the moment the driver had closed the doors on them, they'd set aside the heavy headdresses with the long strands of beads and crystals strung to form a veil.

Sissy didn't know what to say to them, though she had dozens of questions. The silence between them did nothing to soothe her fears.

The driver kept a solid glass partition between himself and her. Real glass. Not bio-plastic. As clear as water and as thick as her fingers. Such luxury frightened her. She might damage something. And then there'd be trouble. Lots of trouble.

Would Laudae Shanet and Mr. Guilliam be her guards or her guardians?

No more hiding behind her hair and makeup. Everyone on Harmony now knew her for a mutant freak. A Lood.

"Why can't we walk?" she finally asked. If she walked, she determined her own direction. If she took off the pointed and pinching shoes and walked barefoot, her toes stroking the ground with awe, she might understand what Harmony asked of her.

How could she find herself if she couldn't feel the planet beneath her feet?

"The people expect a degree of formality from us," Laudae Shanet said. She looked around, appearing as uncomfortable as Sissy felt. "Laud Gregor prefers us to remain a bit aloof from the people."

"Pomp and circumstance," Guilliam muttered.

Sissy grinned at him. Of all the people she'd met in the last week, of all the words she'd struggled to read, Mr. Guilliam seemed the most real, and the most practical.

She caressed the silky texture of the fine dress they'd given her. A light yellow green. She didn't like the color or the way the dress was too long, hitting her mid-calf; the skirt too tight to take a proper step, and too loose in the bodice. The style came out of one of those pricy catalogs no one could afford.

How many months' rent could she have paid for the price of this dress? How many meals could she buy?

"I don't belong here," she said quietly. "I don't know how to act, how to dress. How to talk."

"You'll learn. We'll help you learn." Laudae Shanet patted her knee.

A small note tickled the back of Sissy's throat, in the same tone as Laudae Shanet's voice. Sissy hummed it into life. Her body caught the vibration and found comfort there. She sang a complementary tone, sliding upward into a cascade of melody.

Guilliam matched her note for note in his fine baritone. Laudae Shanet's alto voice wobbled a bit as she, too, tried to sing along with them.

Soon they were singing nonsense tunes and nursery rhymes at the top of their lungs; laughing as much as they sang.

"Ah," Sissy sighed. As long as she could find the notes that blended with Harmony, she was safe. Harmony would protect her. For now.

She reminded herself that High Priest Gregor believed Harmony needed Sissy's weird caste marks for some mysterious purpose. Her place was not to question the Goddess, only to find and maintain Harmony.

The car glided to a stop. Sissy dared a quick peek through the window. Tall crystal columns supported an arched roof over wide double doors of etched glass.

The Crystal Temple. A back entrance hidden from the public by a high courtyard wall.

Mr. Guilliam and Shanet slid out the door opposite Sissy. She moved to follow them, scooting across the seat awkwardly.

Unseen hands opened the door beside her.

"Miss Sissy." High Priest Gregor bowed low in greeting. He wore the formal brocaded green robes of his office, with wide padded shoulders, broad sleeves that flowed beyond his fingertips. A tall, pointed crown of more green and gold with a concealing veil of strung crystals topped him off. The only thing that identified him as different from the other green-and-gold figures arranged in a half circle behind him was his voice.

Her new green dress looked ill-fitting and far too casual for so formal a greeting. She took a deep breath from the inhaler the physicians had given her. The drugs sent a rush of stimulant through her system, brightening her vision and filling her with energy. Instantly her lungs expanded. Air flowed in and out with ease for two breaths.

Then terror clamped down on her again. She needed direction from Harmony.

A male hand reached into the car level with her elbow. "Let me help you, Miss," Guilliam whispered.

Trustingly she placed her own small hand in his larger one. It engulfed hers as he gave a slight tug up and out. She had to follow or have her shoulder dislocated.

As she emerged from the dim car into bright sunlight, a friendly smile peeked out from behind his veil of beads. He had a lot fewer faceted crystals and more plain green glass in his veil than did Gregor.

Carefully Sissy settled her balance on her own two feet, cautious of the new shoes that matched her dress. Green, slender, sophisticated, awkward, with high heels that threatened to throw her forward onto her nose.

"We welcome you, Miss Sissy," Gregor intoned. "Please grace our Temple with your presence." He offered her his right arm in escort.

Sissy nodded, not knowing what else to do. She didn't trust her voice. Her rebellious lungs kept cutting her off in mid word. She took one step forward and teetered on the unfamiliar heels.

High Priest Gregor grabbed her arm to steady her balance. "Are you unwell, Sissy?" He sounded anxious. "The physicians assured me that you could safely leave hospital."

"I'm okay," Sissy insisted. She kicked off the shoes and bent to pick them up.

Laudae Shanet, her hastily donned headdress tilted a bit to one side, beat her to it. "Allow me, Miss Sissy," she said quietly.

A feminine gasp went around the circle.

"You'll hurt your feet, Sissy," Laud Gregor said.

"Nah. Don't never wear shoes at home. I can feel Harmony better with bare feet." Sissy flashed a smile to all the green-robed people in the courtyard. She caught a glimpse of a grin in return from Laudae Shanet.

Twitters and sneers went around the circle of priests and priestesses.

"So be it!" Gregor proclaimed. "Our High Priestess removes barriers between us and our Mother Goddess." Gregor bent and removed his own green half boots.

Sissy cringed away. She hadn't ordered anything. She just didn't like wearing shoes. Truthfully, she'd never been able to afford a pair that fit well enough to be comfortable.

When Gregor righted, he stared at the circle of green-and-gold clad officials. In a neighborhood Temple any one of them would have ruled with absolute power over their congregation. Here they were all subordinate to the High Priest.

And *she* was supposed to become High Priestess, placed above all of them, including Gregor.

"Do it," he sneered, glaring at each of them in turn.

A stick-straight woman in the center of the pack lifted her chin haughtily. "Never." She turned gracefully on her own high heels and stalked back inside the temple.

The remaining four women followed her. All still wore their shoes.

But the six men hopped around, pulling their feet free of their own boots.

CHAPTER FOURTEEN

GREGOR WINCED AS HIS BARE feet touched the frigid paving stones of the courtyard. The first spring flowers might be poking their heads through the soil, but winter had not yet fled Harmony City. He watched Sissy skip over to a patch of grass surrounding a sacred rowan tree at the center of the open area. She buried her toes in the soft greenery and sighed deeply. The joy on her face made his own discomfort flee.

"We have become jaded while we sought comfort over our need to renew contact with Mother Harmony," a young acolyte of about twelve years, barely out of training, whispered to Gregor.

The High Priest glared at the boy sharply. Then relented. He was right. The young offered fresh perspectives on life. Sometimes. Sometimes they were just annoying.

"What is your name, boy?" Gregor whispered back. He couldn't be expected to remember all of them. Each of the seven priests and seven priestesses had seven acolytes. As those acolytes completed their education, they rotated out to surrounding parishes, making way for the constant stream of children ready to move into their places. Nearly half of them would marry into the Noble caste before they reached ordination. Many more fell into support roles, not qualifying for ordination. No one expected him to remember more than the seven who assisted him at any given time.

"Caleb da Gregor pa Crystal Temple, sir," the boy returned.

Wasn't Marilee's last child named Caleb?

Caleb da *Gregor*. So. The boy was his. Or Marilee claimed it.

Someone in records kept track of the DNA mixes, to avoid incestuous relationships. The gene pool among the Temple caste and Nobles was too small to take chances on mutations.

Like Sissy, with that full array of caste marks. She had sprung from the Worker caste, the largest and most diverse. Little chance for inbreeding there. He needed to make sure she bred soon and often to bring new genes into the mix.

"Mind if I borrow your words to remind all of us of the truth Miss Sissy has brought us?" Gregor asked.

The boy shook his head.

Gregor raised his voice and repeated the statement.

Sissy giggled. "Ain't that the truth," she said. And then she smiled. Her entire face lit up with a glow of wonder.

Why hadn't Gregor thought her beautiful before? From the rapt gazes of the men still gathered in the courtyard, they all agreed. That smile could melt the hardest of hearts. Her value to him as a political tool jumped sevenfold. He might even suggest that he father her first child.

Now he just had to convince Penelope and her Laudaes.

"Laud Gregor?" Sissy asked quietly.

"Yes?" He inclined his head to bring it closer to her, indicating a need for privacy. A little difficult considering the top of her head only came to his shoulder.

"Laud Gregor, why are you all wearing green? I thought you'd all be in black until the funeral."

"The empire is in mourning for Laudae Marilee. But today we celebrate you joining our ranks, Miss Sissy. We wear green to honor you."

"Oh." She shrank within herself, seeming even shorter and slighter. "You didn't have to do that. I ain't . . . I'm not all that special."

"But you are, my dear. You are the miracle I've been waiting a generation for." He patted her hand in reassurance.

She withdrew it, as if afraid of his touch.

"Miss Sissy," Laudae Shanet bowed slightly as she stepped between them. "May I show you your quarters?" Her teeth started to chatter and her feet curled away from the cold in the paving stones.

"Sure," Sissy agreed. "You going to share with me?"

"Oh, no, Miss. I wouldn't dream of presuming on your privacy." Shanet gasped and placed her hand over her mouth.

Sissy's face fell. "You mean I gots . . . I have to be alone?"

"I think you'll find that we have plenty of space in the Temple grounds and quarters for each of us to have a private place, Miss Sissy," Gregor stepped up beside her, offering his arm again. "This is not Worker quarters where there are too many people crowded in too small a space."

"You got so much space to waste on privacy, why not share some of it with Workers who need it?" Sissy stood her ground, ignoring his proffered arm. Her breathing became shallow and ragged. She used the inhaler. Twice.

The physicians had warned him that her lungs needed time and care to clear themselves. She might need that charcoal filter changed a couple more times before she could rid herself of all the dust she'd breathed in saving the entire city from disaster.

"I'm certain we can find larger apartments for your family, Miss," Gregor conceded. Her position as the new HPS had to have some privileges.

"Not just my family. All of the Workers," she insisted.

"That is an issue that can be addressed later, Miss. Now come inside before you catch a chill. You have not been well." Gently he took her hand and placed it in the crook of his elbow. Then he guided her inside, with only a little extra force.

"Guilliam," he addressed his assistant the moment he turned Sissy over to Shanet at the door to their quarters. An idea shimmered in the back of his mind.

"Yes, My Laud?"

"See to it that Miss Sissy's family is moved to more spacious quarters. No. Make it a block of joined flats. At no increase in rent. That way her brother and his new bride can have a room to themselves."

If the Worker caste became enthralled with Sissy the way Gregor's acolytes seemed to be, he could use that force.

"Lord Chauncey isn't going to like that, sir." Guilliam looked around anxiously as if he expected the noble to be lurking within earshot.

"Tell Lord Chauncey he will have the eternal gratitude of the new HPS and the entire Temple. Especially my gratitude as HP on the next divided vote in the High Council."

"What do we do with the four families we displace?" Guilliam did not look happy.

"Two of them go into the flats vacated by Miss Sissy's family. The other two . . . hm . . . Lady Marissa is always complaining that she can't get enough Workers in her factory out in the desert. Transfer them there."

"The reason Lady Marissa can't get enough Workers is because of unsafe working conditions. She has more industrial accident deaths than any three Nobles combined. The entire caste will wonder what these two families did to deserve a death sentence. Lord Chauncey won't like losing valuable, trained employees."

Gregor glared at his assistant. Guilliam glared back.

"Make it work, Guilliam." They glared at each other for a long moment. "I will have a discussion with Lady Marissa about improving working conditions in her factories. Perhaps some concessions in more lucrative Spacer contracts." He tapped his caste mark, thinking hard. An alliance with Lady Marissa at the factory level could help his plans within the High Council. Hmmmm. . . .

"And while you are at it, find out how Big Johnny came to *own* the broadcasting facility. All land and business are owned by Nobles and then leased to Professionals. We need leverage among the media. The threat to remove Big Johnny and Little Johnny from the HCB ought to be worth some cooperation."

"It is my understanding, My Laud, that the Johnnys have always owned HCB, back seven generations or more."

"I don't like that. I believe I need to research some precedents here and take it up with the High Council."

"And when will Miss Sissy's family be allowed to visit, sir?"

Gregor smiled. Guilliam knew when to change the subject. That made him valuable as an assistant.

"Sometime. Make vague promises to them and keep them busy with moving and settling in. I'll deal with the visits later. Miss Sissy can't be allowed to remain dependent upon them. Oh, and make certain that all seven of her acolytes are young and haven't been exposed to Laudae Penelope's influence."

"That will take some shuffling, sir. We had expected Miss Sissy to inherit Laudae Marilee's team."

"Just do it. And rotate Marilee's team out. As far out as possible."

"Even the young ones, sir?" Guilliam looked aghast.

"All seven of them. Let it be a warning to Laudae Penelope that even she is subject to rotation if she continues to defy me."

Guilliam started shaking. "My Laud, if you don't mind, sir, I'd like to take rotation now. I don't want to be anywhere near Laudae Penelope and her aunt Lady Marissa when she finds out what you've done."

CHAPTER FIFTEEN

"**Y**OU LOOK WORSE THAN THE night you died, Jake," Director Marella said from the doorway of her office.

Jake looked up from the contemplation of his clasped hands. Pink palms contrasting with the Numidian dark backs. Would he ever get used to the new coloration, or looking at himself in the mirror, now that the nanos had done their work and he'd stopped itching?

He should sit straighter. His slumped back strained. His elbows dug into his thighs.

"I feel worse than I did the night you dragged me into your convoluted web." He went back to staring at how his thumbs fit together when he slid them back and forth, knuckle to knuckle, then knuckle to flesh.

"What happened?" Pam touched his shoulder with something akin compassion. Not an emotion he would have expected from her.

"It's in my report."

"I want to hear it from you, Jake. Every word, everything you saw. Everything you smelled and heard. Everything you thought." Dragging the high-backed, rocking, swivel chair that molded to her body like a padded glove beside him, she sat down. Then she did the unthinkable. She placed her hand over his, stilling his rubbing thumbs.

"I can't."

"You have to."

"Why? Because you order it?"

"If that's the only way I can get you to talk, then yes. I order you to give me an oral report. A full and thorough report." She scooted the chair away from him with a single thrust of her foot.

"Screw you, Pammy. I quit."

"Can't."

"Why can't I resign?"

"If you do, you go back to being Jake Hannigan and face court-martial for willful disobedience of a direct order during combat. I believe that carries the death penalty."

Blood drained from Jake's face.

"Damn you, Director Marella." He half stood.

A glare from her forced him to plop back down. This time straight and defiant.

"Good, the Jake I hired is back. I get tired of you boys slinking in here all full of grief and self-pity. Get over it, Jake. This is a hard business. You can't ever take any of it personally."

"Billy and Mickey are dead!"

"You never lost comrades in combat before?"

"Yeah, but . . ."

"Yeah, but that was all nice and sanitary. They were in their ships, you in yours. You watched data scatter across a screen. You knew they were gone, but it didn't happen right in front of you. You didn't see the blood or smell the death. Just data on a screen."

"Yeah." The callousness of it all stabbed Jake's mind like a stylus through his temple. He hadn't been with his family when they died. Their deaths were no less real, though.

He winced at the brightness of the lights in Pammy's office, and his own churning thoughts. He didn't like himself very much in that moment. "Losing Billy and Mickey was worse than losing my family. I was there. I watched them die."

And that made it all worse. Billy and Mickey shouldn't be more important than Mom and Dad and brother Lance.

"Stop wallowing, Jake. That's how soldiers live with the filth of war. We're fighting a different kind of war. Up close and personal. Now report!"

Jake spilled the entire episode on Prometheus XII. Everything, from the unbearable heat to the smell of Mickey's bowels releasing at the moment of death. Failure. Total failure.

"Anyone see you come in here?" Pammy asked when he'd spewed the last of it.

"Are you kidding? This office is tucked beneath the main dish of the station in a forgotten corner near the power plant. You've got your own space dock. No one comes down here without a specific invitation. Not even your admin. Most of the people on SB3 don't even know this office, your department, or even you, truly exist."

"Never discount the power of conspiracy theory, Jake. Quite a few people know I and my department exist, or believe it so, and are actively looking for this office. So, I repeat, has anyone seen you. Think carefully from the time you entered SB3 sensor range."

Jake forced his mind back to that awful escape from Prometheus XII and the pirates that masqueraded as the law chasing him into orbit.

Those pirates pursued him with the same persistence and finesse as a pack of Marils.

"Someone ought to go back there and see if they have Maril tech in their ships," he added as an aside.

Then timeless sensory warp in hyperspace. He didn't dare take the sleepy drugs flying solo. The shift of the spectrum and the horizon and then the visit from the ghosts of his comrades felt more normal than his time on that cursed planet.

He didn't tell her about that, though.

"I jumped out of hyperspace in the wake of that big luxury liner docked at the VIP bay. So much turbulence from their engines I don't think anyone in control could have spotted the extra blip." He'd needed to coast in their wake to save the last few drops of fuel for docking. "I broke free of them in the shadow of the station. Slipped into your dock without anyone hailing me." Literally gliding in on empty. "Two guys in the bay to lock down the ship. Both yours and both trained to turn a blind eye to whoever gets out of one of your ships."

"And between the bay and here?" Pammy steepled her hands, palms together, and tapped her fingertips together in an odd cascading rhythm. A sure sign her mind worked furiously.

"Nada."

"Any sense of movement in the shadows, a light that didn't track right?"

Jake closed his eyes and walked himself through the short trip. His mind had been centered on his own misery at the time. He had to concentrate. No doors opened from the corridor. No side aisles or alcoves. Just smooth white walls and bright lighting. No shadows.

He shook his head.

"Fine. Let me give you the antidote to those Numidian nanos and get you bleaching to Harmonic traits." She patted his hand affectionately.

"Did you know that when Harmony's original three colony ships took applications they carefully screened for only Caucasian features and mostly light skins?" She prattled on, keeping his mind occupied with something other than his own grief. "They screened out all traces of homosexuality, independence, liberalism, and perversions. Then they created and froze embryos only from their faithful Caucasian followers. They wanted to avoid any trace of prejudice among their people. Promote harmony, they claimed. Prejudiced bastards is what I call them."

She scooted her chair with an expert flick of her toe. A blank wall behind her desk opened with a touch of her thumb to reveal refrigerated shelves filled with huge syringes.

"No. Oh, no. Not again. Please, Pammy. I can't bear the itch again." Jake thought about bolting for the door.

Where would he go?

"Now, Jake. Bleaching won't bother you nearly as much as turning you into a Numidian. Besides, I need you to shower, eat, then sleep for about a day while I make arrangements to sneak you into Harmony space. By the time you wake up, the process will be complete. You won't feel a thing." She grabbed seven of the largest syringes he'd ever seen and flicked her chair right up to him so that their knees touched.

His chair had no rollers. He was trapped. Unless he committed a horrible breach of protocol and manners and pushed her away.

What good would it do? She'd chase him down and jab him with those half-meter-long needles. And sleep sounded good about now. So did a shower and food.

"Join me for dinner, Pammy. We'll have a nice bottle of wine and then fall into bed together. You can keep me company until I fall asleep. You wouldn't want me having nightmares, waking up raving, yelling loud enough to wake the entire station. But I can't promise you forever."

Pamela smiled. "Sounds like fun. I didn't ask for 'forever.' Besides, I own your ass, Jake, and don't you forget it."

He gulped, unsure of just what she meant.

"Another time, Jake. I've got too much to do putting together your cover. Now be a good boy and sit still." Before she finished talking, she had jabbed the first of the needles into his thigh, right through his flight suit.

"YeeOww!"

"That will kill the nanos in you. Now I'll put in the DNA sequence to give you the right caste mark. Hold out your arm, Jake."

✦   ✦   ✦

Sissy stared at the array of crystals and wands on the tiny altar before her. Laudae Shanet had wasted no time in beginning her training. Barely two hours had passed since she'd first set foot inside the Crystal Temple. Hardly time enough to figure out all the knobs and levers in the necessary of her suite. Or to meet the seven children assigned to assist her and learn from her.

Experience with her younger brothers and sisters might help keeping their high energy in check. What could she teach them about being a priestess? She knew nothing and yet she was supposed to lead them all as the *High* Priestess.

Laudae Penelope had demanded the right to supervise this first session.

So the three of them, with their twenty-one combined acolytes crowded into a small side chapel intended for private prayer and meditation. A few simple chairs filled the center. Laudae Penelope sat in one. Her seven assistants ranged behind her, standing in a semicircle.

Laudae Shanet's seven clumped tightly around the right side of the altar. Sissy's watched from the left; their eyes wide with awe. She thought she remembered their names. Or she would shortly, given half a moment to think about it.

Mary, the eldest at twelve, showed signs of transitioning into a young woman. She held her head high and her back straight, very proud to serve the High Priestess even if the HPS was a mutant freak. A Lood.

No one had said the hated word in her presence, but she saw it in their wary eyes and cautious posture.

Martha peered out at the world as if she needed her eyes corrected. A book was never far from her hand, and she quoted them word for word. Or at least the one on ritual.

Sarah sort of blended into the wall. Just another eleven year old wanting to be older with more responsibility than she could handle.

Jilly. Ah, Jilly. She bounced about with much more energy than sense, a pun or sarcastic comment—or both—on the tip of her tongue. "Missy Sissy," she'd crowed at first meeting. "Missy Sissy came to Temple. Missy Sissy tried to talk. Missy Sissy wanted to walk. Missy Sissy down she fell."

The entire array of women and girls looked horrified at the poem. (At the poem or because it was awkward?)

Until Sissy laughed long and loud. "That about sums it up," she said, picking herself up from where she'd tripped on the thick carpet of her office. An entire room just for her office, as well as a bedroom and a sitting room. At least she shared the sitting room with her girls.

She liked the sound of that. Her girls.

Bella was a bit younger than Jilly but stood almost a head taller. Another quiet one who observed before she spoke, and she spoke rarely.

Sharan was the littlest, looking about eight even though she'd proudly announced that she had reached her tenth birthday two months before.

And lastly there was Suzie. Just ten with wide questioning eyes and a tendency to sidle behind Mary.

Sissy had them fixed in her mind now. But she'd forgotten what she was supposed to do with the crystals and the wand.

She wore another of those ugly green dresses that didn't fit properly. This one had an unflattering ruffle at the hips over a slim skirt that barely fit over her thighs. Her high-heeled shoes with sandal straps at the heel pinched her toes and rubbed her instep wrong.

Pointedly she leaned down and slipped them off. She couldn't concentrate wearing the dang things. An ominous ripping sound came from the back of her skirt, right over her butt. Hopefully the ruffle covered it.

Laudae Shanet, bless her heart, removed her own shoes. Her acolytes and the seven girls assigned to Sissy did, too, giggling along with Jilly.

Laudae Penelope, in a gorgeous emerald outfit, tailored to fit her precisely, sat back in her chair, right leg crossed over left, her high-heeled shoes molding to her narrow elegant feet.

Her acolytes shuffled their feet in uncertainty.

"Miss Sissy prefers to perform rituals with her feet in full contact with Harmony," Laudae Shanet said quietly.

Laudae Penelope ignored her. "Show me what you know about crystal ritual," she said in a bored voice.

"I've only witnessed others," Sissy said quietly. The books Stevie had brought her and she'd puzzled through word by word, only mentioned the idea that crystal sounds alerted Harmony and the other gods that someone wanted their attention.

"Well, what do you remember about it? It's the simplest part of ritual. Anyone with *any* education at all should know it." A bit of anger tinged Laudae Penelope's voice. She bounced her crossed leg impatiently.

Fear churned inside Sissy. What if she did something wrong? Would Harmony withdraw her favor and cast Sissy out? Now that her mutant caste marks had been revealed, High Priest Gregor would have no choice but to order her to the slums or an asylum. Maybe he'd take pity on her and exile her to one of Lady Marissa's death factories out in the desert. Working until she dropped from fatigue, malnutrition, and dehydration was preferable to going insane chained to a wall in an asylum.

"Take it slow and tell me what you remember," Laudae Shanet said quietly. "I'll stop you if you do something wrong."

Sissy flashed her a smile of gratitude. She let her left hand touch each of the seven wands. They all felt cold and lifeless. Except . . . She let her fingers caress the littlest one farthest to her left. Warm tingles moved slowly from her hand to her wrist, up to her elbow, then her shoulder. Finally a flood of singing energy filled her mind. She grasped that wand firmly and held it up in triumph.

"No," Laudae Penelope said firmly. "Why in the names of the Seven did you choose that *one*?"

"It . . . it seemed right," Sissy said. Shame flooded her face.

"We always start with the largest wand against the largest crystal to call the congregation to order," Penelope said on an exasperated sigh.

"Like a shift change bell," Sissy replied. Not exactly what the book said. Understanding came slowly. The little wand felt so *right*.

"If you must use such a primitive analogy, yes." Laudae Penelope heaved another great sigh.

Sissy wondered if Laudae Penelope had trouble breathing, too, and had to inhale and exhale with exaggeration.

"Actually, the little wand against the littlest crystal is appropriate to begin other rituals," Laudae Shanet said. She held her head straight in defiance.

A bit of relief dried the tears of shame crowding at the corners of Sissy's eyes.

"Such as?" Laudae Penelope's face flushed and she narrowed her eyes.

Fear built up in Sissy once more.

"A blessing of a handfasting. A gratitude for rain after a long hot summer," Laudae Shanet replied. "A private celebration of good fortune, naming a child, or a small wedding with only family in attendance."

"I need to know that one," Sissy whispered.

"Rural trivia. We don't perform those here at the Crystal Temple."

"Why not?" Sissy asked. "Those are important rituals."

"Important?" Laudae Penelope stood up, nearly exploding with self-importance.

Sissy had her measure now.

"Important to the people of Harmony." Sissy's ears rang as a force outside herself took command of her words. She tapped the little crystal, a shaft no taller than her hand and as slender as two fingers, with the delicate wand.

A tiny chime matched the vibration of the words in her mind that had to come out. Now.

"Those rituals remind us how the Goddess is present in all aspects of life. Big and small. Without Harmony, we would revert to chaos. Harmony has to be at the center of our lives to maintain civilization, peace, and purpose."

Sissy touched the littlest crystal again. A total of seven times, each tap harder than the last. A single clear note became a chord. It swelled, gained volume, echoed. Then it set the other six crystals vibrating. Each in turn loosed its own note in harmony.

Laudae Penelope held her ears to block out the reverberations. She stepped back, knocking over the chair. It clattered loudly, dissonant against the crystals.

Sissy dashed to right the furniture.

"No," Laudae Shanet commanded. "You are the High Priestess. Others serve you now." At her quick nod, the youngest of Laudae Penelope's acolytes bowed to Sissy, righted the chair, bowed a second time, and retreated.

A small smile played across Laudae Shanet's mouth. Then vanished as quickly as it had come.

"Tricks. It's all tricks," Laudae Penelope said as the crystalline tones faded. Poison nearly dripped from her mouth. "Give me an hour and I'll be able to repeat that trick." She turned on her well-shod heel and stalked out of the tiny chapel.

Her acolytes remained, gape-jawed and silent.

"Don't bet on that, Penelope," Laudae Shanet said. "You have just witnessed Harmony's truth." She bowed deeply toward Sissy and backed away. "Use your instincts in every ritual, Laudae Sissy. Harmony will guide you."

"I'm not a Laudae yet. I haven't been ordained."

"Harmony has spoken through you, Laudae Sissy. You don't need an ordination to confirm what we all just heard. You are Laudae Harmony!"

CHAPTER SIXTEEN

IN THE CLOSED COMMUNITY OF Crystal Temple rumors flew faster than thought. Gregor prowled the twisting corridors listening to hushed conversations. Missy Sissy this. Missy Sissy that. All about Missy Sissy and how Harmony had spoken through her, reprimanding Laudae Penelope.

What was his Temple coming to, referring to the new HPS with the childish nickname "Missy Sissy."

Totally unacceptable.

And yet those who used the name seemed more than willing to accept Sissy as she was, mutant caste marks and all.

The priests had begun calling Sissy Laudae Harmony.

"Why hasn't anyone reported directly to me?" Gregor demanded the moment Guilliam stumbled into his office, arms full of files.

"Um, I am reporting to you now, My Laud." Guilliam deposited his burden on the orderly desktop.

Gregor frowned at the clutter. "You were not there. Your report is hearsay and therefore useless. I want to talk to Shanet. Get her here. Now."

"First, My Laud, your signature on these documents."

"What is this?" Gregor demanded.

Guilliam looked at his feet. "The rotation roster that you requested, My Laud."

"I didn't request . . . oh." He flipped open the top file. The first item up was indeed a list of names shuffling personnel among the far-flung parishes across the planet. "I don't see Laudae Penelope's name on the list, Guilliam. But I do see yours. At the very top. I don't remember giving you permission to rotate."

As he flipped through the file, nodding approval of the other changes, he peeked at the one directly below. Ah, the communications reports from deep space. Still sealed with wax and a new electronic thumbprint. No one, absolutely no one, but himself and one communications officer had the clearance to look in that file. Two other communications people had died in "accidents" rather than risk a leak of this information.

"Please, sir. I . . . um . . ." Guilliam looked over his shoulder in search of eavesdroppers.

"This office is secure." No one would dare eavesdrop here, even if they could get past the layers of offices and assistants between Gregor and the outside world. Still, he pressed a button beneath his desk that set up a jamming field blocking electronic listening. Another toy created by the Spacers and shared only with him.

"Sir, they all come to me with their complaints. All of the women. They want me to pass them on to you." Guilliam dropped into the visitor's chair in total exhaustion. "Laudae Penelope wants Laudae Shanet sent to the desert. Laudae Shanet wants Laudae Penelope rotated to serve in an asylum— preferably on the Southern Continent. One acolyte wants to transfer to Miss Sissy's entourage. Three older girls want to serve someone else, anyone else, other than Miss Sissy or Laudae Penelope. Most of them are quaking in their shoes—except they are all going barefoot now like Miss Sissy—in fear of Miss Sissy. I can't sort it all out and serve you as well."

"Has Laudae Penelope spoken to her aunt, Lady Marissa, yet?" Gregor tapped his caste mark, elbow on the desk, obscuring the files.

"I don't know, sir. I can't keep track of them all," Guilliam whined.

"Send Laudae Penelope to the dressmakers to supervise the new formal robes for Miss Sissy's ordination. That ought to keep her busy for a few hours. Then bring Laudae Shanet to me."

"I'll send word . . ."

"No. Fetch her yourself. I don't want anyone else privy to our conversation."

"Yes, sir." Guilliam heaved himself out of the chair. "You can sign the rotation roster while I'm gone."

"I think not, Guilliam. I find you too useful. Perhaps I'll ordain you. Then you can have seven acolytes of your own to help you."

"Harmony forbid. I have too much work to do as it is. Supervising seven brats, taking my turn conducting services, *and* administering your office. No, thank you, My Laud. I'd rather be chaplain at an asylum."

✦ ✦ ✦

Jake yawned and stretched. The bed in the apartment adjacent to Pammy's office was more than big enough for two. He grinned at the thought of Pammy indulging in an orgy in here.

Last night hadn't been an orgy, but it had been well worth the wait. She'd dallied in her office until he'd crawled into the huge bed. He'd taken his time cleaning up and eating. He had to make up for a bunch of missed meals during his long and lonely flight back from Prometheus XII. Eventually he'd given up waiting for Pammy, hoping she'd finish and join him. Then she'd appeared in the doorway, stark naked, with a bottle of wine and two glasses.

"I think I'll give up on skinny young things. They got nothing on you, Pammy," he said to himself as he grinned all over again.

The lights came on. Probably Pammy telling him it was time to get up and go to work. She'd left him sometime in the middle of the night while he slept.

A quick check showed his skin back to his normal fairness. Really fair. More than just a lack of sunlight from too many hours in ship suits. The hairs on his arms and chest had bleached blond, nearly white. He bounded out of bed and into the bathroom.

"I look like some kind of Viking God!" He marveled at the heavy muscles in his arms and shoulders, the tightness of his butt, and rippled abs.

"Wow! Pammy's nanos really did a number on me."

"They certainly did," Pammy said from right behind him. Her eyes looked heavy with languor and pleasure even though she'd dressed in her usual stiff suit.

He rubbed a red splotch on his left cheek. Those microscopic robots hadn't quite finished there, he guessed.

"Now get dressed. I've ordered breakfast in my office." She slapped his butt as she retreated. But she didn't take her eyes off him. A hint of a smile suggested they linger a bit longer in the intimacy of her apartment.

He reached to pull her against his chest.

She backed away. "Work first. I've also scheduled you into the heavy grav gym in . . ." She checked her chrono. "Less than an hour. You're going to have to work to keep those muscles. Nanos can't do everything."

"So what's my cover?" Jake asked ten minutes later, ravenous and eager to face the day.

"We've had a family in deep cover on Harmony VI, the outermost planet of the Harmonic Empire, for almost two generations. I contacted them last night. Military caste. They are going to slip you into their son's place when his unit transfers to the capital two weeks from now."

"What about the son?"

"He wants out. Got a wife with a child on the way. The same ship that takes you in will bring them out."

"Military units are tight. His men will know something strange is going on. They won't recognize me."

"That's the beauty of nanos. Yours were programmed to make you look like the man you are replacing. He'll give you a REM implant the moment you make the transfer. Filled with memories and data. That's tech the Harmonites don't have. By the time you join the unit, you'll know enough to fake your way through. Incidentally, the son's name is Sergeant Jacob da Jacob pa Law Enforcement H6. Easy enough for you to remain Jake. A way of separating you from your father who is also a sergeant. Less likely to forget your new identity that way."

"That implant won't involve another one of your syringes, will it?" Jake shuffled away from her desk.

"No. Their implant will be administered while you sleep. But your new caste mark isn't up to snuff. I think I need to give you a booster." She pulled another syringe from behind the tray of eggs, toast, bacon, and coffee on two plates that sat between them. "And by the way. We think Harmony has a listening post hidden somewhere that monitors all our communications. Once you are in, you are on your own. For your own protection, no signals to me or anyone else in the CSS until you need extraction. I'll try to get a coded message to you if situations change on this end."

"Oh, Pammy. You've got to find a better way to do this." Jake eyed the size of the syringe and cringed.

"Would you rather have a tattoo? They hurt more and getting rid of them is even more painful. It's also more detectable under medical exam. They take caste marks *very* seriously on Harmony."

Jake sighed and took a fortifying sip of coffee. "I hate that I'm leaving you with the memory of that syringe more powerful than my memory of last night."

"Oh, I'll make sure you have more pleasant memories of me before you leave. Now sit still, this has to go dead center on the caste mark."

✦   ✦   ✦

"My sister Sissy should be here. Why isn't she here?" Stevie asked.

Guilliam had to step back from the force of the young man's insistence. He'd been listening to the music that played from a radio in the background, so the young man had startled him. No one listened to music at Temple—they spent so much time yapping at each other they didn't have time to listen to anything else. He enjoyed the sense of quiet that filled him when music played. Until Stevie had interrupted it.

"Missy Sissy is immersed in her studies. Laud Gregor deemed it imprudent to disrupt her just yet," Guilliam hedged. Better to quote the HP than voice his own opinions just yet.

"My girl needs to come home for a bit. Jes so's she knows where home is," Maigrie added. She noisily stacked pots and pans in a box.

"You're only moving two floors up and three landings to the east. Missy Sissy will be able to find you." If Laud Gregor ever released her from the prison of her office and classroom.

"Don't like it. Not one little bit. She's been gone three weeks now. Three whole weeks without my girl. I miss her." Maigrie sniffed. A little tear leaked from her eye. She didn't dash it away.

Guilliam patted her shoulder in sympathy. He'd missed working with people who weren't afraid to show honest emotions. He'd missed the sense of belonging together and burdens shared that happened only in a tight family.

He tried to re-create this feeling with his children and the woman he loved. But they had to keep that closeness a secret under Gregor's rule, had to avoid touching each other in public, had to pretend they didn't live together. Guilliam had gone so far as to maintain sparse quarters next to Laud Gregor, retiring there every night. Then he slipped out by back passages and hidden doorways to where he truly slept and lived.

"I understand your distress, Maigrie, Stevie. I'm doing the best I can to find a way for you to visit Sissy . . ."

"Laud Gregor promised, every Holy Day and holiday." Stevie stood firm, arms crossed before his chest.

"Once Sissy is ordained . . ."

"Tomorrow."

"I can't . . ."

"Then I can talk to Little Johnny outside and tell him why two *innocent* families are moving to Lady Marissa's factory in the desert. Why two families, twelve people, eight of them children, with two more on the way, will die in those barren holes in the desert Lady Marissa calls factories. We don't want comfort at that cost, Mr. Guilliam."

"Now, Stevie—you are right of course. I have no more excuses, no explanations, except that I will do my best to find them new quarters here in the city. Tomorrow is the state funeral for Laudae Marilee. Missy Sissy must be present. Afterward, I will send a car for you and your parents. I don't know that I can authorize more than you three. You will visit your sister tomorrow afternoon."

Guilliam just hoped Laud Gregor wouldn't find out and cancel the plans. Or the redeployment of the displaced Workers.

CHAPTER SEVENTEEN

GREGOR STARED AT SISSY'S LIMP form huddled on the floor of her bedroom. A dry cough racked the body of his new High Priestess in training. It went on and on. She jerked and spasmed. The sound grated on his nerves, making his own lungs itch in Empathy.

Not a single acolyte or priestess lingered in the room to help her or even lend her comfort. Instead, they cowered in fear in the outer chambers. And Sissy was only half dressed in a black slip and stockings for the state funeral due to commence in an hour.

A panicked call from Laudae Shanet had interrupted his own preparations for the coming ordeal of Marilee's funeral. The former HPS had already been buried deep in a cave, returned to Harmony's womb, in a private ceremony. Today was ritual and pomp for the public. And a chance for them to glimpse Sissy, the new HPS.

He stooped to wrap an arm around Sissy's thin shoulders and help her up. She trembled in weakness and despair.

"'I's sorry, Laud Gregor. I be better soon so's I kin help out at the ritual." She must be in bad shape if she reverted to the dialect of her childhood. He hadn't heard a single grammatical mistake from her since two days after her arrival. Just one small indication of the intelligence beaten down by her upbringing.

"Don't worry about that, Miss Sissy," he soothed, rubbing her back to ease some of the tenseness from her muscles. The sharp angles of her shoulder blades and spine bothered him. Hardly any extra flesh on her at all.

He made a mental note to have Guilliam check into the living conditions in Lord Chauncey's domain. If the Workers were as drastically underfed as this young woman, no wonder there was a constant shortage in the factories. He needed to build up support among the other castes to gain approval of his plans for Harmony, not watch them starve to death.

Sissy leaned heavily against his arm. Gently he scooped her up and carried her to the bed. Clumsily he tucked the covers around her and stuffed extra pillows behind her back and shoulders to prop her up and keep her lungs clear.

Unfamiliar actions. For all the children he'd probably fathered, he'd never had the time, interest, or need to care for them. Nannies did that in the nursery, raising all of the Temple children equally. Any one of them might rise to the role of priest, or remain in the nursery as caregivers, or anything in between. Each took the training most suited to their personality and intelligence. Or even desire.

He'd certainly never scored in the highest percentiles on his tests. But his need to play an active part in shaping Harmony had carried him forward into his current position of leadership.

He had an entire empire to nurture, so why was he wasting so much time on one frail little girl?

Because she held hope in her hands and her prophecies.

"You there, Laudae Shanet!" he called into the outer room.

"Y . . . yes, My Laud." She remained firmly outside, not even showing her face in the doorway. Illness came rarely to the Temple. And when it did, an army of medicos descended to isolate it before it spread.

Rarely encountering it, the Temple caste had grown to fear illness. Temple caste had to present a solid and healthy front for the people. Another reason for the anonymity and frequent rotation of the priests. If one developed a sign of weakness in body or mind, few noticed when they were whisked away and replaced by someone younger and more stable.

Their hospital specialized in minor accidents, obstetrics, and geriatrics. Rarely any other condition. Sissy's condition came under the category of accidents. He hoped. Maybe he should give orders that the physicians had permission to consult other Professionals with more expertise.

"Laudae Shanet, send for a physician and transport to hospital. Miss Sissy needs a new filter in her lungs."

"Wh . . . what about the funeral?" Shanet still did not show her face.

"We will carry on without Miss Sissy. Obey my orders, Laudae. Get help for our High Priestess. Now."

"Yes, My Laud."

He heard scurrying feet.

"I can do this, Laud Gregor. I know the ritual," Sissy said weakly. "It's just . . ."

"It's just that you damaged your health saving this city from the worst of a devastating quake." Gregor sat on the side of the bed and rested his hand on her shoulder, discouraging her from getting up.

"If you'd just get me a new inhaler, I'll be okay in a few minutes. Plenty of time to finish dressing."

She wore no makeup and her hair lay lank about her shoulders. Any woman he knew would need at least another two hours to finish dressing let alone work through the dozen prayers to set her mind properly for the long state funeral.

"Where is your inhaler?" He scanned the neat nightstand and dressing table. No inhaler. And precious little else. Not even the clutter of discarded garments and personal hygiene articles. Unusual. Every woman in the Crystal Temple residence went to extreme effort to personalize her quarters within minutes of moving in.

"I used it up," Sissy said shamefacedly.

Gregor fumed. "Why didn't anyone tell me you needed to use it so often that you used up four in less than a month?"

"I . . . I didn't want to bother you. You're a busy man with lots of responsibility."

"*You* are my responsibility, Miss Sissy. Did no one else think to order you a new inhaler?"

"No one seemed to know how."

Another bustle of sound in the outer room. "Help is here, Sissy. Now you do as the physicians tell you and get better. We will carry on without you for a few more days. I'll send you some reading material while in hospital. You can learn while overcoming the boredom of staying in bed."

"Yes, My Laud," she said meekly. But she bit her lip and turned her face away from him.

Did he sense distaste? He couldn't imagine why. Reading history and political science had always fascinated him. Studying the mistakes of the past had taught him early on that he could find the best path for Harmony when no one else could.

As the medical people slipped an oxygen mask over Sissy's small face pinched with pain, Gregor was struck again by her fragility. He'd risked a lot bringing the girl into the Temple. He couldn't afford to have her slip away again from ill health. The Temple and the High Council would see that as Harmony's disapproval of Sissy and therefore of him.

"Take very good care of her," he ordered the men and women with purple encircling their Professional caste mark. "Make certain you get the filter right this time. I entrust the savior of Harmony into your hands."

They nodded and moved her gently onto a wheeled stretcher. Her skin looked as pale as the sheet that covered her.

He bit his lip, pushing aside the panic that roiled in his gut. He couldn't lose her now. Or ever. Harmony needed her.

He needed her more.

✦   ✦   ✦

"It's going to be a few minutes before we can prep you for surgery," a nurse told Sissy, wheeling a cart with a television into Sissy's hospital room. "We thought you might want to watch the funeral."

A real television. Her block of flats had one in the rec center. But it rarely worked, and when it did, the elders monopolized it, pushing the younger folk so far back they couldn't see anything on it. She'd only ever watched a broadcast when a friend from the factory had invited her and Stevie to view a documentary re-creating Harmony's mating with Empathy, bringing their offspring Nurture and Unity, into being. The entire gathering had cringed and cried out at the war between these gods and their rival family Anger, Greed, and Fear. In the end the seven gods had created the people and given them a home with the compromise that all seven entities belonged together in balance.

Discord had been banished from the family and went off to sulk in the desert and other remote locations, ready to stir up trouble at a moment's notice. Waiting to send a chosen one to break the caste system. Sometime. Someday in the far future.

Sissy had wept openly at the beauty of the drama. She had refused future invitations to watch news and other plays, afraid that nothing else could match the first presentation.

But Mama avidly watched a continuing program every afternoon when she finished work at the bakery.

The nurse turned on the power knob and perched on the visitor's chair.

Sissy didn't dare protest and disappoint the nurse by refusing to watch the ritual she should have presided over.

The black screen grayed, then sprang to life full of color and music. Mournful tones belled from a pipe organ. Lighter but equally sad notes from a full orchestra harmonized with the metallic notes. Figures in black and gold and crystal wended their way through the aisles of the Crystal Temple forecourt, each step matching the rhythm of the music.

Gray skies, heavy with unshed rain, cast an appropriate gloom over the scene.

Sissy sat up, enthralled with the sights and sounds. "It's so beautiful," she whispered around the oxygen tube in her nose. "Why'd I dread being a part of it?"

"New to you, love. We all fear new things. We don't often have state funerals. I've never seen a black crystal on the High Altar before. Must be the biggest one ever made. This is a special treat for all of us. Hope you don't mind that we postponed your surgery until afterward so we can all watch."

"Not at all. I want to see it, too." Sissy counted the steps of the chains of priests and priestesses in their black or gray and gold. She thought she could pick out Laud Gregor at the head of the procession. His proud posture and graceful movements betrayed him to anyone who knew him. The elegant woman right behind him, with more crystals than anyone in her veil had to be Laudae Penelope.

Sissy recognized that headdress and veil as the one Laudae Shanet had prepared for her. Envy prickled her shoulders. Penelope had taken the magnificent piece.

"I guess she has more right to it than I do," she grumbled. But Sissy did so want to hear how those crystals chimed when they clanked together at every movement.

She concentrated on finding her own seven acolytes in the sea of small gray-robed figures at the rear. Too much alike. Too many of them.

One woman stood out. She wore a long flowing gown of black and silver, to match her hair drawn back into a tight bun. A nearly transparent black cloth draped over her head and shoulders. The cameras drew close to her, singling her out.

"Lady Marissa, twin sister to our dear departed Laudae Marilee," a man's voice said softly through the television.

Then the camera zipped over to the first rank of observers and pointed out Lady Marissa's twin sons and other high-ranking Nobles. Including Lord Chauncey, a frail old man in a wheeled chair. His black suit and crisp white shirt looked like they cost Sissy's entire yearly salary.

She'd never before seen the man who controlled so much of his Workers' lives in Harmony City, had controlled so much of Sissy's life.

Then Laud Gregor tapped out the first resonant chimes on a huge black crystal at the center of the altar. The crystal picked up the tones from the pipe organ and the plucked strings from the orchestra to harmonize in a chord that twisted Sissy's heart and reminded her of the grief felt by the entire empire at the loss of their High Priestess; of all the deaths that had happened during the quake.

Sissy wondered if she could have brought forth the same tone if she had been the one to tap that crystal.

A clap of thunder added a note of discord. A gust of wind rattled the trees outside her window.

Sissy jumped and gasped. She held her hand to her throat, thrilled at the energy and majesty of a storm. She wanted to rush to the window and watch the panoply across the skies. That was a new word she'd learned. Laud Gregor had used it to describe the full ritual of a state funeral. It seemed to fit the storm that turned the clouds blacker and sent flickers of strange light across her senses.

Something strange and wonderful hovered just beyond the edges of her vision. What? Was Harmony speaking to her again?

"Oh, dear. I do hope the power holds," the nurse said. She bustled over to the window to look out upon the city. "So far no black sections."

The strange flickers inside Sissy's head vanished.

"Laud Gregor told me that Laudae Marilee hated thunderstorms. I wonder why Harmony sent this one to her funeral. Seems kind of a dishonor." Sissy wouldn't allow herself to believe the storm honored her, Laudae Marilee's replacement. Sissy loved storms as much as she relished bright blue skies and lush grass beneath her feet. Whatever weather Harmony threw at them had a purpose. She reveled in it all.

"I wonder why the Temple scheduled the funeral for today. The weather satellites should have predicted this a week in advance," the nurse grumbled. "Surely they could have waited a day for better weather."

A flash of blue-white light out the windows made the interior yellow toned lights flicker. More thunder rolled around and around the heavens in accompaniment. Shouts of distress erupted in the corridor.

On the television screen the throng of funeral attendees pressed back to the scant cover offered by the overhang behind the seven crystal columns—two of them only recently repaired and held together with miracle compounds that hardly showed the cracks at all.

The shouts in the hospital corridor became desperate. Slamming doors and running feet accompanied the sounds of distress.

Another flicker of lights and more thunder. Sissy began to tremble with excitement she didn't understand, could hardly contain.

A ball of golden fur shot into Sissy's room. It levitated to her bed and tried to crawl beneath her light sheet and blanket.

"What have we here?" She climbed back onto the bed and tried to soothe the very wet and frightened cat that pressed itself as close to her as possible.

"Oh, my. Don't touch it, Miss Sissy. It's dirty. The fur will upset your breathing."

"How'd you get in here?" Sissy asked the cat, letting it find warmth and comfort beside her. "You're so skinny, hasn't anyone fed you lately?"

Two orderlies slid to a halt outside her door and bolted in. "We'll take the animal now," one of them said, reaching for the cat.

"Why?" Sissy asked. She kept a protective hand on the critter.

The two orderlies and the nurse stared at her aghast. "A hospital is no place for a cat, Miss. It's dirty, full of contaminants and allergens."

"It sneaked in right after the rain started. We chased it all over," an orderly explained. "The thunder must have frightened it. Wonder why it was out on the streets. Laws against letting pets run free."

"It's frightened and lonely," Sissy said. Just like she was. "He doesn't have a home."

Did Sissy?

The cat butted its head against her side.

She pulled it closer yet. A deep rumbling purr grew from a faint wheeze to a loud roar beneath her hand. The vibrations melded with the pageantry and music on the television screen and filled her with a sense of Unity.

If she closed her eyes, she could almost see the tendrils of power that bound all life together in Harmony with the mother planet.

Once again, words formed in the back of her throat and tumbled out beyond her will to control them. Her voice rolled, deeper, more majestic than her own. It echoed through the room on a sympathetic note to the chiming crystals on the television.

"I claim this cat as a symbolic refugee, as the Temple is required to remain open to all those lost and alone, living without Harmony. We must use Empathy and Nurture to help them find Unity and Harmony."

The hospital professionals bowed to her, mouths agape in wonder.

CHAPTER EIGHTEEN

J AKE CHECKED THE AIR IN his emergency reserve for the seventh time in as many minutes. He hated running solo with a dead ship. No air, no lights, no engines, no sensors. And no gravity. Only his own eyes constantly scanning for signs of another ship, also running dead. Momentum kept him going in the vacuum of space on a planned trajectory.

He'd drifted inside the borders of the Harmonite Empire two hours ago.

If worse came to worse, and the authorities found him, he had the excuse of major ship malfunction and loss of control. The tiny explorer scout certainly looked as if it had sustained a collision with an asteroid or space junk. Pammy had made certain of that.

She built layer upon layer of cover story into his documents. Three different sets of them to cover any contingency. If they all got questioned, Jake had to wing it on his own and hope for a prison cell on Harmony Prime—which he intended to break out of as soon as possible.

If all went right, he'd exchange identities with another man of similar age and build. A quick shot of more nanos should complete the identity exchange.

But where was the guy he was supposed to replace? They should have rendezvoused five minutes ago.

Out here, running dead, a tiny fraction of a degree off the planned path and they'd miss by a parsec.

The ship jolted slightly.

Startled, Jake nearly panicked and hit the sequence to bring the ship back to life.

A tiny buzz inside his helmet. Pilot to pilot, private conversation, limited range and subject to interference and override.

They had to keep each burst of words short and simple. Long-range sensors could pick up the signal if not the actual words.

"We have tethered to you," a man said quietly in his ear over the static of space radiation. His accent sounded strange, slow and clipped at the same time. Final syllables drifted off into nothingness.

"Acknowledged. Sending my own tether over."

"No time. Open hatch." Anxiety clipped the man's words further.

Jake obeyed.

In moments two suited figures drifted from the small storage area behind the cockpit into the copilot and navigator's jump seats.

"Two?"

"My spouse." The taller of the two figures handed Jake a data flimsy. "Illegal marriage out of caste. Baby coming. We had to get out fast. My colonel is suspicious."

"Briefing?"

"No time. Take my ship back. Dream drugs tell you much."

Another buzz in Jake's other ear. Someone was trying to listen.

Hastily, he vacated his seat and propelled himself from one handhold to another until he stood in the hatch. "Luck!" he told the fugitives, grabbed the tether, and slid twenty meters across to another hatch. Not much more than a black outline inside a black blob against a black backdrop. Only his helmet lights showed him anything.

He'd no sooner retracted the tether and closed the hatch than his counterpart risked a quick firing of engines to turn back toward the CSS and safety. Then he killed the engines and drifted away.

Jake allowed himself a moment while his heart thundered in his ears to orient himself to the new ship. Everything seemed reversed, right to left, front to back. Ancient in configuration and yet . . . the specs in the data flimsy suggested this little ship could outfly anything Pammy could drag out of R&D.

He waited another twenty minutes before engaging his own engines and setting the coordinates in the flimsy. Harmony VI, no—wait—they called it H6, lay two days dead ahead of him if he continued to drift.

A suspicious colonel meant he needed to report for duty in twelve hours. Supposedly the wife would just disappear, as must happen if she bore an out-of-caste child.

An hour after that, when Jake knew as much as he could learn while awake, he brought the ship back to life, set the autopilot to wake him an hour from sensor range on H6 and injected a round of sleepy drugs that carried memories and data carefully recorded over weeks, maybe months by Sergeant Jacob da Jacob pa Law Enforcement H6.

✦   ✦   ✦

"Is she gone for good?" Laudae Penelope whispered as she nudged Gil's arm. They stood in a damp huddled mass beneath the overhang waiting for Laud Gregor to sound the final chime of Funeral Ritual. All of the black-clad priests, priestesses, and their acolytes fought to maintain any dignity they could in the midst of the totally unexpected storm. Torrents of rain drenched the High Priest. Still, he persevered and finished the state funeral with aplomb and proper pacing.

"I doubt it," Gil whispered back. He hoped not. In just a few weeks Sissy had brought a sense of lightness and enthusiasm to the Crystal Temple he hadn't seen since he and Penelope had first worked together reorganizing and implementing a new curriculum for Holy Day classes among the other castes. The woman standing beside him had been full of bright laughter and . . . joy then.

When had she become so bitter and shallow? Fashion and protocol dominated her conversations now. Not their lessons and how she wanted to upgrade the educational system throughout the empire.

Blame Marilee for that.

Gil suspected the High Priestess they mourned today had so little intelligence and ambition that she spent all of her time and energy on pageantry with nothing left over for actual work. Lady Marissa had more than enough intelligence and ambition for both of them.

"Bethy reports that the Lood learns quickly but has less formal education than her acolytes," Penelope sneered. She leaned close so that only he could hear her words.

A rare chance for him to hold her hand in public. He took it firmly.

"Expected. In her prior life she didn't need more than a basic education."

"She makes each lesson a rhyming game and plays with her girls as if she were no older than they." This time her voice showed more amazement than contempt. She returned the squeeze of his hand.

"An interesting teaching technique. I presume that both Miss Sissy and her girls find the lessons more memorable." Harmony forbid that Penelope might actually learn something from Sissy.

"Bethy agrees. She suggested we adopt it in the religious curriculum for the very young and the lesser castes."

Gil cringed at her tone. Was he the only person at Crystal Temple who saw an equality in all the castes? Certainly some carried more responsibility, but each filled a necessary niche in civilization. Without any one caste, the rest would collapse. Except maybe the Poor. But there were always those who could not work because of illness, disability, or extreme age. And they gave the other castes a chance to learn charity. Teens of all castes spent many hours volunteering to help among the Poor, burning off excess energy and eating up free time when they would probably think of ways to get into trouble.

Yes, even the Poor filled a place in society. How to convince Laudae Penelope of this, and open her heart to charity and acceptance of others?

An interesting problem.

"Bethy smiles more now," he whispered to Penelope.

Beneath her heavy crystal veil Penelope made an ugly face.

The rain let up a little, and the thunder seemed more distant. The storm passed just as Laud Gregor brought his last prayer to conclusion. He sounded the final note of the closing ritual and bowed to the High Altar. With dignity and grace he backed up and retreated.

Penelope withdrew her hand from Gil's grasp and followed Gregor close on his heels, eager for all to see her position as next in line.

Gil waited for all the Lauds and Laudaes to retreat from the open forecourt around the altar through a tunnel into the privacy of the Temple buildings. Then he took his place as most senior acolyte.

Penelope needed to have her world shaken, he decided. He couldn't think of a safe way to do it, though. Yet.

CHAPTER NINETEEN

JAKE LET THE AUTOPILOT LAND** the little scout. He didn't know how good a pilot Jacob da Jacob pa Law Enforcement H6 was and didn't want to show off too much. He glided it into the bay directed by control, deliberately making his touchdown rough. He could almost hear the guys in the comm tower wince.

They said nothing. They didn't even pipe up when he delayed opening the hatch, though he knew maintenance people waited for him.

Slowly he gathered his thoughts and hoped the REM implant would guide him through the first awkward moments of the unknown.

"Thanks, Spacers," he said quietly to Control.

"Return the favor sometime," an anonymous voice replied. With respect.

Interesting cooperation between the castes.

"Did you get her out of your system?" a man in a black uniform with three stripes on the cuffs asked the moment Jake poked his head out of the hatch.

Jake grumbled something. Morrie da Hawk pa Law Enforcement H6. The name popped into Jake's head from the REM implant. He knew the man preferred to be called da Hawk, Morrie having some bad family associations. The implant didn't know why.

"Her father has disowned her. If she's found, she'll be cast down to the Poor caste, left to starve on the streets, no one allowed to do more than give her alms. Quite a comedown for the daughter of the Fire Marshal," da Hawk said.

Jake kept his face down and eyes averted, not certain how much he actually looked like his counterpart. Hopefully Pammy had a recent image to program her nanobots.

Another flash of memory that wasn't his own. The woman da Hawk referenced helped him/Jacob solve an arson case at Lord Daniel's shoe factory. They'd tracked the arsonist to employment at Lord Nathaniel's fine leatherworks factory. Seems the two lords were rivals for the same supplier of raw materials. Jacob had turned in his report.

The investigation stopped cold at the doorsteps of the lords. Only the arsonist saw Justice Hall and punishment—the death penalty for obeying his lord.

"Her name shall never cross my lips," he said. Of course it wouldn't. He didn't even know the woman's name and only had a brief memory of her face.

"Good. Colonel turned a blind eye to you going AWOL for a full day and night. Now he wants you back at work. There's been a burglary at Lord Daniel's bank. You've got the detail. I suggest you find the criminals and get them to Justice Hall quickly."

Jake nodded. How the hell was he supposed to do that?

"Forensics come up with any data?" That question came straight from the implant. So apparently Jacob da Jacob knew how to investigate crimes.

"Nope. They wore gloves and masks. Muffled their voices and carried illegal firearms."

Jake grumbled some more. "The weapons. We need to track the materials for making gunpowder. And the maker. Not a lot of places in the city capable of making a gun, fewer where someone could make them in secret. I'm betting the maker and the robbers are one and the same." That's what he'd do. Considering the death penalty for getting caught making, possessing, or using a firearm, he wouldn't trust or risk anyone but himself in this escapade.

Da Hawk raised his eyebrows. "Good thinking. Collect your squad and get out there. Make it look like hard work. At this rate they'll promote you to a desk, so you won't think much. Thinking will get you into trouble. Maybe if they promote you, I'll get some of these good cases so that I can earn favor with the officers." He wandered off, apparently satisfied that Jake was ready to go back to work.

"I could really use some favors right now." Da Hawk had sounded weary, as if all the troubles of their caste rested on his shoulders.

Jake was surprised that the Military was so forgiving of an out-of-caste love affair and so leery of independent thought.

✦　✦　✦

Sissy took a deep breath, testing the new implant. If the blamed thing didn't work right, she wanted to know now, before the physicians sent her back to Crystal Temple tonight.

They called it her home. They had it all wrong. Home was a couple of joined flats on the fifth floor of an apartment block filled with her family.

Even that was gone, taken from her. The family lived somewhere else now.

Her lungs worked. She coaxed her chest to expand just a little more, take in a bit more air. She felt a little constriction. Not enough to make her cough.

She buried her face in Cat's fur—the animal never strayed more than a few inches from her, even choosing to use the box of sand in the necessary when she did. As she raised her head, she inhaled again. A little less constriction, a little more air.

Satisfied that the filter did indeed work, she swung her legs off the narrow hospital bed and scooted forward. The moment her bare toes touched the cold floor a chill raised upward and grabbed her lungs.

She coughed and coughed until she could get no air. And then she coughed some more. Tears clogged her eyes and her nose.

Someone thrust the inhaler into her mouth. She gasped the medication more than breathed it.

Instantly her blurry eyes sharpened focus, making fractured images through the water.

"Stevie," she whispered, afraid to raise her voice and induce more coughing. He gathered her into a hug.

"You can only stay five minutes," Mr. Guilliam hissed from the doorway. "She's not supposed to have any visitors at all."

"Who says no visitors?" Sissy asked. Her chest eased and she felt confident in speaking again.

"Laud Gregor's orders," Mr. Guilliam said. He looked anxiously over his shoulder.

"He ain't . . . he isn't a physician. He doesn't know what's best for me."

"Perhaps not. But he thinks he knows what is best for Harmony."

"Didn't you say that as soon as I take ordination I become Harmony?" Sissy wanted to giggle at that. Stevie had come. She'd be okay. He'd look out for her, just like he done—did—when they were little, and in school, and later in the factory. He didn't let the girls bully her about her caste marks and he kept the bigger boys from taking advantage of her.

Mr. Guilliam rolled his eyes upward. "Please, Miss Sissy, I can't afford any trouble with Laud Gregor. And neither can you. Not yet anyway."

Sissy winked at him conspiratorially. He winked back.

"You going to keep that cat?" Stevie asked. He shoved the animal out of the way, so he could sit next to Sissy on the bed. Like he'd always done at home.

"I've given the cat refuge." That was the word she'd shouted in her prophecy, not knowing she knew it until she spoke.

"Costs lots to feed an animal. Got to have a special license. Can you afford to buy meat for it?"

Sissy had no idea what her new salary would be. "Stevie, they feed me meat every day. Sometimes twice a day. I've been holding back bits of it to feed the cat. I can't eat it all without feeling sick."

"Too much meat isn't good for you. Guess it's better to share than waste it."

"Tell me about the new flat, Stevie. Tell me about you and Anna. Tell me about everyone. I miss you all."

"You'd heal quicker at home," Stevie said. "Why can't we take you back home, even for a couple of days? You need Mama's good cooking, not the too rich stuff they give you here. And Grandma feeding you hot possets, and Josh and Ashel telling you silly jokes."

Sissy sighed deeply. She had nurses bringing her hot soothing drinks, the hospital kitchen prepared special dishes just for her, and her acolytes sent her hand drawn cards with Jilly's silly jokes printed on them.

But it wasn't the same. It could be, given time. But it wasn't; not without the shared memories and blood bonds present since birth.

Why couldn't she have both? She had caste marks to give her seven families if she wanted. She only wanted Stevie and Mama, and Pop, and all the rest.

How could she make Laud Gregor understand that she needed both?

Guilliam bypassed the door to his official quarters beside Laud Gregor's suite. Noon. All the men and boys who inhabited this wing should be in the refectory or at their prayers. Still, he walked softly, clinging to the shadows he'd created by disabling random light fixtures and never reporting them to Maintenance. This windowless corridor still had enough light to negotiate the turns and curves, not enough to banish his hiding places.

He loved the warren of tenebrous passages and near forgotten rooms and alcoves. Over the years he'd hunted out most of them. Each generation added on, remodeled, blocked off ancient sections until Crystal Temple sprawled in an amorphous mass. Only the open forecourt with the High Altar and the seven crystal columns supporting the roof at the edges remained the same.

For a people who abhorred change, Temple caste eagerly changed their headquarters and primary dwelling quite often.

He'd discovered much that they'd changed in their worship and culture, too. Only they didn't see it. They didn't search out the secret past as Guilliam did.

Today, he sought a hidden back door to the archive basement. He'd learned early on that access to old records came to his hand much easier if he just spirited them away and returned them unnoticed rather than approach the archivist from the front door. Most of the time the withered old men who ran the place didn't know half of what they guarded. They'd never had the time or interest to crawl around and dig through ten layers of obscurity for the truth.

Today, Guilliam sought records of the earliest rituals for ordaining an HPS. He needed to come up with something special that also had precedence. Surely, somewhere in the dim past, something was done to honor, or even invoke the Gift of Harmony. Originally every HPS had the gift of prophecy, a genetic mutation actively sought and eagerly bred into succeeding generations.

He guessed that Harmony had caused the mutation out of Temple caste because She needed something, someone special.

The populace needed to experience one of Missy Sissy's prophecies to understand and accept her.

At the far end of the corridor that ended in a stone wall with no obvious outlet, Guilliam dug his fingernails into the crumbling mortar of the center block, not much bigger than a brick, three tiers down from the top. It rotated with a rough grinding noise that scraped against his nerves.

He shot a quick glance down the full length of the corridor. No one came to investigate the alien sounds. His pent-up breath whooshed out in relief.

Behind the brick his fingertips found an indentation in another piece of the wall. With the slightest pressure his side opened a narrow door a few inches. He found it easier to squeeze through the opening than to force the little-used door to open further. His green shirt buttons caught on the edge.

Discord, he needed to lose a little weight. Penelope would fuss and chide him if he lost another button during his explorations. Bad enough he usually returned to her covered in dust and grime.

Exhaling deeply while sucking in his gut, he managed to pass the barrier with his buttons intact. He paused to breathe in the dank smell of disuse in the space between walls. If he closed his eyes, he could almost believe himself back in the burial caves of his youth.

Renewed and refreshed, he descended a spiral staircase, its treads worn and indented from centuries of use. Damp slicked the walls. He welcomed the touch of algae that grew only in very dark places, like caves and forgotten corridors. At the bottom he found the locking mechanism for the door into the archives. He had to repeat the squeeze through it and nearly stumbled into a tiny area he'd carved out of the disorganized mess.

Here he lit the candle stub he carried in his pocket. He had to read box labels to know which to search. Whoever had shoved the crates and containers down here had at least listed contents accurately. Day-to-day accountings and diaries of long-dead Crystal Temple denizens.

He needed something older, more venerable. Something going back nearly as far as the existence of the Crystal Temple, built about five hundred years ago on the foundations of the previous Temple. Quakes had destroyed the First Temple and damaged much of the attached castle. The ruins had provided the building material for the present Governmental Palace. But the Crystal Temple had been built of new stone surrounding the High Altar and forecourt.

Not all of the ruins had been cannibalized. Some had been shored up for temporary use, then abandoned as new buildings made them obsolete.

Guilliam needed something from that time. A time when every HPS had the Gift of Harmony. A time when castes emerged out of chaos.

He found something entirely different. Something Laud Gregor needed to know, but Guilliam dared not show him.

> *And the time shall come*
> *When Beloved Harmony*
> *Lashes out in anger.*
> *Out of the ashes of Discord*
> *Will Rise*
> *One who loves us all,*
> *Appeases Harmony,*
> *Brings Chaos,*
> *And restores life.*

Discord! It all made sense now.

CHAPTER TWENTY

"**I CAN'T STAND BEING COOPED** up indoors one moment longer," Sissy said. She gathered Cat into her arms and marched from her bedroom into her office. "I've been out of hospital for three days now. I've rested enough."

Seven girls ranging in age from ten to twelve awaited her. They each had books and notebooks in front of them, studying lessons Laudae Shanet had set for them. Shanet's own seven acolytes, somewhat older, were in the library with their own lessons.

"Miss Sissy, are you truly well enough?" Laudae Shanet asked from directly behind her.

"I'll get better faster breathing real air and letting natural sunshine warm my skin."

"But it's hot out there," Mary, the oldest of the acolytes protested. "I like air-conditioning."

"Well, I don't," Sissy insisted. She'd never had air-conditioning in the Worker flats. Some in the factory because of the delicate components she assembled. Even then she hadn't liked the recycled air and artificial chill. "Stay here if you like. There's a big park behind the buildings. Reserved just for Temple. I intend to make use of it. Maybe take a swim." She'd never had the leisure to play in the public pools much. Never learned to swim. Maybe now she'd make the time.

"Um, Miss Sissy, the Reserve is . . . is not going to be what you expect," Shanet said quietly.

Immediately seven pairs of little ears perked up and seven young bodies leaned closer, listening intently.

Shanet ushered Sissy into the hallway. "The Reserve is walled. It's not open to the public," she said.

"I know that. I've walked all around the outside. We made it a family outing one Holy Day." She strolled toward the doorway at the end of the corridor. One advantage to becoming High Priestess, she had easy access to the Reserve. Her bedroom window looked out on trees. Not that she had much time to contemplate the view. Every time she turned around, someone shoved more books and papers under her nose.

"Read this." "Sign that." Over and over.

And then there were the rituals. A ritual to greet the dawn, another to bless the meals, yet another to gather the entire Temple together to thank the gods for the work they were about to start.

On and on and on. She kind of liked it. But often forgot which prayers belonged to which ritual.

Seemed like these people spent more time eating than working, too.

"Temple caste has different . . . sensibilities from Workers." Shanet looked anxiously at the floor.

"Meaning?" Sissy paused with one hand on the door. Cat ceased purring in her arms. He looked just a bit anxious at going outside. Probably afraid he'd be abandoned again.

She set the cat down and let him scamper back to the safety of her chambers.

"Miss Sissy, I have spent most of my life serving in small parishes. I know how Workers view family and that marriage is sacred."

"Of course."

"Temple caste is different. We do not marry."

"But . . . ?"

"Nor are we celibate. I've borne three children to three different fathers. Two of them I sent to Temple nurseries. Only one did I raise on my own, because my parish was so far removed I could not visit the nursery regularly. Unlike most of my caste, I felt an attachment to the children I carried in my womb."

Sissy wanted to sit down. This was so . . . . so alien.

"We do not view marriage and relationships the same way you do. We have little body modesty amongst ourselves. In some ways, our entire caste is our family. Indeed, we are such a small caste that it is hard to find another member who isn't related in some way."

"What are you trying to tell me, Laudae Shanet?" Sissy grew cold. Suddenly this woman, her mentor, her *friend* seemed like something outside the empire, outside *civilization*.

"I do not want to deny you the pleasure of walking in the Reserve. But I feel I needed to warn you of how others use the area." Resolutely, she thrust open the door and led Sissy into the lush greenery.

Thick grass greeted Sissy's bare toes. She wiggled them with joy and took a deep breath. The sweet spring air caressed her lungs and did not catch for a change. She lifted her face to the sun and drank in its warmth and light.

The sounds of laughter drew her onward toward a screen of bushes. She smelled water, sharpened with cleansing chemicals. The pool.

She aimed her steps for the shrubbery. A spot of bright turquoise and rusty brown diverted her attention. Not quite artificial but definitely out of place in this serene setting.

The colors scuttled closer, flashing and shifting as they moved. Sissy recognized the outline of a lizard. A big muncher lizard. Normally the creature inhabited much wetter and much warmer climes than Harmony City.

Sissy'd seen one in the zoo and been fascinated that such a little thing could eat its weight in leaves every day. She knew the lizard displayed those colors when frightened or fighting. Otherwise it blended into the greenery. If it intended to fight, its spiny crest would flare upward. This guy ran for his life, right toward Sissy.

She bent down to scoop him up.

"No!" Shanet screamed. "It'll bite you. It's poisonous." She streaked toward Sissy as fast as her short legs could carry her.

"Don't be silly, Laudae Shanet," Sissy laughed. The lizard reached her and climbed up her leg and skirt, all the way to her shoulder where it tried to hide beneath her hair. "Munchers aren't poisonous. This guy is just scared." She searched the grounds for signs of a predator.

A rustling in the bushes revealed a mongrel dog, brown with long legs and upright ears. His ribs were clearly outlined beneath filthy and matted fur. It remained ten feet away, eyeing Sissy warily.

"Laudae Shanet, please fetch something for the dog to eat. I'm sure, once he's no longer quite so hungry he won't need to chase lizards. Lizards don't taste very good, Dog." Carefully, Sissy brought the muncher into her arms, disengaging his claws from her dress before they shredded the fine fabric.

"Looks like Cat will have some new companions." Shanet snorted. Then she clapped her hands.

A totally naked boy of about ten appeared from behind the bushes that screened the pool. "Yes, my Laudae?" he asked as if being naked was nothing out of the ordinary.

Sissy had to lower her eyes to the lizard and concentrate hard on searching it for signs of injury. She'd seen naked children before. She couldn't help it, living cheek by jowl with four brothers and two sisters. With one bathroom. She'd changed diapers on most of them.

But this boy's total lack of modesty shocked her, sent her thoughts spinning in a dozen different directions.

Some of what Shanet had told her tried to poke through the storm of her thoughts. Nothing settled in her mind. Other than . . . shock.

Shanet gave the boy directions for food for the dog and a basket for the lizard. He scampered off, not even bothering with a towel to cover himself.

"We'll need a special license to feed the dog. He eats meat," Sissy mused.

"Who do you think grants the licenses?" Shanet asked on a laugh. "We do. Getting meat is no problem for Temple caste."

Other people appeared from behind the bushes. Men, women, children, teens. None of them wore a stitch of clothing.

Sissy's eyes opened wide. Then she turned her back on them all and began walking back the way she had come, still cradling the lizard. The dog trailed behind her. Each step grew faster until Sissy ran for the shelter of her chambers.

"I'm sorry you had to find out about the pool this way, Miss Sissy," Shanet said quietly. "But you had to see it to understand that our way of life differs from anything you've known before."

"Everything about this place is different. Too different. I don't like any of it. I want out. I want to go home to my family."

"This is your home now. And we are your family. There is no going back."

"I want to see my family."

"We'll see if Laud Gregor has made arrangements."

"Where's the nearest 'phone? I want to talk to my mama and my brother Stevie."

"Later. When we've finished today's lessons."

"Always later. Never now. Why can't I talk to them."

Laudae Shanet frowned. "They'll all be at work right now. Wait until suppertime. I'll see if we can arrange something."

But after supper, Laud Gregor required Sissy to read and sign yet more documents. They finished long after everyone else had gone to bed.

✦   ✦   ✦

Jake pulled air into his aching lungs. He pumped his legs harder. Rain dripped into his eyes, blurring his vision. He just made out the line in the scuffed dirt that marked the finish line. Twenty meters ahead. One bloke ahead of him, two nearly at his side and three more closing fast. None of them looked winded, or even determined. And they carried fifty-kilo packs with long swords sheathed at their hips.

None of them bothered tossing the rain out of their eyes. Just another condition to be coped with.

Oh, for the climate control of a space base!

Physical training among the Military caste on Harmony was just something they did. And did very well. So was swordplay. They disdained any kind of projectile or energy weapons as dishonorable and therefore illegal. They had to look the enemy in the eye before they killed them. Jake had no doubt they killed without conscience. Just part of the job. Part of life. Their lot, due to the red square caste mark on their left cheeks.

No sense of glory or accomplishment in any part of their lives. None of the endorphins pumping through their systems from the physical exercise or the heat of battle. Not even a touch of competition. Just get out there and run. Or lift weights, or carry a fifty-kilo pack on your back and climb a mountain.

And obey. Without question or thought.

He wanted more. He wanted his squad to follow him into hell and back because they respected and trusted him, not because they must.

His foot slipped a bit in the wet. Catching his balance, he almost tripped over the sword banging against his leg.

Always those long and lethally sharp swords at their hips.

Swordplay was supposed to be for fun, with blunted or foiled weapons. A way of honing skills and sharpening reactions. At least that was why Jake had engaged in the sport back in civilization.

God, how did these people ever improve if they didn't push? That was just it. Improvement meant change and nothing changed on Harmony. Not ever. The only new tech came out of Spacer needs to protect the frontier from invasion. And they kept it all to themselves. Change might disrupt their archaic caste system, their bizarre sense of honor, and a stagnating economy.

Few of these people could even grasp the concept of money. They still bartered and traded goods and services in the marketplace. All their money went to paying rent to the lord they worked for. An endless cycle of the rich getting richer and the poor running in place.

And little feudal benevolence. Workers were as expendable as the Poor. Always a dozen more to replace anyone injured on the job or sick, or disgruntled.

Jake couldn't let these guys beat him. In his new identity as Sergeant Jacob da Jacob pa Law Enforcement H6—oops they'd changed that last bit with the move to Harmony City on H Prime, now they were pa Capital Law Enforcement H Prime. He had to be better than they were. He'd bring about change by hook or by crook just as soon as he found his way into a Badger Metal processing plant and stole the formula.

In the meantime, he had a race to win. He wondered if winning would change the unspoken protocol of place in line at the urinals, or who got dessert and who didn't, even who got to ride shotgun. He preferred that place as opposed to in the back and slightly elevated position in their lumbering version of a jeep, supposedly so he could survey the landscape better for ambushes. The bloke ahead of him always got the prime spot in the far corner of the restrooms—the cleanest and the most private.

He breathed as deeply as his laboring lungs allowed and pushed his legs harder than he ever had before. Ten meters and he left the two closest men behind. Slowly he closed in on the leader.

Five meters, he drew alongside his only competition in this sprint.

One meter. He nosed ahead. The rain beat at him harder, drenching his clothes and his pack, adding weight, cooling the sweat on him. He pushed harder just to stay warm.

He crossed the finish line half a stride in the lead. And continued going, letting his body slow gradually. His squad of twenty followed him.

Everyone else just stopped in place the moment he finished the race first.

Sheesh! What would they do in battle the first time one of them died. Just give up and let the enemy slaughter them?

But then, none of these men had ever seen combat. None of them. Peace reigned in the Harmonite Empire. Except on the frontier near the jump points. The Spacer caste handled those skirmishes. They got to use energy weapons. Dishonorable weapons because they fought against dishonorable enemies.

Maybe he should activate his emergency beacon and tell Pammy to launch a full-scale attack on the borders. That would shake them up.

He guessed that rounding up the occasional thief or breaking up a bar brawl wasn't really combat. Violent crime was rare here—even the bank robber with a gun had surrendered peacefully when discovered, execution just another alternative to starving to death. He'd been a skilled metal Worker thrown out and relegated to Poor caste when he lost a leg in an industrial accident.

Violent tendencies were another trait weeded out from the initial colonists.

A whistle shrilled behind Jake. He completed the lap in his warm down to come back to the platoon. His nearest competition, Sergeant Morrie da Hawk had shed his heavy pack and waited for him inside a circle scuffed into the dirt, sword drawn.

His reward for winning the race: he got to fight for his life. In the pouring rain, with a slick surface beneath his feet.

CHAPTER TWENTY-ONE

B LEARY-EYED, SISSY TRUDGED into the small chapel the next morning for more lessons and drills in ritual. A kernel of anger formed a
knot in her belly.

After spending so many hours trying to read document after document, and feeling sick at signing things she did not understand, but too
afraid to admit to Laud Gregor she didn't, she'd slept fitfully. Every
time she closed her eyes, she saw jumbles of letters spinning around.
None of them made coherent patterns. And they taunted her with their
randomness.

And she still hadn't been allowed to talk to her family.

Too much. Temple asked too much of her.

Laud Gregor appeared in the doorway looking rested and refreshed,
as if he hadn't sat up half the night. "Out. All of you out!" He banished
Laudae Shanet and Laudae Penelope and all of their acolytes.

"The rest of you," he scowled at Sissy's seven little girls, "go do some
lessons or something, elsewhere."

Jilly led the girls in a rapid scuttle out the doorway. From tiny giggles,
Sissy knew they'd gone no farther than just around the corner.

"Now begin, Miss Sissy. Show me what you have learned."

"Which ritual?" she asked meekly, not daring to look at him. If she did,
she just might let him see her bewilderment, her confusion, and her anger.

"Begin with morning prayers and work your way through the day."
He settled into the chair Laudae Penelope usually occupied. Only, he
relaxed into it rather than perching on the edge waiting to pounce the
moment Sissy made a mistake, just like Cat waiting at a mousehole.

One by one, Sissy followed the prescribed order of crystal tones and
prayers. In less than an hour she had completed the daily rituals.

"And now the ones for Holy Day," Laud Gregor ordered. "You do know
those, don't you? You have to know them all before your ordination."

"Yes, I know them," Sissy replied as she set down her favorite crystal wand. She made sure the delicate thing wouldn't roll off the altar.

The golden cat, curled at her feet, purred in a comforting rhythm in time with her tapping of the crystals. When the last chime died away, so did the deep rumble. Satisfaction.

Dog drowsed by the doorway. His ears cocked to listen for changes in her mood or words.

She loved working with the crystals. Not enough. She needed to go home.

The ache deep inside her to go home grew by the minute until she thought there was nothing left of her. She needed to visit each room in the new flats, breathe the familiar scents of her family. Mama's baking would make the air rich with cinnamon and sugar. Grandma's skin left a sharp papery smell on everything she brushed against, and she did that a lot because of her screwed balance.

Sissy needed to touch each threadbare piece of furniture, memorize the texture. Remember bouncing on Pop's lap in one, climbing up the back with Stevie on another, curling up with a blanket and her youngest sister Ashel when the toddler was sick.

Most of all, she needed to hug every one of her grandparents, aunts, uncles, cousins, and especially her brothers and sisters. And Pop and Mama.

A lump grew in her throat, making her feel emptier than ever.

"I want to see my family," she said softly into the silence that followed the last echoing chime. Cat's ears pricked, but he did not open his eyes or lift his head from its rest atop his paws.

Laud Gregor looked up sharply from the single chair. He didn't miss much, she'd discovered in the last few weeks. They felt like years. Very lonely years. Except for Cat, Dog, and Godfrey the lizard. Without their undemanding presence she didn't know if she could have continued at the Temple as long as she had.

"I'm working on arrangements with Lord Chauncey and his liaison with the Worker caste," Laud Gregor said with reassurance. "These things take time. Now run through the Holy Day prayers with the appropriate chimes."

"No, these things don't take time." She forced herself to look him in the eye. "You make things happen in a hurry, when you want them to. You promised me access to my family. Now you are stalling." She crossed her arms, keeping her hands away from the temptation of working with the wand and the crystals.

Cat shifted in his sleep, mimicking her unease. Dog sat up from his post by the door.

"Sissy, what you ask is unprecedented. I have to get the approval of the entire High Council . . ." he explained with extreme patience.

"No, you don't. All you have to do is give Pop a visitor's pass and send a car for them, or a loxen cart, even a pedicar."

"You don't know. You haven't been here long enough . . ." A tinge of anger colored his voice. Patience and understanding evaporated.

"I do know. I asked. No one of Temple will *tell* me anything. But if I ask questions of the Workers who serve you, they answer truthfully. Now I want to see my family." Pointedly, she stepped away from the altar.

"Sissy . . ." He stood, looming over her.

Cat woke up and stretched front to back, then back to front. He sat upright and began washing a paw. Sissy knew from the angle of his ears that he listened for signs of upset.

Dog whined a question and crept forward.

A rustle of clothing told her that her girls listened avidly.

Sissy stood her ground. "You broke your promise to me. I'm going back to my home and back to work in the factory where I'm needed. And wanted. And where I can get clothes that *fit*. In colors I like." She stepped around Laud Gregor. Cat followed her, pointedly staying away from the High Priest.

Dog took up his place at her left heel, ready to defend her to the death.

"What's wrong with your clothes?" Laud Gregor grabbed her arm and spun her around.

Sissy examined his face for signs of trickery. He looked honestly puzzled.

"What can I say? Can't you see? Tell me who owned these dresses before me, and I'll give 'em back. I'm used to hand-me-downs. I'll take someone else's castoffs if I can just give these back." She plucked at the too tight skirt and the neckline that threatened to slip off her shoulders exposing her small clothes.

"What do you mean, 'hand-me-downs'? I ordered a dozen new gowns and pairs of shoes made to order for you."

"Then you got cheated. And I don't like this green. It's ugly."

"Yes, I see that it is not the most flattering." He crossed his arms, then lifted his left hand to tap his caste mark. A habitual gesture she'd come to recognize. Why did he need to remind people of his superior caste? He was the highest of the high!

"I sense Laudae Penelope's hand in this," he said at last. Five quick steps took him to the comm unit behind the altar. He pushed a button. "Guilliam, send the dressmaker to Miss Sissy's quarters."

"Very good, sir. What color fabric should I tell her to bring?" Guilliam's disembodied voice came through the tiny speaker. Was that a yawn behind the false briskness? Sissy had never known the man to be less than completely alert and aware of everything around him. He hadn't had any more sleep than she. Why?

Sissy shook her head, jarred into distrust at this instant communication within the Temple. At home, people ran back and forth between flats and shops. Nothing was very far away. Why waste money on expensive equipment, and the energy to run them, when talking face-to-face was so much nicer and gave you a chance to visit?

Now all she had was remote conversations over those costly electronics.

"Green, of course. We always wear green," Laud Gregor said.

"What *shade* of green?"

"Um . . ."

"Why do we have to wear green?" Sissy asked.

"Green reminds us of Harmony's bounty," Gregor sighed. "Haven't those women taught you anything?"

"What about the blue of a summer sky, or the yellow of ripening corn, or the red of a love flower? Or . . . or why not purple to match our caste mark? I like purple. I want to wear purple." Sissy grinned as she imagined wearing a simple gown in silky fabric the color of the mountains at sunset.

Mama would love it. Her sisters would gasp with envy.

"Sir," Guilliam said. "There is a precedent. Our records indicate that one hundred years ago, Temple caste wore red and gold. It seems that at the time the choice of color was up to the current HPS."

Sissy's smile deepened. "Then I want to wear purple. Everything in purple."

Gregor's eyes widened in horror. "Do you realize the upset, the massive turnover, the *waste* of time, labor, money, and energy to change the wardrobe of every member of our caste!"

"You all don't have to change if you like green. But I like purple and I want to wear it. Mr. Guilliam just said I can."

"But . . . but this is unprecedented."

"No, it isn't," Sissy insisted. "He just said I could choose for myself. So why can't everyone else? I know. I want each of the seven priestesses at Crystal Temple to wear a different color."

"In the name of the Seven, woman, you can't overturn centuries of tradition on a whim."

"Yes, I can. You want me to be your High Priestess, you'll do it. And you'll let me see my family."

Cat stropped her ankles. He opened his mouth in a cat grin.

Gregor frowned, then ignored her last statement. "But if we show different colors and styles in our formal robes, then the populace will be able to pick out favorites. A cult of personality will develop. We will lose the harmony of anonymity."

"Fine, then all the formal robes can be whatever color you like as long as it isn't this vile vomit green."

"Your formal robes will be darker emerald green once you are ordained," Gregor sighed in defeat.

"That's fine."

"But you must wear shoes. If you go barefoot, you will stand out in the formal rituals."

"Then find me a pair that fit."

"Fit? Shoes always fit."

"No, they don't. Not unless they are *made* to fit."

He sighed again. "Laudae Penelope has a lot to answer for."

"Yeah, she does. So when do I get to see my family?"

"I'll arrange something."

"Guilliam will arrange it. That way it will get done. For tomorrow. Holy Day. After services." Sissy returned to the altar and picked up her wand. A bit of warmth wiggled in her midsection. One win at a time.

Now she just had to figure out why Gregor thought it so important to smile and pretend to give her what she asked for, without giving her anything.

She bet it had something to do with all those forms he had her sign without reading.

Tonight, when everyone was asleep, she'd go back and try to read the blamed things. Having a room to herself could be a blessing sometimes. In this convoluted world of the Temple, a bit of privacy might come in handy.

Even if it was so terribly lonely.

A bird chirruped outside the window. That gave Sissy an idea. For tomorrow. One battle at a time.

CHAPTER TWENTY-TWO

JAKE DREW HIS SWORD TWENTY paces from his opponent. Ten more paces and he dropped his pack. Behind him, he heard twenty swords clear their scabbards. His men readying to protect his back.

Da Hawk's men ranged behind him. Belatedly, they also drew their weapons when they saw Jake's men do it.

Curious. No time to think on that.

Two paces from da Hawk, just barely inside the circle he lunged, without pausing for an honorable salute, letting the mud carry him farther forward than his legs could from that distance.

About the only rule these guys observed was the boundary of the circle and one hand on the sword. Sort of like the Spanish Circle school of fencing. But that was the end of the resemblance. No rules, no right of way, no off target. Slash, jab, score a bloody touché any way you could, so long as you did it first, before the other guy scored on you.

But his men would keep da Hawk from murdering him. Touché only, not a killing wound.

Morrie da Hawk reacted, fast. Faster than Jake thought possible. Parry four, low and inside, riposte to his high six, the shoulder of his weapon hand.

Jake parried and lunged for a low seven, the hip of Morrie's off hand. Morrie sidestepped and brought his sword toward Jake's partially exposed back.

Not about to fall for that beginner's mistake, Jake dropped to his knees and rolled to the edge of the circle three meters out. More than enough room to brace his feet and bounce back up.

His feet kept moving. No traction.

Was that a gentle hand on his belt, helping him up? He'd give that man an extra helping at dinner, even if it meant Jake went a little hungry.

He kept his swing tight, parrying the next jab to his heart.

Morrie breathed hard. Sweat poured from his face, a different color and texture from the rain that drenched them both.

Jake felt the effects, too. But not as bad as his opponent. He had to end this quickly or Morrie, one of the best sergeants in the platoon, and a . . . a friend would be useless for a couple of days.

With a flick of his wrist, Jake bound Morrie's blade, keeping it angled away from his body.

But Morrie was more determined. He gave in to the pressure, letting it carry his blade to the outside with just enough slack to disengage with an undercut and thrust toward Jake's knee.

Jake had seen Morrie do this before in drill. Anticipated it. Caught a circular parry exposing Morrie just enough to slice lightly along his belly.

A gasp of surprise. A line of red following Jake's blade tip. Morrie stepped back, clutching his wound.

"Halt!" Lieutenant Charl da Martin called.

Instantly a medic caught the wounded man beneath the shoulders and eased to him the ground.

The rest of the platoon stepped away, sheathing their weapons. They gathered around the lieutenant, a man younger than Jake, younger than ninety percent of the platoon, but he'd inherited his rank and had an extra hashmark beneath the red square of his caste mark indicating his officer status.

"What you trying to prove, da Jacob?" Lieutenant da Martin asked belligerently. He stood with hands on hips and a scowl on his face.

"Ease up on him, sir," Sergeant Camden da Yehan growled. "He's seen a lot of action, solved some serious crimes of late with bad results. Let him run and fight hard if it makes him easier to live with." A pregnant pause that suggested Jake's hurt went deeper, more personal.

The unmentionable out-of-caste love affair.

"Barely nicked him," the medic called. "Some light pressure bandages and he'll be back on duty tomorrow."

Charl Da Martin grumbled something about emotions having no place within the ranks, then turned to address the gathered platoon.

"Listen up, men. The ordination of the new HPS takes place two weeks from today. Every Noble in the empire will be present, along with their entourages. Every priest and priestess in the empire will be present, along with *their* entourages. That's a lot of people who control a lot of power. We cannot allow the dissent among the desert Worker caste to spread to the capital."

Dissent? That surprised Jake. That suggested large numbers and organization. More than just a single disgruntled Worker causing trouble.

What was so bad in the desert that spawned a Worker revolt?

"Deployment?" Jake asked. A major riot in the capital might prove enough of a diversion to let him break into a Badger Metal factory.

"Patience," he almost heard Pammy counseling him.

He wanted off this rock and back in the civilized space of the CSS. The best way to ensure that was to stay cool and in control of his cover.

"Since you seem intent on proving yourself better than the rest of us, da Jacob, you lead the detachment covering the Crystal Temple fore-court. No one gets into Temple grounds without an invitation, a pass, and ID. Not press—they can use remote hover cams. Not your mother. Not even someone with a sparkling Temple caste mark. They all have to have an invite, a pass, and ID," Lieutenant da Martin said.

"As a side note," he continued with barely a pause for breath. "The media have offered us copies of *all* of their recordings should there be trouble. We'll have evidence to convict."

"Why do they want to cooperate with us? They never have in the past," Jake said. That bit of info came direct from his implant.

"Cooperation is just part of their bid to become a separate caste."

They didn't want to be responsible to, or censored by, anyone but themselves. Just like the press in the rest of the galaxy.

Lieutenant Charl went on to give details of how many men at each gate, how many patrolling the perimeter, what weapons to carry in addi-tion to their swords and which of them to display.

Jake chilled. From the rain, he told himself. Too much rain out of season.

Standard security procedures. If they knew how to do this right, they must have done it before. A lot of times. All was not as peaceful and *har-monious* on Harmony as the government pretended.

Very interesting. Pammy needed to know about this just as soon as Jake got back to civilization. Maybe before, if he could figure out how to send a secure signal.

Time to start prowling around the comm center.

✦   ✦   ✦

Sissy stared at the thick sheaf of papers long and hard. Night had fallen hours ago. The Temple slept, including Cat and Dog. Godfrey prowled his glass cage, kept warm by artificial lights. She had privacy and time to think after a long, long day of study and ritual practice. She could do without the study. History and government bored her. Practicing with the crystals and the prayers and the patterns of movement enthralled her. She'd gladly do that all day long. If Laudae Shanet and Laud Gregor would let her.

Sadly, they wouldn't. She had to learn *so* much before she could complete her training as High Priestess.

Carefully she sounded out each letter of the string of long words. "Whereas the Gov-er-n-men-tal hi-er-ar-chy needs to network . . ." she knew that word well. She'd used it often enough in building nav systems. "Needs to network within a pat-ern-al-is-tic attitude . . . What in the name of the Seven does that mean?" She sighed.

She wished now that she had taken the opportunity for additional education when it was offered to her. But at twelve, when she had passed her mechanical aptitude tests with superior marks, the chance to work in the electronics factory seemed much more interesting and advantageous. Her family needed the money offered for her fine dexterity more than they needed her to continue on with her schooling for another four years. Leave that to Stevie who wanted to do more at work than just build nav units. He wanted to manage the entire factory some day.

"I wish you were here with me now, Stevie," she whispered. "You could help me understand this gibberish."

"I am here. What do you need help with?" Stevie said quietly from her doorway.

"Stevie!" She flung herself across the big room into his arms, the text forgotten in her joy.

He held her tightly with strong hands. She clung to his neck for long moments, cherishing his warmth and the press of his hands on her back. She'd almost forgotten how good it felt to hug someone. All Temple caste seemed capable of was a placating pat on the shoulder.

"Oh, Stevie, I am so tired and confused and lonely. I want to go home. But I can't."

"I know, Sissy. I know. We miss you at home, too. The new quarters are big. Almost too big. We don't trip over each other anymore," he half laughed. A sob choked off his mirth.

"How did you get in here?" Sissy asked. She looked around for signs of the grim-faced Military who prowled the perimeter of the Temple, keeping out lower castes who might taint the Temple with their presence. Or were they keeping the Temple caste in so they wouldn't taint themselves by mixing with outsiders?

"Mr. Guilliam gave me a pass. I can come and go anytime I want. This is the only time I could get free of work and the family." Stevie grinned from ear to ear; just like he had when they were children plotting pranks against older cousins.

"He did? Oh, I am so grateful to that man. He's the one who truly runs things around here. Laud Gregor likes people to think he's in charge, but

Guilliam's the one who actually gets things done and makes sure others do what they's supposed to."

" 'They are supposed to' not 'they's'. You've got to remember your grammar, Sissy."

"I know," she sighed. "It's just so hard to remember everything I'm supposed to do, and not supposed to do. Like cutting *one* piece of meat and eating it before cutting another. Why not cut all the pieces and then eat? That's more efficient. But not as polite. And they know who to bow to and who to stand straight for. So much easier just to bow to everyone. Temple people think different than we do. And they expect me to *know* everything right off without telling me I'm supposed to know it, or how to learn it."

"Every caste is different, Sissy. Different and closed off from all the others. As dictated by the Gods. We each serve the whole in different ways. There's no way you could know."

"They don't understand that. They have all this history and literature and stuff bred into them. We don't need to know that to work in the factories. We need to know how things work, how to make them, and how to fix 'em when people like Temple klutzes break 'em. They just expect all their gadgets and communications and stuff to work while they argue endlessly about the interpretation of events that took place hundreds of years ago. And they don't understand why I don't think that's important."

"To a priestess that is important. Especially to the High Priestess, which is what you are. And you don't bow to anyone. They all bow to you."

"Not yet the High Priestess, I ain't. Not till next month when they perform this big ritual and then have a grand party afterward. A party don't make me smart enough to be a priestess."

"The entire planet gets a day off work that day, Sissy. The ritual is important to all of us. We get to see you elevated to the highest rank in our society. You, Sissy. My little sister will lead the High Council as well as the Temple. You will be able to make things better for people like us. And we get to party, too, in our way. Anna and I want you to marry us afterward. You'll be a priestess and can do that. Imagine me and Anna married by the HPS of all Harmony."

Sissy had to sit down. Fast. "Stevie, I'm glad you and Anna are getting married. I really am. And I'll gladly do the ritual. I know that one real well. I've been practicing that one just for you. But lead the High Council? How can I do that?"

"It's the law, Sissy. HPS presides over them. You have a vote and your vote weighs more than any one of the other Guardians. So you can keep the government on the path to Harmony."

"I can't do that!" she wailed.

"You have to. We're counting on you."

"But I can't even read all the stuff they send me!"

"Then let me help you. What is it you don't understand?"

Together they pored over the first layer of documents. Stevie read them first, then broke them down into simple statements.

"Why'd they have to take three paragraphs to say that trade between the North and South Continents is getting smaller?" Sissy rubbed her tired eyes in frustration. "Di-min-ish-ing. Is that the word you used?"

"Diminishing, yes. Getting smaller. They do use a lot of extra words. Makes them sound more important, I guess. And here, these five pages say that ocean storms are sinking ships. Taking lives. Ocean levels rising on the coasts. Won't be much land left if the seas take it all over. The weather satellites aren't doing their jobs anymore. Aren't telling us all that's happening."

Could that be why the thunderstorm surprised everyone on the day of the funeral?

"Why's that?" Sissy bent closer, suddenly more interested. "And why haven't we heard anything about this? This is important. People are dying out there."

"It doesn't say why. It just says something must be done to correct the loss of revenue to the port owners. Lord Louis wants the government to compensate him for his losses in shipping and tariffs, and rebuilding further inland."

"Com-pen-sate?"

"Pay him back."

"Oh. That don't seem fair. Seems like we should find out why these things are happening and correct that. The families of the sailors should be compensated for their loss, not the lord."

"See what I mean, Sissy. You can change these things. No one else can."

"I don't know . . . who's gonna listen to me?"

"All of Harmony."

"But not Laud Gregor or the High Council."

"You'll have to find a way to make them listen. Like you made Harmony listen when you sang us out of the quake."

CHAPTER TWENTY-THREE

J **AKE STUDIED THE SIGN-IN FORM** at the Communications Tower in
the dead center of Harmony City. He had duty at dawn, so this evening
was his own time. No reason an off duty sergeant shouldn't check out
dispatches from his family back on H6.

Technically this facility belonged to the Spacers. But Military shared it
rather than waste energy duplicating functions. Spacer communications
went off planet. Military monitored all planet-bound communications.

At the last second he signed Sergeant Morrie da Hawk's name instead
of his own. Without a guard to check ID, no one questioned him as he
took the elevator to the seventh floor. He wondered briefly how they got
this building to stand far above its neighbors when none of them stood
higher than seven stories.

Since the big quake, anything left standing higher than seven stories
had been torn down and rebuilt.

The elevator took an uncommonly long time to progress upward. His
stomach plummeted and his head felt light, as if the mechanism rose
faster. Ah, each story must be twice normal height, giving this building
the look of a tower jutting far above its neighbors, but still maintaining
the sacred seven.

He exited into a broad lobby surrounded by closed office doors. No
signs. He guessed that anyone coming here was supposed to know where
to go. Sort of like knowing which line to stand in at the commissary and
who sat where in transport vehicles or in the mess hall. Little things that
people grew up knowing but had given Jake the newcomer several moments of awkward pause until he figured it out.

The first door to his left was locked, as was the next one to it. He'd
come back with his trusty lockpicks if the other five doors didn't pan out.
The fourth door he tried opened at a touch. He held back listening at the
crack.

Two men conversed quietly to the far left of the big room. A quick peek put them in a corner cubicle, crouched over something that looked suspiciously like a communications board.

Jake slid around the door on tiptoe and into the first cubicle to his right. Another comm board. Lots of buttons, nothing like a thumbprint recognition screen. Old-fashioned, easier to hack into.

Sitting with his head bowed to avoid being spotted by the others, he began the long process of finding passwords to get him into the system. Pretty easy, actually. Morrie da Hawk's name and ID number produced access to a variety of menus. Including interstellar messages.

"Now we're flying," he muttered. Over the past two days he'd taken the time to carefully compose his message so that it looked like just a lonely man telling his sister how much he missed the family—and others. Embedded in the phrases were code words to Pammy. Should all the stars align and the seven gods shine on him, she'd understand that when he said that all was well in Harmony City, he meant that nothing is as it seems. And sorry you couldn't come with me, really meant Pammy should consider invasion. As he finished typing the message, he added a last nano thought requesting an immediate reply.

Then he found the menu for selecting a destination. Cities throughout the empire followed by their coordinates. A few simple tricks and he tweaked the coordinates for H6 so that the message would bounce from ansible to moon to asteroid and into hyperspace where a CSS beacon sat quietly waiting for instructions.

Just as he pressed the send button, the voices in the other cubicle rose to hearing level and beyond. More curious than cautious, Jake poked his head above the barrier around him that really only gave an illusion of privacy.

The two men had moved into a glassed, enclosed office with a more complicated comm board. The Military caste man wore the standard black jumpsuit uniform with pockets inside pockets inside pockets and the hash marks of a corporal. Short, thin, unassuming, and young, barely old enough to shave. He could walk anywhere and no one would notice him.

The other man, also in black but of a civilian cut, was striking. Tall, loose-limbed, with a fringe of gray around a shiny bald pate, he carried himself with pride and self-assurance. His purple circle caste mark glistened in the bright overhead lights.

"My Laud, I am obligated to pass this information to my superiors," the corporal said. An edge of panic made his voice rise from tenor to nearly soprano range.

"I am superior to your superiors. Giving me these communications fulfills your obligation," the priest replied.

"But, My Laud . . ."

"Do not question my orders. I can have you stripped of rank and caste. Do you want to end your days in an asylum?"

The boy shook his head.

"I thought not. Tell no one of my visit or the contents of these messages. Do you understand?"

The boy nodded, chewing his lip in agitation.

"I will be in contact." Abruptly the priest turned to leave.

Jake ducked back behind his cubicle, seemingly intent upon the board and screen before him. He waited until he heard the priest's footsteps retreat and the outer door slam. A quick check showed the young corporal hunched into the chair in the office. He stared out the wall of windows over the city, oblivious to all but his own turbulent thoughts.

"Time for a judicious retreat." But Jake would be back to see if he could find hidden copies of those communiqués on a hard drive.

✦   ✦   ✦

"You missed some." Penelope brushed a mat of dust out of Gil's shower-damp hair.

He blushed slightly, more concerned at having her discover his clandestine activities in the archives than how easily his red robe untied.

As her hand traveled down his face in a gentle caress, he captured her hand, pressing his lips to her palm.

"What fascinates you so about those dusty old documents, Gil?"

"You'd be surprised what I can find, Penelope." More than surprised, possibly appalled.

"Like all this upset about colors?" A frown drew long lines on her face, showing her maturity, making her more beautiful than ever.

"Among other things." How to tell her his most recent discovery? Excitement of a new revelation bounced through his blood. At the same time apprehension churned in his gut.

"Come to bed, love." She shrugged, uninterested in the past.

"Penelope." He paused, not knowing how to say what he must say. He wanted to practice on her before approaching Gregor. She might forgive him. Eventually.

"Oh, stop fussing and come to bed. It will wait until morning."

"Everything in its own time."

"Precisely. And now is the time for you to hold me close while we lie side by side."

"What if the out-of-season storms, the quakes, the floods, and volcanoes are not Harmony's wrath, but a natural cycle to planetary stresses?"

"What? You've lost me." She shook her head, boredom glazing her eyes. "You aren't going to leave this alone."

"I found notes written by a scientist five hundred years ago. She documented evidence in layers of rock that suggested the planet goes through cycles of disruption. She'd just lived through the tail end of one of those cycles." And probably died for writing down that evidence.

Penelope froze, one hand half-lifted to cup his face. "Does that mean *SHE* didn't stop the quake? *SHE* isn't a miracle worker?" Hope dawned in her face.

"No, Sissy mitigated the quake and its damage. But the coming of it is something that just happens. Nothing we did brought it on."

"You can't mean that. You can't think that science is more important, more *accurate* than religion!" She looked outraged.

Evasion was better than answering that question. "We owe Miss Sissy a lot. She saved many people."

"She didn't save my mother," Penelope spat.

"You have a right to grieve, but not to blame."

Her eyes hardened.

"Penelope, think about it."

"Later." She flounced into the bedroom and slammed the door.

Gil heaved a weary sigh. Reluctantly he drew his robe closed over his chest and made his way to the room assigned to him.

There was so much more he needed to relate. Obviously he needed to think more carefully about whom he chose to tell.

Life on Harmony wouldn't be easy for anyone when the truth came out.

What if he leaked a little bit of information to Little Johnny.

No. If he broadcast it, even with evidence, he'd face execution. Not even his father could save him.

CHAPTER TWENTY-FOUR

"**S**IT STILL, **LAUDAE SISSY**," Laudae Shanet pleaded. She held a wand of mascara in her hand.

"I know how to put on makeup," Sissy insisted. She wiggled and tried to jerk her head away from the harsh tugging on her hair by yet another priestess.

"We have to make sure everything is perfect. This ordination is a once-in-a-lifetime event for all of Harmony," Laudae Shanet insisted.

"Well, my hair isn't going to be perfect if *she* keeps teasing it into a vermin nest." Sissy finally yanked the comb out of the other woman's hand. She also turned her face away from Laudae Shanet's ministrations.

The two women continued to rail at her. Laudae Penelope threw up her hands and left.

Jilly mimicked Penelope's dramatics so perfectly she set all of the girls into a fray of giggles.

Sissy refused to hear the chaos around her. Finally in frustration she slapped Laudae Shanet's hand away from her face. The mascara slashed across her right cheek leaving an ominous black smear across her caste marks.

The five women in the room gasped. They dropped whatever garment or grooming utensil they held and made a warding gesture, thumbs and index fingers joined in a circle, the other fingers splayed wide in imitation of the sun.

Cat scuttled out from beneath Sissy's chair to a new hiding place. Dog whined from his basket. Even Godfrey set up a racket by rattling his cage.

Sissy burst into tears. The bit of makeup already applied smudged and ran down her cheeks. She buried her face in her hands, her entire body trembling with headache and anxiety.

Today was the day. The day she became High Priestess for certain. She wasn't ready. She didn't want the responsibility. She couldn't even read properly. How could she function as the Head of the High Council? How could she nurture an entire empire?

She wanted her family beside her, right here, right now.

A new wave of sobs threatened the delicate balance in her lungs. She reached for the inhaler. Couldn't find it on the dressing table.

Panic.

Her breaths came in short painful gasps. Precious air became scarcer and scarcer. Each breath more shallow. A strange whistling sound. Pressure built inside her chest. She fought for air. The world tilted and colors shifted. Her eyes lost focus.

Then someone jammed the inhaler into her mouth.

Blessed drugs filled her system, releasing the tightness in her chest. Air followed. She concentrated on each breath, getting as much air as she could. Afraid that the next one would catch and close.

"Again," a gentle voice instructed.

Another shot from the inhaler. Sissy's vision cleared. She dragged another lungful of air into her aching body and dared look at her rescuer.

An older woman with soft silver hair, with precious few black streaks left in it, piled into an intricate knot atop her head looked calmly into Sissy's eyes. Age lines radiated from her mild blue eyes—the same color as her diamond caste mark. A Noble woman. A frown of concern drew her mouth downward. More creases shaped her lower cheeks into the beginning of jowls.

The drugs within Sissy made halos of bright blue and shimmering yellow appear around the woman's head.

She'd seen her before, but for the life of her couldn't remember where. Noble women didn't cross her path often, or at all.

"Who may I thank for rescue?" Sissy asked politely, forming each word carefully so that they didn't catch.

"Ignorant Loo . . . savage!" Laudae Penelope snarled. When did she return? "Don't you even recognize Lady Marissa of the High Council?"

"Now, Penelope, give the woman some credit for manners. How would she know me? We've never met." Lady Marissa kept her calm gaze fixed upon Sissy. "Are you feeling better, dear?"

"Yes, My Lady."

The day of the funeral. Lady Marissa had marched within the ranks of Temple priests and priestesses. Sissy had seen her face on the television for a few brief seconds.

"Do you feel well enough to finish getting ready?"

"I think so. But . . . but do we have to be so fancy?" Sissy waved at the mess of her hair.

"Oh, my no. Something simple, my dear." She moved behind Sissy and took up the brush. Gently she worked it through the tangles, bringing it back to the smooth straightness. "No one will see it beneath the head-dress and for the party, we want you to shine, not the grooming expertise of these fine priestesses."

Sissy relaxed and let the woman, not much taller than herself, massage the tightness out of her scalp with long even strokes of the brush.

"Can . . . may I wash my face?" Sissy asked. She stared at the black smudge across her caste marks. An ominous portent. Did it mean that she was doomed to fail?

A brighter thought, a frightening thought, flitted through her mind. Could it be? Could she be the one foretold long ago, chosen by Discord to break the caste system?

A tickle in the back of her throat. The terrible compulsion to speak in a voice not her own.

She closed her eyes and mouth, letting the words echo around her mind. She dared not speak them now. Not now.

And the time shall come
When Beloved Harmony
Lashes out in anger.
Out of the ashes of Discord
Will Rise
One who loves us all,
Appeases Harmony,
Brings Chaos,
And restores life.

A shudder ran through her. The thought of the chaos that accompanied such a move scared her. People not knowing their place in society, having to determine their own fates, select their own leaders. Blasphemy.

At the same time the idea thrilled her. What if people had choices in life? What if the benefit of a single Noble did not outweigh the good of the entire Worker caste?

"It's good to see you smile, Miss Sissy," Lady Marissa said. "When our High Priestess is in a good mood, surely Harmony must smile on us as well."

Sissy sobered instantly, fully aware of the weight of responsibility the Temple caste placed upon her shoulders today.

✦   ✦   ✦

Laud Gregor scanned the weather report one more time. Clear skies. No storms anywhere near Harmony City. He couldn't afford another disaster like the thunder and pouring rain that ruined the state funeral for Marilee. He tapped his caste mark in agitation.

"Guilliam, where is the report regarding the repair of the weather satellites?"

"Right here." Guilliam handed him the file from the corner of the massive desk.

Gregor flipped it open and read with growing horror. "No repairs!"

"The Spacers decided we are better served with a new chain of satellites rather than repairing aging equipment that might not be repairable," Guilliam replied. He sat in a corner chair and studied the beads and crystals on his headdress. Some of them looked dull and hung askew. With a frown he twisted the connecting chains with a pair of pliers. "Those satellites are more than seven hundred years old."

"In the meantime we are left with faulty reports for the next year until they launch new satellites!" Rage boiled through Gregor. "Don't those people understand how vital accurate weather reports are?" Not only to the shipping industry, agriculture, and construction, but to the Temple as well. How could they appear omnipotent to the people with inaccurate information? Without that aura of infallibility their authority diminished. Without authority at the top, their entire society would break down.

The threat of the Lost Colony declaring independence and petitioning the CSS for membership might spread to the other six colonies. Worse, it might spread to the Worker caste that outnumbered three to one all the others combined.

He began to tremble. Instead of releasing the panic within him, he marched through the chain of offices and reception areas to a west-facing window. Only one way remained to get an accurate view of the weather.

Clear blue skies with a few puffy white clouds greeted him.

He sighed in relief.

"You will note the way the clouds are clumping to the west, piling high," Guilliam said from right behind him. He seemed distracted. Like he needed to say more.

He would say it eventually. At the least opportune moment, when he could contain it no longer.

Gregor had to wait. Guilliam wouldn't spill his information until he was ready. Then there'd be no stopping the gush of data.

"Thunderstorms building. How long?" Gregor brought the conversation back to topic and away from whatever bothered Guilliam.

"A few hours."

"Long enough to get through the ordination?"

"Probably. I've shortened some of the hymns and stretched out the crystal music a bit. It's an older ritual." He handed Gregor a program.

"How long ago?" Gregor cocked one eyebrow upward.

"Last used two hundred years ago. But its origins are much older."

"Let's get on with it, then."

"Certainly, My Laud. You need only don your headdress."

"And Miss Sissy?"

"I hear that the preparations reduced her to tears, but Lady Marissa calmed her."

"Marissa? What does that witch want? She never does anything that doesn't work to her advantage. Why was she even in Sissy's quarters?"

"Laudae Penelope summoned her."

"I smell conspiracy. Is Sissy fit to go through the ritual?"

"Apparently so. Lady Marissa calmed her, got her breathing again, and finished dressing her in the new purple vestments." Guilliam plucked at his own light green robe. It looked a little shabby, in need of replacement.

Gregor smoothed his own new purple garments. Today only he and Sissy wore that color. Everyone else had elected to remain in green. He did like the dignity and tradition of the new color. Historically, only the wealthiest of Temple and Noble caste could afford the expensive dyes and chemicals needed to make purple.

A good reminder to the other castes—especially Lady Marissa and her Nobles—that he and Sissy sat on the High Council and together could outvote all the others.

He frowned. "Place a constant watch on Lady Marissa. I don't trust her. She and Penelope are too close. Bound by friendship and by blood. There has to be an ulterior motive behind them helping Sissy."

✦   ✦   ✦

Jake took his post in front of the fence made of decorative wrought iron, woven in an intricate lace atop a one-meter-high stone wall. He'd already chased away half a dozen teens and adults who'd tried to climb the fence for a better view of the festivities.

Two paces away, the massive gate, made of interlaced crystal wands, stood closed. Not much of a defensive point. One slash with his sword would shatter the fulcrum upon which the gate balanced. Or the shove of a desperate crowd would twist the ornate—but hardly functional locks—and thrust the gates inward.

He directed four men to stand in front of it. Lieutenant da Martin had ordered only two.

The men looked relieved for the extra support at this vulnerable point.

In a judicious move, the government had placed rare and expensive televisions and movie screens at strategic points around the city. Those who couldn't get into the Crystal Temple could at least watch the crowning of a new High Priestess peacefully. That didn't reduce the numbers watching at the Crystal Temple by much.

Once the pageantry started, who knew what would happen? Innocent spectators and troublemakers alike would press forward, taxing him and his men to keep them at bay.

He moved more men from the fringes closer in and kept them moving, listening, and obviously armed.

"Da Hawk, put four men at each of the side gates," he whispered into his shoulder comm.

"Orders are . . ."

"Orders are inadequate. Gates are vulnerable." With that thought he added two more men to the front gate, ordering them to keep moving, back and forth, no more than ten paces each direction.

A short skinny guy with a Professional caste mark and an extra bulge in his jacket pocket presented Jake with a pass.

Jake looked from the printed card, complete with picture and three signatures, to the extra baggage the man hid.

"Kind of warm for a coat," he mused, rubbing his thumb across the card. Was that a smudge?

"A formal occasion," the man said officiously.

"I need your invitation and personal ID to let you inside." Jake gestured with the hand behind his back for the gate guards to be ready.

The short Professional turned red. "I must have left them at home. Valuable souvenirs. I didn't want them lost or stolen."

"Sorry. No one gets in without invitation, ID, and pass."

"Do you know who I am?" The man drew himself as tall as he could. Jake still stood a full head above him.

"I don't care who you are. Orders from HP Laud Gregor, visitor's pass, ID, *and* invitation."

The two moving guards closed in behind Jake. He didn't need to see them. A bit of extra warmth on his back told him all he needed to know.

One of them whispered into his ear.

"John da John pa Harmony City Broadcasting, also known as Little Johnny to differentiate him from his father who owns HCB."

Jake wondered if his dad was as short as this guy. He pointedly tore up the pass. Had to be a forgery or an outdated one altered a bit with the date."

"That . . . that's a valuable piece of paper. I may never get another one," Little Johnny spluttered. "I have orders from the head of my caste . . ."

"And I have orders from HP Laud Gregor himself. All media denied access. You've got hover cams. You, in particular, are on the list to be escorted back to HCB."

Little Johnny gulped. "Mr. Guilliam, Laud Gregor's assistant said . . ."

The orders about triple credentials to get in had come from a Guilliam da Baillie.

"Mr. Guilliam is well respected in the city. For his sake, I'll let you stand on the wall peering in through the fence. But I've got to confiscate the camera." Jake reached into Little Johnny's pocket and retrieved the bulky equipment. A tight fit. Then he passed it to one of the men behind him.

The corporal opened the back and yanked out a long strand of plastic. Film? How archaic! Jake had only read about such things in ancient history texts. Then the guard escorted Little Johnny to a place near a stone fence support anchored to the meter-high wall.

"Good move," the other roving corporal whispered. "Can't afford to antagonize the media any more than we have to."

The crowd hadn't reacted to the interchange. They kept reasonable order. So far.

He didn't trust them. Half the conversations he overheard spoke of awe and respect for Temple. The other half mumbled distrust of all Temple and Noble as well as the imposter or Lood they tried to thrust upon them as an HPS, since they couldn't find a real avatar of Harmony.

Jake had no idea what Lood meant. But it sounded like a deep insult.

He accessed the dream implant for information. "Lood, condensed from Log of Wood, something nonhuman to be reviled and distrusted." Uh-oh. Prejudice in its extreme form. A license to kill. And just who determined the next minority to be declared Loods?

He wondered how many of the rumors about the new HPS were true. Something strange and controversial about prophetic visions and about her caste marks.

The Temple caste had drawn a veil of secrecy about her.

Caste *marks*. Plural. No one he'd seen had more than one. Uneasiness climbed his spine.

God, he wished he could talk to Pammy about this.

"I'm on my own. Have to think for myself. Damn, I wish I could just get the formula for Badger Metal and go home."

CHAPTER TWENTY-FIVE

HER SERENE HIGHNESS, LAUDAE SISSY, High Priestess of the Host of the Seven Guardians of the planet Harmony and her Colonies, slipped her beringed hands into the copious sleeves of her purple brocade robes. She dropped her head slightly as she assumed a meditative pose. The crystals and glass beads of her veil bobbed and swayed, giving her a refracted view of her companion priests and priestesses. They all stood in the dim tunnel opening on the forecourt of Crystal Temple. Tension and anticipation of the high ritual to come throbbed among them like a saber lion pacing her cage.

"We chose a good day. The Summer Solstice. Sun at its highest point. The Moon is full. Harmony balances the beginning of the season of bounty," she whispered, reminding herself of the auspicious ritual she was about to preside over. And endure. "My twenty-first birthday. I'm not ready."

Outside, the conversations of the waiting populace assumed a low thrumming note in anticipation of the crowning of a new High Priestess. The crowd spilled out of the forecourt into the streets beyond.

No other time brought so many together, binding them with the beauty and spirit of ritual. She had to do this right.

Laud Gregor had drilled her over and over. She knew the sequence of prayers and chimes and movements.

Restlessly she shifted her feet, uncomfortable standing so long, waiting for the precise moment Laud Gregor would lead them all forward.

Sissy blinked rapidly. The hummed note of the crowd did not fit. Out of harmony. Out of synchronization. Out of place.

A counter note vibrated in the back of her throat. Desperately, she tried to pull the exterior tone into place.

It defied her. The world tilted around her.

She began to tremble. The beads and crystals in her veil clanked together. *Not again. Dear Harmony, not again.*

How did she make it right?

"Come, Sissy," Laud Gregor whispered in her ear. He could not presume on her person to actually tug at her sleeve, but she sensed his urgency.

She unraveled her attention from the disharmony around her. Her companions had moved ahead of her into the forecourt. She and Gregor must follow. The last to enter.

She took one step and flailed for balance.

"Do you need the inhaler?" Laud Gregor asked. This time he presumed to take her arm just to keep her upright.

"I don't know," Sissy murmured back. The caste marks on her right cheek began to burn and pulse. She clenched her hands tightly around opposite wrists within her sleeves to keep from touching the unique birthmarks.

"Grit your teeth and hang on. Once Harmony has her new avatar, everything will settle down. We will convince the populace that Harmony thrives." Maintaining his fierce grip on her arm, he led her to her place behind the crystal altar at the center of the forecourt.

Media cams hovered all around her from her first step outside the tunnel. They broadcast her every word and gesture to all of Harmony, in every temple and public gathering place in the empire.

Sunshine caught the crystals in her veil and refracted with bright rainbows, nearly blinding her. Only familiarity with the route to her place at the altar kept her on the proper path.

Sissy raised her arms, palm outward as if embracing her congregation from a distance. She chanted:

> "We gather to honor you, Harmony,
> Binder of all.
> We gather to worship you, Empathy,
> Giver of life, knowledge and wisdom
> To all who seek you.
> We gather to Nurture each other
> And our home.
> We gather to create Unity.
> We gather to balance the forces
> Of Greed, Anger, and Fear,
> To banish Discord and Chaos.

We gather the castes in common purpose;
Each in their own way;
Each from their own place.
We gather, Host of Seven,
All of Harmony together
In harmony."

But there was no harmony today. The prophecy of long ago burned at the back of her throat. She pushed it away. But she couldn't ignore the curious too bright light and too sharp detail.

Her notes fell flat, absorbed by the crystal columns upon the crystal altar and the crystal pillars that supported the roof of the temple around the open courtyard.

She tried again to find a balance in the notes as she repeated the chant with all those around her.

The people should match her tones. Their notes were flat by a full half tone.

She shook her head to clear it of the disharmony. The veil clanked again, sharp by a full half tone.

A quick glance to right and left showed the full contingent of seven priests and six other priestesses unaware that something was drastically wrong and growing worse.

Light fractured as it struck the crystals in her veil. Halos burst forth surrounding everything with a yellowish cast. Something about the quality of that light . . .

She looked up. Deep, dark clouds piled one atop the other, moving rapidly toward the capital from the west.

Mary, her senior acolyte, placed a glass wand in her right hand.

She stared at it for the length of a heartbeat, unsure if she should use it.

Gregor nudged her foot with one of his own.

She tapped the tapered center crystal atop the altar. A half meter high and six centimeters at the base, it rose to a sharp faceted point. A clear note rang forth when the glass wand touched the stone.

Better.

Colors that she did not know were off kilter by three shades too yellow, shifted back to the blue side of the spectrum.

Sissy breathed a little easier. She tapped the shortest crystal on the far right of the array.

It sang a sour note, as if the mineral matrix had cracked.

She needed the reassuring tones of a black crystal. None here. This wasn't a funeral.

A media cam homed in on her movements, broadcasting the ritual and her distress to the entire planet.

She frowned as her chest tightened, constricting her breathing. Her people would never believe that she and the rest of the Temple could control the forces of chaos and change if she faltered or altered this special ritual. Her first. The most important that would set the standard for the rest of her life.

She drew a deep breath and acid tingled on her tongue. The faintest hint of electrical energy.

She tapped the center crystal again. It harmonized with the current in the air and kept her balance oriented. She tapped it again.

Good.

The clergy, in their bright green robes and sparkling headdresses faltered at this alteration in the sequence. They consulted the notes they'd hidden in their sleeves. Notes written by Mr. Guilliam and handed out at the last minute.

Sissy ran the glass wand along the entire array of crystals, bringing forth a strange cacophony of sound. The crystal altar itself picked up the tones and echoed them through the congregation.

They faltered in their singing as well.

Everyone in the empire must now know that something was wrong. Terribly wrong.

And she, Sissy, priestess and avatar of Harmony, could not fix it.

The hairs on her arms and the back of her neck stood up, quivering with the electricity.

She recognized it now. The beginnings of a storm. A big one. A violent one. The sky darkened as the clouds streaming in from the west and south swallowed the sun.

The crystals upon the altar were not enough. She needed more sound. More harmony to balance the air pressures. She needed the Unity of every atom in the universe to dissipate the energy of the storm and break it up.

Inspiration lit her mind. Clenching her wand, she broke through the ranks of clergy, military guards, and congregation until she could touch the first pillar at the edge of the open area.

The courtyard sang with a bright gong the moment she touched it.

She ran to the next pillar and set it ringing with her wand. It sounded a step lower than the first, still in tune, still in harmony.

Before the reverberations could die away, she ran to the next pillar and the next, tapping each with enough force to bring forth a full chord of notes.

Her fellow celebrants had no choice but to follow her lead. The ritual was set. What Sissy did, the rest must repeat.

Gregor slapped each pillar one step behind her, then each of the priests and priestesses followed suit. And so did the gathered throng of representatives of all seven castes, the Temple, the Nobles, the Professionals, the Military, the Spacers, the Workers, and the Poor.

All seven caste marks on Sissy's cheek began to burn and pulse with the elemental music she created. She caught glimmers of the same phenomena on the single caste marks on the cheeks of each person she passed.

Resolutely she cast off her headdress. The clanging crystal beads fractured her vision and sang out of tune.

A collective gasp ran through the entire forecourt. She didn't care. She had to do this. She had to save Harmony City from the gathering storm that swirled above them in ever tighter spirals.

Sissy kept running, kept bringing forth the notes, running counterclockwise in opposition to the storm. Cold wind slapped her face and tangled her hair. She lifted her face to meet it, challenge it.

After one circuit of the seven pillars, she wove a new pattern among them. Inside, outside, dark daylight, darker shadows. High notes, light and lilting; deep notes, solemn and weighty. She wove the music that bound Harmony to her orbit around the sun Empathy; that bound the solar system in its place within the galaxy; that allowed the galaxy to hold its place in the universe.

All part of one cosmic plan with one origin and harmonic ties to all other parts of the whole.

Sissy slowed as she returned the pattern of the music and the dance to the altar. The others continued to flow around her. She raised her arms once more, beseeching the cosmos to right itself. She breathed in rhythm with the growing cone of mixing notes that equalized the clashing air masses. Her body lost all sense of weight and anchor. She drifted among the stars, spinning, spinning, spinning into the darkness.

A clash of thunder added its own note to the whole. Lightning flitted across the heavens. Rain poured down to drench her in blessing. She felt herself unwind, spread out, join the tendrils of energy that bound all the stars together.

CHAPTER TWENTY-SIX

JAKE'S JAW HUNG OPEN. He couldn't believe what he saw. Blue lightning engulfed the High Priestess in a bubble of crackling energy. She stood in a puddle that collected on the dais within seconds of the downpour.

Electric energy and water. A recipe for disaster.

"Shit!" Jake pulled out his Badger Metal sword and slashed through the old-fashioned lock on the gate. Shards of crystal exploded in all directions sending the crowd ducking and screaming. But they didn't go home, they just backed up. This ordination must be more important to them than the discomfort of the sudden—and unpredicted—thunderstorm.

Two men followed him in and turned to face the crowd, swords drawn. The rovers took their place at the opening, also brandishing their weapons. Covering his back, as they should. Keeping the crowd at bay should anyone of them start thinking and move forward.

In a situation like this, crowds tended to develop a single mind, moving in concert, obeying some inner laws.

Rain drenched the forecourt, cascading down from the oval altar dais. Small puddles pooled and became a single lake five centimeters deep.

From the intensity of the clouds, Jake wondered if it were more than just another storm.

The HPS looked at him with intense interest. Her eyes reflected starshine.

It was like looking at his own soul through the wisdom of the ages.

"Seek a new path. The old ways are not for you," she whispered. Then she touched the half ovoid of the crystal altar.

All that blue energy poured out of her and grounded.

Jake grabbed her as she slumped.

"Choices open before you. You cannot take the easy trail and survive." Then she passed out.

What the hell did that mean? He was seeking a new path, that of a spy in deep cover. And it sure wasn't easy. Pammy had made him forsake his life as a fighter pilot.

Was there something else out there for him? Something bigger and better? More *important!*

Jake scooped up the slight lady in his arms. As light as a child. He cradled her tenderly against his chest, afraid her frail bones would crumble under his touch.

"Follow me," the man dressed in purple directed Jake. He drew off his own headdress and veil, handing it to a green-robed assistant. A gray fringe around a bald pate. Tall, lean, loose jointed.

The priest at the comm tower. Laud Gregor himself.

He'd figure that out later.

The HP led him into the tunnel that connected the forecourt with the temple. He paused at a shadowed door while he fished a key out of a hidden pocket of his robe. His hands trembled so badly he couldn't get the key in.

"My Laud, may I?" asked the assistant in pale green. He produced his own key and had the door open in a heartbeat.

Jake didn't need direction to lay the young woman on the lounge near the wardrobe. He felt for a pulse on her cold hand.

"We'll handle it from here. Our thanks, Sergeant." The HP shouldered him aside and pulled up a stool to sit holding her hand. "Summon the physician, Guilliam."

The assistant nodded and departed. A marmalade cat slithered in and hid beneath the lounge. A brownish mongrel dog sat at her feet, muzzle resting on the robe, and whined.

Jake followed the assistant out. The rest of the participants in the strange ritual had organized some of the chaos in the forecourt. They sang a hymn that had the ring of finality and blessing in it. Then they waded through the throng to form a receiving line as the crowd exited.

No one stopped Jake as he circled the altar again and again seeking signs of scorch marks. Nothing. Somehow the girl had controlled the lightning. Maybe even summoned it. She'd certainly looked like she reveled in the storm as she spun in circles, arms out, face lifted to receive the rain—like a bizarre kind of baptism.

He would not, could not believe that the circling winds had lifted her upward a full meter, then set her back down again, quite gently. That defied belief, defied physics. Defied—well everything.

Curiouser and curiouser. "Damn, I need to talk to Pammy. She'd make sense of all this."

But he was on his own with twenty men looking to him for direction.

And the most elite governor in the empire sneaking around the comm tower.

✦   ✦   ✦

"Get that sergeant's name and unit. We'll give him a medal of gratitude for his help. Maybe even Laud his caste mark so he can serve the entire Temple," Gregor said idly to Guilliam when he returned to the private vestry with a physician in tow.

Laudae Sissy stirred and moaned upon the narrow lounge. Her cat levitated to her side. It tested its steps and settled delicately on the girl's chest, purring louder than the retreating thunder.

Outside, rain continued to pound upon the forecourt. Fortunately the thunder and lightning had gone away after that first awesome blast that shook the entire Crystal Temple to its foundations.

"She's coming around," Gregor said quietly. He shooed away the physician with a gesture. He still felt as if the air tingled around him. The fine hairs on his arms and back wanted to bristle.

The physician bowed and retreated two steps from taking Sissy's pulse and blood pressure.

Stripped of her headdress and formal robe, she appeared too slight, too young, and too fragile for the weight of her responsibilities. Today was an auspicious date. He'd chosen this date for many reasons.

Or Harmony had chosen it for him. He banished that thought. He was in control of the Temple and all its rituals.

He smoothed Sissy's dark hair away from her face. Thick tendrils tried to cling to the caste marks on her right cheek.

"Come here," Sissy whispered. The words came out choked as if she'd spent a long time in the desert without water or shade. She lifted one finger away from petting the cat—barely—and beckoned the physician closer.

The man knelt beside the couch and bent his head in reverence.

Sissy turned her head slightly to look at the man directly. She stared at the purple circle around his green triangle caste mark. Her brown eyes glinted silver. "Serve where your heart leads you. You cannot fulfill your destiny here in these rarified halls."

Her head dropped back, and she closed her eyes once more. When she opened them again, all traces of the starshine had vanished. She was once more an ordinary young woman who happened to have the weight of the world in her being.

Cat decided she'd heal without his help and hid once more. Just in time.

"What do you mean she's ill?" Penelope's strident tones grated on Gregor's already taut nerves. "She's faking it just to get attention, trying to make her betters look incompetent."

In her wake followed the five other members of the High Council, all wearing the blue diamond Noble caste mark.

Gregor cringed.

So did Sissy.

"Out of my way." Penelope pushed past the Military guard at the door—not the rescuing sergeant. She had divested herself of her formal regalia, but instead of a simple green dress she sported the latest fashion in bright green trousers and a coordinated print blouse that nearly outshone the chunks of gold jewelry at her throat, wrists, and ears.

The guard shrugged an apology. He blushed with embarrassment nearly the same deep red as his square caste mark. No one should have been able to penetrate his guard.

Unfortunately, Penelope and her cohort outranked the man. He could lose his head for barring their entrance.

Too many of the lower caste faced execution, alone, without their families or loved ones, at the mercy of a soulless beheading machine, because a Noble took offense.

Gregor nodded his acceptance of the man's plight. Penelope was a force of nature not to be denied.

"This is the final burden of Empathy, My Laud High Priest." Penelope spat the title. By invoking it, she made this a formal complaint that must be dealt with rather than a personal request. "She deviates from formal ritual, she spouts nonsense and calls it prophecy . . ."

"I beg your pardon, Laudae Penelope." The physician bowed. "Laudae Harmony spoke true. I have long wished to take on the challenge of working in one of the city hospitals."

Penelope, Gregor, and Lady Marissa all gasped.

"You would taint your person by working outside your caste!" Penelope screeched.

The five Noble leaders made the splayed circle warding with their hands for this breech of solemn law.

"This is my true calling. I have spoken of it to no one. Yet Laudae Harmony knew what was in my heart and advised me to find my proper destiny. Consider this my formal resignation, My Laud. I shall depart Temple grounds before dawn. If you deem it necessary, I'll de-Laud my caste mark to reflect my calling." He bowed himself out.

"This is too much. Now she has cost us the most gifted physician of our generation. The Workers and the Poor do not deserve him." The most senior Guardian Chauncey, having sat on the Council longest, and ten years older than Gregor, shuddered in disapproval of the physician's announcement. "We must investigate the presence of a mutant in the highest places of government, the avatar of our beloved home world. We must investigate *your* choice of this child as our High Priestess, Gregor."

Beside Chauncey, Penelope mouthed the words the patriarch spoke. She'd planned this confrontation for a long time.

Strangely, Lady Marissa remained silent, reserved and slightly apart from this verbal fray. Her son stood just behind her left shoulder, ready to whisper advice or information as needed. Gregor didn't know which of her twin sons it was. They exchanged place frequently and looked exactly alike.

"It is not our place to question the visions of Laudae Harmony." Gregor bowed his head. He had to bite his cheeks in vexation. He knew this day would come. Just not quite so soon.

"This aberration of nature cannot continue among us," Lady Sarah added. She represented a minor family that had made a powerful alliance by having her marrying Penelope's brother—a dilettante with no priestly calling. That tied her to Marissa as well.

"Sissy cannot be trusted with important rituals," Sarah continued. "This Lood brings change and disorder to our ancient and respected traditions. You have been negligent in this, Gregor. I call the High Council to remove you and your protégée from office." She neglected to add a title to Sissy's name. As severe a breach of protocol as anything they accused Gregor of.

"If found guilty, both of you must face trial as traitors to Harmony," Nathaniel concluded. That aged but unbowed Noble normally represented compromise on the High Council. "The penalty for treason is death by beheading."

Everyone in the room shuddered at the thought of the hideous and humiliating punishment.

"Only a full conclave of my caste may remove me from the rank I have earned." Gregor stood and faced Penelope, his true adversary. The heat of anger flushed his face and hardened his gaze.

"My Lords, My Ladies, Laud and Laudae, you must look at this!" Guilliam burst into the private room. He couldn't have chosen a more opportune moment. He brushed past Penelope as if she wasn't there. Their arms touched briefly. She did not react.

Strange.

"You are presumptuous and ill-mannered to burst into the presence of the High Council uninvited," Penelope snarled, as if she were one of them rather than their puppet master.

Gregor raised his eyebrows. "So are you, Penelope."

"But you have to see this." Guilliam waved a handheld computer in his superior's face. A very expensive instrument loaned to Gregor by the Spacers. He had no intention of returning it.

Gregor grabbed the computer and held it at arm's length to focus better. He viewed the forecourt from the perspective of a hover cam near the roof. He watched the entire ritual as well as a piece of the skyline. At the moment Sissy broke free of the ritual to begin her dance among the crystal pillars the cam shifted its angle upward. The sky grew blacker with tinges of yellow to the mist. Then a piece of the cloud spun lower and lower, a tornado forming before his eyes.

A second and a third spiral pushed downward. Then five more. An unprecedented storm in a year of unprecedented planetary upheaval.

The swirling winds whipped at clothing and hair, anything loose on the ground, pulling things upward into its voracious maw.

Then the reaching whirlwinds pulled back, withdrew, spat out what they had engulfed and faded back into the rapidly dissipating dark cloud cover.

"What is this?" He handed the computer back to Guilliam.

"She did it, sir." He pointed to Sissy. "She countered the storm and made it break apart."

The High Priestess sat up and took the computer into her own hands. She sighed happily and handed it back.

"Let me see that," Penelope demanded. She grabbed the instrument and stared at it long and hard. "You faked this. You had to. No storm would gather so intensely and then just go away. You are all conspiring to destroy the order of our society by supporting this charlatan. Everyone knows a tornado rotates counterclockwise. She ran the same direction so she couldn't have countered it."

"Then you should listen to the latest news reports coming in from all over the city." Guilliam faced Penelope and the High Council squarely, standing his ground as Gregor had never seen him do before. Usually he whispered compromise while fading into the background. "The tornado touched down in three places just outside the Crystal Temple and caused only minor damage. All the meteorologists are puzzled because the storms circulated clockwise. They only do that in extreme and unusual circumstances. My homage, Laudae Harmony, you saved our city once more from devastation. Every member of every caste in the city is waiting outside the gates for a glimpse of their new High Priestess. They want to express their awe directly to you." He knelt and bowed his head.

Sissy touched his hair briefly in blessing.

Penelope stormed out of the vestry, lips clamped tightly into a thin line, cheeks flaring red, and eyes smoldering with plans. "I curse the day you came to us, Sissy of the Worker caste."

The High Council looked back and forth between Penelope's retreating back and Sissy, not knowing which represented the stronger power.

"I bless the day I found you, Sissy of *every* caste," Gregor said loudly and bowed to his priestess. "I had planned to speak to you privately about changing your name to something more appropriate. But I believe you have earned the right to become, Estella—Laudae of the Stars—as well as our own Laudae Harmony."

The girl blushed and shook her head, eyes wide with bewilderment.

Sissy accepted Laud Gregor's assistance to sit up. A wave of dizziness made her pause before swinging her legs over the side of the lounge. It passed quickly and she rose, still holding his arm.

"The man who carried me away from the altar?" Sissy had a vague memory of a tall, blond man with kind eyes. She'd said something to him about choices and paths.

"Sergeant Jacob da Jacob pa Law Enforcement HQ H Prime," Guilliam said.

"I would speak with him."

"He's gone," Guilliam said. "I'll call him back."

"Later," Gregor countered. "Laudae Estella has an empire to greet."

"I have a wedding to perform." Sissy paused in her careful steps toward the tunnel. "My brother . . ."

"You are in no condition to perform another ritual," Gregor insisted. "I shall do the honors for your brother, My Laudae."

"No. I will." She shook off his support. Her balance held. The swirling confusion of prophecy had vanished the moment she touched the altar and grounded the storm energy. "Mr. Guilliam, please bring my family to the forecourt."

"My Laudae," Gregor protested. "A wedding should be a private, family affair. If you perform the ritual in the forecourt, the entire empire will view it through the hover cams."

"So be it. I want my first official duty as HPS to be one of joy, invoking Nurture and Unity. Very symbolic. Very important." Resolutely she walked forward.

At the tunnel exit she found a smile deep within her and flashed it to the waiting throng. Cheers rose up around her.

Then suddenly Mama and Pop were there, gathering her into a hug. More of her family joined the embrace.

The cheers of the waiting empire drowned out all other thoughts. Her heart swelled in gratitude and tears of joy touched her eyes.

CHAPTER TWENTY-SEVEN

"WHY AM I HERE, GIL?" Penelope asked quietly.

Gil drove a roomy town car. Penelope's seven acolytes rode in the back, squished together and fully occupied with their own gossipy conversation. He doubted any of them eavesdropped on their elders.

"Because you are the Director of Religious Education." A more logical pairing than Shanet who welcomed the opportunity to remain in Temple and complete some of her own work.

"I know that." She rolled her eyes upward. "But why did you insist I visit a public school today? I have meetings and new texts to review."

"Our new HPS is visiting this school with her acolytes. We need to keep an eye on her." Sissy rode ahead of them in a much bigger car with a Professional driver. Gil had personally selected the driver, Bertie, for his dedication and hereditary loyalty to the Temple.

Sissy's acolytes had plenty of room, except they had to share space with the cat, the dog, the lizard, and a newly acquired kitten with only one eye.

Penelope crossed her arms under her magnificent bosom and frowned.

Gil wanted to gaze fondly at her figure. He didn't dare take his eyes off the road.

Two rapid turns took them around back of a huge factory complex to a smaller building. Bertie parked Sissy's car in the middle of the street in front of a modest double door.

Fortunately, this district didn't get much wheeled traffic that would have to inch around it.

Gil politely pulled his car as far to the right as he could manage. He spent several long moments adjusting his position.

Penelope frowned at him. He didn't bother explaining that he thought it important to disrupt normal lives as little as possible. Sissy's presence alone would do that. Why add a traffic jam to it?

Frequently craning his head into a new position, he searched for signs of Little Johnny and his ever-present hover cam. There, at the corner, ready to move closer when he could follow unobtrusively.

Penelope and Sissy might not appreciate media presence at this visitation. Gil thought it important.

Bertie exited Sissy's car and scooted around to the offside door. He paused a moment, took a deep breath, and opened the door for Sissy.

She ignored his proffered hand of assistance and bounced out. Her girls followed in a whirlwind of exuberance. Dog took the opportunity to run around the car three times at top speed before settling at Sissy's heel. The cat and the lizard remained inside.

Kitten? Gil made a swift survey, automatically counting heads and bodies, just like he did with his own five children—the two youngest, twins, assisted Penelope. Ah, there, one of the middle girls cradled the kitten in her arms.

All present and accounted for.

The hover cam caught it all.

The double doors opened to frame Lady Marissa, her twin sons behind her. She stood with all the majesty and grace bred into her from countless generations of inherited power. A mature woman full of confidence and arrogance. She directed a benevolent smile toward Sissy and held out her hand in greeting.

Gil didn't believe in her sincerity for one moment. He immediately cast off his jovial family personality of Gil, and became Guilliam, the watchful and wary chief administrative acolyte to the HP of all Harmony.

"What is she doing here?" he asked. "This is Chauncey's domain." He didn't want anyone stealing time in the media coverage away from Sissy.

"I don't know," Penelope replied. She smiled and rushed to greet her aunt.

But Marissa's entire attention was on Sissy. The older woman gathered the HPS into a familial hug. Then arms draped about each other, they ambled inside.

Guilliam hurried to catch up, making sure all of the acolytes preceded him. Interesting how the youngest of the girls in both Sissy's and Penelope's gaggle tended to cross to the other group and pair off according to age. Since Penelope's girls ranged in age from nine to seventeen, and Sissy's from nine to twelve, the oldest girls kept to themselves.

He had to remind himself that these children had spent a lot of time together during Sissy's training. And Sissy tended to treat all of them as one big happy family.

A quick look made sure that Little Johnny observed it all.

Just inside the doorway, Penelope grabbed Guilliam's arm and pulled him aside.

"What is that smell?" she whispered and wrinkled her nose in disgust.

"An old building filled with too many bodies," he replied.

"Sharper than that. It smells . . . it smells like an over-ripe diaper." She'd know. She'd changed enough of them over the years, keeping her children close. Balking at her mother's and her aunt's insistence that she place every child in the Temple nursery, Penelope had nursed them as long as possible, entrusting them to the nursery only when fully weaned and out of diapers.

Guilliam approved. He'd been raised by his mother along with two sisters and a brother. And they all had the same father. Penelope had confessed to him early on, that she had *ached* for a mother and close family as a child. Lady Marissa had given her more love and attention than Marilee.

"Old plumbing not maintained," Guilliam explained.

"But that's . . . that's uncivilized. Why don't these people do something about it?"

"They can't. Not without Lord Chauncey's authorization. And he doesn't release funds for new pipes or plumbers to fix them."

"We'll see about that." Penelope stalked after the retreating backs of Lady Marissa and Sissy.

"I want to visit a classroom," Sissy said.

"But I've arranged with the director for you to meet a few specially selected children who show great promise in advancing to supervisory positions," Lady Marissa said. She frowned and clenched her teeth.

"Later. First I want to see what has changed since I went to school here." With that, Sissy marched to the nearest door and flung it open.

Guilliam could just see a mass of small bodies, all dressed in coarse brown coveralls. The subtle sounds of whispers and restless shifting ceased abruptly.

Penelope moved forward to peer over Sissy's shoulder. She began to shake with anger.

Guilliam hurried to her side and pressed his hand against her back, not caring who witnessed the intimate touch. "Easy. No sense in making a scene in front of the hover cam."

"How can they survive like this? Twenty, thirty, no, fifty children in a room designed for twenty. Five to a book. And only one teacher who looks totally exhausted."

"That's the way it has always been in the Worker caste. They make do with what they have. No one thinks to give them anything better, especially if it costs their lord money."

"Something has to change. Now. It's inhuman to treat children like this. They're just children." She placed a hand on the shoulder of each of her two youngest girls.

"Change has already started. With Laudae Sissy. You're the Director of Religious Education. You can follow her lead and correct some terrible wrongs."

"I intend to. But first I need to talk to the director of this school and make certain they're at least following prescribed curriculum."

She turned on her heel and made her way toward a partially open door with the word "Director" painted on it. The once-red paint had faded and chipped to be almost indiscernible.

Lady Marissa scurried after her.

The hover cam followed.

Sissy turned to Guilliam and flashed him one of her charming smiles. "Did it work?"

"She's beginning to see the light."

"Good. Now let's go meet some children."

"Where are we off to today, Laudae Estella?" Gregor asked as he inserted himself beside his High Priestess in the back seat of her car.

Seven little girls, all dressed in lavender, scooted and rearranged themselves to accommodate him. His knees brushed the shoes of the littlest one sitting across from him. She had to stop swinging those feet to avoid kicking him. A deep frown marred her picture-perfect blonde beauty as she sought another outlet for her restlessness.

"I did not expect you accompany us to the . . . children's hospital and then some playtime in the park," Sissy said as she deposited her cat in the little girl's lap. Instantly, the animal's purring soothed her squirming.

Dog reached up his muzzle to rest on her purple-clad knee and whined for a pet. She gave it to him, all the while keeping her gaze firmly away from Gregor.

The car moved forward smoothly and picked up speed so gradually that Gregor hardly felt the transition. He'd chosen the right driver for her.

"Visiting the sick is the work of lesser clergy, Laudae Estella."

She winced. "My name is Sissy. Plain Sissy. I never was a fancy person and I don't need a fancy name."

"But the people need an elegant High Priestess with an elegant name."

"The people need comfort and prayers, and I don't see anyone else at

Crystal Temple attending to those duties. So I must. And from what I've seen so far, the people like a plain and simple High Priestess they can talk to."

He nodded to her logic. "They also need someone to inspire awe that they can look up to."

"Plenty of folks at Crystal Temple pretend to inspire awe. Seems kind of repetitious, um, redundant, for me to try and fail."

Gregor looked out the window while trying to find his next riposte. As he watched, they sped past the children's hospital in the Professional neighborhood adjacent to the Crystal Temple.

He leaned forward and tapped the driver's shoulder. Sissy had left the dividing glass down, inviting familiarity and eavesdropping. "You passed the hospital."

The driver nodded and kept on going.

"Laudae Estella, where are we going?" Gregor turned a stern countenance upon her.

She gulped and looked away.

"I'm waiting for an answer."

"I'm going to visit the asylum." She stuck her chin out in stubborn defiance.

"That is not authorized." He shuddered with revulsion.

"I'm your High Priestess. I authorize where I go, when I go."

"But it's dangerous!"

"Then we will stop and collect a Military escort. But I am going."

"Why, in the Name of the Seven?"

"Because it is the place I fear most. It is the place where I would have been sent eventually if you had not brought me to Crystal Temple," she whispered.

"You are safe now, Sissy." He used her familiar name as he patted her hand. "You are HPS of all Harmony, protected and beloved." Now maybe they could turn around and go back to the safe confines of Crystal Temple.

"I have to do for the castoffs what everyone would be too afraid to do for me. I need to eliminate the fear of mutations."

No, you don't! he wanted to scream. Without that fear, people would view the mutations as natural. Next, a person born out of caste would assume the higher caste. Mixing would follow. A disruption of the orderly process of society. He couldn't allow that.

"Turn around, Bertie."

"Sorry, My Laud. Laudae Harmony's authority is higher than yours." The driver closed the partition between them and kept driving.

Gregor sat with his mouth agape. Never in all the sixteen years he had presided over the Crystal Temple had anyone, *anyone,* of any caste offered such insubordination.

How should he react?

Dammit, the man was right. Sissy did outrank him. As decreed in the original Covenant of Harmony.

He seethed while he considered appropriate punishments.

Within moments they drove down an increasingly narrow and dirty alley. Gregor kept his eyes moving constantly, starting at every movement, every misshapen shadow. Who knew what violent criminals and what dregs of society lurked here, where order had disappeared?

"Laudae Estella, this venture is a very bad idea."

"Only if you make it so."

The car stopped and she hopped out before Gregor could react. He contemplated sitting here while the inmates killed her. But that would look bad.

Discord! A hover cam sat just above the doorway, watching him. Who had told the media the HPS would be here today, at this time?

He had to follow her. And she knew it.

"All seven of you girls sit right here. Do not move. Lock all the doors and windows." The automatic cooling system should take care of the midsummer sunshine. "You, Bertie, come with us. I order you to protect Laudae Estella with your life."

"Who is going to protect you, My Laud?"

"I intend to run at the first sign of trouble."

CHAPTER TWENTY-EIGHT

THE SMELL OF RANCID SWEAT, FEAR, urine, and other unmention-able things assailed Sissy the moment she crossed the threshold of the asylum. Worse than the school. Worse than the streets of the Poor district.

Her hands shook, her knees trembled, and chills filled her with dread.

This was her fate.

And all of Harmony was probably watching.

As she had arranged, a physician met her at the door. The same physician who had tended her when she fainted at the ordination. The same physician who had asked to serve where he was most needed rather than where he was most praised. His caste mark looked raw and angry where the purple circle had been removed.

He guided her down a long, narrow, and dimly lit hallway to an office. The hover cam followed at a wary distance.

Stark white walls enclosed her in an imitation of light and joy. By the time Sissy sank into a stiff wooden chair, she could barely breathe. Her heart pounded so loudly the physician's words sounded as if he whispered them from outside the closed and barred window.

Above her, she heard pitiful moans. Wails without hope. No exit. No escape from this place.

Death would be kinder. Even the merciless execution dictated by the gods. Alone, chained to a block, waiting for the unpredictable robotic machine to sever your head on its own timing. Never knowing when. It could come in five seconds or an hour.

Never knowing when. Only that it must. And no one would remember or mourn you.

"Laudae, how may I serve you?" the physician asked. He sounded kind and caring.

"Tell me what you are doing for these people," she croaked out.

Laud Gregor stomped into the office. He glared at the hover cam. "Remove yourself," he sneered. He swatted at the device until it flew into the hallway. Then he slammed the door on it and took a second chair, as straight and uncomfortable as her own.

"We try to keep them calm and comfortable and feed them when they will eat."

Sissy wrinkled her nose. So did Laud Gregor.

"Are they allowed to bathe, have clean clothing?"

"That is more difficult. I don't have the staff to supervise and assist. Our funds are very limited."

"Why?"

"Why?" the physician echoed. "Because—because that is how it has always been. The castoffs and leftovers get the castoffs and leftovers."

"Is bathing so difficult a chore that they cannot manage it themselves?" Anger boiled inside Sissy. If she stayed angry, she wouldn't fall into despair.

"Laudae, this is not necessary, nor your concern. Let others . . ." Laud Gregor said.

"It is most definitely my concern. The helpless and the hopeless have no one else to turn to but me. Surely, Physician, the inmates can bathe themselves and keep their quarters clean. Why are they not allowed to do this?"

"You have to understand, Laudae, these are not normal people. Training them is useless. I doubt they'd know how to mop a floor or wash clothing. They can barely wipe themselves," the physician said. He hadn't offered her a name, as if he were too good to give it to a Lood such as she.

Sissy stared at him aghast. And continued to stare long after he could reasonably expect a comment.

He began to squirm.

"Laudae, we must leave," Gregor urged.

Sissy continued to sit and stare at the physician.

"I quote accepted wisdom rather than the truth," the physician finally admitted. "This place is filthy because the rest of Harmony expects it to be filthy. They do not wish to admit that my patients are anything more than animals." Perhaps he hadn't offered her a name because he presumed she knew it. Everyone at Crystal Temple probably did. Except her. She hadn't been there long enough to know him.

"My dog takes better care of himself, keeps himself cleaner than you allow these patients to be cared for."

"Laudae, we must leave. Your acolytes await you in the car." Gregor stood and placed his hand beneath her elbow.

Sissy wanted to comply. She wanted to run away to safety and blind acceptance of the asylum and its filth. She wanted to run to the haven of her family and bury her tears in her mother's apron.

A particularly loud wail from above set her teeth to chattering. The patients couldn't run away.

"Who do I talk to to get more money into this place so they can at least get cleaning supplies and take care of the stench?" She turned her hardest glare upon Gregor.

"You have but to say the word, and the money will be found. But we have to leave now."

"Laudae, money will do little good. Each person in a long chain of administration will take a percentage as their due. Little or none of it will actually reach the asylum." The physician hung his head in shame.

"That is not acceptable."

"It is reality."

"I will do something to help these people!" Sissy insisted.

"They aren't people," Gregor retorted as he took a firmer grip on her arm and dragged her back the way they had come.

"If they are not people, then neither am I," Sissy insisted. She tried digging in her heels. Gregor merely nodded to the Bertie, the driver who awaited them outside the office. He added his strength and determination to removing her from the premises.

"You are a person because I have decreed it," Gregor replied through clenched teeth. "Never forget that. You owe *me* your loyalty, your obedience, and your life."

The hover cam recorded it all.

CHAPTER TWENTY-NINE

J **AKE RAISED HIS HAND TO** signal the local barmaid for a refill of his light ale. Light being relative. Back on SB3 this brew qualified as liquid bread.

The woman ignored him, keeping her eyes on the floor while she limped from table to table.

Every caste mark in the place was a red square. Even the bartender and her servers. They'd all gathered on Rest Day, the first chance available after the ordination, to celebrate the new reign of the Laudae Estella as HPS. The frail young woman had filled the newscasts for the last two weeks. She visited the sick and the impoverished in the worst parts of the city. She played with children in the park.

And she gathered stray animals every time she flashed that engaging smile. Dogs, cats, birds, a ferretlike creature native to the planet before human colonizers terraformed it. At last count her menagerie had grown to fourteen. Double the sacred seven. Everyone called that a good omen.

The city remained quiet. But Jake sensed an air of caution. Not everyone approved of Laudae Estella and her seven caste marks.

While he waited for the barmaid to acknowledge him, he took his turn at the dart board. The rules here differed somewhat from back home. Instead of a complicated point system marked off in different segments of a circle, he faced a male silhouette and had to take out different target points in order.

Jake tuned out the raucous music in the background, lined up his dart, and threw, hoping his eye-hand coordination held true. That's what it was all about, honing skills so one didn't have to think on the battlefield. These guys seemed to like drills, endless repetitious, *boring* drills. Often set to music to help them find their inner rhythm, like a dance.

Worse than flight drills at SB3.

Only these guys played for keeps. No blunted or foiled blades for them. Every man in Jake's squad had spent at least a few hours with the medics since he'd arrived. He even had a couple of scars himself now. Superficial wounds to arms and legs, nothing as potentially dangerous as the belly swipe he'd given da Hawk—his friend.

Jake's dart embedded itself in the left thigh of the outline. It wobbled a bit, not truly secure; still, he got the points.

"Disabled the left leg, seven points," da Hawk called out.

Corporal Camden da Chester tallied the score.

Meticulously, Jake worked his way around the target—he wouldn't think of it as a *human* silhouette. Another seven points for the right thigh. Same for upper arms, hands, and belly.

Seven times seven. He'd started to dream about sevens.

"Now for the kill shot," da Hawk breathed. "You're in the lead. No one else has got a full seven points on every target."

Jake closed his eyes and told himself this was just a game. Just another game. It had nothing to do with killing people.

He let the dart fly, almost hoping he missed.

"Woo hoo! Dead center on the caste mark. You made him a Lood. Double points for that," the corporal chortled.

Jake felt sick to his stomach.

He really needed a drink.

He heard the word Lood whispered a lot. Sometimes in disgust. Most times in fear. And sometimes right after Laudae Sissy made an appearance on a newscast. Not often, but enough to make him wary.

No sign of the barmaid. He tried to catch the eye of the middle-aged matron who ran the place. She didn't seem inclined to flirt or refill his pewter tankard.

Jake studied the dregs in his mug. Flirting was definitely not a good idea if he wanted to maintain his cover. A man with a broken heart wasn't likely to flirt with the motherly types, or the buxom lass with a limp who actually served the drinks. Jacob da Jacob supposedly ached so much he ran extra laps and pumped iron in the middle of the night.

What he really did was search the city for traces of a Badger Metal factory. He wanted out of Harmony. He'd take a court-martial and a demotion any day over the constant watchfulness of being a spy.

Where was the damn barmaid?

She swung around a corner from the back room and worked her way closer to Jake's dart board, still keeping her eyes down. That lady might have an artificial limb—probably hacked off in a training exercise. Everyone served active duty until they couldn't. Then they took support roles, like bartenders or admin jobs.

The bartender and her helpers had come with the regiment to H Prime. Military caste closed ranks and kept themselves separate within their divisions as badly as each caste did.

Finally the barmaid filled a pitcher and limped over to Jake. She plopped it on the table in front of the scorekeeper. A little of the precious liquid slopped over the edge. She hastily whipped a cloth and spray bottle of cleanser out of her apron pocket. Her hands made quick work of mopping up the mess. "Sorry, sorry, sorry," she whispered with each swipe. When the table was cleaner than before she had spilled a little ale, she walked away without making eye contact.

"Pity she's not worth looking at anymore," da Hawk said. But his eyes followed her across the room.

Jake raised his eyebrow in question rather than protest that the barmaid was one mighty fine looking woman.

"Not quite a Lood, but now that she's maimed, she's useless to us," da Hawk continued. Bitterness tinged his voice and his countenance. He took a long quaff of the thick ale.

Jake edged da Hawk away from the dart board. A young private moved into Jake's place, eager to best his sergeant's score.

"You were close to her before . . ." Jake prodded, uncertain he wanted to know more. But he had to. For the friendship building between them.

His REM implant flashed him the information that he and da Hawk had only begun that friendship about a year before, about the time da Hawk took on widowed status and Jacob da Jacob met the love of his life—an out-of-caste woman. The hopelessness of their relationships had drawn them together.

"We were married. Applying for leave to have babies," da Hawk said so quietly Jake almost missed it.

Jake grunted. *Were* married. Da Hawk was officially widowed, and yet his wife still lived.

"Yeah, that stump of a leg is hideous. Deep sword cut didn't get treated in time. Went gangrenous and had to lop it off. The general dissolved our marriage instantly. Gave me leave to find another mate. Haven't had the heart for it yet."

"She's still useful as a barmaid. She can still listen and talk. Still hold your hand when you're hurting. Still have your babies."

"Shush." Da Hawk looked around anxiously. "Don't let an officer hear you say that. She can't serve anymore. She's useless to us. Not allowed to breed."

"She was injured . . . not born a mutant. Her kids won't have missing limbs."

"You can't know that!"

Want to make a bet on that? Jake buried his protest in his mug. *Stupid, ignorant, mind blind, inbred* . . . Undereducated. That was the key to control in this empire. No one got more education than they absolutely had to have to function in their designated jobs. Science and genetics didn't belong in an army that still used swords.

The media couldn't be allowed separate caste status, uncontrolled by Noble and Temple because they might inform and educate the populace to the truth.

CHAPTER THIRTY

"HEADS UP AND BEERS DOWN!" Lieutenant Charl da Martin shouted from the doorway, interrupting Jake's litany of disgust.

Instantly the entire platoon stood in rapt attention to their officer's orders.

"Weapons at the ready! We've got a riot at Low Port Asylum."

Murmurs of surprise rippled across the bar. The private at the dart board blanched, his freckles standing out on his cheeks like—like mutant caste marks.

"Seems the HPS visited there this morning and was told there was nothing she could do to make the plight of the inmates better," da Martin continued, barely breathing between sentences. Like he had to spill all the information at once before he lost his nerve.

"The inmates have decided to do something about it themselves. They've taken hostages. We've drawn the lot to quell it. The lives of the hostages are optional to suppressing the inmates."

Every soldier in the bar loosened daggers, checked boot knives and drew their swords. Then they all jog-trotted in Charl da Martin's wake with their blades resting on their shoulders.

Jake suppressed his questions. Nowhere in his briefing had he heard about an asylum. So, not something these people talked about. Not something they bothered with on an everyday basis. But, from the grim looks on the faces of his company, an asylum was something they all knew about. Possibly dreaded.

He positioned the freckle-faced private in the middle of his squad to keep him from bolting, or fainting.

The men and women running beside him looked straight forward, following their lieutenant. A frisson of alarm climbed Jake's spine. They should be wary, alert to possible dangers around them. Riots had a way of spilling outward from their source, infecting all in the path.

The scrubbed street looked deserted. Unusual at this time of day, shift change from day to evening. Workers should spill from the factories and docks toward home, family, and dinner. Instead, the few people he spotted cowered in shop doorways and apartment block entrances.

Another platoon joined his at the next intersection. All grim-faced. Determined. Looking straight ahead. Swords naked on their shoulders.

Two hundred ninety-four weapons ready to kill.

A huge stone building loomed ahead at the end of the narrowing street. Warehouses crowded closer and closer. Little space separated them. Down those narrow, litter-filled alleys, barely wide enough for one person to walk, he caught glimpses of vast oceangoing vessels docked in the deepwater bay at the river's mouth. Dirt encrusted the gutters and crumbling mortar.

An ugly rancid smell permeated the air. More than fish and brine. Worse than filth.

Neglect.

Fear.

Despair.

This sector smelled of hatred. The people outside hated what was inside. The people inside hated those who were free.

Low Port. Just beyond the end of civilization, cleanliness, and caring lay the asylum.

With dread, Jake knew that this place held the castoffs of society. A place to hide what Harmony didn't want to admit existed. A vast place. How many people called it home? Hundreds? Thousands?

He shuddered and suppressed the hot bile churning in the back of his throat.

Unnatural silence felt like a thick, hovering presence holding its breath. Waiting, ready to pounce.

A crossbar on the *outside* held the double doors closed.

"Workers evacuated and left the inmates locked inside, along with their hostages," da Hawk said with a shudder.

Lieutenant da Martin stepped aside from his lead position. The first two privates awkwardly lifted the heavy bar and set it aside. The next five took a guarded stance and held their swords in both hands *en garde*. All of the soldiers around Jake took similar poses, those in front kneeling so the blades of the men behind came over their shoulders.

A kind of hedgehog formation that herded the rushing enemy onto the wickedly sharp, meter-long, Badger Metal blades. Blades that never dulled no matter what material they cut through: wood, cloth, crystal.

Flesh.

Bone.

Chills ran through Jake. He had to clench his teeth to quell his shivers. No rules. No boundaries. No stopping at first blood.

He remembered Billy and Mickey on Prometheus XII. His insides trembled. He clenched his teeth and locked his knees to hide the fear rising in him.

The first two privates stood on either side of the door handles, each grabbing one. Lieutenant da Martin counted silently to three. The privates yanked and withdrew, bringing the door panels with them.

Bodies rushed free of the building. Ragged, filthy, scabrous, reeking bodies burst into the alley, yelling, screaming. Hair tangled, hands clawing, clothing flying in tatters behind them. Eyes desperate. Or insane.

Driven insane by desperation?

The first wave of beings leaped in all directions at the soldiers, impaling themselves on the swords. Twenty-one uniformed men struggled desperately to free their blades.

A second wave followed. They climbed the backs of their dead inmates, clawing at the line of men still trying to yank their weapons free.

Screams of pain as fingernails and teeth met eyes and noses.

Then more screams as the second tier of men brought their daggers to bear for close infighting.

But a third wave of inmates burst free. They kicked aside anyone in their way, fellows or soldiers. They didn't seem to care what or who stood in the way of their path to freedom.

In absolute terror, Jake hacked and slashed at the distorted features of an inmate. He watched as his victim's face froze in surprise, blood spilling from a gut wound, and his mouth.

The absolute intimacy of the act nearly sent Jake to his knees.

Another desperate body flew at him. Jagged nails raked his face. Hands made strong by desperation tried to dislocate his shoulder.

He had no time to think, only to act, to defend himself.

Thank the Host of Seven for drills.

He jabbed with his dagger and slashed with his boot knife. Then he had to brace with his foot on the chest of his first victim while he pulled his sword free.

Dead *PEOPLE* fell in bloody heaps. Hundreds of them. Soldiers pressed on, slowing as their arms tired and gore dripped from their blades. They, too, suffered injury to exposed faces and hands.

And more inmates plowed forward, leaped. A few grabbed weapons from fallen soldiers.

Jake found himself parrying wild slashes from a dagger. He lunged and ran the woman through. A pregnant woman.

Time slowed as the awful horror of his act penetrated his crazed and frightened mind.

"Fall back," Jake ordered his men. They had to keep space between themselves and the demented people pouring at them in never-ending numbers.

One pace, two, then three they retreated, separating themselves from the wall of dead bodies and demented beings. And still they fought for their lives.

As Jake watched, he saw five inmates descend upon Lieutenant da Martin and rend him limb from limb.

The charnel stench threatened to choke him. His eyes burned. Heaviness filled his shoulders and arms.

And still he wielded his blade.

They fell back again and again. Bodies filled the street from gutter to gutter, five and six deep.

Acid burned Jake's gullet.

He slashed blindly.

He wept.

A strong hand on his shoulder. He whirled to face this new danger and had to forcibly stay his blade.

"It's over, Jacob da Jacob," Morrie da Hawk said sadly. Blood dripped from a slash across his brow and an ear nearly bitten off.

"Over?" Jake had to shake his head to clear his mind of the blind terror and need to defend himself.

"The only inmates left are the ones chained to their beds, most likely cowering beneath them." Da Hawk pulled a handkerchief from his pocket and pressed it tightly against his ear. His face blanched and he swayed.

Jake propped him up with a shaking shoulder.

"They'll make an officer of you yet, Jake. You pretty much led the entire fight. Saved my arse a couple of times," Morrie muttered.

Then Jake swallowed hard and forced himself to look at what he and his men had done.

Arms and legs sprawled at unnatural angles. Eyes stared blankly at the empty sky, mouths open in surprise, or slightly smiling in the joyful release that only came with death.

What kind of life had these people lived that they embraced death with joy?

"Don't take it so hard," da Hawk said. "They're just Loods."

"They were *people*."

"No, they weren't." Da Hawk looked puzzled. "Don't let any officer hear you say that. No one with a mutant caste mark is a *person!*"

Except the High Priestess of you all, you hypocrites! Jake wanted to shout.

He looked closer. He saw smudged and indeterminate caste marks on left cheeks. Double marks on the right cheeks. Worker brown Xs, Professional green triangles, Poor black bars, even a Noble blue diamond, and a Spacer yellow star. Not perfect but still discernible. Then he spotted two faces clear of any mark.

He turned to ask da Hawk's opinion only to watch the man kick at those two bodies. "Less than Loods," he muttered.

"They were people once, and I just killed a lot of them," Jake whispered. "*I* just murdered a whole lot of innocent people."

He joined the ranks of young men emptying their guts in the gutter.

CHAPTER THIRTY-ONE

"**D**EAD. DID YOU SAY they were *all* dead?" Penelope whispered to Gil.

He'd just crawled into bed after a very long day and night in the aftermath of the riot. No one quite knew how to deal with the cleanup. Should they order an investigation of the Military action? Or should they look more closely at the administration of the asylum itself for the cause.

And what to do with all of those dead bodies?

Never before in all of Harmony's history had so many died so violently in so short a time.

"A few dozen inmates survived. Only because they were chained to their beds and had not the strength to break their beds as the others did. The instigators killed two of the Workers they held hostage. The others are barely sane from the horrors they witnessed and endured," he whispered back, afraid he'd wake the youngest children. They still had three sharing their quarters, the twins who served Penelope and their older brother, taking advanced schooling before assignment as an acolyte.

"What . . . what could drive them to such desperation?" Penelope asked, head buried against his chest.

He wrapped his arms around her naked body. Her warmth and her scent banished the awful images for a moment. If he pulled her close enough, could he hold the outside world at bay?

"The inmates aren't just Loods. They were human once. Intelligent, thinking, feeling human beings who love Harmony and Empathy as much as we do." His teeth began to chatter. But not from the cold that ran rampant through his veins. "The asylum was licensed for eight hundred inmates, two to a room. There are nearly seventeen hundred dead. How did they pack so many people in the building?"

"I almost understand Sissy's fear," Penelope whispered. She, too, shivered with the cold of shock. After a moment of silence she added, "Sissy isn't what I expected her to be."

"Me either. I find her delightful. A breath of fresh air in our rather stagnant lives."

"You're right. Bethy smiles more now that she's with Shanet and working closely with Sissy. I enjoy our daughter when she smiles and bubbles with enthusiasm for her lessons and her work."

"She was rather grim with teenage anger." Gil almost chuckled. This was what he needed. Reminders of his family and the everyday life that continued despite the massacre of thousands of asylum inmates. Would continue.

Must continue.

Otherwise . . .

"I'm frightened. Things are changing and not always for the better. Hold me, Gil," Penelope begged. "I need to hear your heart beat."

Gratefully, he complied. "I'm scared, too."

Sissy took a deep breath for courage and gathered her seven acolytes and Dog into the motorcar. A little crowded. Manageable with only Dog from the growing family. Cat wouldn't set foot outside. Godfrey the lizard, Milton the weasel, and the other pets needed to stay in her quarters until they recognized the place as home. The pressure of small bodies against her in the car reminded her of home: younger brothers and sisters, parents, grandparents, and always visiting aunts, uncles, cousins, all joined together in laughter, tears, reminiscence, and excitement over current activities.

And support in times of trial. More and more, she found herself treasuring the companionship these girls gave her, storing up the memories for when everything was taken away from her.

Someday, possibly soon, she would lose everything.

The riot at the asylum last night had shown her that.

And when it happened, she wouldn't get to go back to her family and work at the factory.

The entire city reeled with uncertainty in the aftermath. Laud Gregor and the other Temple people walked warily, speaking in hushed tones, avoiding discussions of *that* in public.

Sissy had to fight her own fears to leave her rooms. She'd feared exile to an asylum all her life. She would become one of the crazed, desperate people ready to die rather than face another day locked away, chained to a bed, never again to see Empathy's light or feel Harmony's caress on her feet.

If Laudae Penelope had her way, she'd remove Sissy from Laud Gregor's protection and send her to an asylum.

Sissy had to force herself to take her girls on their daily outing. She had to show her face in public, project calm and stability when Discord threatened Harmony.

"Where to, Laudae Estella?" Bertie, the driver, asked when the nearly silent children had all settled inside the motorcar. They might not understand the riot and massacre, but they picked up the mood of their elders.

Sissy cringed a little at her new name. No one listened to her when she told them to forget the nonsense of calling her that. Laud Gregor had decreed. Therefore she had a new name. Like it or not.

"To the park beside Lord Chauncey's factory."

"Laudae Estella, is that wise?" Bertie looked frightened.

"I played in that park as a child. Then I worked in the factory for nine years. I deem the outing wise." Something in the man's demeanor made her nervous.

"Perhaps the park beside the lake would be a better choice," he suggested.

Sissy had never been to the park reserved for the highest of the Professional caste families. She'd listened to stories about it with envy. Now she had the right to go there.

"Very well, Bertie. Just so long as we can spend the afternoon playing in the fresh air with green grass and tall trees all around us."

"Yes, My Laudae."

"But we've got grass and trees in the Temple Reserve," Mary, the oldest of the girls, protested.

"The Reserve is walled in. I like the idea of an open field better."

She didn't like the casual way men and women cast off *all* of their clothing to swim in the pool in the Reserve. Nor did she like the way men and women paired off and returned to their chambers for the night. Or even the afternoon!

That was a part of Temple life she'd never accept, never participate in.

She'd never be able to swim in the pool or share the Reserve with her girls. Not without drastic changes. Changing attitudes and long traditions was beyond her.

She swallowed her distaste and concentrated on memorizing the route to the park.

"May I keep the next cat that comes to you, Laudae Estella?" Suzie, the youngest of the seven, asked. She petted Dog with vigor as he moved across the floor, resting his muzzle on successive knees eager for as much love as he could gather. Storing it up in his memory as if he, too, feared being outcast very soon.

"Perhaps, my dear. We'll see what happens.

✦   ✦   ✦

Jake led his squad of twenty men jogging through the city streets. He made the twenty-first. Three sevens. He was sick and tired of doing the math in his head. Why couldn't they count in a civilized base ten! Or a wild card three. Or something different!

He had an uneasy feeling. The city felt tense; a combination of uncertain and uncomfortable. With a touch of fear embedded deep in the lizard brain. Not quite anger. Not yet.

He didn't trust it. When a Military unit fidgeted the way the city did today, trouble usually followed.

Each apartment block elected three to five men as their part-time constables to keep order. The lords had their own security people to police the factories and businesses. The Professional caste hired muscle when they needed protection from criminals. But for the city as a whole, only the Military had the authority to maintain order.

So he ran his men as hard as he could through the streets, to help banish yesterday's horror from their consciousness and to keep tabs on the city.

Fully armed with packs, he drilled his men openly, letting the populace know they could depend upon the Military caste to protect them.

The jokes about a thousand fewer Loods to worry about fell flat and sounded like false bravado.

All the while he felt half sick to his stomach. Even the talk of promoting him didn't quell his uneasiness. Such a promotion required serious thought and lots of paperwork and research of precedence since his "family" came from enlisted stock rather than officer. A promotion required DNA manipulation to upgrade his caste mark.

Would the medicos discover the nanobots that gave him the caste mark in the first place?

Should he use his emergency signal—embedded in his wrist—and abort the mission? How badly did the CSS need Badger Metal anyway? Maybe Pammy's scientists had decoded Grecko's computer and come up with a substitute.

Not bloody likely.

Damn, he wished she'd reply to his first message. Give him a clue as to his next move. Something more than a few words from Jacob da

Jacob's parents that sounded like a loving family missing a key member but decoded to "Frontier getting hot. Get the damned formula and hurry up about it."

Pure Pammy.

He rounded the big lake at the center of the city. The beach opened to a wide field. Picnic benches, swing sets, and game courts spread out across the ten or so acres. So much like the neighborhood where he'd grown up on Earth he almost stumbled, certain he'd drifted through a jump point.

A splotch of purple on the fringes drew his attention. The same purple Laudae Estella had worn at the ordination.

Curious, he led the men onto the sidewalk. They lined up, two abreast and trotted behind him like good little soldiers should. He could have taken them into the street. Motorcars were rare here, but a number of mass transit loxen-drawn buses, carts, pedicars, and sedan chairs moved along. Pedestrians darted in and out of the slow traffic.

The big black motorcar with the uniformed driver must be from the Temple. Sure enough, as he passed and nodded he recognized the purple circle surrounding the man's Professional caste mark.

He shifted his attention to the slight young woman with seven little girls—also dressed in shades of purple—sitting in a circle examining a bird with bright yellow-and-red plumage. Laudae Estella let the bird perch on her outstretched hand. A brindled mutt crouched beneath the nearest picnic table with all their shoes, preparing to pounce on its natural prey. The bird seemed oblivious to the dog, completely enthralled with the HPS.

A number of other children had crept closer. Not so nicely dressed, with green caste marks.

She created an island of quiescence.

Jake almost laughed at the sight. Innocent children and animals trusted the new HPS. It was the hidebound and fearful adults she had to fear.

"Sarge," Corporal Camden da Chester drew alongside him. "That dark blue motorcar seems to be circling the park. I've counted three times."

Jake yanked his gaze away from the enticing vista of Laudae Estella rising gracefully with the bird still in her hand. It caressed her palm with the side of its broad beak.

"Only Nobles can afford cars like that," Jake mused. "Or Temples."

Sure enough, the car slowed as it approached the gaggle of giggling girls. A window rolled down.

Jake veered off course. Sped up to an all-out run. Ten long strides later he hoisted Laudae Estella up by the waist. The bird squawked and floundered to the ground. The moment the HPS' feet left the ground, Jake sprinted as far and as fast as he could toward the lake. Away from the car.

Behind him, he sensed Camden da Chester and some others gathering the children.

A concussion slammed him to the ground with his burden. Half a heartbeat later he heard the explosion.

CHAPTER THIRTY-TWO

S ISSY KICKED OUT AT THE STRANGE man carrying her away. Where was Bertie? Were her girls safe?

She gathered a deep breath to scream. Air caught in her lungs. Her back arched in the first spasm of a cough.

A blast of pressure and noise knocked the cough from her chest. Then she was on the ground, with grass trying to grow into her cheek. And the man atop her.

Dog added his own weight to her back. He growled deep in his throat.

"Forgive my presumption, My Laudae," the strange man said as he rolled off her. "Are you okay?" He ran his hands along her back, impersonal, assessing, much like a physician would.

"I . . . I think so," Sissy choked out. The cough erupted with her words.

He slapped her back, pushing the bad air and a wad of dust-laden phlegm from her throat.

The spasm passed quickly. She closed her eyes a moment, trying to figure out if she actually hurt somewhere or merely felt the aftermath of shock. A tickle at the back of her throat demanded another cough. She fought it for three heartbeats. Pressure built up in her chest. No air penetrated the blockade of the cough. She couldn't fight it any longer.

A long hack followed by a wheeze erupted from her.

The man pounded on her back, harder.

Finally she settled into normal, if shallow, breathing. "What happened? My girls? Are they safe?" She tried to roll over, but Dog kept her pinned in place.

"A small concussion grenade," the man spat. "Highly illegal and very expensive."

Sissy didn't like the sound of that. Nor did she like the way the man stood over her, sword and dagger drawn, knees bent, and ready to fend off a host of attackers.

"My men are protecting the children. All safe."

Sissy breathed easier. "Explain the concussion grenade."

He spouted a lot of words Sissy did not understand, like gunpowder and catalyst and ignition.

Wait, she did know that word from her work with Spacer electronics.

"A concussion grenade won't kill you, but it can damage your hearing. Someone sent you a warning, My Laudae."

Apparently satisfied that the threat had passed, the man sheathed his weapons and offered his hand to help her up.

"My girls?" she asked again, brushing grass seeds off her simple dress.

"Up and moving, mostly, but they look scared. They could use some of your famous calm reassurance, My Laudae."

Sissy scanned the scene. Bertie crouched beside the car, wary and uncertain. The moment her gaze lighted on him, he stood and marched toward her. The girls were scattered all over the park, each with an attending soldier. Other children screamed and cried in bewilderment, they clung to the soldiers as well. A scattering of parents or caretakers soothed some. Others wandered alone and lost.

Sissy started toward the first of the abandoned ones. She couldn't leave them alone.

Her rescuer dogged her footsteps, alert and wary.

"I think the warning was meant for the other castes as well as for me," she said. Her insides wanted to tremble and turn to liquid. She didn't dare succumb to the need to run away and hide in some dark corner where no one could find her. "Their children aren't safe as long as I am the High Priestess of Harmony."

"That's how terrorists operate, My Laudae. The best way to counter them is to carry on with your life as if they don't exist. Don't let fear rule your life. If you do, then they win, even if they haven't killed anyone."

She had five unknown children clinging to her skirts by this time. All wore the Professional caste mark.

"Do I know you?" Sissy turned to face her rescuer. Something in his tone, his authoritative manner reminded her of something. She couldn't quite put a name to him or a circumstance to their meeting. But she knew she had encountered him before.

"Sergeant Jacob da Jacob pa Law Enforcement HQ H Prime, My Laudae." He stood at attention, fist to his heart in salute.

"Your name is unknown to me, but not you. How do I know you?" She cocked her head and tried to silently wrap her tongue around the name, like an almost familiar taste.

"At your ordination, My Laudae. I carried you to the vestry after the blue lightning . . . grounded out of you." He looked almost puzzled.

"I thank you, Sergeant Jacob da Jacob. Twice." She put her palms together and bowed as she did in front of an altar. "You have questions."

"My Laudae, how did you survive the lightning? You called it and controlled it. Anyone else would have been fried."

Sissy had to stop and think. "I have no memory of that. I sang, I rang the chimes, I sought to banish Discord. I had to find the *right* note. I had to restore Harmony." She searched for the right words.

"Harmonic vibrations . . . changing the air pressure . . . that explains how you controlled the storms, channeling the energy elsewhere. But the lightning . . ."

"Energy is energy. It all vibrates."

"Interesting," Sergeant Jacob da Jacob said. "Very interesting." He looked as if he were ready to speak again.

Uncomfortable with his questions, having to question how and why she reacted to Harmony, Sissy moved toward the next distressed child. She knelt before him and enfolded him in a comforting hug. The way she wished she could soothe everyone in Harmony City. Especially those who feared her because she was different.

The way she wished someone would soothe her. Stevie, Mom, Pop, anyone of the family would do. Just so long as they hugged her tight and sent the nightmares away.

"Laudae, Laudae, please come." Mary ran up to her, tugging at her sleeve. "It's Jilly. She won't wake up." The oldest acolyte ran back toward the picnic bench where they'd left their shoes . . . hours ago. Only minutes ago.

Sissy bounced to her feet and ran after her. She had to push and shove soldiers and children aside.

Jilly lay on the ground, round face white and pinched, arms and legs rigid and straight.

Sissy breathed a little easier; she'd expected twisted and broken limbs, blood.

Yes, there was a little blood on the inside of Jilly's left ear.

"Jilly, wake up," she murmured as she knelt beside the child. "Jilly, can you hear me?"

The little girl's eyes flew open. She stared straight up, her gaze fixed on something beyond. Something Sissy could not see.

Then Sissy noticed a peculiar silver glaze over her eyes.

Jilly whispered something, so softly Sissy couldn't understand the words.

"Say that again, Jilly. Louder," Sissy ordered. She knew this was important. She bit her lip not wanting to admit she knew what was coming.

"Discord has chosen. Discord will win. Look deep, look long for the answers, for the thing that will subdue Discord before She wins."

Jilly closed her eyes and moaned. A moment later she looked up again. This time her clear gaze lighted on Sissy. "I'm sorry, Laudae. I didn't mean to trip and fall. I'm sorry my dress got dirty." All trace of silver in her eyes had disappeared.

"Not to worry, little 'un. Dresses can be washed and mended. So long's you aren't hurt, I don't care about dresses." She patted the girl's hand, soothing her childish worries.

"None of you will repeat a word she said," Sissy ordered. "A terrorist seeks to silence my gift of prophecy. We will not endanger another with the same gift. I want your oath of silence about Jilly. All of you. Right now."

"I swear I will tell no one outside the Temple of this," Bertie said, holding his hand over his heart and bowing his head.

"No. You must tell no one. Not even Laud Gregor," Sissy insisted. She closed her eyes in dismay at her sudden distrust. In that instant, she knew without a doubt that Gregor would betray her as quickly as he had elevated her if it served his interests.

Looking around her, she knew she could trust these soldiers and her acolytes more than she did the High Priest of all Harmony.

"But surely . . ." Bertie protested.

"No one. If Laud Gregor needs to hear that Jilly bears Harmony's gift, then I will tell him. No one else. If your superior officers question you about more than the explosion," she addressed the Military encircling them. "Then you must direct them to me. Now swear your secrecy and your loyalty to me. All of you."

She held the gaze of Sergeant Jacob da Jacob the longest. He was the last to nod his head and salute.

CHAPTER THIRTY-THREE

M ARY APPROACHED SISSY SLOWLY, carrying a heavy headdress of gold-and-black brocade with a veil of dangling crystals and gold beads. She bit her cheeks in concentration while carrying the precious ornament.

Sissy had dressed herself in a robe of black and gold over a new black dress. A special, dressy gown of silky fabric that molded to her bodice and then fell in comfortable swirls down to her ankles. She'd pinned her hair back behind her ears with black-and-gold clasps. The headdress she needed help with.

For the state funeral honoring the fallen Military during the riot she didn't want to chance a repeat of her ordination breakdown due to the well-meaning attentions of the other Laudaes in her preparations.

Normally the girls laughed and giggled, making a learning game of every task set for them by Laudae Shanet and Sissy. Not today. Their young faces looked pinched and pale. Worry and bewilderment clouded their eyes after the incident in the park two days ago.

The older girls walked wary circles around Jilly. Not a single pun or joke or prank came from that little girl. She looked more frightened of herself than the other girls did of her.

"It's not proper, Laudae Sissy," Mary whispered as she set the heavy crown and veil upon her head. "They shouldn't be burning all those dead Loods on the day we bury the brave soldiers who gave their lives at the asylum."

"No, it's not proper. The bodies should be taken out to the desert and the fields and returned to Harmony through the scavengers. Then we should gather their bones and place them in the funeral caves, the womb of Mother Harmony. They are children of the Goddess as much as we are," Sissy replied. She couldn't bring herself to condemn the poor in-mates driven to insane violence. She herself could so easily have been one of them. Might be one yet.

"There are too many of them," Sharan, the littlest of the girls, though not the youngest, said with solemn wisdom. She was always solemn, rarely smiling or laughing with the others. "Leaving so many bodies lying about would encourage the spread of disease and taint the water table."

"They were Loods, not deserving of burial in a cave," Martha, next in age to Mary but taller and closer to maturity, protested. "Only Noble and Temple caste deserve interment in a cave."

Sissy bit her tongue rather than reprimand the girl by instructing her that all people deserved a return to the symbolic womb of Harmony.

"Laudae Estella, Laud Gregor requests an audience," Sarah, a middle acolyte announced as she bowed to Sissy. She betrayed nothing in her face or posture. She never did.

Sissy could never tell the child's true mood.

"I shall see him in the office." Sissy sighed and waved Mary away with the heavy headdress. Then she gathered the skirts of her robe and passed through her private sitting room and public reception room to her office. A place she visited as rarely as possible. Too many unread memos and documents littered the desk, the floor, the chairs. Stacks of them. Mountains of them.

Could she burrow a cave in them and hide from the onerous duty they represented.

"My Laudae." Laud Gregor bowed to her formally. "I have consulted with my advisers and they agree with me that the climate of the city is too violent for you to preside at today's funeral." He, too, wore his black-and-gold funeral regalia, minus the headdress and veil.

It seemed no one liked wearing the heavy headgear any longer than necessary.

"I must preside today," Sissy insisted. "If I cower in fear, then those who want me removed have won without a fight. I refuse to give them that pleasure."

She had to remember and keep repeating the wisdom of Sergeant Jacob da Jacob. If she said it often enough, she might come to believe it. She doubted she'd ever actually conquer the fear that quivered within her. She just wouldn't let it rule her life.

"Laudae Estella . . . Sissy, please reconsider. We honor brave soldiers, not a member of the High Council. We do not need a full court of seven priests and priestesses."

"Yes, we do. Those soldiers gave their lives to protect the entire city. We owe them nothing less than a full panoply."

"You are determined? I cannot persuade you to take the path of safety? A bodyguard perhaps? Or a team of guards?"

"Life is not safe. Life is what we make of it. Cowering in fear is not living." That felt as if someone else gave her the wisdom to utter those words. Not a full prophecy, just . . . help from Harmony. "I will preside today and I will accompany the bodies to the burial caves."

"Um . . . we actually had planned a private interment." Laud Gregor refused to meet her gaze.

"Interment? I'm not sure of the word. It sounds like burial, not placement in a cave."

"My Laudae, you do not understand."

"Enlighten me."

Laud Gregor flung his head up, finally looking her in the eye. He narrowed his eyes in surprise. Surprise at the firmness of her tone.

She'd learned a few things in the past three months. Primarily that the only way to wade through layers of half truths and stalling techniques was to remain resolute. Or go to Guilliam.

Was Guilliam the "advisers" Laud Gregor had consulted?

Laud Gregor thrust his chin out and tapped his caste mark. "This is something you do not need to know."

"Yes, I do. I am High Priestess."

"I made you High Priestess for a reason. Do not question me." Anger flared in his eyes.

She nearly backed off.

"Enlighten me as to how far from Harmony's Covenant our burial practices have strayed," she demanded. "Enlighten me, and I may accept a bodyguard. A single bodyguard that I shall choose, for when I leave Crystal Temple." Compromise. Living in a large family with limited space had taught her how to do that.

"A bodyguard it will be, then." He drew in a deep breath and continued. "Generation after generation from times most ancient have filled the caves," he replied grudgingly. "We now bury the dead or scatter their ashes nearby. Guilliam," he called to the hovering presence in the reception area. "Find ten Military officers with Temple credentials for Laudae Estella to choose a bodyguard from."

"Not yet, Mr. Guilliam," Sissy jumped in. "Laud Gregor, how are the interments marked so that families may honor their ancestors and join with Harmony next to them? How are *scattered* ashes so marked?" She nearly cried that her family's annual trek to their ancestors' cave to place flowers and notes near the entrance, to spend time recounting the year's events, introducing new members of the family, and mourning those who had joined the ancestors in Harmony, was a wasted effort.

"Such rituals are for the living. If the dead have joined with Harmony, they are beyond caring," Laud Gregor insisted.

"How can you say that?" Sissy forced herself to breathe steadily and evenly. In and out. In and out. She wouldn't let the weakness grab hold and stop her. "Laud Gregor, you and your entire caste are guilty of violating our oldest Covenant with Harmony. And you wonder that our planet, our home, rebels against us with quakes and storms, with violence and fear. With Discord."

She had to pause lest her anger get the better of her.

"We are your caste as well, Laudae Estella."

"My name is Sissy. I am of every caste. Clearly, Harmony sent me to right things between Her and Her people. The soldiers will be buried in the caves. The ashes of the asylum inmates as well."

"Don't be ridiculous."

"We will begin correcting our mistakes here and now, or I contact the media and inform all the people of the empire just how far off track we have strayed. I shall inform them how the caste system has violated every rule and promise. How the Temple caste has invited Discord."

"You wouldn't dare!"

"What have I got to lose?"

"Your life."

✦   ✦   ✦

Jake tugged at the tight collar of his class A red tunic. He'd donned the uncomfortable uniform first for his promotion ceremony, followed immediately by the formal funeral of the men lost during the riot. And now a preemptive summons by the HP and HPS themselves.

Burying fallen comrades was probably the only thing more uncomfortable than this uniform. One thing Military types had all over the universe was an uncomfortable class A. On top of that, his newly augmented caste mark itched as badly as Pammy's nanos.

Actually the Harmony medicos did use nanobots to alter an existing caste mark. They didn't run any checks, just gave him one shot right below the red square to give him an officer's hash mark. A second shot added a purple circle to the whole. Temple credentials. Upgraded and Lauded in the same procedure. Rescuing the HPS twice brought some perks.

Now he had to present himself to the HP in class A reds along with six other lieutenants. Most of them barely old enough to shave. Little consolation that they also fidgeted and tugged at too-tight tunics and choking collars. But he did like the shiny purple medal of valor dangling from his chest. None of the other guys had anything so bright or ornamental.

Jake moved so that the sunlight coming in through the big window

of the reception area made his new medal sparkle. Why not indulge in
a little childish one-upmanship? He had to have some fun in this job or
he'd go insane.

As insane as the inmates at the asylum.

Pammy would not approve.

Pammy wasn't here.

A sense of urgency plagued him. He hoped that his promotion and
lauding would help him gain access to the Badger Metal factory he'd
located out in the Serim Desert. The only registered factory on the continent. Another one on the Southern Continent.

What about unregistered factories? Could some enterprising renegade
have set one up on Far Continent?

Ridiculous. Harmony didn't have enough renegades to take those
kinds of risks and make them profitable.

Far Continent was uninhabitable with active volcanoes, steamy and
poisonous jungles, and very unstable plate tectonics. Harmonites had
chosen to expand into space rather than take the risk of living there.
Other than that, the planet had only a few islands separating North and
South and a lot of ocean. A whole heck of a lot of ocean, more than on
Earth or anywhere else.

He'd only learned that much about Harmony during his prowls of the
city looking for the blasted factory. He'd found maps in the Harbor Master's office and weather satellite views in the comm tower.

The single door to this holding chamber opened on silent hinges. Jake
snapped to attention and slammed his right fist over his heart in an automatic salute. His comrades followed suit a tad slower.

The HP and HPS stood inside the room before the last of the raw
lieutenants came fully out of his slouch. The tall and aesthetically slender
HP frowned. But then, Jake had heard he usually did. The monochrome
dark green street clothes he wore only emphasized his height.

The same clothes he'd seen on the same man in the comm tower.
Again he wondered what business the HP of all Harmony had in the
Spacer facility in the dead of night. He had the authority and plenty of
reasons to visit in broad daylight, and be greeted with deference by the
heads of the Spacer and Military castes.

Why the consult with a lowly Spacer comm officer?

The little HPS, still wearing her oversized padded black robe, looked
tinier than usual next to her tall partner. Jake wanted to reach out and
enfold her in a protective bubble.

"My Laud, My Laudae." Jake converted his salute to a bow. These
people seemed big on bows.

"Do you know why you are here?" HP Gregor asked. He escorted Laudae Estella to the room's only chair.

She perched on the edge as if ready to bolt and kept her eyes down.

"No, My Laud. Colonel Malcolm da March ordered us to report to you here," Jake replied before the others could open their mouths.

"Due to recent events, the High Council deems it suitable for Laudae Estella to have protection when moving in public. You shall have the privilege of being her honor guard," Laud Gregor explained.

Laudae Estella's eyes flew open at that. "I shall choose one of you. And only one," she insisted.

Laud Gregor frowned more deeply. The lines beside his chin revealed aging. Jake put him in his sixties at least. He hadn't seen many old people around. Either they died young or got shut away when they lost their usefulness in the workplace.

Laudae Estella withdrew a paper from her wide sleeve and handed it to the closest lieutenant. "Read this and then tell me what it says."

Jake watched the man's face as he scanned the page. His eyes moved too fast. He couldn't possibly be reading every word.

"This memo addresses the problem of . . . of," he paused and looked hastily at the HP. "The problem of integrating a network of scientific data within the matrix of . . ."

"Next." She gestured for the first man to pass the paper along.

He read the verbiage out loud, looking enormously pleased with himself.

The HPS ordered him to pass the paper along to Jake after only one paragraph.

Jake took his time, seeking significant words. He couldn't find many of them. "My Laudae, it's gibberish. Whatever the author wants to say is so clouded in extra words I cannot find the true meaning without prolonged study," Jake admitted as she shoved the paper into the hands of the fourth man in the room. But even as he began to read, Sissy dismissed his efforts.

"I want that man," Laudae Estella said firmly. She stood and pointed toward Jake. "He's the only honest one here." With that she exited, holding her head high.

But Jake saw a small smile tug at her mouth. This gal took her triumphs where she could, and she'd just bested HP Gregor at his own game.

He bit his cheeks to keep from grinning broadly. He could almost hear Pammy in the back of his head. "Keep it professional, Jake. And use this promotion to get out to the Badger Metal factory."

CHAPTER THIRTY-FOUR

I'M SORRY THE SPACE IS so small, Lieutenant Jacob da Jacob," Laudae Estella said. She hurriedly scooped two piles of papers together and pulled them off the cot. One doorway of this long narrow room gave access to the HPS' private sitting room. Another, straight opposite it, opened into Laudae Shanet's.

The rest of the room was taken up with the cot across one wall beneath the window, and an open closet on the other.

"I've had smaller quarters with shorter beds," Jake replied. "And call me Jake. Everyone else does. Makes it easier to separate me from my da." An entire room to himself with a bed long enough for him to stretch out. And it had a real mattress.

"I can try to find you a better mattress or, rather, Mr. Guilliam will." She held the ragged bundle of papers against her chest.

Jake dropped his duffel on top of the bed. The mattress bounced a little. Real luxury compared to the short, hard bunks aboard a space station, or the shorter and narrower pallets he'd just left behind at HQ.

"We aren't exactly set up for privacy." The HPS blushed prettily. "We've been using this space for storage, just a pass through."

"Don't quite know what I'll do with all the room. Security-wise, it's close to you, and my presence will inhibit bad guys from using Laudae Shanet's suite as access to you." He couldn't suppress his smile at her embarrassment. "Compared to sharing a room with six other sergeants, this is very private."

"I thought the same . . ." Her mouth opened in surprise, then quirked up into a half grin. "I have a large family. Six brothers and sisters. We shared two small flats with both sets of grandparents. All our aunts and uncles and cousins wandered in and out all the time." She dropped her head.

Had he truly seen a tear glisten in the corner of her eye?

"You miss them terribly, don't you, Laudae Estella?" he asked softly. He could have said the same for his own parents and brother. Only his family was dead, while hers was just across town.

Maril bombs had taken out his family dirtside. They didn't have a chance because the intense attack had ripped the atmosphere to shreds. If they'd survived the buildings collapsing on them, they'd have suffocated out in the open.

Ever since, Jake had preferred space stations and ships, where he had a chance of saving himself with an EVA suit. And music piped over the comms to drown out his thoughts.

"I don't get to see my family much since I moved here." She scanned the room as if looking for something she'd forgotten. "Call me Sissy, please. I hate the name Laud Gregor imposed on me."

"Laudae Sissy, I can take you to see them."

"You can?" she gasped.

"Don't see why not. You name the day and time, and I'll order the car."

"But Laud Gregor . . ."

"Always puts obstacles in your way. Why do we have to tell him?"

She flashed him that famous smile that lit the entire room with joy. No wonder the people of Harmony loved her. It was the Noble and Temple castes that feared her. Feared her because the people loved her.

Temple and Noble drove big cars. No one else. Temple liked black. Nobles drove blue.

His law enforcement team looked into that. They wouldn't let it rest, in fact, having a personal stake in Laudae Sissy's safety. If Jake or any one of them had acted a heartbeat slower, they might all be disabled with deafness from the concussion grenade.

They also saw the presence of the illegal concussion grenade as a personal insult. He trusted Corporal Camden da Chester to follow through.

Seven giggling girls, all dressed in lavender, tumbled through the open doorway.

"Girls! You can't just enter Lieutenant Jacob da Jacob's room without knocking on the door," Sissy admonished them. "We need to respect his privacy."

"Don't see why. No one respects ours. Gotta be a priest or priestess to have a room to yourself," an older girl grumbled."

"You going to sleep with him? That's an awfully small bed for two," one of the middle ones remarked.

Jake vowed then and there to learn all their names before evening. Little Miss Impertinence was top of the list.

Laudae Sissy went pale. Then she blushed. She looked away.

"Jilly, that is totally uncalled for. Not only is it none of your business, but Lieutenant Jacob da Jacob is out of caste."

"But you've got all seven caste marks, so you can cross all caste lines any time you want," Jilly said.

"No more. We will discuss this no more. We must leave Lieutenant da Jacob and let him settle in. In private." She herded the girls toward the door.

"My name's Jake," he called after them.

"Jake, will you order the car for tomorrow? There is something I have to do that Laud Gregor will not approve of."

"Consider it done, My Laudae."

"And don't tell . . ."

"I have to tell Mr. Guilliam so I can get the car."

She looked disappointed.

Jake's heart nearly broke at the sight of her sagging shoulders and downcast eyes.

"The same thing will happen when I want to see my family."

"No. I promise. Once I find out the procedure for ordering a car, I can . . . um . . . work around the system to protect your privacy."

"Thank you."

That smile again. And suddenly the world sat bright and hopeful around Jake again.

"Can I get a radio to play some music?"

"Oh, yes. Please. I do miss the music we had at home. No one here listens to anything but their own pompous . . ."

"Music will help mask private conversations," he said quietly. And keep him from thinking of anything but his mission.

✦   ✦   ✦

"I forbid you to do this, Laudae Estella!" Gregor thundered. The poor girl actually shook with fear as she prepared to step into her car. Guilliam had told him only moments ago of the planned expedition.

"You do not have the authority to stop me from my duties," Sissy insisted.

"Someone else, anyone else can ritually cleanse and bless the asylum. Send Shanet." The asylum held terrors for Sissy beyond what it could for anyone else. Yet she insisted upon going there. Again.

"I cannot order someone else to do this. The people have demanded this ritual. For their peace of mind as well as my own, I must do this."

"They've been influenced by the media. Little Johnny is the only one who really demands this."

"We all need this, no matter where the demand began. And I have to do it."

No arguing with the girl when she set her chin like that. Especially when she sat so regally, making him appear a mere petitioner standing at the car door.

Gregor sighed.

"At least leave your acolytes behind today. They do not need to be exposed to the asylum at their tender ages. Pile them with enough lessons to keep them busy for a week."

"Already done. I do this on my own. For myself as well as the people." She looked at her trembling hands and stuffed them under her.

Her bodyguard Jacob da Jacob stood stolidly holding the door open for Gregor to join her or leave. For all his impassive face and posture, his eyes never stopped moving and one hand always hovered near a weapon.

Gregor had no doubt he heard every word and digested it.

The brown-and-white mongrel dog leaped over Sissy's lap to settle beside her. His tongue lolled and he drooled happily. The wary angle of his ears suggested his happiness was all an act. He was as ready as Jacob da Jacob to rip out the throat of anyone who threatened their mistress.

"I have to do this," she said, as if by repeating it often enough she'd truly convince herself. "The people need a . . . a sense of . . ." Sissy stammered.

"Closure," Jacob da Jacob said quietly. He did that a lot, ever since he'd moved in, providing her with vocabulary when her education failed her. And she always remembered every new word she encountered.

"Yes, closure. They need to see the cleansed asylum blessed. The Poor and the outcasts of our society, those on the fringes, need to see it as a place of refuge instead of a house of horrors." She sat gracefully in the back seat and nodded for da Jacob to shut the door. Close out Gregor, the HP of all Harmony.

Gregor stayed the man's arm. He felt strong muscle and sinew through the thick black dress uniform sleeve. And something more, a sheath with another wickedly sharp blade hidden there. He took Sissy's protection seriously.

The look he gave Gregor told him that he viewed even the High Priest of Harmony as a potential enemy.

Why didn't that reassure Gregor?

"Laudae Estella."

Sissy frowned at him and set her chin.

"Sissy, please. This is a minor ritual. Let someone else do it. Certainly a Temple presence is necessary, if you say so. But not yours. Guilliam will do a nice job and be very diplomatic."

"There is no one in this rarified edifice who understands the asylum as I do."

Her caste marks sparkled as color infused her face. In just a few months they'd taken on the crystalline sheen of those who were born and bred within the Crystal Temple. Perhaps the physicians had augmented them some way the last time she had surgery. The scintillation intensified with her emotions. When she turned her head to look at him directly, her eyes shone with the peculiar reflection of prophecy.

"The time has come to open the haven to all. Exterior markings mean less than you think and more than you imagine." She closed her eyes and slumped back against the seats as if exhausted.

"Excuse me, My Laud, we will be late if we do not hurry," Jacob da Jacob said. His words might be polite, but his manner suggested that he was the one in charge. He easily pushed Gregor aside and slammed the car door shut. Then he slid into the passenger seat beside the driver, slamming that door as well.

"I will be in the car directly behind you, My Laudae," Gregor said. His voice sounded meek in his ears. The girl had a power over him he didn't understand. When she spoke with the authority of Harmony he had to obey, had to believe. But he didn't like it. Not one little bit. By bringing Sissy to Temple, he'd begun a chain of change that could lead to a quake storm. Maybe he should have sent her to asylum with the other Loods when he discovered her mutant caste marks.

He still could if she continued to disobey him.

CHAPTER THIRTY-FIVE

J AKE BOWED WHEN LAUDAE SISSY rapped her little wand upon a portable crystal. The three nurses and two physicians also present followed suit a bit behind Jake. The asylum director, an officious little man with thinning hair and a sharp nose, and wearing a freshly pressed business suit, looked at his pocket watch impatiently.

The people of Harmony might need this cleansing ritual to happen, but that didn't mean they wanted to watch it. The press had sent one hover cam. No one else had showed up. No Little Johnny behind the cam. Not even HP Gregor had made his promised appearance.

Jake didn't want to be here either. His insides turned to liquid every time he thought about the massacre and his part in it.

That didn't stop Laudae Sissy. She saw a need for the ritual and plowed forward. Her dog dropped his head almost to the pavement in imitation of Jake's bow, sending his hind end into the air, scrawny tail stiff like an antenna.

The crystal's ding sounded muffled, like it was swallowed by the tall walls of the asylum and the cramped warehouses around it. The High Priestess, in the full black-and-gold funeral regalia, frowned at the crystal. She set it on the freshly scrubbed door stoop. Then she rapped it again.

This time the chime came out clear and bright. It bounced around the stone barriers a bit, then settled.

Jake bowed again. This time he snaked out a hand and pushed against the director's back. "Show some respect," he whispered.

The director glared at Jake until Sissy fixed them with a gaze that told them both to be quiet and show some respect for the spiritual forces she invoked.

She tapped the crystal again and sang a familiar hymn Jake had learned as a child. Her clear soprano gave special life to the tired tune. The words had changed, but not the intent. Regret piled upon guilt, sorrow at the passing of another, forgiveness and healing. All there. All appropriate for the occasion.

Then she poured a flask of specially blessed water into a golden ball suspended from a chain. Tiny holes perforated the scrollwork around the ball. An aspergillum. That was a word Sissy had to teach Jake. She began swinging the chain in small arcs. Drops of blessed water arced out to spatter the pavement and walls.

Jake let the water fall on his hands. If anyone needed cleansing here, in this place, it was him, not the inanimate street and buildings.

The director sneaked a peek at his watch again.

Jake confiscated it with a yank.

The man opened his mouth in protest. A drop of holy water landed on his tongue. He closed his mouth with a snap and a bewildered expression.

Sissy stepped up to the open doors and paused. Her hands trembled. The chain on her aspergillum rattled and water spewed out in uneven splotches.

Jake took the three long strides necessary to stand at her side. Ready to hold her up, catch her if she fainted. Whatever.

He didn't expect her to thrust a stubby green candle into his hands.

"Light it," she whispered. "I . . ." Her voice trembled as badly as her hands.

Jake grabbed a lighter from her open kit beside the door and set flame to the wick. It caught easily and sent a cheery little light upward along with a whiff of perfume. It reminded him of a damp morning in the forest where his scout troop had camped.

"New growth, new life, a new beginning for the people who come to this asylum." Somehow Sissy managed to impart the meaning of sanctuary and haven to the word rather than a torture chamber to shut away the unwanted. "Now light the blue one."

Jake obeyed, setting the green one down and then placing the lit blue one next to it in the beginning of a half circle that would mark the full double doorway.

"Clean water of the deep blue ocean, washing, renewing," Sissy said.

And he smelled salt spray at the beach, sharp and clean.

Then she directed him to light the yellow for the sunlight that promoted growth. She led the ritual through seven colors, seven phrases of cleansing and renewal, seven scents, each carrying a pleasant memory for him. Each seemed to wash away a bit of the filth that coated his soul.

When they stepped through the doorway, he was able to smile again.

Immediately he was struck by the vastness of the open hall beyond the entrance corridor with its soaring ceiling, and the morning sun rising behind the stained glass windows at the far end. A dais rose three steps at the end, with a long table. Like an altar.

Sissy didn't pause. She'd found her momentum and conquered her fears. She set the aspergillum in motion again, singing small prayers and invoking each of the seven gods to bless the asylum and the people who dwelled and worked here. From the hall they progressed upward and outward to dormitory wings. All empty now. All freshly scrubbed with bleach and disinfectant.

But the scent of the seven candles still burning at the doorway overrode the sharp reminders of the physical cleansing. This was a spiritual cleansing. Any ghosts that might have lingered fled before Sissy's holy water and her songs.

They fled from Jake as well. When they'd made full rounds and returned to their starting point, Jake felt lighter, cleaner, taller with the weight of seven worlds lifted from his shoulders.

"You've made this place into a Temple," he said quietly as he packed Sissy's kit.

"As it should be. All places are sacred. Our own acts defile them. Mr. Director." She turned her attention to the weaselly little man.

"What now?"

Immediately Jake was in front of him with hands ready to wrap around his throat. "How dare you show such disrespect for High Priestess Laudae Estella?" he snarled.

"L . . . Laud . . . Laudae Estella?"

"Who do you think came all the way out here to clean up your mess?" Jake's mess, too. The Military's mess. *Harmony's* mess.

"We presumed she was an acolyte. That's all this place, those Loods deserve."

"They are people, not logs of wood," Jake yelled. "Flesh and blood, and I was forced to murder some of them!"

"Jake." Sissy's delicate hand on his shoulder brought his mind out of the red swirl of anger. He stepped back. His fists remained clenched.

"Mr. Director, your staff may begin moving their patients back to their home," she said quietly.

"Patients? That's an awful fancy name for mindless mutants."

Jake's fist connected with the man's jaw. He staggered back, blood streaming from his nose.

"I'll have your rank and your job for this, Lieutenant."

Jake merely raised an eyebrow.

The director turned and ran to a small dark green car parked halfway down the block.

"I don't want to lose you, Jake. I trust you," Sissy said. Behind her crystal veil she gnawed her lip.

"Not to worry, My Laudae. You preside over the High Council. All you have to do is suggest he was impertinent to you and he's out of work."

"Can I truly do that?"

"There's a lot of things you can do. Including making this place a hospice instead of a prison. You've already started the work with your ritual. I don't know what magic you worked, but it truly is a miracle, the difference in how the place welcomes you now rather than repels you."

"It wasn't me. It was Harmony. It was the gods at work."

"And you are truly their avatar. They chose you to correct some terrible wrongs and bring your people back to the path of Harmony." Now where did that nonsense come from? He wasn't here to make Harmony stronger. He was here to bring them down by stealing the Badger Metal formula.

Or was he? Maybe. . . .

CHAPTER THIRTY-SIX

I DO NOT NEED YOU following me to a meeting of the High Council, Lieutenant Jacob da Jacob," Sissy insisted as she walked rapidly through the maze of corridors. Interesting that they followed a very similar pattern to the circuitry of a nav unit.

"Call me Jake, Laudae Estella. I am charged with protecting you," the lieutenant replied.

"From the High Council?" She stopped in her tracks. He bumped into her, apologized, and backed off three steps. Barely enough space to maintain politeness.

"I saw the car in the park, Laudae. How many people outside the Noble caste can afford a large, dark blue vehicle?" He paused for emphasis, looking grim and dangerous in his daily black uniform.

"Have you found the owner of the car?"

He snorted something derisive. "No central registry of vehicles. Fifteen vehicles of similar make, model, and color in the capital. Who knows how many in the outlying areas."

"If I gave you the authority to question the owners of the vehicles . . . No. Not yet. I think such inquiries should come from Laud Gregor's office. Give your information and a list of questions to Guilliam. He'll see that it's done. Diplomatically." She proceeded toward the Council Chamber, in the most ancient portion of Crystal Temple where it joined the State Palace.

"Laudae Estella, you are about to enter a closed room with five Nobles. The only person on the High Council I trust with your safety is Laud Gregor. And then only because he has an agenda. I don't know what it is. Frankly, I don't care as long as he has more to gain by keeping you alive than seeing you dead. Please allow me to accompany you and protect you as I am charged."

Sissy had to think about that a moment. "Very well. Come if you must, but stay by the door where you are out of the way and can watch everyone. I'm interested in their reactions. I've never attended a meeting before. Now I, too, have an agenda. The first item of which is to fire the director of the asylum." She donned the heavy headdress she'd carried the entire length of the sprawling complex, then took a deep breath and faced the double doorway to the Council Chamber.

"I'll call you Jake if you'll call me Sissy," she said just as she thrust the doors open and blew into the chamber with as much aplomb as she could muster.

And came to an abrupt halt three steps inside the chamber. A long empty table with seven tall chairs around it sat abandoned and dusty in the center beneath an equally neglected stained glass skylight. Bright summer sunshine glinted and fractured into many colors on the table. The dust particles stirred by her entry sparkled and danced in streams of red, blue, green, yellow, and purple light.

The crystals in her veil picked up the many colors and fractured them again, creating the image of ghosts seated around the table. Long-dead ancestors of the current HC.

She blinked away the illusion and shifted her attention to the knot of people gathered around a smaller round table in the corner. Harsh electric lights banished shadows there.

Sissy's crystals continued to work their magic separating the light into a full rainbow. She saw flares of life energy shimmering around each of the six High Council members. Instantly, she recognized patterns of emotions reflected in the auras.

Laud Gregor, green with envy and ambition. Lady Marissa, calm and confident in blue, Lord Chauncey, cold and resentful in alternating layers of orange and white. She didn't know the others by name, only that each had secrets and desires that had nothing to do with the good of all Harmony.

"The Council table is over here, beneath Empathy's beneficial and natural light," Sissy said coldly. "There are no drafts here, and we need not waste energy with artificial light. Now if you will join me, I shall open the gathering with the proper ritual. She produced a crystal and a wand from her sleeve and set them before her place at the head of the table, right in the middle of a shaft of purple light.

Then she marched to the side of the oldest and most frail gentleman and offered him an arm of escort. "My Lord, you will be warmer and more comfortable over here, where you belong."

"My thanks, Laudae," he replied shakily as he rose beside her. "I can walk on my own. 'Bout time we returned to tradition. Something important about ceremony and order." He grabbed an ornately carved cane from beside his chair and hobbled over to the big table. "I'm Nathaniel, by the way. Nice to finally meet you in person."

Off to the side Sissy heard Jake chuckle as he took a protective stance beside the door.

Gregor bit back a sharp retort. Instead he pasted on a smile and said, "Lord Nathaniel, we moved to this isolated corner because the light through the skylight bothered your eyes."

"Well, that unshielded electric light bothers me more," the old man countered. He plunked down into his assigned chair right next to the end where the HPS presided.

Gregor grabbed the chair opposite Nathaniel, on Sissy's other side. He couldn't allow her to totally take control. Not when he'd finally maneuvered some benefits to the five Nobles so that their greed would overtake their caution.

Lady Marissa pushed Lady Sarah aside to sit next to Gregor. "Whatever you two are up to, you won't get away with it," she hissed.

"Laudae Estella's presence is as much a surprise to me as to you," he snarled back at her.

She raised her eyebrows. "Interesting. And what of the grim and handsome Military by the door?"

"A precaution."

Sissy interrupted Lady Marissa's next comment by snapping her wand against the single crystal. A light tone, sweet. It reverberated against the skylight just enough to draw everyone's attention to her where she stood, face upturned, bathed in glorious sunlight. She followed the note with a prayer sung in perfect pitch starting with the crystal note and soaring outward.

For a brief moment Gregor relived his own early days as a priest, full of faith. Wasted time spent searching for the elusive ideal until he realized that faith lay in the prosperity of Harmony. He could unleash his ambition in good conscience because he knew how to expand and strengthen the empire while honoring the seven gods at the same time.

The larger and stronger the empire, the more glory for Harmony, and the more power he controlled. A nice circle of opportunity.

Just before Lord Nathaniel started fidgeting in impatience, Sissy concluded her prayer on a lingering high note that seemed to drift into the heavens of its own accord.

Impressive, indeed. She'd learned a lot in the last four months.

"As I was saying when we were interrupted," Gregor jumped in before anyone else could take control of the meeting. "Our frontiers are under heavy assault from two alien races. We have to increase defenses before our borders crumble and foreign ways begin to corrupt our empire."

"Two alien races?" Lady Marissa asked. "Last I heard we had only the Marils to fear."

"The Marils are an awesome force, avian, but akin to we humans. Two arms, two legs, they stand upright. The others," he allowed himself a shudder to mask his lie. "The others are hideous snake creatures. Totally alien. Bent on our complete submission. They call themselves Css." He drew out the sibilant into a serpent's hiss.

Sissy shot a glance over her shoulder to where her guard stood. Did she know something? Or had the man made a gesture betraying Gregor's lie.

He had to proceed, push for results. If they challenged his information, he'd just plow forward, right over the top of them.

"We have lost a lot of Spacer personnel in the past month. Not enough reserves in their caste to fill all the gaps."

"What can we do?" Lord Chauncey asked. He leaned forward, eager for a solution.

"I propose that we allow the Military to join forces with the Spacers. They serve similar functions, keeping order and defense. They both know how to fight and quell violence."

Daniel nodded. The others looked a little puzzled.

"If we shift more Military to planetary defenses among the colonies under attack, that will free Spacers to man the fleet."

"And who shall fill the empty dockets among the Military?" Lady Marissa asked, too blandly. She was up to something.

"Worker caste can do administrative and clerical jobs for them, drive vehicles, clean things. We have a surplus of Workers here in Harmony City. Shifting some of them to Military bases will ease the housing shortage as well as remove stress on the sewage, water, and energy systems. If necessary, we can even bring some of the able-bodied Poor back into the Worker caste."

"If we eliminate the Poor entirely," mused Lady Marissa, "we would have a place to separate the media from the Professionals. Make them an ally to the HC."

"No." Sissy stood up, fists planted on the tabletop. In her padded robes and jangling headdress she seemed taller, more formidable, and powerful than he'd ever seen her. Cloaked in mystery, she commanded the absolute attention of every member of the HC.

"Mixing of castes is strictly forbidden by all seven gods. Spacers and

Military take care of their own, much as we . . . the Workers do. The elderly, the infirm, parents on maternity leave, can be put back into service in noncombat positions. As they have always done in time of war. As for making the media a caste of their own . . . that requires much thought and examination of old records for a precedent."

"Agreed," Lord Nathaniel shouted. He pounded his feeble fist on the tabletop. "We have drifted away from Harmony's path. Look at us! We, the Guardians of Harmony, have pushed aside our opening ritual in our designated places in favor of speed." He pounded the table again. "No mixing of castes. Ever. This young lady has brought us back to Harmony. What she says, I say."

Gregor gritted his teeth. "These are extraordinary times, My Lords and Ladies. I do not ask for this lightly. Do we dare risk invasion by monsters when a small, temporary compromise will save us all?"

"When you put it like that . . ." Lady Sarah murmured.

"We'd have a lot more Spacer troops if we could establish contact with the Lost Colony," Lady Marissa said. "That was one of your schemes, too, Lord Gregor. Starting up a seventh colony. Thirty ships and crews, each with one thousand people. But we lost contact with them one day into hyperspace."

"I regret my misjudgment daily, My Lady. That has nothing to do with aliens invading our empire." Gregor pulled himself into stiff indignation.

Did she know that he planned to send the Spacers to the Lost Colony that wasn't as lost as they claimed? Had she found a reference to the single communication from the new planet when the ships landed?

The colony had no right to declare itself independent of Harmony and abolish the caste system.

No right whatsoever.

And now his secret listening post had intercepted communications between the Lost Colony and the CSS. He had to put a stop to that right now. If the Lost Colony allied itself with the enemy . . . He didn't even want to think about the repercussions.

He had to reestablish his authority over them. Soon. Before some of the other colonies developed similar ideas.

That accomplished, he'd send Spacers and Military to the frontier. Certainly, the Marils and the CSS had been making more frequent forays against the borders over the last few months, but they hadn't reached invasion force yet.

Yet.

"Show me the communications from the frontier and the battle reports. I want to know the name of every person lost in this war so that I may make memorial to them at the burial caves," Sissy said. She tapped the wand against the tabletop in agitation.

What was she thinking? He couldn't tell with the veil masking her expression.

He knew from experience that she could see from behind the strands of crystals and beads perfectly well.

He'd cobble together some fake reports, making sure he enshrouded them in so much verbiage she'd never understand them. He could easily substitute the names of the crews from the Lost Colony for Spacers killed in battle.

"Speaking of memorials," Sissy continued, hardly pausing for breath. "I propose a scientific expedition to the burial caves."

Gregor reared his head up, shocked out of his musings.

"It has come to my attention that after thousands of generations, the caves are full and that members of the Temple caste have been burying our ancestors in unmarked plots nearby." She paused just long enough for that outrage to sink in.

Before Gregor could form a reply, Sissy continued.

"Surely after all these thousands of years that we have been burying our dead in caves, the bones will have turned to dust. Graves can be consolidated and remarked, making room for the newly dead."

"What?" Nathaniel spouted. "What perversion is this?"

Did he mean the expedition or the change in funeral rites?

"I shall, of course, lead the expedition to make sure all of our ancestors are handled with respect and that they are returned to the womb of Harmony with proper prayers," Sissy continued.

"Agreed!" Lady Sarah chimed in.

"Agreed," the others added.

"Done," Lady Marissa had the last word. She fixed Gregor with a gloating glare.

"I call for an end to this meeting so that I may prepare reports from the frontier for each of you to peruse and determine that my suggestions are the only course of action left to us." Gregor stood, bowed, and retreated with as much dignity as he could muster.

This nonsense of Sissy attending HC meetings had to stop. If she couldn't agree with *him,* she shouldn't be there at all.

Once more he regretted bringing her to Temple.

Maybe letting her muck about in the caves for the next few years was the answer.

"Laud Gregor, one more thing," Sissy's mild address stopped him short, frightening him more than anger.

"Yes, My Laudae?"

"Two things, actually. I will take the ashes of the fallen inmates of the asylum with me, for proper burial. But before I go, I will appoint a new director of the asylum. If you have any recommendations, I will entertain them. At the moment I am considering the senior physician of the facility. He showed admirable compassion in the cleanup and actually attended the blessing and rededication."

"Whatever." He dismissed the notion with a wave as unimportant.

"The old director will need new employment. He is available to any of you lords and ladies. Something in the Serim Desert or possibly the Southern Continent?" she asked mildly. But there was a touch of Badger Metal hardness beneath her words.

Discord! Gregor decided right then and there he did not want to be on the receiving end of Sissy's ill will. What kind of monster had he created?

CHAPTER THIRTY-SEVEN

"**U**M . . . **LAUDAE ESTELLA,**" **JAKE** said as he followed the HPS back to her quarters.

"What did I say about calling me by that artificial name?" She rounded on him, hands on hips, beaded veil flashing and clacking.

"Laudae Sissy." Jake bowed solemnly. Heat flushed his face.

"I prefer just Sissy, but I suppose you have to use a title around here." She resumed her march back through the maze of corridors.

About every twenty paces an alcove offered an altar or a meditation bench. Most of them looked dusty and abandoned. A lot like the large ceremonial center of the Council Chamber.

More evidence that the idyllic life full of faith and spirituality presented to the public crumbled as badly as law and order within Harmony City.

Maybe the threat of invasion wasn't as false as it sounded. Though that whopper of a lie Gregor told about the CSS being hideous snake monsters made everything he said suspect.

"Laudae Sissy, are you serious about leading an expedition to the caves?"

"Of course. Just as soon as I can find scientists and historians willing to go with me."

"Then I have to warn you; you might find some puzzling things. Unexplainable things." Why did he have to warn her? She'd discover soon enough that none of the bones in the caves could be older than seven hundred years.

The shock would devastate her. He couldn't stand the thought of seeing Laudae Sissy confused and bewildered, more at sea than she already was.

Pammy, I've got to get out of here before I muck it up by caring.

"What kinds of unexplainable things?" She stopped and turned again.

"I cannot tell you."

"I am the High Priestess of Harmony. You can't keep secrets from me."

Wanna make a bet? "I learned some things that are not in history books."

"You aren't going to tell me more, are you?"

"No, my Laudae." If he did, she'd have him executed on the spot. She had the authority even if she didn't know she did. "I will tell you that Laud Gregor lied to the HC."

"I know that. I've always been able to tell when someone lies. Which lie most concerns you?" She resumed walking.

Jake looked around uneasily. Gregor could have listening devices hidden anywhere.

"My Laudae, if you must talk about this, can we go somewhere more private?"

"The dogs need a good long walk. You will accompany me." She said nothing more until she'd divested herself of the formal robes and headdress and gathered the five mutts in her menagerie.

The daily walk had become routine. The girls usually tagged along, rejoicing in the break from their lessons. Today Sissy did not invite them.

Jake drilled Laudae Sissy on vocabulary and spelling while they walked. Ostensibly they extended the drills to the girls as well. But they were really mostly for Sissy.

The set of her chin told him today they would use the privacy to discuss more important things.

The animals barely needed leashes, willing to follow Sissy wherever she led. Two small dogs pumped their short legs triple time to keep up with the lumbering pace set by the brown-and-white mongrel and an all-black shaggy monster, named Monster, that weighed more than Laudae Sissy. Jake ended up carrying the littlest of the pack, a little white fuzzball not much bigger than his open hand.

With the dogs walking obediently, Jake could keep his eyes and ears open and his free hand on his weapon.

"Which of Laud Gregor's lies most concerns you?" Sissy repeated her question soon after they'd cleared Temple grounds and walked city streets. She shifted the leashes so that she had one large and one small dog on each side of her. The better to keep an even pace. Dog and Monster didn't compete for the lead that way. Lady, the little gray poodlish dog surged in front of them all, definitely the alpha bitch.

The neighborhood they walked through prospered—highly placed and Lauded Professionals resided here. Large houses with landscaped yards and tall trees lined the streets. Small, energy efficient cars sped about or parked in long driveways.

"Are the frontiers truly under assault, Laudae?" Jake asked. "And . . . and I haven't always lived in Harmony City. I grew up on H6. Really close to the borders. I've seen both Marils and CSSers. The Marils are avian."

"The snake monsters?" Sissy paused to let the dogs sniff and water a series of trees and bushes.

"As human as you and I."

"How is that possible? Human life arose here on Harmony. Are there more lost colonies? Colonies that rebelled and now attack us?" Her hands trembled. The dogs, ever alert to the slightest change in her mood, stopped their attempts to water a tree higher than their predecessor, cocked their ears, and took wary stances.

"Possibly." Let her figure it out when she discovered that human life on Harmony was not native and fairly recent. If her scientists and historians told her the truth.

"Why should I trust you, Jake?" she asked quietly.

"Because you can tell if I lie."

She looked at him sharply, focusing on the air above his left ear. He concentrated his thoughts on one word: Truth.

"You speak the truth, but not all of it," she said. A puzzled frown made her look younger and more vulnerable.

Jake had a sudden urge to build a defensive perimeter around her. *Don't play hero. Just do your job,* he admonished himself.

"You read well, Jake," she said at last.

"I'm no scholar, but I can read well enough."

"Tonight, you will teach me to read better." She whistled to the dogs and walked on.

"Excuse me. I'm no teacher."

"But you know how to read complex reports and tell if they are gibberish or hold a kernel of truth. I cannot. My brother comes to help me sometimes, but he is newly married and works hard. He can't come every night. And I believe Laud Gregor works hard to keep my family away from me. I need your help, Jake."

"Where'd you grow up, Laudae?" Jake asked. He kept his eyes roaming for signs of anything out of place. Trouble was, he didn't know this town, these people, well enough to be certain what was out of place.

"Lord Chauncey's industrial flats and electronics factory. I built nav units for the Space Fleet." She examined her fingertips. "I've got special magnets implanted in my fingers so I can diagnose microcircuitry. Never really needed them. I just knew when they were right and complete." She sounded sad, nostalgic.

"My family still lives and works for Lord Chauncey." She heaved a sigh.

"How much education did they give you?" Jake asked.

"I began work in the factory when I turned twelve. I qualified for more education. But . . ." She fingered her caste marks.

"That would have exposed you to people outside your immediate circle. People in authority who would have reported you as a mutant."

"A Lood."

Jake choked back the nightmare of the asylum riot once more. He'd almost banished it from his sleep, thanks to Sissy's cleansing ritual. Sissy had lived with similar nightmares every day of her life. What if she'd been one of those pathetic wretches he'd killed?

The world went white around him as he relived the horror with greater intensity. This time with a horrible variation.

"I know how to read battle reports and casualty lists. I'll help you." *I'll help you survive in this hypocritical, cruel world.*

If he had to bring down the whole civilization to do it, he would.

A glimmer of an idea blossomed in his mind. A way out. For both of them.

Was he up to the challenge?

Sissy suppressed a yawn while she patiently memorized the words that Jake had underlined.

"Don't you ever sleep, Laudae?" he asked around his own yawn.

"It's only midnight," she said. At least she thought the clock on her desk said midnight. Her eyes refused to focus that far away.

"Time you two had a bite to eat and then turned in," Laudae Shanet said from the doorway. She carried a tray with a pot of steaming herbal tea and plates of sandwiches.

"My thanks, Laudae," Sissy said. She reached for a meat-filled sandwich. "Join us, please," she insisted when her mentor made to leave.

"Miss the family gatherings at meals, do you?" the older woman asked. She settled into a comfortable chair next to Jake and put her feet up on the low table at the center.

"How did you know? Everyone here is so intent on privacy they never share meals."

"Rarely gather together at all except around the pool or in bed," Lady Shanet muttered.

Jake stopped chewing his cheese sandwich and took a long gulp of tea that must have burned his tongue.

"I miss the closeness of a neighborhood Temple and joining families in my congregation for a Holy Day," Shanet continued. "That's the only way Temple get families, is to adopt one from the congregation."

"You never marry," Sissy said.

"*We* never marry," Shanet agreed. "You are one of us now. Never forget that, even if you don't approve of our ways."

"How sad and lonely." Sissy couldn't imagine going her entire life without parents and siblings and cousins and . . . and a spouse and children. The spouse before the children. Though she knew some Workers who experimented in bed before the wedding, such intimacy outside of marriage was highly frowned upon.

"Yes, it is sad. And can get lonely if you let it. I'm surprised you didn't call our way of life indecent. It is by Worker standards. Military, too," Shanet said.

"Yes. We take pride in our families, in training them to serve the empire," Jake said quietly. He looked embarrassed.

"Temples claim they don't need marriage," Shanet said. She slumped down, putting her hands behind her head and settling in for a nice long chat.

Only this wasn't one of the late night chats about history, rituals, government, and gossip. A tension in Shanet's neck and shoulders, despite her casual posture, alarmed Sissy.

"The entire caste is supposed to be one family," Shanet sighed. "Could be true if Gregor didn't move us around so much, never letting us get attached to a congregation, or each other. He claims it's so the congregations can't develop a cult of personality. I wonder sometimes if it's so we never learn to trust anyone enough to band together against him."

"Is there disquiet in the provincial Temples?" Jake sat forward, attentive and wary.

"Some."

"You have more to say, Shanet," Sissy prodded.

"Lots more. But for now I have a . . . let's call it an amusing tidbit of gossip." She, too, sat forward, worry lines radiating from her eyes.

"In other words, a warning," Jake said. He immediately sat up and scanned the room.

"Rumors fly here at Crystal Temple," Shanet said, almost casually. "We live for gossip."

"I know," Sissy snorted. She'd used the rumor mill herself several times to learn what her teachers forgot to tell her.

"Hottest rumor now is speculation as to when you will take a lover, and who it will be. Bets favor Laud Gregor getting to you first. He'll want you to have children. And he'll manipulate their caste marks if Temple doesn't dominate at birth."

Sissy forgot to breathe. Shame warred with anger inside her. She'd never even thought about *that* outside of marriage. Oh, she'd thought about it when she met a handsome man. But always, always, she pictured a wedding first.

"Maybe I shouldn't be here for this discussion." Jake's face flamed.

"Stay, Lieutenant. There's more to protecting this girl than just keeping an assassin from doing someone's dirty work."

"Like what?" Sissy asked.

Jake sat down again.

"Like hurrying up the expedition to the burial caves and keeping her in one of the country Temples for a few weeks. Let the heat die down. Give her time to find her feet before she makes that decision. And it should be her decision. I don't want her taking in the first offer just to get it over with. I may be Temple, but I believe there should be love and respect involved. Not the randy dalliances we see here."

"I think you should accompany us, Laudae Shanet," Jake said quietly.

"I cannot interfere in caste matters. Only in her physical protection."

"Jake says we'll find some things that can't be explained in the caves," Sissy said. The stack of papers in front of her were equally unexplainable.

Her eyes blurred every time they strayed to the pile of battle reports and casualty lists. They didn't make sense. The numbers were off. She might not read very well, but she knew numbers and patterns.

Patterns.

"Jake, did you notice the duplication of names on these lists?" She held up a sheaf.

"Some . . . but in large numbers there are often duplications. Especially among Military where units stay together. The residence name after a family name becomes meaningless. We usually don't bother with it."

"Duplication to the point where the same ten names are repeated three times in the same order? Seems to me in the heat of battle people would be wounded or killed randomly."

"They would." Jake and Shanet shifted to read over her shoulder.

"Here." Shanet pointed. "I served as Chaplain to this unit ten years ago. They didn't die in battle on the frontier, they accompanied the Lost Colony three years ago. No one has heard of them since."

"He's sent you fake reports," Jake growled.

"Because there have been no battles. He wants to add the Military to the Spacers, and push Workers into support roles for them both for some other reason," Sissy mused.

"Maybe he knows the Lost Colony isn't lost. Maybe they've separated themselves from Harmony and the caste system." Something guarded in Jake's hooded eyes alarmed Sissy. "Or he could be planning an offensive against the Marils, or the CSS," Jake suggested.

"Or he knows about the unrest in the provinces and needs the troops to suppress a rebellion," Shanet said.

"I've got to stop him." Sissy tucked the stack of papers under her arm and headed for Gregor's suite.

"You can't." Jake grabbed her shoulder. "Not yet. He'll deny everything and blame some innocent clerk for the error."

"You do need more proof, my dear," Shanet added.

"But he's . . ."

"Been playing these games a lot longer than you have. Wait until you explore the caves before you confront him. Please, Laudae, don't do this yet," Jake pleaded.

"And what will I find in the caves?"

"More proof that he's lying to you and to everyone."

◆ ◆ ◆ ◇ ◆ ◆ ◆

CHAPTER THIRTY-EIGHT

"**LIEUTENANT JACOB DA JACOB,**" Guilliam whispered to the passing Military.

"Mr. Guilliam." Sissy's bodyguard paused and bowed slightly, stiffly, as if he resented the disruption of his errand. He carried a stack of books and a sheaf of documents awkwardly in his left hand, leaving his right hand free to draw a weapon. Even now he caressed the hilt lovingly.

"There is something I must show you." Guilliam looked around, the passage to Laudae Sissy's quarters was empty but for the two of them.

"Can it wait? Laudae Sissy . . ."

"Is quite busy packing. She won't miss you for quite some time." Guilliam tried a smile.

Jacob da Jacob looked like he didn't believe him.

"I just checked with her," Guilliam offered.

"These books . . ."

"Will be quite safe outside her door. You may leave them. I've given orders that no one use this corridor until Laudae Sissy has departed for the mountains." Guilliam wished he'd been tapped to go with her rather than Laudae Shanet. He longed to return to the caves. They didn't have to be his home caves. Any cave would feel familiar, comfortable, welcoming.

A warmer reception than he was receiving from Penelope of late. She had a lot on her mind and wasn't willing to talk to him until she figured it all out.

"This is important, Lieutenant. What I have to show you pertains to what Laudae Sissy will find in the burial caves."

"What do you know?" His head reared up, gaze wary.

"Follow me."

"If we are going to be coconspirators, you might as well call me Jake." He set the books and papers on the floor beside the closed doorways.

The sounds of girls and women laughing and arguing lightly filtered through the panels. Jake looked as if he wanted to be a part of that intimacy but feared it as well. As should any normal male. Guilliam had learned long ago that he couldn't penetrate something so intensely feminine as clothing discussions. And the more females involved, the less he had a chance of understanding.

"Follow me, Jake. And my close friends call me Gil." He led the way back into the old part of the Temple where the stones were thick, the mortar crumbling, and nooks and crannies prevalent.

"Where are we going?" Jake kept close behind him, eyes constantly searching.

Gil decided to take a different path to the archives, a longer and more convoluted one. He turned down one short corridor, then crossed to another and doubled back to his starting place. Another circuit through a different path, all looking the same unless you knew what to look for, and Gil knew precisely what to look for.

By the fourth time around, he hoped that Jake was thoroughly lost and confused. Only then did he slip into one of the little alcoves that sheltered a dusty altar.

"Kind of close quarters," Jake said as he squeezed between the altar and the wall.

Gil grunted. He'd lost another button.

Jake peered over his shoulder trying to see how Gil manipulated the stones.

Gil coughed heavily, nearly doubling over. He used the movement to cover how he pressed a button at the rear of the altar. No sense in revealing all of his secrets to this overly inquisitive bodyguard.

"I don't see any Badger Metal in the candlesticks or statuary," Jake mused.

"This sector of the Temple is old. From before the invention of Badger Metal," Gil said. The scraping of stone upon stone almost drowned out his words.

"I thought Badger Metal was a gift from the Gods, at the beginning of time."

"Um . . . ah, here we go. The passage is narrow. You may light one of the candles and bring it with you."

"You don't need light?" Jake asked. He produced a battery torch from one of his innumerable pockets.

"I've been here before. Darkness doesn't frighten me." He breathed deeply of the stale and damp air.

Jake grumbled something as he flashed his light around the narrow landing and down the spiral stairs. "Watch your step, Gil. Those stairs look slick."

"They are. I was about to warn you of the same thing. We will descend to below harbor level for a time. The path will be partially flooded. At low tide in midsummer it should be nearly dry."

Another grunt from Jake. For a man who read so well and used words so easily, you'd think he could be more articulate.

"What are we looking for?" Jake asked as they stepped off the last stair.

"We have a ways to go first." Gil started off on another long looping journey that crossed the main passageway several times. He'd never encountered any cave-dwelling creatures down here. He almost hoped they'd disturb a colony of bats, the more to confuse Jake and discourage him from repeating this journey on his own.

By the time they neared the back entrance to the archives, they were both soaked to the knee with slimy black water.

"Lieutenant . . . Jake, I know by this time that you are utterly trustworthy and loyal to Laudae Sissy."

"I keep my promises. Oaths mean a lot to me."

"So, I noticed. That is why I am willing to trust you, and no one else, with this knowledge."

"No one? Not even Laud Gregor?"

"Not yet."

"Then why show it to me?"

"Because Laudae Sissy will need you to know this when she encounters . . . certain mysteries in the burial caves. I trust you to feed her the information as she needs it. All at once, and she will dismiss it all."

"It's that important?"

"It is that important and so controversial as to be heresy."

Jake's throat apple bobbed as he swallowed deeply. And again.

"You could send us both to the executioner."

"Only if you reveal this information to the wrong person at the wrong time. So I have your oath of secrecy?"

A long moment of silence. All the time, Jake's eyes scanned the entire area, seeking, thinking, weighing the consequences and his options.

"This is so secret I have not even told the woman I consider my spouse." By the name of the Seven he hoped Penelope never had to find out.

"I thought Temple forbade marriage among themselves." Jake looked intensely curious.

"Some of us do form lasting, monogamous relationships. We raise our children in a loving home, we support each other through good times and bad, nurse each other through sickness, and rejoice together over life's small miracles."

"You just don't talk about it. What about Laud Gregor? Does he know?"

"No, he does not. We go to great pains to make certain he doesn't notice the family units inside his Temple. I am not the only one, believe me."

"And you make certain family units don't get separated in his constant rounds of rotation."

"Precisely." Gil suppressed a small smile. Laud Gregor was easy to manipulate when it came to rotations. Gil just had to judge when was the right time to present them.

"Then how did Gregor get to be HP? So many of you against his policies and all."

"The Temple decided against marriage some generations ago. Laud Gregor finds it convenient to continue it. That way he doesn't have to commit to anyone but himself. He doesn't see a lot of what he doesn't want to admit exists."

"A tyrant in the making."

"Laud Gregor is a good HP in most things. He's able to look at many events and find patterns. He thinks beyond immediate gratification and simple solutions."

"He's a good politician. But is he a believer?" Jake asked.

As if faith were a prerequisite for ruling an empire.

"I believe that Laud Gregor is one of the faithful. At least he started that way."

"Is that why you can't trust him with this knowledge you are about to show me?"

"He will have to know eventually. But I will choose the time and place he discovers it."

"Again I ask: why trust me? Why trust anyone with this knowledge?"

"Because I need to know that someone will know if anything happens to me. Now do you agree to absolute secrecy until Laudae Sissy needs to know, and then only as much as she can absorb at one time?"

"Agreed." He said it at almost the same moment Gil saw acceptance in those wary eyes that saw all too much.

Gil opened the back door of the archives and stepped through. Jake followed him through the maze of boxes, crates, and shelves in silence. They reached a small open space in a far corner, the driest and most comfortable, where Gil had placed a reading chair and portable light. The fact that anyone had bothered to run electricity down here still amazed him.

"These documents are very old and fragile. There are no copies." That was a lie. Gil had made two sets of copies and hidden them well in other parts of the old Temple. He'd sent a third copy to his parents in the far west with orders for them to secrete them deep in the burial caves, in a specific niche, beneath the two skeletons that resided there.

Jake scanned the pages quickly. "How long may I keep them?"

"I give you twenty minutes to read as much as you can. Then I have to replace them and take you back."

With quiet efficiency, Jake began reading in earnest, not wasting time with questions or protests.

The minutes crawled by for Gil. He busied himself with organizing boxes nearby. Just as he was about to call a halt to Jake's perusal, the lieutenant looked up. His hands trembled and he looked paler than usual in the harsh light. The acrid scent of fear sat on his skin.

"You have much to think about, Jake."

"Laudae Sissy is right about one thing. This entire planet is sacred. Always has been and always will be."

Gil bowed his head in acknowledgment. "I'll take you back now."

"Don't bother with trying to get me lost again. I know how to navigate blind. The chamber beneath the High Altar should be just behind that wall. I wonder if there is secondary access." Jake wandered over to the wall in question and peered at the mortar closely.

Gil felt ill. "If you return here, please do so secretly."

"You can bet your ass I will. This information is going nowhere." Unerringly, Jake led the way back through the maze and into the tunnels.

CHAPTER THIRTY-NINE

"**D**AMN YOU, GIL, FOR TRUSTING me with this," Jake grumbled under his breath. How could he concentrate on watching the steep mountain road for hidden assassins when all he could think about was the diary he'd read yesterday.

All of a sudden, he had too many answers to questions he'd never thought to ask before.

He closed his eyes a moment. When he opened them again, the colorful lizard sitting in his lap stared balefully up at him. Godfrey, the muncher, stretched clear across both of Jake's legs with its tail dangling between the two seats in the front of the Temple limousine.

Godfrey rotated its bulbous eyes independently. Then as Jake watched, it faded from rusty brown and turquoise to a dark green that almost matched his black uniform.

"How does she find these critters?" he asked Bertie the driver.

"They find her." He flicked a glance at the lizard and shuddered with distaste.

"But how did it get here? It's not native to this continent." From Jake's reading, the beast originated on Far Continent. A few cropped up occasionally in the equatorial islands. The fact that it was running loose on Northern Continent at all meant there was seagoing traffic to forbidden zones.

Was Far Continent forbidden or just forbidding? He couldn't remember.

He cursed Gil again, for giving him more to think about than his tired brain could absorb. *Discord!* he needed to talk to Pammy.

Bertie shrugged. "Escaped from a zoo? Brought in illegally as a pet? I have no idea. But it found Laudae Sissy, and now it lives with her. Just like all the others. Strays and wounded alike. They know a haven when they see one."

Sissy and Shanet cuddled and cradled a myriad of other animals in the back seat. The acolytes of both women, in the two cars following them, had even more, including Monster, the shaggy black dog. Neither Sissy nor Jake trusted anyone in the Temple to care for the menagerie, let alone allow them to live, if left behind. If released, any one of the animals could become food for a desperate family that hadn't eaten meat in a year or more.

If Pammy could see him now. . . . Jake shook his head in dismay. When he'd signed up to be a spy, he never would have believed he'd end up babysitting Godfrey. The weasel, Milton, didn't get along with Godfrey. And Godfrey didn't like Milton any better. In the wild they were natural enemies. Milton could have ridden with the girls. Godfrey could have. Sissy wouldn't dream of separating herself from her two rarest and most delicate creatures. So she had Milton. He had Godfrey.

He'd rather put up with fourteen giggling girls than Godfrey. Though the lizard was quieter. The girls treated him as one of their own, subject to pranks and pillow fights, and an easy touch for help with their lessons.

Godfrey dug twelve needle-sharp talons (his left hind foot was wrapped in a bandage to hide a maiming injury) into Jake's legs, preparing to shift his considerable bulk to a more comfortable position.

"Delicate, my ass," Jake mumbled to himself. Godfrey had talons as long as his palms and Milton had a mouthful of needle-sharp teeth. Either one could tear him apart if he weren't wearing inflatable gel pad armor within the layers of his uniform. The pads had strands of Badger Metal woven into them to prevent piercing that might let the gel leak or to mix with the catalyst that hardened it into overlapping scales that could stop most projectiles and dissipate energy weapons.

The Badger Metal in the weapons he carried and the uniform he wore would buy him a lifetime of ease in the CSS. How in all the hells did he find the formula out here in the middle of nowhere? He needed a live factory and not an endless cave system filled with dead bodies.

He needed Sissy to visit a factory, not burial caves.

He just hoped the niggling idea of a better solution for everyone was worth the risk and the time he put into it. For all he knew, the Marils could have launched a full-scale invasion of the CSS while he babysat a headstrong young woman, her seven acolytes, and her menagerie.

He'd almost welcome the attack after what he'd read yesterday.

"Jake?" Sissy tapped his shoulder.

He looked around, giving her his full attention.

"What is that rock formation? The different colored layers are so unusual. And look how they break at that odd angle and thrust upward." She pointed to the cliff at their right.

"I can look it up in the library when we get to the Temple, My Laudae. But I believe the layers are caused by volcanic action over time. The break could be a fault line. One side of it went one way and the other the opposite during a quake," he replied, dredging up some long forgotten geology lesson from high school. Damn, he should be piloting fighters or even cruise liners across the space lanes, not giving the HPS basic education.

"Lieutenant Jacob da Jacob," Bertie said quietly when Sissy had settled down.

"Yes?"

"Could you speak to the Laudae for me?"

Jake's body stiffened with alarm. Bertie had as easy a relationship with Sissy as anyone. "About what?" He set Godfrey alongside him, freeing himself to react to any threat the driver might point out.

"I . . . I'd rather not remain with Laudae Sissy at the burial caves."

"We're going to be there for weeks. We'll need a driver to get to and from the local Temple and the nearest town . . ."

"You are qualified to drive. I checked."

Drive fifteen different fighters through space.

Jake didn't enlighten the man that his Harmony Military caste credentials were fake and this lumbering land yacht was beyond his capabilities.

"It's just . . . that the caves make me nervous. My family never followed the practice of annual memorials among our ancestors. Best let the dead stay dead. Don't mess with them. And now *she* is going to disturb them all, shift their bones around." Bertie paled and began to sweat. "I'd like to get out at the next pass point and walk back to the last village."

"Honoring our ancestors is one of the most basic and time-honored traditions." Even back on Earth they had All Saints Day, preceded by the fun and nonsense of Halloween. Every human colony and allied world had some variation of the rituals to honor those who had died.

How a civilization honors its living is reflected in how they honor their dead. Jake had read that somewhere. He wished he could remember who'd said it now. Some long-dead president, he thought.

How had Harmony honored the dead of those who came before them? The *original* inhabitants.

"And my family does honor our dead. But from the safe distance of our homes, barred against intrusion. We pray for their safe and continued repose. We light candles and incense and ward every door and window and hole in the roof with charms. We do not disturb the dead," Bertie insisted.

Jake wondered if this was a very old tradition on Harmony. Stay away from the caves and forget what really lies there.

Bertie slowed the car, seeking a place to pull off the road and stop.

Not very likely. The rutted dirt road was little more than an indentation between the multilayered wall to the right—a series of short terraces—and a very steep drop-off down to a churning river canyon on the left.

"Does the Laudae know how you feel, what you fear?"

Bertie shrugged as he braked and swerved around a pothole. The road had deteriorated the last ten kilometers. An arcing dust trail followed them, plastering the other two cars in grit.

Jake checked the rearview mirrors. He couldn't see the other cars at all. The hairs along his spine stood up straight. If they got separated . . .

"Pull off the road, Bertie. We need to wait for the others to catch up."

"Only if you let me get out and you continue driving."

"I don't care. I don't like this. It doesn't feel right. Are there other sects like your family that don't believe in this mission?"

Maybe someone else had read Gil's precious documents and needed to keep them secret in order to . . . to maintain power.

Bertie slowed to a stop. There wasn't any place wide enough for the car to pull off, nor for another car to pass them.

It smelled like a trap.

"Many in the Professional caste feel that the custom of trekking to the caves every year is primitive, something to soothe the uneducated Workers . . ."

"But do they fear the dead like you do?"

"Some . . ."

Jake opened his door. It only gave him two handbreadths before it wedged into the two-meter-high terrace. He wiggled his way out and ran around to the other side where he didn't have much more maneuvering room, but could at least get the door all the way open. The river valley looked to be nearly two kilometers below. He opened the back door anyway.

"Laudae Sissy, I need you to vacate the car immediately," he ordered.

"Jake?" She looked pale and uncertain. Her breathing came in short and sharp gasps.

He handed her the spare inhaler he kept in his thigh pocket.

The moment she'd shot herself full of medications, he grabbed her arm and dragged her free of the car. He planted her feet a meter behind the car, then returned. "You, too, Laudae Shanet."

"The animals . . ."

"Can fend for themselves."

With the women safe and the animals gathering around Sissy of their own volition, Jake turned his attention to Bertie. The driver gripped the steering wheel with both hands so tightly his knuckles turned blue.

"Bring the lizard, Bertie. We hike from here," Jake ordered.

"If it's all the same to you, Lieutenant, I think I'll stay here and wait for the other car."

"Nope." Jake hauled the door open and faced the man. "You come with us and die at the hand of the executioner, or you stay here and die on my blade." He held his dagger at the man's throat.

"I had nothing to do with this, Lieutenant." Bertie still held the steering wheel as if his life depended upon it.

Maybe it did.

"Nothing to do with what?" Jake nicked Bertie's neck with the tip of the knife. Didn't take much pressure to bring a bright drop of blood to the surface. A second drop pushed it out and formed a small trickle onto the grooved blade.

"Please, kill me quick."

"Why should I give you that honor?" Jake pushed the knife a tad deeper. The trickle of blood became a rivulet.

"Jake?" Sissy asked from behind the car.

"Stay put, My Laudae. For the love of your life, stay right where you are." He prayed that for once she obeyed him. She might be a little slip of a thing, bright, and inquisitive. But she was also stubborn and as bull-headed as he was himself.

"I think we should do as he says," Shanet said quietly.

A bright flash of orange and brown the color of the dusty road told Jake that Godfrey had found his own way back to Sissy. He allowed a tiny morsel of relief to trickle into his system.

Failure was not an option. His life and mission depended upon keeping Sissy safe.

Dammit! He *wanted* to keep her safe. He couldn't bear the thought of an assassin depriving the universe of the shining light that was Sissy.

"Tell me what is going to happen here," Jake said quietly to Bertie.

"I . . . I don't know the details."

"Yet you volunteered to die with the High Priestess of Harmony rather than let her muck about with some old bones. Are you afraid of what she'll find there?" Like proof that human life did not originate on Harmony.

Like proof the original colonists had massacred the original inhabitants with no more thought than they had eliminated the Loods at the asylum.

That would disrupt their entire belief system. Destroy the entire political system with it. Bring chaos in its wake.

Leave them all vulnerable to invasion by the CSS. And the Marils. Depending on who got here first.

Jake almost hoped it was the Marils.

Laud Gregor jumped to the top of his suspect list.

And Sissy would still probably die in the aftermath.

He couldn't let that happen.

When had this become about Sissy rather than his mission?

"Talk, Bertie. It's the only way to avoid the humiliation of the executioner's sword. You can die cleanly by my blade and have your soul remembered with honor, or you can go to whatever hell you believe in. Painfully. Long and slow."

"I only know this car is rigged," Bertie said so softly Jake almost didn't hear him. "I . . . I want to see the expedition to the caves destroyed, not hurt Laudae Sissy. I'd never hurt her. Please believe me."

So he'd started talking at an oblique angle to rouse Jake's suspicions.

"Rigged how?" Jake resisted the urge to back away from the car.

"Suspension."

Jake looked at the washboard road riddled with potholes. No problem for people on foot making a pilgrimage. Or a loxen-drawn cart. But for a car, especially a big car that didn't maneuver easily, the undercarriage had to suffer damage with every jolt.

The next jolt might very well be the one that set off whatever parasitic device rode with them.

"You sit right there and don't move," Jake ordered through gritted teeth.

Bertie nodded.

Jake got down on one knee, knife still poised to stab upward at the least sign of movement. He didn't know much about the construction of these vehicles. He couldn't see anything that didn't belong.

Still . . .

He cursed long and fluently. He didn't have to change his vocabulary to fit this culture. Both societies regarded body waste and bodily functions as fit for such epithets.

He rose, knife poised over Bertie's heart. When his invective wound down, he said quietly, "Laudae Shanet, please help Laudae Sissy climb that embankment and begin walking toward the Temple at the end of the road with all due speed."

"But . . ."

"No buts, Laudae Sissy." An icy calm spread through Jake. "Get out of here as far and as fast as you can. The animals will follow you at their own speed."

"The other car . . . my girls . . ."

"Are safe. That is why they dropped back so far they haven't caught up with us yet."

"We'll send help back to you, Lieutenant," Shanet said as she pushed Sissy up the sharp embankment. Thankfully, the eroded rock had lots of hand- and footholds. A wave of cats and dogs swarmed behind them. The red bird with the thick beak picked up the tiny, half-blind kitten and carried it to the sparse grass of the terrace above.

"If I'm not five minutes behind you, there won't be enough left of me to help."

"Saving her now will only delay the inevitable," Bertie said. "Others will come. But it won't be me. I couldn't bear to hurt her. To live long enough to see her hurt."

Jake caught a flash of fanaticism in the man's eye.

"What others? Who set this up?"

"I cannot tell you."

"Tell me or die?" Jake raised the knife from the man's heart to his throat.

"I'll die anyway."

"How? How are you going to die?"

"The steering. It will give at the next bend or the one after that."

Jake spared a quick glance at the steep cliff and the crumbling track they called a road. He had less than a meter between his feet and the edge. Ahead, the road curved sharply right, seemingly ending just . . .

Bertie gunned the engine. The car flew forward.

Jake barely had room to step out of the way. He watched in horror as Bertie cranked the wheel to the right. The car kept going forward. It left the road behind, seeming to float in the air as it arced out over the valley, then plunged down, and down, and down.

He heard Sissy scream something as he raced to the curve. Each step took forever, didn't cover enough ground. As he sought some kind of path downward, he heard the crash.

Far below him, the car crumpled, wedging the entire engine compartment into the front seat.

"We have to help him," Sissy panted beside him.

"No use. No one could live through that."

"But . . ." Tears streamed down her cheeks.

Jake pulled her gently to his chest, cradling her head in his hand while she cried and pounded out her rage and grief.

CHAPTER FORTY

GREGOR MADE HIS SLOW WAY toward the HC Chamber. He breathed deeply, refreshed that Sissy had taken herself and the chaos that followed her off to the mountains. He paused a moment and cherished the silence. No yipping dogs, yowling cats, twittering weasels, or chattering birds. No squeals from her girls as she let them run and play haphazardly throughout the complex. No worry about what she would do next to upset his plans.

If only he could find ways to keep her in the mountains. Or just touring the entire planet.

His mind brightened. That was a worthwhile idea. The people loved Sissy the moment she blessed them with her smile. Since the spectacle of her ordination, attendance numbers at Temple had increased. Having the popular support had never mattered in the running of the government before. But he could see the advantages.

Yes, Laudae Estella, High Priestess of all Harmony, must spend the next year visiting all of Harmony. Including the outer colonies.

Provided war didn't break out. He couldn't take a chance on his Sissy getting caught up in battle.

The flurry of communications flitting around the frontier suggested H6 would be the first target. His source inside the comm tower kept him informed of the increased activity. Admiral Nentares of Spacers and General Armstrong of Military did not see fit to share this knowledge with him.

No trip to H6 anytime soon. He needed Sissy. But sometimes she complicated his life beyond endurance. Like the proposal he intended the HC to pass today reimbursing Lord Chauncey for losses to his shipping business due to out-of-season storms. Sissy had vetoed it last time around. She wanted the families of the dead sailors reimbursed for *their* loss. As if Workers had any value. There were always twenty more to take their places.

The issue was getting the HC to agree without Sissy. If he could pass that through them without her vote or signature, he proved that he controlled the High Council and therefore all of Harmony.

Lady Marissa would lose a fraction of her influence.

Gregor stepped confidently into the huge ceremonial chamber. Four of his fellow Council members already occupied the tall chairs about the table. Only Lady Marissa was absent.

Inwardly Gregor smiled. Probably planning a grand entrance, and she'd assume the place at the head of the table where Sissy should preside. He slipped between the chair and the table in front of the miniature altar Sissy had placed there. Bowing formally to the altar and to the others, he smiled at the prisms arcing out from the crystals beneath the skylight. He, too, knew how to make the best use of ceremony and ritual.

Then he took up a wand and tapped the littlest crystal. A small chime tickled his senses. The Nobles ceased their muted conversations and turned their attention to him.

He tapped the next largest crystal and the next, bringing forth a wonderful chord. By the time the tallest crystal added its bass note to the music, the chamber had filled with peaceful tones.

"Harmony, we invoke your presence," he intoned, beginning a common prayer. A sense of peace washed over him, as it always did in Harmony's grace. He just wished that politics didn't keep intruding on his need to commune with the Gods.

The double doors burst open. Lady Marissa stood framed in the archway. The corridor should have backlit her, making her appear mysterious and majestic. But sunlight filled the chamber and cast her in shadow.

As one, the Nobles frowned at her disruption.

Gregor continued the prayer as if her arrival mattered nothing.

"Oh, stop mouthing your useless platitudes, Gregor," Lady Marissa said, stomping into the Council Chamber. "You don't believe in that nonsense any more than I do."

He wondered how she'd have approached them if they'd waited for her.

"On the contrary, Lady Marissa, my faith is my life. That is what makes me the only person who can preside as HP." He returned to the crystals and took a deep breath before beginning the next long prayer.

"There has been another . . . incident at the Funerary Temple," she said, a gleeful smile lighting her face.

"What do you know?" Gregor clenched his fist around his wand. He didn't ask what she'd heard, but what she knew. Why?

"Radio communication from the mountains is spotty at best. I know

only that Laudae Estella is safe. I have dispatched a contingent of the
Military by helicopter to return her to the safety of the Crystal Temple."
Lady Marissa looked smug.

"You don't have the authority . . ." Lord Nathaniel said. He remained
calm and seated, as if she'd merely issued a parade permit without con-
sulting the city authorities.

"I have every right to see to the continued safety of our HPS," Marissa
replied. She flounced into the empty seat beside Gregor. His place if
Sissy had been here to preside.

"I must go with them," Gregor said. He carefully put down the wand
so that it would not roll and break. The movement disguised the shaking
of his hands. He'd worked too long and hard to get to a place where he
could dominate and manipulate the HC; he couldn't risk it now by losing Sissy. Having her replaced by . . . Penelope. Or worse, someone like
Shanet.

Or Lady Marissa.

"Then you'd best hurry. I heard the first helicopter take off almost five
minutes ago," Lady Marissa said airily. "We'll continue without you. What
is first on the agenda? I believe your proposal to send more Military to
the frontier and reallocate Worker personnel to fill in the gaps . . ."

"This session is closed until we have more information about the wel-
fare of our High Priestess who, by rights, should preside here." Gregor
deliberately tapped the largest crystal, letting its tone fill the room. "Empathy, we invoke you, and thank you for your blessings as we depart."

The Nobles pushed back their chairs. Ritual was too deeply ingrained
in them to question him. The moment Gregor knew Marissa could not
call them back, he dashed for the door.

Sissy had to be all right. Too much depended upon her. Upon his control of her.

✦　✦　✦

Sissy ran from Jake's tired recounting of Bertie's last moments. Poor
Bertie, trapped between loyalty and faith.

She ran uphill, snaking a path beside the road. She ran with tears
blinding her to all but the biggest obstacles in her way. She ran until her
sides ached.

The wind pushed and pulled her in several directions at once. She
heard it sighing among the mountain peaks as if crying for Bertie.

And still she ran.

But she could not escape herself, or the wind reminding her of all the
grief poured out in this place of funerals and good-byes.

A man had died in her place.

By all rights she should be dead now. Not Bertie. Kind, sweet Bertie. Always cheerful. Always loyal.

Too loyal.

Panting, she dropped to her knees in front of the altar in the Funerary Temple. She should be grateful. All of her girls, and Shanet and her girls, the animals, and Jake were safe. And yet . . .

Poor Bertie. How did she pray for his soul? How did she guide his spirit toward Harmony?

Shakily, she brought her palms together and bowed from the waist in deep homage to both the altar and the man she mourned.

Sometime later she became aware of Jake sitting in one of the straight chairs. His long legs sprawled out before him. He slouched as if he'd waited a long time.

"You done crying yet?" he asked.

She choked out some kind of reply. Her throat closed, and new tears threatened.

"Laud Gregor and half the HC are on their way. You need to present a face of calm if you want to continue with the work here."

She nodded. "I never asked for the responsibility of being HPS."

"I know. They thrust it upon you with little or no training. You need to show them you are better than the emotional child you want to be and they believe you to be."

Her stomach twisted. "They took me from my family. Bertie was kind to me. Like an uncle. I needed him."

"All Harmony needs *you*. Harmony needs you strong, clear thinking."

The whop, whop, whop of an approaching aircraft assaulted her ears, a definite discord to the fragile calm she had reached. She gritted her teeth. "I'd like to ban those contraptions."

Jake gave her a slight grin. "I don't think the Military would let you. Nor the Nobles who use them to flit among their far-flung properties."

"If they could just tune their motors to a crystal so they didn't offend my ears."

"Making the enemy cringe at the noise is good tactics."

"We have no enemies among ourselves. Our enemies are all out there." She waved a hand toward the sky.

"Believe that if you must. The Military has a need for weapons."

"Is that what I am? The enemy?" Finally she could face the issue at hand, above and beyond Bertie's death.

"To some."

"Why? I never wanted this."

"You challenge preconceived notions and prejudices."

"I represent change." She remembered her prophecy from her hospital bed. "Is change evil when it brings us back to Harmony?"

"Some people see any change as evil, even those who have drifted so far off Harmony's path they'll never get back. But the drift happened so slowly they don't realize it's happened."

Sissy stood and straightened her rumpled slacks. Almost as an afterthought she kicked off the sturdy shoes she'd worn to hike between the Temple and the caves. Then she walked slowly out into the bright summer sunshine to greet Laud Gregor and the rest of the High Council. The moment they came within earshot, she opened her mouth and prayed that what she said would carry the weight of prophecy.

She had no bubble of "otherness" welling up inside her. When she needed it most, Harmony had deserted her.

"Clouds of Discord gather in response to unfounded fear. What I do here opens a path to Harmony that has been closed."

Laud Gregor stopped short and stared at her. He examined her face.

She kept her eyes lowered, not daring to let him see that she spoke from her heart and not with the voice of their Goddess.

Lady Sarah and Lord Nathaniel dropped to one knee to pay homage to her.

Lady Penelope stepped out of the second helicopter just then, a sneer on her face and anger boiling, judging by her posture.

Lady Marissa remained in the background. She raised one eyebrow and silently applauded Sissy's performance.

CHAPTER FORTY-ONE

"**S**TAY OUT OF THIS, MY ASS,**"** Jake muttered as he hugged the outside wall of the Funerary Temple residence hall. "They don't know who they are dealing with." Military officers were supposed to know how to obey orders. Jake had never been good at that, in any of his incarnations.

Evening shadows made his skulking progress easy. The ever-present wind covered any sound he made.

Not a very big place. Rooms for one priest, one priestess, two dormitories for their acolytes, and three guest suites. One of the suites had pull-out sofas and bunks for acolytes. For tonight, the resident priest and priestess bunked together, and acolytes shared beds to make room for a couple more people. Cramped quarters at best.

Easy to find his way around the building to the outside window of the biggest guest suite.

Small windows to keep heat from escaping in the winter. And not very good for eavesdropping with their double-paned insulation. Especially with the wind whisking away half the words. The sun dropped behind the tallest peak on Harmony. Instantly the thin air cooled. Then chilled. In midsummer.

He ignored his discomfort. Getting a clue regarding Laud Gregor's agenda was more important than seeking the cozy warmth of a wood fire in the great room. More pull-out sofas and bunks there to handle some of the overflow.

Reminded him of summer camp in the Rockies.

Including the shouting matches between counselors after lights out.

He sidled beneath the window he sought. Two voices. Both angry. Laud Gregor's deeper tones. Sissy's softer soprano, no less angry despite the quieter volume. His experience with Pammy had taught him that women tended to be more dangerous the quieter they got.

Laud Gregor could be in trouble. Big trouble. Couldn't happen to a more deserving guy.

"I came here for a reason, and that reason still stands," Sissy said. Her words came through the glass and the log walls loud and clear.

Almost too clear. Jake looked around. Either the chinking between the logs conducted sound or . . . or the window was open a crack. Sissy did love her fresh air.

"It's too dangerous!" Gregor shouted.

Jake didn't need the open window to hear him.

"This misguided cult cannot represent more than a few fanatics," Sissy said, some of the heat fading out of her voice. "Surely you can manage to round them up and reeducate them."

Jake noted that she did not mention putting them in an asylum. He wouldn't wish that on anyone, even the cleansed and rededicated facility Sissy had blessed. She'd made promises to keep track of how the inmates were treated. Abolishing the entire system was still outside her control. Left to her own devices long enough, she'd find a way to integrate the abandoned ones—Jake refused to call them Loods—back into Harmony society.

"We don't even know where to begin!" Gregor exploded.

Uh-oh, he was losing control. Would he drag Sissy by her hair back to the capital if he lost the argument?

Jake couldn't allow that. If his own agenda—his, not Pamela Marella's—were to succeed, he needed Sissy to get into those burial caves and start making new assumptions, reassessing the value of continued isolation.

"Anything interesting happening?" Laudae Shanet asked from the region of his elbow.

Jake started. Bad sign; he'd become so engrossed in his own musings he'd lost track of what was going on around him. He placed his finger to his lips. He pointed to the open window with the other hand.

Shanet nodded and raised her eyebrows in question.

"I suggest you question Bertie's family, find out who he's been talking to," Sissy said. She sounded farther away, as if she had moved to the other side of the room. "Better yet, ask Jake how to investigate. He's Military. It's their job to find out these things."

"We can't trust anyone outside the HC."

"Then why is Laudae Penelope here? Last I heard she was not a member of the HC. I suggest you return, with her, to the Crystal Temple and begin looking for answers. You might even look to her for some of those answers."

"That is ridiculous. Penelope is selfish, vain, and disappointed. But not vindictive. She would never violate the precepts of our faith to . . ."

"Wouldn't she?"

A long silence while they considered the possibility. Jake's money was on Penelope as the instigator of the plot. He'd never liked the woman, or trusted her where Sissy was concerned. She didn't need to believe in the cult of fear to use it.

Never trust the easy answer. He could almost hear Pammy's lecture while she prepped him for this mission.

If not Penelope, then who? Who else stood to gain by Sissy's death?

Damn, he didn't know the personalities well enough.

"Start your investigation tonight. Back at Crystal Temple," Sissy ordered. The quiet authority in her voice didn't surprise Jake. It probably knocked the wind out of Gregor.

Well, not all of his wind. He had plenty left to shout.

"Tonight! Fly through the mountains at night!"

"Surely the pilots know how to do that. If not, you'd better start walking. We don't have room for you here."

"Our little girl has grown up," Shanet whispered.

Jake almost laughed out loud. Indeed, Sissy had grown from the shy little mouse to a powerful woman. And she grew more beautiful every day as she became more and more comfortable with that power.

Or was it truly the blessing of Harmony shining through her?

He didn't know anymore. And frankly didn't care. He did know that he was falling in love with her.

Damn. Dangerous. That would make betraying her all the more painful. For both of them.

Double damn.

"Does she know that you love her?" Shanet whispered.

Jake couldn't mask his shock.

"I don't need to read your mind, not that I could. It's written all over your face every time you look at her. Or think about her."

"No, she doesn't know, and she'd better not find out. I'm out of caste to her," he ground out.

"Are you? Think about what her full array of caste marks stands for." Shanet slipped away into the growing darkness.

Pammy'd have his hide for this. So what? She might think she was the puppet master in this charade. Sissy could give the spymaster a run for her money. Jake had cut Pammy's strings the moment he realized stealing the formula for Badger Metal wasn't the only course of action.

Now if he made Sissy realize that his agenda benefited Harmony as much or more than the CSS, then it wasn't truly betrayal. Was it?

✦　✦　✦

Sissy listened to the heavy throp, throp of the helicopter leaving. As the noise retreated to the east, she gave in to her shaking knees and collapsed into the overstuffed chair by the hearth. A wood fire crackled cheerfully. The sweet smell of the smoke drifted up the chimney.

She breathed deeply of the thin air. Easier to fill her lungs up here. The physicians had told her that at this elevation the air couldn't retain as much moisture as it could closer to sea level, near Harmony City. Neither could it hold dust and pollution.

What would happen if she stayed up here all summer escaping the heat and dirty air of the city? She'd be healthier. Her mind and body could rest. She'd have the chance to practice her reading, with Jake's help.

She'd be cut off from her family completely.

A shuffle of footsteps at her doorway alerted her. "Come in, Jake," she called. No need to speak up near him. He'd hear her. She trusted him to hear her no matter the distance or the thick walls that separated them.

She trusted him more than anyone else from Crystal Temple, including Shanet who had been kind to her. Perhaps she trusted him simply because he was not Temple caste.

No, it was more than that. She trusted Jake because he was . . . Jake.

She'd faced her own share of disillusionment when she realized that priests and priestesses were as human as any Worker. Perhaps less so with their ambitions and greed. Their sense of superiority made them look down on the rest of the world, put their own wants and needs above the rest of humanity.

Sometimes in the dark of night she wondered if Temple caste truly believed in the faith that sustained her.

"True belief is the path to Harmony," she repeated an early Holy Day lesson. "I was selected to bring the people of Harmony back to that path."

"And what if the path divides and divides again until the choices overwhelm you?" Jake asked quietly from the doorway.

"What do you know?" she asked, startled.

"Too much and not enough."

"A politician's answer. I expect more directness from a soldier."

"Perhaps my path is dividing and dividing again. People do grow. Sometimes beyond their caste."

"Now you are a philosopher."

"I report what I see. I have only to look at you to believe that the castes might be fluid. Change in a person does not necessarily have to go downward in caste."

She gasped. Never had she heard such a blasphemy uttered. Never. And yet . . . she had gone from Worker to Temple in a single night.

"Have you ever stopped to think why there have been no advancements in technology in the past five hundred years?" he asked, assuming a limp posture mimicking her own in the chair opposite.

"There is nothing left to invent."

"Isn't there? What about improvements in communications, telephones in every home and business, more televisions so that everyone can watch news events unfold or participate in everyday rituals at the Crystal Temple. In color instead of fuzzy shades of gray."

"I don't know enough science to speculate," she hedged. This conversation was headed into dangerous territory, but like a mouse caught in a cat's gaze, she had no choice but to follow his lead.

"I do know enough science to know that new inventions are swallowed up by the government, never allowed to filter down to the people." Jake examined his fingernails.

"Why . . . ?"

"Control."

"Lower castes need direction from above."

"Do they?"

Sissy had to think about that one. Certainly many people she knew in Lord Chauncey's factories and blocks of flats seemed perfectly happy having others make decisions for them. But for people like her brother Stevie, or supervisor Tyker, or . . . or herself, there was always the need to ask why.

"And while you think about that, also wonder why there are no written records older than five hundred years—that means records prior to that never existed, were lost, or suppressed." He heaved himself out of his chair. "Good night, High Priestess of Harmony. I'll send in your girls for their evening prayers. Sleep well. But if you don't, then use the time to think."

CHAPTER FORTY-TWO

SISSY TOSSED OFF THE HEAVY blanket and sheet. Night air cooled her sweating body. Her fevered mind drifted back and forth between nightmare sleep and reality. Today, yesterday, tomorrow, or some far-off realm of the mind twisted and combined.

She heard the whop, whop, whop of approaching helicopters. One crashed into the mountain above her in a fiery explosion. Another loosed a burst of weapon fire she couldn't understand.

Winged, feathered creatures, the size of humans and with features very like her own, fought the mechanical flyers and lost. Laud Gregor shouted at her that nothing could change. Not now, not before, never again.

She must continue on this path that drifted farther and farther away from Harmony.

The crevices and ridges of the mountain became a face. Harmony's face. The cave opening became her mouth, breathing in at dawn and out at sunset. Her glaciers melted into her tears. The tears increased to a roaring torrent, overfilling rivers, flooding out farms and cities, raising the oceans until they pushed the cities farther and farther back toward the mountain.

A mountain waiting to crush them all.

Sissy tried to climb the face of the Goddess, comfort her, stem the cascade of tears. Breathe with Her. She needed to reassure Harmony that she would bring the people back to the true path.

Laud Gregor grabbed her hair and dragged her back.

The blank walls of the asylum awaited her, ready to consume her body and soul.

Harmony protested with a quake that rent the continent into a dozen separate islands.

Her shaking bed finally brought her out of the tangled dreams. She sat up with a jolt; the moving mattress a mere memory.

Had they endured another quake? Or had the mattress shifted when Monster and Cat landed on it and crawled toward her, whining anxiously for her well-being.

She gathered them close.

"It was so real," she murmured as she buried her face in Monster's fur. "I felt every one of those creatures die. I felt their agony at the loss of their home." Mere dream or prophetic vision?

Or had she viewed something real? Something that had happened, or would happen in the near future.

"What does it all mean?"

She lay back down and tried to sleep. Every time she closed her eyes, she relived the entire messy dream.

Dawn crept under the shutters of her windows. The wind sighed as it entered the cave, the mountain breathing in.

She might as well get up and face the day.

And think.

Morning brought clear skies blurred by thick humidity and the sharp actinic taste of thunder brewing. Jake felt the tension in Sissy and the girls when they broke their fast with eggs from local chickens, unleavened cakes made from half a dozen whole grains, and sweetened with an orange-colored fruit that might have been a peach when it started on Earth but mutated to something else in the terraforming process.

Sarah snapped at Sharan. Bella quibbled with Mary. Suzie cried at their noise. Martha yelled at them all to be quiet. And Jilly, bless her, quipped, "What do you get when you cross a book with a disobedient acolyte?"

"I don't know, Jilly, what do you get when you cross a book with a disobedient acolyte?" Sissy prompted. Her usual smile was missing. Dark circles made her eyes look hollow. She hadn't slept any better than he had.

"A sore bottom," Jake snarled.

The girls stared at him in puzzlement.

"You'll all get spanked with a book if you don't stop arguing." He smacked his fist into his open palm. The noise gave him a headache worse than the sound of the arguments. Tension clawed at his shoulders and shortened his neck.

When did he become the dad of this crew? His own father had never stepped in when Jake and his brother Lance had squabbled at the table, or resorted to wrestling in the dirt to solve their differences.

Jilly giggled and ran off, remembering to turn and bow to Sissy when she reached the doorway.

Mary dared a light chuckle. The others followed suit.

They quieted their bickering a moment.

"Finish up, girls, and then you can have an hour of free time before lessons," Sissy said as she pushed aside her plate, still half full.

"Can we go to the caves?" Martha asked. The others all nodded in agreement.

"Not yet. We have to let the scientists in first. It's been so long since anyone has ventured beyond the opening, we don't know if they are safe," Sissy said.

"Oh." Suzie pouted.

"You'll get your chance, girls. Just not today. The scientists are due right after lunch," Jake placated them.

The girls scampered off.

"You need me for anything?" he asked Sissy.

She shook her head. Her gaze kept drifting out the windows toward the path to the caves. Then upward staring at the mountain.

"I'd like to scout the area and learn the lay of the land before we have company."

"Go ahead." She waved him off. Her mind had already jumped somewhere else.

He hesitated a moment. "Want to talk about it?"

"Talk about what?"

"Whatever kept you awake last night."

"No." She continued looking out the window. Sadness clouded her eyes. And puzzlement.

Maybe now wasn't the time to talk to her.

At the entrance to the great room, Jake checked his weapons. Arm sheaths snug, quick release snappy. Boot knives in place. Two pair of throwing stars in each hip pocket. Dagger and sword in place. He checked each for sharpness though he knew the Badger Metal blades never dulled. Then he donned a hat to shield against glare and enhanced spectrum glasses to probe shadows.

When he left Harmony, he wanted to take those glasses with him. Better than any equipment available to the CSS troops. Standard issue here.

Another anomaly. Harmony was a mishmash of technology. First-rate for Spacers and Military where needed. Everyone else had to make do with rudimentary stuff. Society wasn't willing to spend the energy on giving tech to the populace.

Early morning sun just topped the lower peaks to the east when he stepped outside the Temple complex. Long shadows with diffuse edges spread out behind rocks, trees, and irregularities in the landscape. Too much humidity to sharply define anything.

To the west he noted tall white clouds with dark undersides piling up. Would the sunshine disperse them or would heating the land push more energy into them?

Energy. Tech. Energy. All about control. The Nobles and Temple controlled the energy, and therefore they controlled the economy. Control the economy and the supply chain, you control the masses.

The glasses helped him peer into the shadows. He spotted a few birds, including Sissy's red bird with the thick beak, perched in the trees. Cats sprawled in the sunshine, soaking up the sun's energy. Dogs panted in shadows. Godfrey laid claim to the top of a rock nearby. Milton wove slithering circles around him.

Jake would have only spotted half the wildlife without the glasses.

Slowly he walked a spiral around the buildings, memorizing the land and all its obstacles. As his circles widened, he approached the path up to the caves. Heat signatures flashed on the path.

Then he heard whispers and giggles.

The girls. All seven of them tried to hide from him as they crawled up to the gated entrance. "Much more energy than sense," he muttered to himself. "Shanet'll have a fit if they get all dirty, scrape their knees, and ruin their clothes. Sissy won't mind, though."

So long as they didn't get hurt.

He set his feet onto the winding path, keeping the girls in his periphery. One S curve after another he followed them up.

As the embankment steepened, he lost sight of them. Even his glasses couldn't see through several feet of dirt and rock.

He turned the next corner cautiously, keeping his eyes on the next level for signs of what the girls were up to.

The next step brought him to his knees as he stumbled over something. In a flash he had knives in hand and he'd surveyed the immediate area in a full circle.

A bright giggle brought his alert level down and his attention closer to the ground. Jilly huddled in a depression in the embankment. His glasses had trouble sorting her from the surrounding dirt and rock that had masked her heat signature and helped her blend in with the shadows. With her hand covering her mouth to suppress her laughter she nearly tumbled into his path.

"Did you trip me, little girl?" Jake demanded in his sternest voice.

Jilly nodded.

"Do you know what the punishment is for such insubordination?" He made the knives disappear.

She shook her head.

Before he could think of a suitable reply, six more small bodies landed on top of him from above. Good thing he'd sheathed his knives. He fought free of a flurry of lavender skirts and white petticoats.

They all rolled right and left trying to get a grip on the ground and regain their balance. He got a foot in his chest. The armor reacted with a small burst of hardened gel.

For some reason Bella thought this hilarious and curled up in a ball of giggles. Suzie took advantage of her immobility with an assault of tickles.

This triggered the other girls to try to tickle Jake through his armored uniform.

He succumbed to a fit of merriment at their tries though he couldn't really feel much through the uniform layers.

In turn, he found a suitable victim in Martha and let her have a taste of her own medicine.

Jake's attempts at tickling turned into fierce hugs of love and gratitude. No way could he take himself too seriously among this gaggle.

No way could he conceive of abandoning and betraying this brood of precious little girls when the time came to leave Harmony.

Instantly he sobered. How in all the hells could he think of leaving?

Lightning split the air. A crack of thunder released the tension.

A thick shower of rain subdued their wrestling match.

"Race you back to the Temple," Jake called. He grabbed up the two littlest and pelted back the way he'd come.

The others followed. They all landed in the foyer dripping wet, filthy, and smiling. By the time they'd shed their wet shoes, the rain had stopped and the sun reappeared. The humidity dropped and they all relaxed despite a bit of chill.

As he knelt to help Suzie peel off her stockings, Jake's heart swelled with so much emotion he felt his chest couldn't contain it all.

He had to cherish every bit of it. Store it up in his memory for the horrible time to come when he returned to his very lonely life in the CSS.

When he left, he'd betray these wondrous children as well as Sissy.

Damn, there had to be a compromise. Something he could do.

"Don't worry, Jake." Jilly patted his hand. "It will all turn out all right. Harmony promised me that you will find your path."

CHAPTER FORTY-THREE

JAKE WATCHED THE TEAMS of scientists spill out of their troop transport trucks like a litter of puppies allowed out to explore on their own for the first time. They tripped over their own feet in their enthusiasm. They didn't even pause to set up their camps. En masse, they dashed to the burial cave opening one hundred meters uphill from the little Temple complex. They climbed the narrow switchback trail that defined pilgrimage. The emphasis being on the *grim*.

The trail where Sissy's seven acolytes had taught him a lot about love and family only a few hours ago.

The local priest and priestess and their acolytes stopped the scientists short of surging upward beyond the first switchback. Their sheer numbers provided a formidable blockage on the narrow path.

Thirty-five scientists and historians stumbled into some kind of arrangement by rank and seniority. Shanet and her girls mixed among them at carefully selected intervals with candles and incense and crystals.

Sissy presided at the top by the gate in full purple ceremonial regalia, including the heavy headdress and crystal veil. This was Sissy's show.

Jake hovered as close as she'd let him. No way was he going to allow her out of his sight while the scientists mucked about with the bones of their ancestors. Not only did he need to protect her from any fanatics who might have slipped into the science teams, but he needed to be close by to whisper truths into her ears when the bone analysis began.

Jake took a few precious moments to scan caste marks on the newcomers before they came together on the wide ledge in front of Sissy. They pressed a little too close for comfort in their eagerness. He shouldered the leaders aside, not needing to see Sissy's face to know she feared the eager press of them. Her breathing grew heavy, and she flung her head right and left.

"Easy, guys. Time enough to do your work after proper rituals," Jake said when a slender man with the yellow star of a Spacer pushed back at him.

Thirty out of the thirty-five wore yellow stars with a slash beneath them indicating officers in the Space Corps. Four green triangles of Professionals, physicians. And one Military red square. A forensic investigator, a colonel and therefore very senior. Probably an expert with the equivalent of a couple of PhDs.

Not an archaeologist or anthropologist among them. Those sciences hadn't developed on Harmony. What need had they to dig up ruins when there weren't any. Everything they *wanted* to know about their past was written down, beginning with the lies penned by the survivors among the first colonists.

The numbers of scientists matched the roster and personnel files he'd studied late into the night. That didn't mean some of them hadn't allied with the "no bones" cult. Or been sent by someone with a grudge against Sissy, or against the mission.

Sissy subdued their excited chatter with a tap to a large crystal set into a niche beside the gate. She turned to face them, arms uplifted. A shaft of sunlight caught the crystal beads in her veil and sparkled. Bright rainbows arced about her in a holy aura of majesty.

Then she tapped the crystal on the opposite side of the gate. The ringing notes and the wind wandering around the peaks filled Jake's ears.

The scientists immediately shut up. Superstitious awe replaced cold calculation in their eyes. Despite their extensive educations, even these guys fell victim to Sissy's magic.

"Harmony, Mother of us all, from your womb we are born. To your womb we return. Bless this endeavor to bring your people back to your cradle so that we may join the web of the universe and find rebirth," Sissy intoned.

For a single moment, with the sunlight just so, Jake almost saw strands of colored light connecting her upraised hands and spreading out in a beneficent net, enfolding the scientists, including them in the energy that bound the universe together. Dust motes sparkled in that web of light, stardust, echoes of the big bang that started it all.

"We are all star stuff," he whispered.

One and all the scientists circled their thumbs and forefingers, splaying their fingers in the symbol of Harmony's womb joined with Empathy's sun rays.

Jake mimicked them, suddenly compelled to be a part of whatever wonder Sissy performed.

Still, he kept his eyes open and his attention on the men and women who followed her ritual. Was that a narrowing of focus in the eyes of the lady physician hanging at the edge of the crowd?

Sissy tapped the crystals again and raised her arms to include everyone in her blessing. "Let us begin this work of renewing our Covenant with Harmony. Jake, if you please."

From a clip on his belt, Jake produced the three iron keys that opened the three locks on the gate. He had the two spare sets (the only extra sets) in the thigh pockets of his uniform. And hadn't he had a swell time coercing the local priest and priestess to relinquish those keys. But while Sissy presided here, no one, absolutely no one, got into the cave without Jake knowing about it.

He manipulated each of the three locks, all the while wondering why there weren't a sacred seven of them. Then he pointedly replaced the keys on his belt. He felt covetous stares boring through him to those keys.

Locks open, he stepped aside and let Sissy push the gates inward. The hinges groaned with disuse. A few flakes of rust floated to the ground, sparkling in the sunlight as if they, too, participated in Sissy's magic.

Then she walked inside, Jake at her elbow, the scientists pushing and shoving for position right behind her.

The cool dimness nearly blinded Jake before he remembered to reach for a torch to his left and light it with the matches the priest had given him. No electric light allowed inside. Only natural flame.

The priest wouldn't allow his spectrum-enhanced glasses inside either.

Natural air currents sent the smoke drifting outward.

The sole Military scientist grabbed a torch on the right. He tried to push forward, to be the first to get a look at the anthropological treasure inside.

Jake frowned at him, making sure the guy got a good look at the purple circle around his caste mark. That outranked his colonelship to Jake's lieutenancy any day.

Sissy led them along a short tunnel to the first grave niches. The wind increased in the narrow passage. Then it died completely as the way opened and the path sloped downward. She looked eagerly right and left, dragging her fingertips along the right side of the cave wall. When the space opened to a vast cavern, she paused long enough to taste the moisture gathered on her fingers. Then she drew off the heavy headdress and peered into the gloom.

Jake thrust his torch forward to aid her vision.

"Oh, my!" she gasped.

The scientists pressed forward. Jake stepped aside for them. This might be Sissy's party, but this was their playground. When the last one had descended the ten steps cut into the ground, Jake took a moment to look.

"I'll be damned."

Acres of open cavern with a dais and altar in the sunken center. All around, everywhere he looked, floor to ceiling and down additional tunnels to more caverns were niches filled with bones, some full skeletons, others mere dust. Thousands and thousands of them. Whole families lay together. A little bronze plaque gave the name, caste, and position of the deceased on the closest graves. Farther along, the plaques became older, corroded, missing, or never in place.

"This . . . this place goes back to our prehistory," whispered the forensics colonel. "And there are thousands of these caves spread out all over Harmony."

"Impossible," Jake whispered.

Only Sissy seemed to have heard him. She cast him a strange glance as she frowned. Then she daintily lifted the hem of her robe and strode confidently down the steps to the central nave and up to her rightful position behind the altar.

✦   ✦   ✦

Gregor took over closing the rituals from Penelope. How had he ever considered the woman to succeed Marilee? She had no flair, no sense of timing, and he suspected she was tone deaf, not caring to chime the crystals in any sort of rhythm or tonal quality.

Three Holy Days without Sissy presiding, and the populace of Harmony City knew it. Attendance at rituals had dropped to lower than pre-Sissy days. Those who came responded listlessly and departed as soon as possible.

Gregor had dressed all the clergy in purple, added crystals to every veil, and ordered shoes off at the tunnel entrance, and still the people knew their HPS had left the city.

Temple could not control the masses, as dictated by their Covenant of Harmony, if they could not keep them enthralled. Sissy did it just by walking into a room and smiling. Penelope had to work at capturing the attention of the younger priests, even in the nude. Rumor had it she hadn't had a lover in months, perhaps years.

From all reports, Sissy hadn't either.

That had to change. Gregor needed Sissy to produce children—preferably babies with proper Temple caste marks—soon. He had to prove to the HC that she could breed true to her adopted caste and that her mutant caste marks were a sign from Harmony, a symbol of her gift of Harmony and rightful place as HPS.

Gratefully, he retreated to his office and the mountains of paperwork that always accumulated. Throwing his headdress across the room, he shed his robes and dumped them on the floor. Guilliam would growl and fuss at this uncharacteristic mistreatment of the costly regalia, but Gregor did not care.

He considered calling Sissy back to the capital. No. He had the HC on the verge of agreeing to his troop rearrangement. He had to wait until the fleet entered hyperspace, beyond recall. Then Sissy could not interfere with the retaking of the Lost Colony.

She would never understand the need to maintain the symbolic seven. Certainly Harmony's empire of home world and six colonies made seven. But Temple always worked with one ordained clergy and *seven* acolytes. Harmony needed seven colonies to make the same symbolic grouping.

An idea struck him. Seven gods. Why not a primary god with *seven* companion gods. Yes. He needed to elevate Discord to godhood. Balance among the gods. Harmony as primary with Empathy, Nurture, and Unity at her right hand, Anger, Greed, Fear, and *Discord* on the left as her seven acolytes!

Symbolism held power. He knew that. Marilee had understood that, included it in all her lavish pageantry. No one else in the current regime had the same grasp of the need for control through symbolism.

How to do it? A rewriting of the Covenant of Harmony. A restaging of the creation myth.

What if Sissy's expedition found a new interpretation of the original myth.

He smiled to himself as he sat at the desk and prepared to write a dispatch to his contact among the scientists. She'd find a way to "discover" an ancient mural in the oldest portion of the caves. She'd already reported finding a hidden side cave behind a rockfall. Surely she could arrange to get in there and plant the evidence before anyone else.

Harmony would benefit from this. He knew it in his gut.

The discovery would also keep Sissy fully occupied and out of the capital for a few more weeks until the fleet was underway to retake H7 from the rebels.

The top file on his desk caught his attention. Guilliam had recommended once again that Gregor transfer Penelope and himself outside the capital. After today's lackluster performance he should get rid of her.

His last argument with Sissy sprang to his mind. Why had Penelope inserted herself into the HC when they went to the mountains to rescue Sissy? Simple ambition to be seen as a part of the government? Or something more sinister?

He tapped the file while he thought. Penelope in close proximity to the HC was dangerous. Penelope on her own, outside his careful surveillance, could be more dangerous.

"Guilliam," he called his assistant through the comm unit.

"Yes, My Laud?" Guilliam appeared in the doorway within seconds.

"I need someone to watch Laudae Penelope without her knowing."

"I'll see to it, My Laud. Any suggestions?

"Find her a new lover. Someone young and energetic."

"And not overly picky." Guilliam frowned. Then heaved the deep sigh of a martyr.

Confident in Guilliam's efficiency, Gregor returned to the never-ending paperwork.

CHAPTER FORTY-FOUR

GUILLIAM HELPED A TREMBLING Maigrie from the helicopter. Her knees buckled a little when she touched ground. Her spouse Jaimey looked whiter and more shaken than she. Guilliam let Stevie help his father out of the vehicle. A strange and awesome flight for people unused to transportation other than their own two feet.

Then all three spotted Sissy at the same time. Huge smiles broke out on their faces and firmed their balance. Sissy stood just outside the Temple complex with her girls. Her entire being seemed to glow with pleasure.

Arms spread wide, she ran toward them. The slowing helicopter rotors kicked up enough wind to blow her hair back from her face. Her caste marks seemed brighter than Guilliam remembered, as if they more clearly defined her.

He stepped aside to give them all room for a group hug. They clung to each other for long moments, hands gripping tightly, not wanting to let go. Laughing and crying with joy.

"Cherish the moment," Guilliam whispered to himself. "I don't know how often I can pull this off."

"Our thanks for managing it at least once, Gil," Jake replied in his ear. "Anyone question you commandeering a helicopter?"

Gil tried not to jump. How had the man gotten so close without him noticing?

"Temple business." They grinned at each other, conspiring friends. "I do this once, everyone presumes someone else ordered it. I do it twice, on Holy Day when all the Lauds and Laudaes are supposed to be in their quarters preparing for services or in quiet prayer, questions get asked."

Eventually Sissy managed to drag her family back toward the guest quarters, arms draped around the waists of both her parents, Stevie following close behind. He seemed nearly as wary and suspicious as Jake.

"Almost makes you want to be one of them," Jake said. He watched the pilot descend from the helicopter rather than looking at the family.

"He can be trusted," Gil advised Jake.

"How far?"

"I don't understand." Gil drew in a lungful of hot dry air, hoping he truly did not understand Jake's meaning.

"How far do you trust him? With your life, certainly, if you got into a helicopter with him. But then the media wouldn't make much of a to-do about your death. Do you trust that pilot with Laudae Sissy's life?" Jake took a stance between the pilot and Sissy's family.

"I trust him," Gil said firmly.

"Well, I trust no one." Then louder, he addressed the pilot, "You can grab a cup of tea and a hot lunch in the camp." He jerked his head down-hill toward the orderly array of tents set up for the scientists and their equipment.

The pilot looked a little disappointed as he nodded and angled his steps in the direction Jake indicated.

Not until the pilot actually sat before a campfire with a cup of hot tea in his hands and half a dozen physicians and the Military colonel gathered to gossip did Jake hasten to catch up with Sissy.

"She chose well in you," Gil panted. He hadn't hurried this much in years, and the thin mountain air didn't make breathing any easier.

"I do my best," Jake replied. His breathing was absolutely normal. But then he was younger, fitter, and had had nearly a month to get used to the elevation.

"I'm surprised the science teams are not inside the caves today," Gil mused.

"Holy Day. With the HPS of all Harmony in their midst, they don't dare violate her orders to rest and renew our Covenant with Harmony today."

Gil inspected the snug rooms inside the Temple complex. Thick walls and small windows as insulation against the winter cold, a large hearth in each of the main rooms—empty in the height of summer—and bright carpets and curtains, made a cozy, and homely welcome. He could almost picture himself here with his children. But not Penelope. She'd never be comfortable here.

He sighed with a touch of regret.

"Any chance I may take a tour of the caves today?" he asked Jake. "For me, it would be a welcome relaxation, not work."

He could have sent Sissy's family up here with only the pilot for escort. He probably should have, to avoid scrutiny of the transport orders. If he had, he wouldn't have the chance to walk in a real cave, breathe the cold air, smell the dust, touch the bones of the ages, revisit memories from his earliest childhood. Feel the cave breathe.

And then experience the glorious sense of rebirth when emerging from the darkness.

Penelope would never understand. Sissy, with her intense contact with Harmony, might.

"Laudae Sissy will probably jump at the chance to show off what she's accomplished." Jake grinned. "Come, I'll get you some hot tea and lunch." He ambled down a long windowless hallway toward the sounds of plates and cutlery banging and bright voices laughing.

"Why did I know I'd find Laudae Sissy and her family here in the kitchen?" Gil said.

They'd gathered around the central worktable, making themselves at home. Cooks and servants, usually very territorial about their work space, made room for them, pushing extra treats of jam and precious spices on them.

"But why didn't Anna come with you, Stevie?" Sissy asked, ladling stew into bowls.

Stevie blushed and looked away.

"Stevie?" A bit of bedrock entered Sissy's voice, demanding an answer.

"Tyker called in Anna's team to work an extra shift," Stevie muttered.

"On Holy Day?" Sissy sounded outraged.

"New Spacer contracts. Have to be filled immediately," Jaimey said around a mouthful of bread and creamy butter.

Guilliam was willing to bet this simple meal seemed the height of luxury to the Worker family.

"That is no excuse for violating Holy Day. Mr. Guilliam, what is happening in the capital?" Sissy looked up at him.

"I am not aware of any change in policy. The order to work extra shifts had to come from Lord Chauncey. He's on the High Council."

"I do not like this. Jake, after lunch will you help me draft a letter to Laud Gregor? This must stop. I don't care how important those Spacer contracts are. We cannot allow Workers to be abused this way."

"I can help you," Stevie said. He glared at Jake jealously.

A moment of tense silence hung on them all, like an unwanted ghost.

At last Jake executed a slight bow. "I'll gladly turn that chore over to you, Stevie. Mr. Guilliam has requested a tour of the caves. I'll accompany him."

The tension evaporated.

"And we can talk privately about what is and what is not in those caves," Jake whispered.

CHAPTER FORTY-FIVE

ON FIRST DAY, SISSY LED her girls into the caves. They all wore purple-and-lavender coveralls for protection from the dusty work. Sissy looked forward to the long day ahead, refreshed by her reunion with Mama and Pop and Stevie. At the same time she worried that she needed to be back in Harmony City, monitoring everyday life.

This business of factory owners requiring Workers to complete extra shifts on Holy Day needed to stop immediately. How could she be sure Laud Gregor would see to it if she wasn't presiding over the HC meeting?

"What's down here?" Jilly asked, darting away from Sissy and the other girls into a newly opened side tunnel within the maze of caves.

"Come back here, Jilly," Sissy called. Then she looked to Jake for help when her most energetic acolyte chose not to hear her.

He nodded curtly and went after Jilly in long strides. Not hurrying, but not wasting any time either.

"Why can't we go down there?" Sharan asked, looking up from where she and Suzie made rubbings of the letters and glyphs on freshly cleaned brass plaques.

"Because we don't know what's down there yet," Sissy explained. She transferred a badly encrusted plaque from one solution to another, using Badger Metal tweezers.

Her training in meticulous detail work made her the best person for this delicate cleaning process. She seemed to know instinctively how long to leave a piece in each solution and when to vary the acid level.

And each day, the acid baths made a little more of the residual Badger Metal stuck on her hands slough off. Almost completely clean now. Sissy saw this return of full feeling and dexterity as a gift; a thank you from Harmony for doing her work.

"How are we supposed to find out what's down there if we don't go down there?" Mary asked. She peered eagerly at the dark length of hollowed-out rock, leaning forward, but keeping her feet safely planted beside Sissy. She and Martha took the square pieces of brass from the last soapy basin, rinsed, and dried them.

Jilly was supposed to polish them with a soft cloth and special rubbing compound. Bella and Sarah then made exact copies of the engravings in as neat a hand as possible. But Jilly couldn't sit still today. She'd rubbed the top layer of brass off unevenly and left other sections dull.

Jilly came skipping back to the main cavern where they worked. Her simple lavender coveralls in sturdy everyday cloth—already too short at the ankle by three inches and they had been new when they first came to the caves a month ago—showed as a bright spot before the rest of her became visible. She clung tightly to Jake's hand.

Sissy often found those two together of late, heads together as they puzzled out a lesson, or shared secrets, or plotted pranks.

"Jake says there's a new cavern at the end of the tunnel. A very old one. And lots of places that look like they might be other caves once they remove the rub . . . rubble. Is that the right word, Jake?" Jilly looked up at the soldier with adoring eyes.

Jake nodded. "Looks like they've opened enough space in one of them to poke a torch and a camera through."

Sissy had to smile. More and more they all seemed to mesh together. Like a good team.

Or a family.

She sighed. Someday Jake would leave them. When his services were no longer needed. When they both realized that an out-of-caste relationship could never work.

Jilly's eyes rolled up, and she swayed in place. Her face screwed up as if in great pain.

Jake grabbed her around the waist, keeping her from falling.

Sissy rushed forward and knelt in front of the girl.

"Discord hides in the open. The Gods cannot see him, only follow his trail of destruction . . ." Jilly mumbled. Then she closed her eyes. Her face relaxed and she found her own balance.

"What did she say?" Mary asked. She kept the other girls back. "We couldn't hear her. She mumbled and slurred her words."

"Nothing of import," Sissy replied. She hated lying to the girls. But she had to protect them from this latest prophecy. Here, deep within the womb of Harmony, both she and Jilly had experienced this special gift more and more often. Rarely did they remember what they said.

Jake recorded it all in a notebook he kept sealed within a secret pocket in his uniform full of pockets.

"Laudae, I've found something!" Spacer Scientist Barba du Annalyse pu Science Fleet called from far down the tunnel.

"Let's go see!" Jilly exclaimed, completely recovered and oblivious to the concern of her elders.

The scientist eagerly waved to Sissy to join the group huddled around a tumble of rock halfway back to the new cavern.

For four weeks they had all skirted the fallen rocks warily. They had so many new things to explore, so much other work to be done, the rockfall hadn't pricked anyone's curiosity. But Scientist Barba loved rocks. How they were formed. Why this one lay next to that one. The elusive minerals hiding in a matrix of other, more common minerals. She'd finally succumbed to her curiosity and started sifting through the tumble. Milton the weasel had joined her, eager to explore tiny places in the dark.

He'd eaten his weight in cave mice every day. The cats caught and played with other rodents while the dogs lazed in the sun at the entrance.

Sissy joined the throng of scientists, as eager as they to see what lay behind the rockfall. "Stay behind me, girls, until we know that the rocks are stable."

Three men rolled away a three-foot-tall boulder. Above it, they could already see a blacker-than-black opening into yet another cavern.

"Why would they seal off some rooms and leave others open to all?" Sissy asked.

"This is the oldest section," Barba said, mopping sweat off her brow with her sleeve. "Maybe, in olden times, before the Covenant with Harmony they had different customs." She shrugged.

"Before the Covenant *with* Harmony?" Sissy asked. According to every myth she'd been told growing up, and all she'd read since, the Seven Gods created humanity with the Covenant intact. There should be nothing before that.

"Prehistory gets confusing when facts disagree," Jake muttered in her ear. He was never far away from her, even when he helped the scientists sort and catalog their findings.

"Facts cannot disagree," Sissy insisted.

Jake just looked at her long and hard. His expression made her stop and think. He used it often. And every time she came up with more questions than answers.

"We're clear," Barba exclaimed. Sweat glistened on her face in the torchlight. Why was she sweating now? She hadn't put her back into rolling away the big rock.

The girls edged closer. Sissy glared at them to back off. They ignored her, but obeyed Jake's hasty gesture.

"Laudae, I think you should be first inside," Matteo, a Spacer scientist, offered her a torch.

Sissy gulped. What had Jilly said about Discord hiding?

"I'm right behind you, Laudae," Jake said quietly.

She knew he'd already loosened his weapons. If anything hid in the dark, he'd be on it in seconds.

"It helps if you put the torch in first and look around." Physician Gaila du Jenn pu Crystal Temple Hospital thrust her own light through the opening. The coroner was rather quiet and so caught up in her work she didn't socialize much. Sissy had hardly spoken to her.

Sissy followed suit with her own torch, then peered cautiously through the arched opening. A perfectly carved arch, not a rough natural break in the wall. The dust of the ages swirled and rose before her. She stopped breathing.

"I see color on the walls."

Enthralled she took one step into the new cavern. She had to squeeze around a tumble of smaller rocks that still clogged the entrance. Forgetting the dust, she gasped at the spectacle. Her lungs froze. She fought the cough, oblivious to the scientists who crowded in behind her, pushing her out of their way in their hurry.

Seven girls followed them, darting beneath outstretched arms to be the first ones to touch the brilliant colors painted on a smooth wall.

Jake handed Sissy an inhaler and stood by her shoulder. Together they watched as the bevy of professionals "oohed" and "aahed" over the mural that spanned a good ten feet of the fifteen-foot wall and ran from four feet off the floor nearly to the ceiling, twenty feet up.

"What is it about?" Sissy asked when she got her breathing under control. "Bella, Martha, keep your hands down. You don't know if you'll damage the paint!"

All she could see were faded splotches of rusty red, chipped sky blue, and lots of different shades of green.

"Looks like a version of the Creation," Barba said, standing back to look at the entire picture while her colleagues examined tiny portions with magnifying glasses.

"We need photos," someone shouted.

No one seemed willing to leave the spectacle to fetch the equipment. Sissy looked at Jake.

"I'm not leaving the room without you," he said quietly.

"Oh, for Harmony's sake." Sissy marched out of the room, and turned left toward the central cavern.

Two more scientists passed her, running, each with a camera in hand. They didn't even look at her, too intent on their destination to notice.

"Knowing them, two cameras won't be enough. They'll want them all," Jake grumbled. "Girls, we need your help!"

All seven of them crawled around the blockage and assembled at his side.

They returned to the new cavern, arms loaded with cameras, light bars, (the rule against artificial light had to be modified to accommodate the cameras) battery packs, and everything else they could think of that might remotely be required. The entire crowd of scientists centered on one tiny section down in the right-hand corner.

"What?" Sissy shouldered her way in and under to pop her head up in front of them all. Her eyes focused on an array of figures, each with a sacred glyph above their heads, like halos.

There was elegant Lady Harmony wearing green in the center, slightly raised above the others. Empathy, a bright male in golden robes, and Anger, a short blocky man wearing red stood to her left. Nurture, small and delicate in blue, and Greed big and flamboyant in orange to Harmony's right. Unity, a swirl of many colors and blurred outlines, and Fear, a hard knot of anxious bilious yellow knelt before Harmony. As they always did, in every icon in every Temple throughout the Empire.

The symmetry was off, though. A black figure standing just below Harmony's dais, facing out in defiance, looked as if someone had tried to chip it out, obliterate it, then been interrupted before finishing.

"Discord," Sissy breathed. "Discord included in the sacred family."

The torches smoked. Darkness crept in from the edges of her vision. Her face and hands grew cold.

She couldn't find up or down, right or left. Nothing fit or stood in place anymore.

Discord hides in the open.

◆　◆　◆

"It's done," a husky, androgynous voice whispered into Gregor's portable telephone.

"What do they think of it?" he asked, suppressing a yawn. Three hours past midnight. Dawn only a few hours away. He should be in bed. Asleep. He thrust aside the mound of paperwork he'd dallied with while waiting for this call.

"They can't agree on anything. Half cling to the old myth that the scene depicts Harmony banishing Discord. The other half are considering rewriting history."

"And the Laudae?"

"Hasn't said a word. She just sits, staring out the window. No lights on in her room, but I can see her outline in the moonlight."

"Suggest to someone who will suggest to someone else that perhaps it's time she comes home."

"That will just make her more stubborn about staying."

"I know. Amazing how peaceful the Temple is without her." Meaning how malleable the HC was without her interference. He hadn't even had to bring up the issue of Holy Day work shifts to bring Lord Chauncey back to his way of thinking.

As long as Chauncey voted the way Gregor wanted him to, Gregor would let the extra shifts work. Any deviation, and Chauncey faced heavy fines and possible removal from the HC.

Gregor stretched and yawned again. "Keep me posted. Good work. I'll arrange a bonus for you when you return."

"I want the bonus in my bank account by open of business today." The husky voice turned hard.

"That was not our agreement."

"It is now. I went to a lot of risk setting this up. Sooner or later that snoopy Military is going to try to analyze and date the paint."

"The bodyguard is supposed to be guarding Laudae Estella, not asking questions."

"Not him. The other one. The forensics officer. He's got the skills and the equipment. Next thing you know, he'll try to tell us the oldest bones are not human. He'll announce that humans came to this planet from the CSS seven hundred years ago."

Gregor froze. That was information only he and one other had access to. He'd learned it from his predecessor and been sworn to secrecy. The other one had stumbled on it accidentally.

"The money will be in your account by noon. I can't do it before then."

"Noon. No later, or I tell Laudae Sissy what you are up to."

CHAPTER FORTY-SIX

"**H**AVE YOU HEARD FROM Bethy?" Penelope demanded. She leaned across Gil's desk, giving him a spectacular view of her cleavage.

Gil gulped and pushed away his first thoughts. Almost eighteen years with this woman and he never got tired of her.

"No. She is supposed to report to you," he answered, carefully putting aside his current report. It would wait. Except that there were fifteen others beneath it awaiting his attention.

"She calls by radio relay every afternoon. But not today." Worry lines drew Penelope's mouth into a deep frown.

Gil checked his clock. Well after dinnertime. Late enough that he worried, too. "Communications in the mountains are spotty. A gathering storm could interrupt . . ."

"That hasn't stopped her in the month she's been gone."

"Oh."

"I'm worried, Gil. Gregor is up to something. If Bethy gets caught in the backlash . . . I'm scared."

"Gregor would never hurt another Temple, especially not a young girl."

"Not directly. But if Sissy outlives her usefulness to him, or he changes his mind . . . He's ruthless. And unforgiving."

"I know. I'll make inquiries." He half stood, just enough to brush her lips with his own. "At this point, no news is good news."

"Are you sure, Gil?"

"Yes," he lied.

"It's just that after the driver died, I worry. I wanted Sissy out of the Temple, not assassinated."

"I know, Penny. Sissy has requested some unusual supplies for her scientists. I need to call to verify them. I'll make sure Bethy is okay at the same time."

"Do it now."

"Now?" He surveyed the masses of paperwork left to complete before he could justify retiring for the night and act upon the invitation of Penelope's breasts.

In an instant he decided that some things were more important than paperwork. He pulled Penelope into his lap (no fear of being observed together, Gregor had gone off to a party with the HC and a few select Nobles) and the 'phone in front of him.

After many long delays, relays, and clicks and pops on the line, he managed to connect to the Temple residence in the mountains.

Bethy herself answered. "Daddy, have you heard?" she asked breathlessly.

Gil hoped her shallow breathing was excitement and hurry and not the thin mountain air affecting her lungs.

"Heard what, sweetheart?" He tried to picture his daughter in her current location and only came up with the memory of the day she'd proudly displayed a gap in her mouth when she lost her first milk tooth; all bright smiles and dark curls floppy about her round baby face as she bounced about the room.

Penelope rested her head against his, listening as closely as he.

"We've found a truly ancient mural. It's got some . . . anomalies. Is that the right word?" She asked the latter in an aside.

"Anomaly sounds correct. So you've been too busy to call home. What kind of anomalies?"

"I'm not supposed to say until Laudae Sissy makes a formal announcement."

"And who do you suppose is going to write up the report she announces?" He had to smile.

"But, Daddy!"

"Tell him, sweetie," Penelope coaxed.

"Hi, Mama, I should have known you ordered Daddy to call."

"Stop stalling and tell us, Bethy," Gil commanded.

She did.

He went absolutely still inside. Something was wrong. He couldn't put his finger on it. Just something out of place. He needed to . . . to what? Dig up the original Covenant Stones?

Not a bad idea. Then he groaned at the amount of work required to get that to happen. Unless he found a back entrance into the chamber. Jake had suggested the corridor outside the archive basement.

Penelope ran her fingers through his hair.

The Covenant Stones had been hidden away for centuries. They'd wait another day.

"Be careful, Bethy," he warned, very uneasy in his mid region. "This is dangerous information. The 'no bones' cult might take this as a license to make Discord an equal to Harmony."

"I know, Daddy. That's why Laudae Sissy doesn't want us talking about it to anybody. So you'd better not tell anyone either. Even Laud Gregor, until Laudae Sissy says so."

"Our lips are sealed, Bethy. Watch your step and your back. You never know who up there has a different agenda from Laudae Sissy."

✦   ✦   ✦

"I need your help," Colonel Jeoff da George pa Law Enforcement HQ H Prime whispered in Jake's ear.

Jake pretended to startle out of a light doze. He never slept hard, less so now that he guarded Sissy day and night, taking what rest he could on a cot placed across the door to Sissy's bedroom. He'd charted Jeoff's quiet footsteps from the moment he entered the residence wing of the Temple.

Jeoff's hand covered his mouth, just enough to keep him from crying out.

"What?" Jake mouthed against the hand.

Jeoff motioned Jake to follow. On silent stockinged feet they threaded their way through Sissy's sitting room crowded with sleeping acolytes. Jake carried his boots.

Once outside the residence, Jeoff sat on the stoop to pull on his own boots. Jake sat beside him to do the same. Chill mountain air cut through the thick cloth of his uniform, sending goose bumps up his arms. He yawned and shivered slightly, more to put the colonel off guard than to express his own discomfort.

Jeoff was young for his advanced rank. Not more than mid-forties. Still vigorous and strong, with a full head of tight sandy-blond curls and only the beginnings of a middle-aged spread around his gut. This guy worked in the field as much as at his desk. Someone to be wary of.

"What?" Jake asked again, this time aloud.

"I need a closer look at some of those bones, without mind-blind Temple enthusiasts peering over my shoulder."

"So go look. Who's stopping you. It's three in the effing morning." Another yawn. This one real.

"I can't do it alone. I need good lights and someone to hold them for me. Someone to bear witness that I'm not tainting the evidence I find." Jeoff heaved himself upright.

Jake continued sitting, playing with getting his boots on just right. Stalling for more information. "What do you expect to find?"

"That the oldest bones, everything over five hundred years, are not human. And that those at the five hundred mark were slaughtered. By human weapons."

"Let's go." Jake smiled. At last. Someone more interested in the truth than faith. His agenda just took a baby step forward. The next step would be to convince Sissy. "You might also want to date the paint on that controversial mural."

"Started the chemical analysis an hour ago. Do you know something I should know?"

"Don't want to taint your tests. Let the facts speak for themselves."

"You aren't just a bodyguard."

"I am a bodyguard. Now."

"And before?"

"Law Enforcement HQ H Prime, before that on H6." He didn't add that he'd only been on H6 three weeks before coming here.

"There is something more you are not telling me. I'll figure it out. I always figure it out. I have a one hundred percent success rate at solving crimes based upon forensic evidence."

"Then look at the evidence and let it tell you everything you need to know." Jake hoisted to his shoulder a battery operated light bar from Jeoff's pile of equipment and headed uphill.

The local clergy weren't happy about all the electric equipment going in and out of the caves. Sissy's command to give the scientists every tool available overrode their objections. Barely.

Something about desecrating the dead. Not fanatical "no bones" but worth watching. He had Morrie da Hawk doing background checks on them from the city data banks.

Jeoff followed Jake with a big black suitcase and another light bar. He handed Jake the suitcase that measured nearly a meter square. "I outrank you. I think. At least play at being my subordinate. And I'll run a DNA test on you in the morning. Just to make sure you are as human as I am."

"I can guarantee you that I am as human as you are," Jake said behind a smile."

✦   ✦   ✦

Gregor parked the little dark blue electric car in front of the comm tower. The spot was reserved for the colonel, but he wasn't about to need it at three in the morning.

A single light glimmered in an upper-story window. His listener was hard at work, deciphering the coded messages recorded throughout the day.

The CSS tried hard to mask their signals. They changed codes and frequencies often. Gregor's technician was only half a step behind them. He always caught up. And he was an absolute genius cryptographer. He'd even broken the Maril language. Something the CSS had yet to do.

Gregor used the top secret code on the keypad beside the door to unlock it and deactivate the alarms. He wasn't supposed to have that code.

Who would question the HP of all Harmony? He had a right to every secret in the empire. He had the right to keep some of them secret, too.

At the foot of the stairs Gregor slipped off his shoes. As a top military facility this building warranted the energy expenditure of an elevator. He chose the stairs, up to the tall seventh story. No sense alerting his listener to his presence with the sounds of mechanics.

Counting every step as if his life depended upon keeping track, Gregor pulled himself slowly upward, pacing himself. At the fourth floor he began to sweat. By the fifth he breathed hard. At the sixth he had to stop and wait for his lungs and heart to catch up with him. He hated getting old. No matter how fit he kept himself, the years kept taking their toll. A little here and little more there. Pretty soon the Temple would begin to whisper he had outlived his usefulness as High Priest.

Not yet. He had too much to do before he retired or died.

But the cryptographer had outlived his usefulness.

If Gregor could just get the HC to agree to his plans, he'd have the Lost Colony back under control, the frontier secured, and life could continue on Harmony as it had always done: with a High Priestess with Harmony's gift of prophecy and every member of every caste firmly in place, obedient to the Temple and Harmony's Covenant.

Then he could rest, retire gracefully to a beach cabin on the Southern Continent and spend his days sailing and fishing. No exile to the archives for him. He'd not finish his days as a ghostly husk wandering those dusty halls.

Time to get moving, before the city awoke.

He climbed the last set of stairs and listened at the insulated door. No sounds penetrated. He pushed it open, muffling the sound of its heavy closing behind him with a handkerchief. Almost as an afterthought he retrieved the square of white cloth.

He stepped into a narrow corridor lined with offices. Light shone beneath the door at the corner room. This time he loosed the thin blade from his belt sheath before opening the door. Electronics bleeped and blinked. His listener sat hunched over a computer screen humming lightly to himself.

The tune grated on Gregor's nerves. Sissy's hymn of thanksgiving that she sang at the closing of her brother's wedding ritual. He hated that tune.

Two more silent steps and he whipped the knife across the man's throat.

Blood spurted forward and sideways. The listener slumped into lifelessness. Gregor remained behind him, until the blood finished spraying. He couldn't have any trace on himself or his clothing.

"You couldn't keep your mouth shut. You had to tell someone what you overheard on CSS chatter," he sneered at the dead man. "No one, absolutely no one, can know that we are of the same blood stock as the CSS. Human life arose on this planet, with Harmony's Covenant intact, and nowhere else," he muttered.

Out of long habit he spoke a prayer for the departing soul as he printed out all of the latest reports. Then he removed all traces of the long-distance listening and his name from the man's equipment.

He wiped the military issue knife clean of his fingerprints and pressed it into the listener's hand. A cursory examination would look like suicide. If they decided murder, and they had a way of tracing the weapon, they'd find it came from Laudae Estella's bodyguard. But all those Military knives were alike.

Then he typed a note of regret into the man's computer, turned out the light, and returned to the elevator. His need for silence was gone. No sense in taxing his body further by walking down the stairs.

CHAPTER FORTY-SEVEN

SISSY TOSSED AND TURNED with endless nightmares of Discord popping up and poking his bony fingers into her back, tangling in her hair, tickling her feet. And with every touch came sharp electric shocks through her body that reflected the disruption and chaos throughout Harmony. She flinched, and factories closed. Workers were thrown out of work. She cried in pain, and riots erupted over a shortage of food. On and on until Discord ruled Harmony.

Sissy/Harmony could no longer spread her wings to fly away or give blessings.

A noise brought her out of the depths of her dreams in a cold sweat.

Bleary-eyed and anxious, she heard Jake tiptoe away from her door.

Something in the furtiveness of his step chased away the dream fog of unreality. She followed him and Colonel Jeoff up the hill.

"What are you doing, Jake?" Sissy asked when she caught up with them.

Jake jumped away from his crouch over one of the niches in the newest cavern. The one with the disturbing mural that had interrupted her sleep with nightmares.

It looked like they were desecrating some of the oldest bones in the complex, dismembering them under the unholy blaring lights.

"Crap," Jake sputtered. He stood straight and tried to stand between Sissy and whatever Jeoff was doing. "Laudae, what are you doing up?"

"I couldn't sleep. Apparently neither could you. What are you doing? I will not tolerate disrespect for our ancestors." She moved forward, fists clenching and unclenching.

How could Jake do this? She had trusted him with her life! Now he betrayed that trust by . . . by . . .

"These aren't our ancestors," Jeoff said, rising slowly from his stooped examination. He held up a long slender bone, no thicker than one of her crystal wands. Much too skinny compared to other bones of that length she had blessed and relocated over the past month.

"Put that back!" Sissy demanded.

"Why? It's just the wing finger bone of a juvenile animal," Jeoff shrugged.

"Something akin to a Maril," Jake added. "The only ones we've seen . . . out on H6 at the edge of civilization, have wings that are just long flaps of skin beneath their arms, no longer needing the elongated fingers to support them. But that's the warrior class that travels off planet. Who's to say the ones they left at home don't have fully developed wings."

"This can't be true! Why would our ancestors bury aliens in their sacred ground?" Sissy felt faint with outrage.

"Because our ancestors weren't even here a thousand years ago," Jake said quietly. "We came from somewhere else and settled this place. There were only a few Marils here. We conquered them and made the place our own."

"No. No, no, no, no." Sissy sat down hard upon the uneven cave floor. Her entire world rocked. She couldn't focus her eyes or her thoughts.

And yet that disturbing mural showed Harmony with arms raised, her gown flowing away like wings . . .

"Have you got enough evidence, Jeoff?" Jake asked even as he bent over Sissy, testing her pulse and handing her an inhaler, if she needed it.

Sissy slapped his hand away. "How can this be?"

"Don't know. But it is. There are no human bones anywhere in this cave older than five hundred years," Jeoff said. He carefully placed an entire skeleton into a special box, bone by bone.

"The other caves . . ."

"I doubt you'll find anything different there," Jeoff said.

"Our civilization is older than five hundred years . . ." Sissy insisted.

"Is it?" Jake asked quietly. He remained kneeling beside her, ready to assist her in any way she wanted. Except in giving her the answers she wanted.

"You've never lied to me before, Jake."

He remained silent.

She searched his face and posture for clues. "You aren't lying to me now. You truly believe this."

"Yes, My Laudae."

Was there a special significance to the way he said her title, almost like he caressed the words with his mouth?

"If you have scientific proof of what you say, Jeoff . . ."

"I do, Laudae. Or I will as soon as I can get to my lab in the city."

"I will see this proof. None of us are to utter one word of this discovery to anyone. I'll have your heads if I hear the faintest whisper of a rumor."

"I will need three days for the analysis," Jeoff said. And I do believe that mural is a fake. I'm running the chemicals to date the paint."

"If the mural is a fake, or has been altered, then someone is manipulating you, Laudae," Jake added.

"Someone wants me to decree that Discord is equal to the other gods and not just a demon. Why, Jake? To what purpose?"

"I don't know, Laudae. But the answers do not lie here."

"They lie in the stone tablets beneath the altar in the Crystal Temple." She sat a moment longer, thoughts skittering here and there like a kitten chasing a dust ball. "We leave at dawn."

"I'll notify . . ."

"Tell no one. The girls can follow us later in the day. I want this mission to continue. Laudae Shanet can bless the transfer and consolidation of bones. Whoever is trying to alter our faith needs to be surprised by my return to the Temple." And this new theory about Marils needed to be kept secret.

✦   ✦   ✦

"Laudae Sissy wished me to inform you that she has returned to Crystal Temple," Guilliam intoned from the doorway of Gregor's office.

The need for sleep tugged at Gregor's muscles as the hour neared afternoon refreshment. But he jumped and started at every sound, too nervous to settle until he'd heard through normal media channels an official verdict on the death at the Military facility. No evidence existed to trace back to him. Yet the Military forensics teams had made enormous strides in solving the increasing number of murders and other violent crimes throughout the empire.

How? Why had violence become a normal part of their society in the last twenty-five years?

So violent had they become that he doubted he could mention in public an offer of peace and trade from the CSS.

"Laudae *Estella* was supposed to inform me six days before leaving the mountains," Gregor frowned at his acolyte in disapproval.

"She didn't. She's here."

"Why?"

"You'll have to ask her."

"So I shall. Bring her here."

"Um . . . I don't believe I can do that." The man looked too damn smug. He knew something. Gregor needed to know what. Right now.

"Why not?" Anger boiled in Gregor. He fought it down. He couldn't allow his fatigue and nervousness to color his actions.

"Because she has ordered a construction team to open the High Altar."

"What!" Gregor exploded upward, covering the distance to the doorway in three long strides. He resisted the urge to throttle Guilliam with his bare hands. The man cowered away from him. That was enough to satisfy him. It had to be.

One murder he could get away with. Could explain away to soothe his conscience. Two he could not justify. To himself, to the world, or to the gods.

"The High Altar is sacred space. It may not be violated by anyone. Not even the High Priestess."

"Laudae Sissy seems to think otherwise."

"Then you will have to change her mind."

"Not in the mood she's in, My Laud. It's not worth my life. But if you would sign my transfer to one of the outer colonies, I'll consider talking to her."

"Your life isn't worth the trouble." Gregor stomped past his assistant. "Summon every priest and priestess in the place. And all of their acolytes. I want witnesses to this."

"Laudae Sissy has already done so, My Laud. A crowd of Workers and Professionals has gathered around the fence to watch. I've spotted three hover cams inside the fence and two more outside."

Gregor chilled as all of his blood rushed away from his head and his hands into his feet. He couldn't allow his plans to come to naught all for a headstrong girl.

A girl he had elevated to the highest position in all of Harmony.

He'd raised her. He *would* bring her down if he had to.

✦   ✦   ✦

"I's sorry, My Laudae," Shan da Gan pa Darrell of the Worker caste said quietly. He shuffled his feet and held his soft cloth cap in his hands. With every word he rotated the cap, as if studying the brim would ease his burden. "I can't do as you ask. I's sorry."

"Why not?" Sissy wanted desperately to hold on to her anger. In the face of the man's misery she could only empathize with his plight. With half of Harmony City watching through the fence, and the other half through the hover cam that circled the altar, she needed to maintain an aura of calm and Nurture. She wore her majestic robes, but had left off her masking headdress, wanting no doubt in anyone's mind who had ordered the altar opened.

"T'aint right, My Laudae. The High Altar, she be sum'at special. To tear her apart . . . cain't do it."

"I'm not asking you to tear it apart. All I want is access to the stone tablets beneath it." Sissy tapped her foot impatiently. Surely there was some way around this man's superstition.

"The man is right," Laud Gregor called from the entrance to the forecourt. "The High Altar cannot be tampered with. Ever. For any reason." He sounded as angry as Sissy had been when Jeoff had told her the black paint around Discord on the mural was only days old. The rest of the mural dated back over a thousand years. And yet the oldest human bones in the caves were indeed only five hundred years old.

Contradiction piled upon contradiction upon fakery upon malice.

And the hover cam recorded it all.

With an effort, Sissy drew herself up as tall as she could stand. If all of Harmony watched her today, then she had to show them something special. She pulled all of her previous prophecies to the front of her mind. There were a few for which she couldn't remember the exact words; others near blinded her with clarity.

She touched the altar with her fingertips for confidence. Let the world know why she had been chosen by Harmony as the High Priestess.

"I am the harbinger of change," she said quietly. The world seemed to still around her. The hover cam focused in on her. "Better to control the trickle of change than clean up after the flood."

Jake held his breath as Sissy spoke. Her eyes remained clear of starshine. But . . . but the moment she touched the altar, a blue glitter seemed to cover her lightly.

Electric sparks left over from the lightning on the day of her ordination, he told himself. That was all it could be.

Wasn't it?

The hover cam backed off, changing the lens opening rapidly, trying to focus on something elusive.

A disconcerted gasp ran around the crowd of Workers, Professionals, and Temple who had gathered to watch the battle of wills.

The moment Sissy lifted her hand, he rushed to her side, ready to hold her up, carry her if necessary.

She remained standing, glaring at Laud Gregor, or was she flaying him with her eyes.

Jake placed a hand discreetly under her elbow. She slapped it away. "I am not an invalid," she hissed at him.

He backed off. So did the camera.

Laudae Penelope stepped forward from the knot of HC members. They seemed to have pushed her. All of them together or just one of them? If only one, which one?

Her delicate perfume floated before her, something earthy and enticing. Artificial. She reminded him a lot of Pamela Marella, in her posture, her physique, and her artifice.

He suddenly lost all sense of attraction to either woman, though they were both damned beautiful. Sissy's own natural scent of flowers and greenery filled his senses and his needs.

He wondered briefly if the watchers recognized the essential difference between the two women. Natural or artificial, confident or pompous, caring or self-centered.

Then Penelope did the totally unexpected. She melted back into the throng of the HC and pushed forward the two men who stood to either side of Lady Marissa. Noble twin sons who aided Marissa much as Guilliam worked for Gregor.

"I won't be the puppet of the HC any longer. I won't take the blame for their hatred," Penelope said, just loud enough for those in the forecourt to hear, but not beyond to those at the fence.

What about the ever-present hover cam? It still focused tightly on Sissy.

Marissa's son, no telling which one glared at Penelope, no more happy to be the mouthpiece of the HC than she was. The other kept his eyes on the ground.

Number One took a deep breath, straightened his shoulders, and faced the center of the forecourt squarely. "If you, Miss Sissy, can't control and contain coming changes," the man said, pointing accusingly at Sissy, "we will remove the Lood taint from the sacred Temple. By force if necessary."

Not on my watch, Jake growled to himself.

How was he supposed to do that if he planned to leave Harmony?

CHAPTER FORTY-EIGHT

S **ISSY FORGOT TO BREATHE.**
Silence descended upon the courtyard, like a heavy blanket soaked in ice water. Sissy heard Jake loosen his sword in its sheath. No one else moved.

Finally, Laud Gregor drew in a deep breath. He turned on the entire HC with eyes blazing and fists clenched. "You are dismissed, Penelope. As are you, Bevan and Lukan." No titles.

Sissy had the feeling something important had just happened.

"You haven't the authority . . ." Penelope protested.

"But Laud Gregor and I combined do," Lady Marissa said. Her sweet voice wafted over them all like a warm breeze, removing the ice in Sissy's veins.

The hover cam zipped over to her.

"Get that damned thing out of my face," Lady Marissa screamed. She flung her arms out. Her right fist punched the vulnerable lens and smacked the device into one of the crystal columns.

It connected with a loud crack that sent shivers through Sissy. Then the camera flopped to the ground. The lens fell out and shattered.

The column looked undamaged.

Lady Marissa relaxed her face from ugly viciousness to calm grace.

"But . . . but . . . I've refused to be their mouthpiece any more," Penelope spluttered. She looked anxiously toward Marissa's twin sons for support. All three were victims of someone else's prejudice and ambition.

Fully recovered from her temper tantrum, Lady Marissa smiled sweetly. "Best retire with dignity while you can, girl." She patted Penelope's hand as if she were a child and not a fully grown and mature woman old enough to be Sissy's mother. Marissa jerked her head at her two tall sons to follow their cousin.

"Good advice," Jake whispered into Sissy's ear. "This discussion should be conducted in private."

"No, it shouldn't be kept private," Bevan, one of Marissa's twins, announced to the crowd. "The world needs to know that High Priest Gregor prefers a Lood as his High Priestess to a woman who was born to the Temple, raised and educated to the Temple, and who has achieved a sacred seven times seven years."

"My Laudae," Guilliam stepped up behind Penelope. His proprietary hand on her waist suggested a long intimacy that surprised Sissy. "My Laudae, if confidence in the Temple is shaken by this encounter, then a major alteration has occurred. She will truly be the harbinger of change. Of chaos. She will have won and you lost. Irrevocably."

Penelope stood for a long moment her mouth opening and closing soundlessly.

Sissy breathed deeply. She had never doubted that Guilliam ran the day-to-day events of the Temple. Now, she realized he was much more. He was the anchor around which that life in the Temple revolved. He maintained a solid column of stability and whispered wisdom where it was needed, when it was needed. The rest of them merely reacted to his prodding.

She found humor there. For all of Penelope's and Gregor's pretensions, Guilliam was the true power here.

If Guilliam knew so much, then he probably could open the High Altar without construction tools or damaging the crystal. What else did he know and keep secret?

She should have gone to him first.

Penelope whirled about and stalked back through the tunnel toward the Temple interior with Lukan and Bevan following in her wake.

"We will discuss this in Council Chamber," Bevan called from the archway that framed his tall figure majestically.

"Now is the time to speak to the HC," Jake whispered.

Sissy almost laughed. As Guilliam advised and manipulated Gregor and Penelope, so Jake did the same for her. And Marissa's sons advised their mother.

"Must I remind the High Council that our meetings are private, and outsiders are forbidden to speak?" Sissy said. She fixed Laud Gregor and Lady Marissa with a fierce gaze. "Laudae Penelope and Lady Marissa's sons are not members of the High Council."

"Neither is your bodyguard." Lady Marissa looked at Jake as if she feared him. Her right eye twitched and she drew her right hand into a tight fist.

Murmurs of discontent whisked through the crowd beyond the fence like a whirlwind. A handheld camera flashed again and again.

"My bodyguard does not speak in Council. He enters the chamber only to ensure my safety. If you will guarantee with your life that no harm comes to me during the meetings, he will remain outside the doors." Sissy tried hard to keep her chin from trembling in fear. Jake had reminded her often that only a Noble could afford a large, dark blue car and throw an illegal concussion grenade from it.

The crowd pressed closer to the fence. Ghoulish gawkers feeding on the negative emotions, or concerned onlookers ready to defend her?

"My Lords and Ladies, Lauds and Laudaes, this is not the time or place—" Gregor insisted. With a gesture he began herding them all back toward the tunnel. Guilliam became his sheepdog standing behind the various factions and pressing them in the correct direction.

"Harmony bless you, Laudae Sissy!" someone shouted from the depths of the crowd.

"Keep her safe, Military, or answer to us!"

Shouts of agreement rose and echoed against the crystal columns. "Sissy! Our Sissy!" The noise filled the courtyard more completely than a dozen glass wands chiming against the altar crystals.

Then a new shout erupted from the front of the crowd. "Show us the tablets!"

✦   ✦   ✦

Jake paced nervously before the entrance to the HC Chamber. Penelope sat in a thronelike chair three meters down the corridor. She twitched and fidgeted as if lasers pricked her butt. Was she in trouble for working with the HC against Sissy? Or for refusing to do so any longer? And what had changed her mind?

He didn't even know if he was supposed to address her as Laudae anymore. Not that he dared not use the title if he spoke to her.

She'd tried to enter the chamber with the rest of the HC. A single glare from Gregor to Guilliam and the assistant had gently touched her arm and her waist to escort her to the throne.

Then Guilliam had disappeared down a side corridor shortly thereafter.

Lady Marissa's sons were nowhere in sight. So were they banished or not in trouble at all?

For that matter, why did any of the HC need assistants to speak for them? Probably so no one of them would take the blame if their plots backfired.

Too many players. Not enough intel.

The intimacy of Guilliam's touch upon Penelope had not escaped Jake.

Right now, he was more concerned with Sissy than the convoluted relationships. He heard murmurs and shouts through the thick doors. All undecipherable. At least the High Priestess had donned her elaborate crystal headdress before making a grand entrance into the chamber. She needed to assert her authority with these martinets.

If only he had a simple handheld computer, he'd sensitize the internal receivers and listen remotely.

Penelope looked impatiently down the side passage Guilliam had taken. Hmmm.

Guilliam knew of back tunnels and secret rooms.

He might very well have sophisticated listening devices planted in every room. Including the HC Chamber.

If Gregor had access to the listening post in space that intercepted messages through the CSS, then it stood to reason that his assistant had access to similar ground-based equipment.

The continuation of calm murmurs assured him that the discussion inside wasn't about to explode into violence. He decided to explore a bit and find Guilliam.

He lengthened his route of pacing. No sense in alerting Penelope of his intent.

"You won't find him," she said bitterly as he made his third pass. One more and he'd include the side corridor as a natural extension of his path.

"I beg your pardon, Laudae?" He opened his eyes wide, like Sissy did, trying to appear innocent.

"We've all tried to follow Gil, looking for his observation post. He just disappears." She shrugged and went back to her fidgeting.

"Secret passages?" Jake asked, again trying for innocence. He knew damn well how to find at least one of them. Maybe others.

"Probably. The place is a weasel's nest."

"Intriguing." Jake sauntered down the old hallway. Now he knew what to look for. He'd find Guilliam come vacuum or radiation. Or both.

The corridor narrowed as it skirted behind the HC Chamber. The electric light panels became more widely spaced. The light wood paneling, pervasive in the rest of the Temple, gave way to dark stones. Massive stones mortared together. They looked a lot more ancient than five or even seven hundred years. Like maybe the original colonists had usurped an older building after they slaughtered the inhabitants.

Jake felt as if the walls closed in around him. The dim light took on weight and texture. His breathing became strained. He kept his left hand on the wall that should be the back side of the chamber. His right hand he wanted free to pull his sword.

About halfway to where the hallway ended in a sharp corner, he pressed his ear against the stones on his left. A quiet susurration of sound; the murmur of voices. The HC continuing their discussion or the memories of an ancient people trapped in stone?

He shook off the superstitious nonsense and proceeded to the end. To his left, he found another of the ubiquitous small alcoves with a neglected altar. Cobwebs connected every surface to the stones. It reminded him of holovids of ancient castles back on Earth.

Guilliam had used a similar one to access the basement tunnels.

Jake turned back to the altar.

Strange. He'd seen a lot of dust, lots of insects. But no spiders. Whatever made these cobwebs seemed unique to this particular spot. Was the atavistic fear of arachnids so ingrained in racial memory that Harmonites shied away from cobwebs even though they knew nothing of spiders?

He released his stiletto from his arm sheath and gingerly touched the stringy mass with the tip. It remained intact, like a synthetic fiber. He swapped the stiletto for an edged boot knife. That blade sliced through the sticky web easily and wrapped around the knife like a bandage. Hmmmm. Shredded bandage fiber with its self-stick adhesive still ingrained.

A few moments later Jake had cleared away all of the web. Tufts of it clung to his uniform, his hair, the backs of his hands. Along with a lot of dust. Great piles of the stuff. Artificial piles of it meant to deter a finicky investigator, like Penelope. A lot of Temple folk, mostly the ordained clergy, seemed deathly afraid of getting their hands dirty.

Once clear of debris, Jake spent several minutes moving the crystals atop the altar, feeling under the lip of the top piece, shoving at the plinth and the main column of the structure. Then he stepped back and frowned.

Guilliam would want quick and easy access to anything behind the altar. He wouldn't want to disturb his camouflage. So . . . Jake shifted his attention to the walls surrounding the altar. Was that just a crack in the mortar or the outline of a low door?

Jake squeezed between the altar and the wall. Guilliam was about his own height, but bulkier of build. He'd be hard-pressed to push his middle-aged belly through here. Jake just barely fit in the space. No one would suspect Guilliam could slide in here.

This place must be important.

A little pressure on the wall beside the crack and it swung inward on well-oiled hinges.

"Eureka!" Jake almost shouted. Then he remembered his need for stealth. He slipped inside and waited for his eyes to adjust to the brighter light that flashed on the moment the door swung shut behind him.

He found himself in a small room, not much bigger than the altar alcove. Three walls were covered with the flickering lights of monitor screens. Twelve in all. Each showed the activity in a different room. Including the HC Chamber.

No Guilliam. No room for another exit. This must be only one of many observation posts.

A quick glance showed Sissy standing at the long Council table. The crystals on her veil clanked together as she moved her head right and left. The crystals chimed louder than her words. Guilliam needed a better microphone.

"How can we know our entire faith is not based on a lie if we do not have the original tablets to consult?" she asked.

"We have copies in the archives," Gregor said mildly. His face had a studied blank look that Jake knew meant he was lying.

"How do we know the copies are true and accurate?" Sissy insisted. She placed her clenched hands on the table and leaned forward.

"You doubt the integrity of our people!" Gregor shouted. He stood up, trying to convey outrage. But his shoulders were too relaxed.

"Give me a reason to have as much faith in them as I do in all seven of our gods." Sissy stared him down. "Show me the copies. Bring them forth for all the people to read and inspect. Do it every Holy Day. If you hide them, then you have a reason to keep them secret."

"Perhaps so you can change the rules as you deem necessary?" Lady Marissa cocked one eyebrow at the High Priest.

"The copies are old. Fragile. Exposure to the air will damage them irrevocably," Gregor protested.

"Then why aren't there copies of the copies?" Lady Marissa continued. She sounded as if this were just a mild discussion of what flowers to put in the centerpiece at dinner.

"Wonder why we never thought we needed to read the Covenant before?" Lord Nathaniel asked.

No one listened to him. The others kept their rapt attention on the three leaders at the head of the table.

"I am going to the archives now. Your clerks do not have the authority to hide anything from me. I will see these copies. All of them. New and old. I shall compare them for discrepancies." Sissy marched toward the door.

"Good on you, My Laudae," Jake murmured.

Oops, he'd better hurry back, sticky web, dirt and all. He needed to be beside Sissy every step of the way. Make sure she understood what she read. And keep Laud Gregor from slipping in a forgery.

Or slipping a knife between her ribs.

CHAPTER FORTY-NINE

S ISSY TAPPED HER FOOT impatiently. "And you wonder why I distrust your archivist?" she said quietly to Laud Gregor.

Dust filled her nose and threatened her breathing. Books and piles of
paper littered every surface, piled haphazardly, teetering on the brink of
falling. Even ancient rolls tied with bits of fraying ribbon had been tossed
carelessly into the jumble. The archivist and his method for finding anything were apparently absent.

Tall, gaunt, and balding, he looked as if he never saw the blessed light
of Empathy and ate knowledge rather than food.

He bore an uncanny resemblance to what Laud Gregor would look
like in twenty years.

"How do you find anything in here?" Lady Marissa asked. She and
Lord Nathaniel were the only members of the High Council who had
followed Sissy and Gregor to the archives in the very back of the oldest
part of the Temple. Lord Chauncey seemed to be avoiding Sissy at all
costs.

"Apparently they remember where they put everything and don't
need to keep records," Lord Nathaniel quipped, then spoiled the humor
by coughing. He doubled over in an uncontrollable spasm.

Jake handed him one of Sissy's inhalers. The old man took it gratefully.
Then he hobbled out, using his cane and Lady Marissa's arm to keep him
upright.

"It seems the High Council does not agree with your need to read the
copies of the Covenant," Laud Gregor said mildly. He kept the infuriat-
ingly blank look on his face, betraying no emotion.

"I expect to see those copies on my desk by dinnertime," Sissy said
curtly. Angry at her repeated failure to accomplish anything, she spun
about with a clank of the crystals in her veil and marched back the way
they had come.

At the first junction of corridors she turned to Jake and whispered, "I'm lost."

"To the left, I think. There's more light down that way." He pointed to where the massive stonework gave way to lighter woods, big windows, and well spaced lights.

"What do I do now?" she asked the air, not really expecting an answer.

"Wait until everyone is asleep," Jake replied.

"You know something?" She kept walking, making sure her voice didn't carry beyond his ears.

"I suspect something. We'll investigate the High Altar in privacy. There should be a spring or hidden door to access the tablets. Or possibly a door from the basement."

"There are basements?" Sissy shuddered. She'd heard of basements and the filth they hid. "And you discovered this how?" She looked at the dust and globs of white stuck to him in odd places.

"Let's just say the Temple building has as many secrets as its inhabitants."

"I believe that."

✦   ✦   ✦

"Guilliam?"

"Yes, My Laud?" The assistant appeared at Gregor's elbow, just as he knew he would.

"Talk to the archivist and all his clerks. I want all copies of the Covenant rounded up and on my desk in one hour. No more. Less time would be preferable."

"Will you take the copies to Laudae Sissy?"

"Not until I have read them all and corrected any mistakes." Mistakes that deviated from what he knew was best for Harmony.

"Yes, My Laud. While I take care of that, Admiral Nentares da Andromeda pa HQ H Prime awaits you in your office." Guilliam scuttled off into the bowels of the archives.

"The head of the Spacer caste? What does he want?"

"You'll have to ask him," came Guilliam's disembodied voice from behind a tall case containing a haphazard collection of rolled documents and dusty books.

Gregor mumbled and grumbled to himself as he wended his way back to his office. He formulated exact phrases to counter any accusations that might arise. He'd heard nothing about the deceased communications officer. The Spacers had not seen fit to release that information to the media.

"What's with that verbal dustup in the courtyard?" Admiral Nentares asked the moment he and Gregor shook hands. A man near Gregor's age with a full head of brown hair, cropped short. He had the slight build of his caste, a more efficient metabolism and compact size for convenience in long-term space travel in cramped ship quarters. Gregor towered over him, yet he almost felt the need to salute his overwhelming aura of command.

"A minor disagreement over proper ritual procedure," Gregor dismissed the "dustup" easily. The entire city probably knew the minute details by now. He refused to acknowledge them; refused to give the media that kind of control over Temple. What he decreed as truth was the truth, no matter what the hover cams reported.

"What brings you here, Admiral?" Gregor took his seat behind his desk and waved the admiral to the less comfortable chair before it. He wanted the symbols of authority and hierarchy in place.

"Two things. First, you know that we have equipment and personnel monitoring deep space communications." The admiral sat stiffly, his back never touching the chair. "Redundant systems."

"I have heard rumors of such."

The admiral raised his eyebrows slightly. Did he know that Gregor had thumbprint-sealed detailed reports on his desk every day? He did until an unfortunate comm technician died. He'd have to find a replacement.

"We have deciphered anomalies in the communications of our enemies," Nentares said. He kept his voice level and his eyes probing Gregor.

"What kind of anomalies?" Gregor sat forward, hands clasped. "New assaults on our frontier?"

"We have noted a serious buildup of Maril fleets, almost the beginnings of a blockade. What concerns me more is that the CSS has sent an offer of peace, and the opportunity to consult with them on neutral territory."

"Bah, we don't need them." He'd had that report three days ago and decided to ignore it. "We don't care about a blockade of our frontier. We are self-sufficient."

"Apparently the Lost Colony cares."

Everything inside Gregor stilled.

"The Lost Colony hasn't been heard from since they entered hyperspace three years ago. A tragic accident."

"You and I both know the Lost Colony cut off communications deliberately. They arrived at their destination and set up housekeeping independent of us. They have thrown off the caste system and elected a republican government."

"Blasphemy!"

"Blasphemy that the Lost Colony has rejected the caste system, or is it blasphemy that I know about it?" the admiral quirked half a smile.

Gregor allowed silence to speak for him.

The admiral met him stare for stare, silence for silence. At last Gregor had to say something to keep the turmoil in his gut from exploding.

"The fact that you dare ask the question tells me how far you have strayed from Harmony's Covenant. Have you knelt in prayer and lit a candle to the gods this day?" Gregor assumed his most patriarchal demeanor. "We can retire to a private chapel."

"I make my prayers diligently every morning," Nentares snarled. "With a priest who understands Spacer ways and has seen the frontier. A priest who knows that the CSS are as human as you and I and not the hideous snake monsters you pretend."

"The populace needs to know only that the CSS are as much the enemy as the Marils. Both are alien to our way of life."

"Granted. Which brings me to the second matter of concern. Another way in which life on Harmony has strayed from the path of the Covenant." Nentares fixed Gregor with a new look that he could not interpret.

But Gregor knew what was coming. He leaned back in his comfortable chair and crossed one leg over the other, ankle to knee, assuming a more casual air. The better to belie his nervousness. There was no law that could touch him if Nentares somehow proved that he had murdered the comm technician. But if it became known, then public confidence in him, in the Temple caste as a whole, would be shaken and possibly irreparably damaged. "Tell me what troubles you."

"One of my communications officers was murdered last night."

Only last night? It seemed a lifetime ago.

"Unfortunately, murder and other violent crimes are on the rise," Gregor said with eyes closed as if in grief. "I blame it on the increasing number of Loods among us. They should be euthanized at birth."

"Including your new High Priestess?"

"That is one we are lucky we missed."

"What others are we lucky we missed?"

Another long silence. Gregor didn't have to explain himself. To anyone.

"My scientists tell me that the number of genetic anomalies born each year increases. My caste incorporates them into our population."

"Research into this area is forbidden. So is failure to report the anomalies." Gregor's foot across his knee began to twitch. He planted it on the floor. Firmly.

"Try and catch us with legal evidence," Nentares replied.

Another long silence. Admiral Nentares broke it this time. "The officer who was murdered. His assailant tried to make it look like suicide."

"Oh?" Best not to say anything lest he inadvertently betray himself.

"Typed a suicide note on the man's computer. But it contained a grave spelling error."

"Surely a man in the throes of extreme distress cannot be responsible for his spelling."

"This was one word the man would not misspell, but someone from another caste would."

"Such as?"

"His pa assignment in his name."

Gulp.

"Do you have suspects? Motive?"

"We do. But no proof. Whoever entered the secure building knew the pass code and knew enough to wear gloves. No fingerprints."

"Weapon?"

"A common knife available anywhere in the city. Left at the scene."

"I can see why this concerns you. A drastic breach of security. But why bring it to me? If you need help with the investigation, I'm sure the Military forensic people will assist."

"The murderer deleted some files from the computer. But he did not reformat the hard drive. We recovered them."

Gulp.

"They were top secret files designated for your eyes only."

"What are you saying?" Hedge. Stall. Divert. How?

"I'm stating facts."

"Then stick to facts. I'm interested to know the outcome of your investigation. Send a message directly to me when you arrest the murderer."

"You'll be the first to know, My Laud." Nentares rose and saluted, turned crisply, and marched out the door.

"If any of your Loods stray into normal society, they will be arrested and confined, Admiral," Gregor said just before the man stepped through the doorway.

"Little chance of that, My Laud. We fix them, we don't discard them. People are too valuable to discard. Or murder casually." Nentares kept moving, beyond Gregor's sight, beyond Gregor's words. Beyond Gregor's reach.

CHAPTER FIFTY

"**G**ENERAL ARMSTRONG DA BEAURE PA HQ H PRIME sends his compliments and requires your presence at HQ within the hour," a young male acolyte announced to Jake just as he and Sissy approached her quarters.

"Tell General Armstrong da Beaure that I cannot leave Laudae Sissy unguarded," Jake spat at the boy. He wondered what mischief the child had gotten into that he drew runner duty for the front office.

"He thought you might say that," Sergeant Morrie da Hawk said from the end of the corridor. He lounged against the wall as if he had nothing better to do than keep everyone waiting. "The powers that be sent me to fill your place until you return." He sauntered forward, casual and unconcerned, keeping his hands out to the side, well away from his sword and dagger.

Jake raised an eyebrow at that. Of all the people from his unit at Law Enforcement HQ H Prime, Morrie da Hawk was the only one he knew well enough to trust.

But he did not bear a purple circle around his red square caste mark.

Jake stared at Morrie in indecision. If the head of the entire Military caste sent for him, then he must have something important to say. His duty to Pammy and the CSS demanded he find out what that was.

On the other hand, he'd sworn oaths to protect Sissy with his life. If anything should happen to her while he was gone . . .

Would his life be worth living without her? With the guilt of having left her vulnerable and unprotected.

"I can take care of her," Morrie said quietly.

"Go, Jake," Sissy said removing her headdress. "You must obey the head of your caste."

"My Laudae, what if . . ."

"I promise not to leave the Temple before you get back." She dismissed his concerns with a wave of her delicate hand.

"You will not leave your quarters without me," he replied sternly.

Sissy rolled her eyes, then nodded her agreement. "I have plenty of paperwork to keep me busy and chained to my desk for the rest of the day and half the night."

"I promise you, My Laudae, I will return as fast as humanly possible. Do not open your door to anyone. Do you hear me, not anyone."

She nodded and gulped.

"A better class of uniform might be advisable," Morrie added. He bowed respectfully to Sissy and opened the door for her.

"Generals must love making subordinates uncomfortable," Jake growled as he headed for his own narrow room between Sissy's suite and Shanet's less spacious and opulent one.

An actual motorcar awaited Jake at the Temple's back entrance, a dark-green two seater. It barely had enough power to move faster than a loxen cart. But it was extremely fuel efficient. He probably could have walked to HQ faster.

The entire headquarters staff had been put on alert for him. From the lowest private guarding the door, to the reception sergeant, to the lieutenant assisting General Armstrong da Beaure, they each ushered him forward with all due speed and a minimum of protocol. Jake barely saluted before the burly general shoved a thin file folder into his hands.

"We need this to get to Laudae Sissy with all due speed," the general said.

"Um . . . aren't there protocols . . ."

"With all due speed and without question. She has to see it, be made aware of the implications. You are dismissed, Lieutenant." The general resumed his perusal of the next folder on his desk. "There is a private message for you in there, too, received from your mother on H6," he added, not looking up. "Something about your father being sick. You are not to request leave to visit. You won't get it. Our HPS is more important than an aging sergeant."

Jake saluted and backed out. A message about a sick parent from Pammy meant trouble. Big trouble. Did he need to abort with his mission less than half complete?

He had just opened the folder to read the material when the assistant grabbed his arm and nearly dragged him back out the way he'd come. He had to close the folder to keep the two sheets of paper from flying out.

"With all due speed," he repeated as he slammed the door of the waiting car.

The same car that had brought Jake to HQ. He didn't think he'd been inside for more than two minutes. Only a few people in the chain of command had seen him enter or leave. He was willing to bet each and every one of them reported only to General Armstrong da Beaure and they all owed each other extreme loyalty above and beyond rank and caste.

Something was up. Something important. He opened the file again. Two columns of words. The one on the left appeared gibberish jumbles of random numbers and letter. Code. The same code he'd memorized for any emergency message that went direct to Pamela Marella. The column on the right was the translation.

"The CSS offers peace with the opportunity to discuss trade and a mutual alliance against common enemies," he read silently. Then he matched the code against the translation. Exact. Word for word.

And the private message? Translation: "Get the formula and get out now. War getting hotter by the minute."

Not exactly what he'd planned. He went back to the first message.

"Now why do they need this to go directly into the hands of the HPS?" Jake muttered.

"To make sure she gets it and it isn't lost in transmission," the driver replied quietly. "We're working closely with the Spacers on this. It's important that Laudae Sissy know what's actually happening and not what Laud Gregor wants her to know."

Sissy stared at the stacks of paper requiring her signature. She hated signing before she'd read and fully understood the documents. If she took the time to read every piece of paper brought to her, she'd never finish. Even if she read faster, she'd never find an end to them.

With a sigh she lifted her pen to sign that she approved the latest requisitions for the Temple kitchens. That, at least, she understood. Though why they needed so much sugar she did not know. Her mother would.

An ache of loneliness invaded her heart.

She rested her head on the desk a moment. If she could just picture Mama and Pop and Stevie behind her closed eyes . . .

The image of Harmony, arms raised, sleeves flowing away from her like wings appeared in the distance. Tiny. Moving forward, gliding through the air like some predatory bird using the air currents.

Sissy blinked and found herself looking down upon the land. Upon the people. Her people.

They looked up at her, pointed, and began shouting. She almost understood their words.

Then she peered closer. Not her people. They were different. Strange fur covered the tops of their heads instead of a sleek cap of iridescent feathers. These people had no wings.

A sharp pain pierced her neck and side.

She cried out in pain and rose higher, into air that grew thinner. Not enough air to breathe.

Then she looked down. A huge arrow pierced her side. Blood streamed away from the wound. Where it touched the ground, it turned to acid, burning lush greenery into withered and charred stumps, became desert.

The land protested with tremendous shakes. Volcanoes spewed their innards like a drunk unable to contain his drink. Thunderstorms built higher and higher, sending sheets of rain.

A crack of thunder so loud her ears hurt . . .

Sissy woke up with a crick in her neck and an ache in her side. Beside her, a book had crashed to the floor.

Just a dream. A strange and terrible dream that left her with a sour mouth and shaking hands.

She got up and poured herself a glass of water from the pitcher on the side table. It had gone warm and flat. It tasted vile. She spat it out.

Even the endless reports requiring her signature were more pleasant than this.

She needed to ask Jake about the old requisition of charcoal and saltpeter. Months old. Why was it on her desk, it should have been taken care of long ago.

What in Harmony's name was saltpeter? She knew salt of course. And pepper. Essentials in cooking. But saltpeter?

Why did the kitchen need charcoal? They cooked over flammable gas piped in from the waste of one of the metal smelting factories.

"Jake?"

No answer. Strange. Jake always answered her call. Jake always hung at her elbow, never more than ten paces away.

Then she remembered. Jake had been called to HQ. Another Military had taken his place for a few hours.

Where was he? "Sergeant Morrie da Hawk," she called.

No answer.

She looked around, a bubble of panic beginning to form. She was alone in her office. A quick look and she knew that her girls had not yet returned from the burial caves. The sergeant was also absent of any room in her suite.

The corridor echoed emptily.

Sissy ducked back inside and slammed the door. Jake had told her not to move from her quarters until he returned. For once she had to obey him. Where could she hide?

✦   ✦   ✦

Jake tore open his tight uniform collar as he made his way from the Temple entrance near the center of the sprawling complex toward Sissy's quarters. He'd never realized how isolated her suite was until he needed to hurry and explain to her the significance of the paper he'd tucked inside his uniform tunic.

Should he just hand that all-important paper to Sissy? Or should he devise some sort of prelude to prepare her?

The shadows within a ubiquitous side altar shifted.

Jake stopped short, hand upon his sword grip. Maybe this was just Guilliam emerging from one of his secret listening posts. Somehow, Jake didn't think so.

He had the sword half drawn when the dark shadow took the form of a masked man. Only his dark eyes visible in his all black clothing. In his hands, Badger Metal sword and dagger gleamed. Silver threads with a bluish cast glistened within the concealing clothes. Badger Metal armor.

Jake gulped as he parried the first blow with his offside forearm.

Hot pain sliced through the flesh. His masked opponent twirled and set up another blow.

Jake used the time to get his sword free and meet the attack. Awkward. His balance was off. The pain in his offside hand upset his timing.

Concentrate. Put the pain behind. Watch the eyes and the tip of the blade.

Parry, riposte. Meet the next attack. Counter with a bind. Hold. Hold. Hold. Slide into a circular parry.

He'd done this before. The exact pattern. He'd fought this assassin before. Who? When?

In the weeks he'd worked with Law Enforcement, he'd trained with nearly every Military in the division.

Did anyone else know swordsmanship?

The attacker bounced back three steps.

Jake skipped into a short advance followed by a long lunge.

"Oh," the assailant gasped as the tip of Jake's Badger Metal blade nicked his ribs, just below the heart. Just a scratch, barely enough to bruise let alone draw blood.

Jake's thighs protested the stretch. He pushed the sword forward as far as he could.

The assassin backed off, turned, and disappeared around a corner.

"Coward, come back and finish this!" Jake awkwardly brought his feet together, recovered his balance.

"Too easy," he muttered as he raced to follow. At the next corner the man had disappeared. Jake had to get back to Sissy.

He pelted around the opposite corner. He found Sissy's door locked. Back off. Cradling his cut left arm against his chest, he slammed his good shoulder against the panel close to the lock.

A splintering of wood and a pop of metal. He crashed inward, sword drawn and ready.

Empty anteroom. Empty office.

Hastily he searched the suite. "Laudae?" he whispered into each and every corner and closet, behind the major pieces of furniture.

"Dammit, Sissy, where are you!" Cold sweat popped out on his back and brow. "Sissy!"

"Here." The tiniest of whispers.

He followed it, fearing to find her broken and bleeding.

His heart nearly stopped in his chest when a small, long-fingered hand slid out from beneath the bed.

"Sissy!" He laid the sword down to grasp her hand and elbow. Oblivious to his own pain he drew her out from her hiding place.

"You're safe," he breathed. No trace of blood or break.

"Discord! What happened to you."

"Just a scratch." He nearly laughed with relief as he held her tightly. She felt so right nestled there beneath his shoulder. Her warmth, her scent. The other half of himself. "You're safe, My Laudae. That's what's important. Where's Morrie da Hawk?"

"Right here." The sergeant stood in the doorway to Jake's room. "Thought I'd explore a bit. Someone conked me on the head. I just woke up in one of those little alcoves." He rubbed the back of his neck and winced. He swayed unsteadily.

Jake's fist met the man's jaw. Morrie staggered backward. "I told you never to leave her alone. Now get out before I finish the fight the assassin ran away from.

CHAPTER FIFTY-ONE

JAKE LAY ON HIS COT waiting for the Temple to grow quiet. He stretched his full length and his feet stayed atop the mattress. Plenty of room for himself and another.

Stop that. He had no business thinking about sex just before a mission. And sex with the one woman he craved would never happen. His job and her caste would keep them separate for all eternity.

Unless one of them brought the entire Harmony culture crashing down around their ears. Not as unlikely tonight as it was six months ago when he arrived.

That scenario no longer fit his plans or goals. A strong Harmony allied to the CSS made more sense. Much more sense for all concerned.

Except for him and Sissy.

He could hasten the downfall of Harmony just by taking Sissy to the basement archives and letting her read that early colonial diary. The writer had survived the cyclic planetary instability that lasted nearly two centuries, and then a war of attrition against the original inhabitants. A war they started because the human newcomers knew that Harmony expressed her displeasure at the presence of the Marils using the planet as a holy retreat center.

In their human pride and arrogance, with religious fanaticism thrown in, they had completely wiped out tens of thousands of Maril religious leaders and petitioners seeking peace and renewal.

No wonder the Marils had declared war on the entire human population.

The big question was why they had waited three hundred years to do it.

Better to wait a bit before letting Sissy read those accounts. How the settlers had solved their problems of reduced numbers due to drought, natural disaster, and war wasn't any prettier. In her current mood, Sissy just might declare war on the entire Temple and Noble castes.

The slice on Jake's left forearm burned beneath the bandage. A stark reminder of why he was here in this bed listening to every nuance of sound, alert to danger, even when he should be getting as much sleep as he could before the next adventure, or crisis.

Damn, he'd forgotten to give Sissy the document that he'd been given at HQ. In the morning. Too late tonight to think straight.

He closed his eyes, only half awake, and identified the various comforting and familiar sounds. Sissy and her girls—now returned from the burial caves—saying their bedtime prayers. He could picture each of the girls making a response to a catechism question. Mary first, reciting the words by rote without feeling. Then Martha, giving passion to each phrase as if her life depended upon it. Sarah, hesitant and afraid of making a mistake. Jilly the clown twisting the words into an outrageous pun. They'd all giggle together, then Sissy would remind Jilly gently that jokes were out of place right now.

Bella would mumble something and try to hide, perhaps suggesting that Mary and Martha should answer for her. Sharan and Suzie as the littlest and the youngest would pipe up that they knew the answers. They'd tussle a moment for the right to answer for Bella.

The click of dog claws on the wooden floor. The slither of Godfrey in his glass tank with the heat lamp. A scurry of Milton as he sought the best sleeping place in the pile of blankets at Sissy's feet. Jake never heard the cats unless they wanted him to.

He smiled. Strange how quickly he'd become attached to the girls and the critters. Children and pets had never had a place in his life before. He never believed he'd live long enough, live a settled enough life, to accept children into his life. Perhaps one day father a few of them.

Silence from Shanet's side of the door. That felt strange. She and her girls, all older than Sissy's and much less individual, were still in the mountains. Again he smiled at the adolescent need for conformity. All seven of Shanet's acolytes strove to look, act, and talk just like their six peers. Might as well be clones of Bethy, the oldest, who took the lead in fashion and dictated catch words and slang.

He stretched again and listened to the building beyond this little enclave.

Shuffling footsteps in the long corridor beyond. The creak of the building settling. A gush of wind beyond his window.

Sissy climbing into bed, shifting position.

A crackle. What?

More like a snap.

Definitely out of place. He came alert from his light drowse. He listened again.

Then the smell of smoke drifted past his nose. Just a wisp. Not the sweet woodsmoke of an evening fire, or the softer scent of a snuffed candle. This had an acrid undertone. Chemicals.

"Fire!" he shouted and was on his feet in less than a heartbeat.

He thrust open the door connecting his room to Sissy's without waiting for a polite knock. "Fire! Get the girls."

Thicker smoke here. Heavier air. Dark smoke curled under the doorway to the office. He didn't need to test that door to know the main fire was behind it. He could hear the crackle of flames eating at the wood. Smell the dark threat in the smoke.

His heart pounded and his mind gibbered in fear. The greatest worry of the spacebound. Fire, eating up precious oxygen. Fire, weakening bulkheads. Nothing but vacuum and radiation beyond. Trapped. Nowhere to run. Nowhere to hide.

Fire!

He forced himself to calm down. Panic used up air more quickly. He had to breathe. He had to get Sissy and the girls to safety. They were dirtside. He had places to run and hide from the fire.

"Everyone out of bed!" he shouted as he banged open the door to the girls' dormitory. The smoke hadn't reached here yet. "This is not a drill. We have fire."

They rubbed their eyes sleepily and stared at him in bewilderment.

"Come on now, get up. Go to Laudae Sissy. Follow Laudae Sissy out through my room into the other suite." He flipped back their blankets and yanked each girl upright. When they resisted, he slapped bottoms and pushed them toward Sissy and safety.

A few more steps and he could close the door on this nightmare, summon help. Turn over the responsibility to Professionals. Already he heard klaxons in the distance. Help was coming.

He couldn't breathe in the smoke. A tendril of flame licked beneath the door to the office.

Instinctively, he dropped to his knees and crawled. Eyes watering, breath labored, he banged his head into something solid.

"Godfrey," Sissy choked. "I have to get him. And Red Bird. They can't get out." She tripped over him in her haste to go back into the smoke and darkness.

"No." Jake pulled himself up, using the doorjamb to brace his heavy, reluctant body. He wrapped his free arm around her waist and pulled her back. "You can't save the animals. It's too late."

"They're helpless. Trapped. Alone," she sobbed out her worst fears, *his* worst fears, kicking and clawing at him. Tears rained down her face.

By sheer force of will he dragged her out.

"Trapped. Alone." She collapsed against his arm, back spasming with her cries.

"I'll get them!" Jilly said as she ran back into the smoke-filled sitting room, ducking beneath Jake's arm.

"Jilly, no!" he cried.

Swallowing his own fears and weakness, Jake shoved Sissy toward the knot of her cowering acolytes and dove after the errant Jilly.

He found her slumped against the sofa, coughing and gagging, hands burned raw from a brief touch on the metal corners of Godfrey's cage. "Damn, I hope I can get you out in time."

"Jilly! Oh, no." Sissy took the limp girl from Jake and cradled her against her chest.

"We've got to get out of here." Jake leaned against the door to Shanet's suite. "Damn, damn, damn. It's locked." He shoved harder.

Nothing happened.

He stepped back and slammed his foot into the wood panel with a hideous yell. The panel buckled. Another kick and yell that set the girls to covering their ears, and the wood splintered around the lock.

Klaxons in the distance grew louder. Shouts from other suites. And the roar of the fire as it gained momentum.

Sissy pushed the girls through to the other suite and from there toward the corridor.

"Safer to go out a window!" Jake yelled as he dragged Mary by the collar of her nightgown toward the far room.

Still cradling Jilly, Sissy followed him. Her own breathing became labored. She was so tired. And Jilly was so still. One more little effort. Then Jake would hand her an inhaler. A few more steps.

Darkness crowded around her as the noise and chaos grew.

She smelled fresh air. A cool breeze caressed her face. Someone took Jilly from her. She missed the heavy burden. Then she was climbing through a window and tumbling on the damp grass of the Reserve. Her girls crowded around her, crying and bewildered. They needed comfort more than she did.

But she couldn't breathe.

"Jake?" she gasped.

He pounded her back. "Sorry, love. I didn't think to grab an extra inhaler."

"Jilly." Sissy forced herself to crawl toward the unmoving lump on the grass. The rest of her girls followed, clinging to her nightgown, crying and sobbing worse than she. "Jilly." She touched the charred and bloody *thing* that had been Jilly.

Jilly's eyes fluttered. She drew in a shallow breath, coughed it out again.

"Don't try to say anything. Help is on the way."

Sissy spotted uniformed people pouring into the Reserve from a doorway near the center of the Temple. They carried big boxes and had packs and cylinders slung on their backs. Jake waved them over.

"Laudae," Jilly whispered. She grasped at Sissy's garment, tangling the fine fabric in grubby hands.

"Don't try to talk, sweetie. Help is coming."

"The Covenant is broken," she said in a hollow voice, unlike her own. Her eyes glazed as she stared upward toward the stars. "The Covenant can only be restored out there. The stars are the answer." A huge rattling last exhalation. Her head lolled and her eyes went vacant.

"Jilly!" Sissy screamed in anguish. "Not my Jilly."

"What in Discord's name did she mean?" Laud Gregor asked as he ran ahead of the medics with oxygen and bandages.

The rest of his words were drowned out by a whoosh of flames. The roof of Sissy's bedroom collapsed.

CHAPTER FIFTY-TWO

GREGOR THREW HIMSELF ATOP Sissy, hoping against hope that she had suffered no further damage. As much as he hated the things she did, she was still more valuable to him alive than dead.

"We've got to get out of here!" the bodyguard croaked. He coughed out the last word. Soot smudged his face. He had a scrape across his cheek that went nearly to the bone. He didn't look capable of saving himself. Yet he still gathered up the six remaining girls and shoved Gregor aside to reach for Sissy.

"I've got her. You take care of the little ones," Gregor said, pulling himself upright.

"She's my responsibility, My Laud." He looked grim and determined.

"You can hardly stand, man. Let me take care of her."

Lieutenant Jake continued to pull Sissy upright. He paused and took a deep breath before lifting her into his arms. The breath turned into a deep cough that nearly doubled him over.

Gregor waved over the medics. "You can trust me to take care of my High Priestess," Gregor whispered into Jake's ear.

The man looked up with wary eyes as a medic strapped an oxygen mask over his face. Grimly he pulled the mask aside. "Anything happens to her, anything but good, and I will kill you, My Laud."

Gregor fell back one step. The man scared him as few things in life did. As High Priest he might be above the law; that didn't matter to Jake. Jake, Gregor had a feeling, made his own laws. Duty and honor were more important to him than caste or hierarchy.

"We will sort this out later. For tonight, I take you all under my personal protection," Gregor replied, sensing that appealing to the man's honor was the only way to get through the smoke and confusion.

"Come, Sissy, my girl." Gregor put his shoulder beneath the girl's arm and hoisted her up.

"Jilly." She half reached back for the dead girl.

"The medics will bring her."

"She was special."

"All of your girls are special. That's why I chose them to serve you."

"No. More than that. Jilly was touched by Harmony. The Gods chose her to succeed me."

Gregor paused in his trek across the grass toward the pool, a safe barrier between them and the raging fire.

"Her last words . . ."

"Were prophecy. The Covenant is broken. It can only be reforged out there." Sissy looked up toward the stars.

"Do you know what that means?" Gregor had an awful feeling he did know.

"Not yet, but I will."

Gregor had little doubt of that. She had an uncanny knack for seeing the truth behind a facade. He had to make certain he controlled what she discovered as the true meaning behind Jilly's prophecy. For that, he had to keep Sissy close. Very close. In his suite at least, in his bed if possible.

"Until we do know the meaning behind her words, we must keep her prophecy a secret. We must keep her ability to prophesy a secret. You must be the only one with the gift of Harmony."

But if Harmony sent a second with the gift, that must mean that Sissy was in danger, that life on Harmony was very precarious. When did he lose control?

Jake sat cross-legged on the ground and gathered as many of the girls into his lap as he could in a group hug. A pitiful six girls. There should be seven. An emptiness opened in his gut. As bad as the day his commandant had told him how his parents and Lance died. He saw the same loss in the eyes of the girls.

He'd barely settled when Sissy pushed herself away from Gregor and joined them. She sat opposite him and pulled Suzie into her lap. The group settled so that all of them were together. Arms and legs tangled and indistinguishable. Important only that they all touch each other.

A unit. A family.

One by one, the mobile pets found them. Cats and dogs, the weasel. But not Godfrey the lizard from another continent that had gotten lost and found haven with Sissy. Nor Red Bird, the exotic bird locked in a wire cage. Both should have died in the wild long ago, prey to larger and more aggressive animals. Sissy had given them a few extra months of comfort.

A tear slipped down Jake's cheek. He blinked rapidly, trying to hold back the flood of emotion. The dam of his pride and duty wasn't strong enough. Sissy and the girls had drilled too many holes in it. For just a moment he indulged in the luxury of allowing his true self to surface and dominate.

His grief unleashed a torrent among them all. Enough that he could shift a bit of his own deeper, away from the surface. His senses expanded once more. With new sharpness he noted the position of every person within the immediate vicinity. Gregor, the medics, Gil flapping closer wearing a red silk dressing gown to cover his nakedness. Penelope close on his heels wearing an identical gown.

"I guess Penelope has chosen her color for formal robes," Sissy whispered on a giggle that ended with a sob.

"Jilly's prophecy," Jake started, not knowing quite how to finish. "I know what it means." He said the last quietly, not meant to travel beyond their circle. The chaos of fighting the fire should cover his words.

Sissy's eyes widened. The girls quieted, snuggling closer and listening avidly.

"Admiral Nentares, the head of the Spacer caste spoke with General Armstrong da Beaure pa HQ H Prime, the head of my caste," Jake continued. He took as deep a breath as he could without coughing. "The Confederated Star Systems have sent an offer of peace and trade. Generous terms to Harmony. An alliance against the Marils."

But were the Marils truly the bad guys in this war?

"Are you suggesting we let foreigners in to taint our lives?" Sissy looked aghast.

"Maybe. Maybe we only need send a single representative *out* to them."

"Better to control a trickle of change than clean up after a flood," Sissy quoted her own prophecy.

"If we don't do something, both the CSS and the Marils may invade in order to get Badger Metal." He needed to get into the factory. Out in the desert. Isolated. Protected. Impenetrable.

"Laudae." Mary tugged on Sissy's sleeve. "Someone tried to kill you. Several times. Does that break the Covenant?"

Both Jake and Sissy stared at the girl, amazed at her perception. All of them shifted their attention to the flames that reached ever higher, despite the streams of water Professional firefighters poured on them.

"Forgive me for leaving you, Laudae, I must speak with others of my caste. Others who can determine if that fire was accidental or deliberate." Jake gave Sharan one last hug and shifted the little girl to Sissy's lap.

"Jake, what do you know?" Sissy asked, accepting the additional burden of another small girl within her embrace.

"I smelled chemicals when the fire started."

"An electrical . . ."

"Chemicals." That meant arson. And a murderer getting desperate enough to endanger the entire residential wing of the Temple.

The Covenant with Harmony was indeed broken.

"My Laudae," Guilliam spoke gently, touching Sissy's shoulder.

Sissy acknowledged him with a nod. She couldn't bring herself to look up, to let him see the extent of her grief and confusion. The emotions were too personal, too private.

"My Laudae, the fire is almost out. You should go inside now, where it's warm and dry. We're preparing rooms in the old palace." As ever, Guilliam got things done while Laud Gregor stood around looking important.

"I thank you for your kindness, Guilliam." Sissy stood up, bringing her girls upright with her. Jake had disappeared into the darkness at the far fringe of the Reserve. "But I am taking my girls home. Where I know it is safe."

"I don't understand . . ."

"To the flat where my family dwells." Sissy set her posture into the haughty stubbornness she'd witnessed Penelope assume.

"My Laudae, there's no room there. No privacy. No . . ."

"It is my home. We will make room. And privacy is a thing of the mind. We will cope. Now will you summon a car, or shall we walk?" She looked pointedly at the bare feet and scanty clothing of her acolytes.

Suzie and Sharan whimpered slightly, wrapping their arms about themselves in the nighttime chill.

"I must consult Laud Gregor."

"Consult all you want, after you arrange for a car."

"Jake? How will he find you? You need to wait."

"Jake will find me, no matter where I roam in the universe." That felt almost like a prophecy. She had to ignore the strange implications of those words and continue with what needed to be said. "I need to get my girls to safety. The Temple is no longer a haven for me or anyone else. Someone, some group of someones, fear me so much they are willing to fracture the Covenant with Harmony by destroying the Temple to get rid of me."

Something clicked in her mind. The strange requisition for charcoal and saltpeter. She knew without knowing how she knew that those chemicals had something to do with the fire or the grenade.

Someone in Temple had close ties to the "no bones" cult.

"Until the Covenant is reforged and these dangerous criminals removed, I cannot reside in the Crystal Temple, nor preside over its rituals." Resolutely, she began walking toward the gate in the hedge that led to the street. "As High Priestess, I close the Crystal Temple and revoke its authority."

CHAPTER FIFTY-THREE

JAKE TIPTOED INTO THE UNLOCKED apartment registered to Sissy's parents. False dawn lightened the horizon outside the windows. By that light he spotted a blanket-wrapped lump on the floor surrounded by six smaller sprawls of little girls secure in their sleep.

Gil had given him directions. But Jake had known deep in his heart that Sissy would come here with her girls. She wouldn't risk staying at the Temple. Hell, she didn't *like* living in the Temple when all was peaceful and quiet.

"Shsh," he breathed into Sissy's ear as he lay down beside her and confiscated half her blanket. The chill of shock and too many hours without sleep had him shaking. A cup of hot chocolate, or coffee, would work wonders on his system, but that blessed balm was one of the few human luxuries that hadn't made it to Harmony. Too addictive. The founders of Harmony had left a lot of wonderful things behind in their quest for a peaceful society.

"Jake," Sissy sighed and relaxed into him.

Her warmth went a long way toward relieving his chills.

"Laudae Shanet will return to Harmony City tomorrow. She and her girls will watch and listen carefully at the Crystal Temple, keep you informed of what Laud Gregor is up to." He didn't tell her that he'd told Shanet how to find the listening post.

"Good. I miss her."

"I also talked to Jeoff. He'll be the first one into the fire scene as soon as it cools enough to pick through the rubble."

"What good will that do?"

Jake wrapped his arm around her waist so he could whisper more quietly. She felt better nestled against him than he'd imagined. But his dreams had always set this moment in a more romantic and private situation.

Oh, well, beggars can't be choosers. He'd take what he could get.

"Jeoff will find out if the fire was arson. He might even be able to find evidence to point toward the perpetrator."

"This is good." She turned within the circle of his arm to face him. Her breath tickled his neck and roused new sensations in him. Sensations he had to suppress.

"Go to sleep, Sissy. We'll sort the rest out in the morning."

"It is morning. Pop and Stevie will be up soon to go to work. They'll trip over us. Just like old times before they moved to bigger quarters." She yawned.

Jake groaned. "I was looking forward to ten minutes of real sleep."

"I can promise you ten minutes." She half smiled and snuggled closer. "I like having you beside me. I feel safe with you, Jake. I trust you. Just like I trusted you to find me here. Harmony led you to me."

"I will keep you safe, Sissy. Always." *My love.*

✦   ✦   ✦

"Who is this person?" Gregor asked Guilliam.

They followed the blond Military man wearing black overalls through the stinking, steaming rubble of the residential wing.

Gregor kicked aside a charred black lump. The outer layer of charcoal crumbled away to reveal the staring blue glass eyes of a doll.

He gagged, thinking again of the little girl who had died of smoke inhalation. A little girl who had shown signs of the gift of Harmony. Prophecy.

Her words still haunted him. They could only reforge the broken Covenant out there, among the stars. Coming on top of his visit from Admiral Nentares he felt he had to listen.

Later. Right now he had to deal with the Temple in shambles, worse than after the quake.

"Colonel Jeoff da George pa Law Enforcement HQ H Prime," Guilliam answered quietly. "He's the most expert in his field, forensic investigation." He dogged the Military's footsteps, peering over his shoulder with avid curiosity.

"What's he looking for? We had a fire. Fires happen. Especially when we burn candles and incense," Gregor protested. He didn't want to think about any other possibility.

Bad enough that Sissy had removed herself from the Temple. Not just to go to another Temple. But back to her parents' home. If she was right, that someone had deliberately set the fire . . .

Then a prophet of Harmony had been murdered. Another seriously endangered. The Covenant was broken.

No, he would not believe that. He dared not believe that anyone powerful enough to gain entrance to the residential wing would have so little faith in the Temple, the Covenant, their entire government and culture, that they would commit the ultimate sin.

"This is what I'm looking for," Colonel Jeoff announced. He crouched before what was left of the wall that separated Sissy's public office from her private sitting room.

"What am I looking at?" Gregor asked. All he saw was black.

"The way the char marks fan out from this point." Colonel Jeoff described an arc with his arm.

"Now that you point it out . . ." Guilliam said. He crouched beside the Military and peered at the black-on-gray stains.

"That's the flash point. Where the fire started." Colonel Jeoff dug out a small knife from his pocket along with a sealable plastic bag. He scraped some of the black residue off the wall into the bag. "Once I get this back to the lab, I'll be able to tell the composition of the accelerant. That will point to the perpetrator."

"Then this is definitely arson?" Guilliam asked.

"From the smell, I'm guessing gasoline. Hard to come by unless you can afford a car and have a license to buy the stuff. That makes it arson. I'm also detecting gunpowder. Highly illegal and almost unknown except among the Military and Spacers."

Gregor felt sick.

Suddenly he saw a way out. "Lieutenant Jake is Military. He'd know about this gunpowder. Who told you to come today?" Normally the Senior Firefighter would have petitioned for permission to investigate anything suspicious. This man had arrived and started poking around without even announcing his presence. Fortunately, Gregor and Guilliam had been staring at the ruins, wondering how to go about salvage and reconstruction when he showed up.

Whoever called him might very well be the person who set the fire.

"My Laud, I am not allowed to speak of that. You will have to ask General Armstrong da Beaure pa HQ H Prime," Colonel Jeoff said. He shifted position, still crouched, and collected scrapings from a different area.

"I shall ask him. No one may keep secrets from me." Not even Laudae Sissy. "Guilliam come with me." Gregor stalked off, desperately afraid he was losing control over his caste—indeed, over all of Harmony.

"My Laud." Guilliam touched Gregor's sleeve and nodded to their left, the direction of the garage where the Crystal Temple stored several vehicles and had a refueling station for their exclusive use. Easy for one of their own to siphon off a little extra for a dirty job.

They didn't keep records of consumption.

But that was not what had caught his assistant's attention. A long black car had just pulled up. Laudae Shanet and her seven teenage acolytes spilled out. The priestess who had taken Sissy under her wing marched toward him without pausing. From the set of her chin and the length of her stride, Gregor knew she meant to stir up trouble. Lots and lots of trouble.

When had so many things gone wrong all at once? When did he have to answer to a priestess who didn't even have Crystal Temple sparkles in her caste mark?

"Deal with her, Guilliam. I have calls to make from my office."

✦   ✦   ✦

"Sissy! It's for you," Ashel, the youngest of the du Maigrie girls called from the front door of the apartment complex.

"No so loud, Ashel," Maigrie called back to her daughter. She cringed and winced as if she had a headache.

Sissy cringed and winced in empathy. Her mother had been hesitant and fearful since Sissy and her six remaining acolytes had descended upon the household in the middle of the night. Her mother didn't like involving her family in anything the least bit controversial. She'd rather hide in the shadows.

Like she had hidden Sissy her entire life.

"Sit," Jake ordered when Sissy tried to disentangle herself from the circle of her girls combined with her youngest brother and Ashel. "I'll check it out."

Sissy returned to the simple finger games and teaching rhymes she'd shown her acolytes, amazed they'd never learned them. But then these girls had the advantage of special schools from an early age. Something Worker children could only dream of. They entered school at the age of seven, learned basic reading, writing, and maths, then started working at the age of twelve.

Temple children began working a little earlier, if you called following a priest or priestess about and running their errands work. They continued their lessons in history, geography, and politics along with their studies of religion and ritual well into their twenties. Even those who never aspired to ordination had the advantage of as much education as they could absorb. Sissy was playing a constant game of catch-up, learning right alongside her acolytes.

"I knew you'd not sit idle and brooding," Shanet said from the doorway.

Sissy jumped up. Before she could run to embrace her friend, she found herself engulfed in hugs and tears from Shanet's seven assistants.

"We brought clothing," Shanet said. She proffered a pile of black cloth edged in purple toward Sissy. "I had to invoke your name to break through the line of laudaes demanding fresh clothing, untainted by the smell of smoke. They had no concept that you had lost everything. No interest in anything but their own minor discomfort. They've barely acknowledged your right to be in mourning." A tear leaked out of her eyes.

Sissy pulled the older woman closer.

"Clothing is needed. Food is needed more," Maigrie grumbled. "I haven't the coupons or credit to feed all these extras. I haven't a license to buy meat for all them animals." She stood in the doorway to the kitchen wringing her hands. The smell of hot cinnamon, sugar, and yeasty flour filled the four-flat complex with warmth and the scent of hospitality.

"I had no idea." Shanet looked amazed. Then a flash of resolution crossed her face. She fumbled in her pockets. "Bethy, paper and pen?" she asked her senior acolyte.

The teenager produced a notebook and pen from her own pocket.

Shanet filled two pages rapidly with her neat handwriting and handed it back to the girl. "Take this to our driver. Go with him and help procure everything on the list."

"Would help if Laudae Harmony signed it," Bethy whispered. Briefly she lifted her eyes to Sissy and then lowered them again. "Local merchants don't know us."

"The locals don't even know she's alive," Kandy, the next oldest to Bethy, added. "No one has seen her since before the fire."

"Stevie reported crowds milling about the squares, watching the news. A lot of rumors. More rumors than truth," Jake mused. He tapped his fingers against his thigh in an arcane rhythm.

"The people need to see you, Laudae Sissy," Shanet said.

"No," Maigrie wailed. "They'll kill her!"

"She's right," Jake said firmly. "I can't protect her out in public."

They all looked at each other, shivering in fear.

Sissy hugged the pile of dresses, undergarments, and shoes close to her chest. They looked much too fine for this neighborhood. Her old brown coveralls felt comfortable, familiar. Loose and unconfining. Like stepping backward in time to before her life had become so complicated and dangerous.

But her girls kept picking at their borrowed clothing as if the coarse weave irritated their skin. Suddenly her own back itched and she craved the tailored fit of one of the silky dresses.

"I'll get cleaned up. Then we all go out to the square. We let the hover cam take a few pictures. We use Temple credit for food, the animals can stay at the local Temple, then I come back here."

"Laudae, no." Jake grabbed her shoulders and shook her slightly until she looked up into his face.

She didn't like the fear and anger she saw in his eyes. For the first time since meeting him, she understood that this man had killed people with his myriad weapons. He would kill again on her behalf. Without guilt.

"I don't want that kind of power," she whispered to herself.

But he heard her. "What kind of power is that, Laudae?"

"The power to impel you to kill people."

Shock made his jaw drop. He let go of her shoulders and stepped away.

"Jake?"

He walked to the window overlooking the community square, turning his back on her. "Do what you must, My Laudae. I will do what I must."

Sissy mastered her need to run and hide in the back of the closet. "Girls, we will wash and change and then walk out."

Jake's shoulders stiffened, and his jaw clenched.

"We will do what the Crystal Temple should have done. Reassure all of Harmony that we are safe even if there is evil afoot elsewhere. And don't worry, Mama, I'll take care of my family as I take care of all Harmony."

"For as long as Temple and Noble let you," Jake muttered.

CHAPTER FIFTY-FOUR

"**M**Y LAUD." GUILLIAM APPROACHED Gregor's desk with a smirk only half hidden behind his usual formal demeanor. "I think you need to turn on the television."

"I'll watch the news later. . . ." Gregor surveyed the damage reports on his desk alongside estimates of rebuilding half the residential wing. The Construction sect of Professional caste wanted a year and twice the amount of money the wing had cost to build in the first place. Unconscionable. They weren't dealing with uneducated Workers who could be bilked of every credit they'd earn for the rest of their lives. He'd give them half the money and three months to do the work.

That should teach them to keep within the guidelines of "reasonable profit" outlined in the Covenant.

"Now, My Laud."

The firm authority in Guilliam's voice grated on Gregor. Maybe it was time to rotate the man out to the rural Temples, teach him a little humility. All of Harmony needed to learn a lot of humility. Maybe he should find a way to elevate that attribute to godhood instead of Discord.

Nevertheless, Gregor swiveled his chair to the small unit on the credenza behind him. He expected the usual afternoon serial dramas beloved by the masses that featured ancient times with the gods and goddesses blatantly interfering with daily life. About every three years he had to call the head of the media sect of the Professional caste and warn him that the stories had strayed from accepted doctrine. He didn't approve of the near irreverence of common actors portraying deities.

What he saw instead shocked him even more than seeing a half-dressed actress playing Harmony, disporting in bed with Discord.

Sissy stood at the center of a community square waving to a throng of mixed Workers, Professionals, Military, and Poor. No one seemed to be keeping order, and the crowd chanted ceaselessly, "Sissy, Sissy, Sissy!"

The normally soothing voice of the man who usually read the evening news overlaid the pictures with excited tremors. "We are pleased to report that despite rumors of her death, our Laudae Harmony survived the tragic fire at Crystal Temple last night. She is alive and unharmed. Harmony be praised. Laudae Sissy lives!" The voice cracked with tears.

"Put a stop to this, Guilliam, and bring her home." Gregor switched off the annoyance and returned to his work. "The people need to be reminded that their High Priestess is Temple caste and presides over the HC from the Crystal Temple, not from some hovel in Lord Chauncey's factory complex."

Anxiety ate at Gregor's innards. Sissy taking refuge out there was only a symptom of how much control he'd lost over the people and the government. Harmony needed her back. Now.

"She is home, My Laud."

Gregor glared at him.

"Very well, My Laud." Guilliam heaved a sigh worthy of martyrdom. "I shall seek audience with Laudae Sissy and ask her to return to Crystal Temple."

"Her name is Laudae Estella."

"Try convincing the empire of that, My Laud. They love their Sissy." He turned. His next words filtered through to Gregor as a muffled grunt. "And they don't love you or the HC."

"The Covenant doesn't require the people to love their governors," Gregor insisted. Still he felt stung by the realization.

"Who knows what the Covenant says, My Laud." The outer door slammed behind Guilliam's retreating back.

Jake paced the confines of the family flats. Four tiny apartments, each with two bedrooms and a bath, opening into a big sitting room. Three of them had miniscule alcoves with a two-burner stove, sink, and a half-sized cooler. The fourth unit had a monster kitchen, easily as large as the sitting room. Maigrie presided there, turning out mountains of baked goods. Cinnamon rolls, cookies, pies, and luscious cakes. But no chocolate.

For some reason Jake craved chocolate. His teeth ached for the taste and texture of rich dark chocolate. Not the cheap watered-down waxy stuff so popular among kids that was more milky filler than chocolate. He wanted the pure soft, melt-in-your-mouth, with just a touch of bitterness dark chocolate.

He felt like his mind would explode and scatter into stardust if he didn't get some soon. He had to settle for endless cups of the roasted root coffee substitute they used on Harmony. At least it had some caffeine.

Something bothered him. Something more than raw nerves irritated by the coffee. Sissy had ventured out and come back unharmed. The people loved her.

She seemed only in danger near the Crystal Temple or among the upper castes.

He didn't have enough information.

Back in the CSS, he'd have access to numerous databases that detailed relationships, money interests, weapons registrations, and many other bits of unrelated information that could be pieced together to make a pattern.

Here, he doubted such databases existed. Law enforcement relied on interviews, and gut instinct, with a little assist from forensics to solve crimes. Jeoff might have more information by now. Jake had no way to contact him. Telephones were few and far between. And he didn't dare leave Sissy alone long enough to go find one, or even to travel across the city to Law Enforcement HQ H Prime.

So he paced, checking the view out the window seven stories down, the locks on all four exterior doors, and the mood among the children who littered the floors, the chairs, and every path he tried to take.

Grim children with wide, frightened eyes. No Jilly to lighten the mood with a joke or a funny face or a wickedly sarcastic imitation of her elders.

A sharp knock on the door startled him. He jumped to reach it before the children flung it open without safety precautions.

Ashel glared at him, stamping her foot. Answering the door was her job, one she performed with enthusiasm.

Jake growled at her. She ran screaming for the protection of her mother's apron. Maigrie screamed with equal shrillness. The crash and clatter of kitchen tools hitting the floor echoed throughout the apartment.

Everyone cringed. Including Jake.

He unsheathed his dagger and opened the door a crack. Suddenly he felt foolish. An enemy wouldn't bother knocking. Still he needed to make a show of fierceness, to soothe his own nerves, if not Sissy's and her family's.

"Forgive me if I've come at a bad time," Gil said, blinking rapidly, as if confused.

Or masking other, malicious emotions.

"Mind if I search you for weapons first?" Jake didn't wait for an answer. With the dagger at Gil's throat, he used his free hand to pat him down.

The fact that Sissy made no protest at his rudeness showed just how on edge they all were.

"You're clean. What do you want?" Jake snarled.

"May I speak with Laudae Sissy?"

"You may," Sissy called. She moved from the floor and her teaching games to a threadbare overstuffed chair. She sat with her back to the window, the late summer sunlight making a corona around her like a halo. She'd learned a few things about majesty in the six months she'd spent at the Crystal Temple. As High Priestess, she was as close to being reigning queen of Harmony as anyone could be.

Except she had the oligarchy of the HC to contend with.

The imagery was not lost on Gil. He knelt on one knee, head bowed before her.

"Laudae, I've come to beg you to return to the Crystal Temple."

"Why?" she asked.

The burden of continuing the interview became Gil's. Jake knew he was a master at twisting words to his own purpose. Better at it than Gregor.

"The people have lost confidence in the Temple and the HC. We need you to return as a symbol of solidarity and stability."

"A lie. I've had enough of lies."

"You are the only one who can cut through the lies to the core of the truth."

"Every time I try, someone tries to kill me. The breach of the Covenant that represents is . . . is . . ." She looked to Jake for the proper word.

"Anathema," he supplied.

She still looked puzzled.

"Blasphemy," he tried.

She nodded. "Blasphemy at the highest level. I refuse to return to Crystal Temple until the per . . . per . . . arsonist is found."

"Perpetrator," Jake said too late.

She shrugged and settled for her own word.

"But . . . but that may take weeks! We may never know." Gil began to shake. "The Spacers and the Military are already suggesting that any action taken by the HC is not valid until you return to the Crystal Temple."

"You've shut down the government, My Laudae," Jake smirked. "That takes guts. Means no one gets paid. No one can authorize emergency responses. No one can organize defense if the Marils invade. If the HC realizes this, maybe that will hurry up the investigation. Or at least get them to cooperate."

Gil blanched and gasped. Sweat broke out on his brow. He wrung his hands.

Was he that good an actor?

"Will they invade?" Sissy asked Jake, ignoring Gil.

"If they monitor our communications as closely as the Spacers monitor theirs, then they may be tempted. Of course, the few Spacers I've met are independent enough they may respond with or without authority."

"My Laudae," Gil whispered. "Please, at least move to one of the smaller city Temples. That way you make a show of tacitly approving a continuance of Temple rituals. You cannot deny the people, all the castes, the comfort of continuing on Harmony's path."

"Temple life continued when I was at the burial caves and when I was in hospital."

"Both times you left Crystal Temple you went to Temple-approved places. You remained connected to the Crystal Temple symbolically and spiritually."

"Here, you've snubbed them all," Jake said. "Kind of ironic considering your origins and that they disdain every caste but their own."

"Enough, Jake," Sissy reprimanded. Though her tone shared a bit of mirth with him.

"Please, Laudae. Do not continue on this destructive path," Gil pleaded.

"I will remove to the closest Temple on one condition."

"Which is?" Gil looked up with a modicum of hope in his eyes.

Jake scowled. He wanted Sissy to be strong and independent. He wasn't sure she knew how to do that without being foolish.

"That everyone at Crystal Temple and the HC cooperate fully with Jake in his investigation of the arson. I mean answering every question truthfully when he asks. No deferring to underlings, no delays, and no dismissing him as insignificant. And we find the person who requisitioned the makings of gunpowder through the kitchen."

Gil sat back on his heels.

Jake grinned from ear to ear. His Sissy had learned a lot.

"Laudae, there is no precedent for that."

"There is no precedent for a reigning High Priestess condemning the entire Temple and demanding they face the criminal laws like anyone else."

"My Laudae, no!"

"Yes!

"And the time shall come
When Beloved Harmony
Lashes out in anger.
Out of the ashes of Discord
Will Rise
One who loves us all,
Appeases Harmony,
Brings Chaos,
And restores life."

"I . . . I must consult with My Laud Gregor."

"Do that. Tell him I will go to the local Temple as a gesture of . . ."

"Of good faith," Jake gave her the phrase.

"Of good faith. But if he does not agree to my demands and does not guarantee my safety with his own life, then I will disappear. I will break the government and the Temple. Chaos will reign and I will have fulfilled the prophecy of Discord's chosen one."

"Very well, My Laudae." Guilliam backed out.

"Remind me not to make you angry with me, My Laudae," Jake whistled through his teeth.

"As soon as my girls and I settle in at the nearest Temple, you will return to the Crystal Temple and begin your investigation. Bring in any expert you think you need. I will give you written authority for . . ."

"Blanket authority. Covers everything." At last! He could requisition the formula for Badger Metal.

That no longer seemed important.

If he got his hands on the formula, he was obligated to return to Pammy and the CSS.

That no longer felt like home.

Now that Sissy had put the fear of the gods into these people about invasion maybe they'd listen to the CSS proposal for peace. He liked that idea more and more.

Except . . . when he left, he'd have to say good-bye to Sissy. Forever.

CHAPTER FIFTY-FIVE

GREGOR PUSHED THE LEVER OF the heavy mover forward, just as he'd been shown. The machine lumbered forward, its scoop lowered. At the proper place, the construction Worker sitting beside him signaled he should stop and operate the scoop. He switched to a knob and wiggled it around until it got under a small bit of charred debris. Then he wiggled it some more and the scoop tilted back.

A hover cam captured it all. Little Johnny stood out of the way, watching carefully, taking notes, and directing another media Professional with a stationary camera.

"Too much, My Laud," the Worker shouted over the noise of the machine. He dropped his hand over Gregor's to guide his movement.

Gregor had to bite his lip to keep from jerking his hand out from under the other man's. Now was not the time or place to stand on formality.

If he'd had his way, Little Johnny and his camera would have been banned from this symbolic operation. Guilliam had convinced him the people needed to see him doing something positive to counter the rumors flying through the city about the rift between Sissy and Crystal Temple.

Just a little more jiggling and the debris rested solidly on the scoop. A pitifully small amount considering the vastness of the fire's destruction. But it was a ceremonial beginning of the cleanup.

Two full days had passed since the fire. Two full days without a word from Sissy. Just those blasted images on the television of her accepting the adoration of the people. The media still reported her living with her family and often showed her with her adoring brother Stevie. She even performed a special blessing for Stevie and his spouse Anna at the announcement of a new baby on the way.

A small ceremony that the entire empire watched through Little Johnny's hover cam.

"Now guide the lever backward just a little."

Gregor obeyed the instruction. When he had backed the machine away from the debris field, he stopped everything, unfastened his safety harness, and jumped down. The foreman walked over to him, hand extended. Gregor handed him his bright green hard hat rather than shake the proffered hand. He'd endured enough familiarity from the lesser castes. No more today.

A semicircle of Temple observers clapped their hands a few times to signal their appreciation of his work. He bowed slightly. None of them wore black for the lost acolyte. He frowned at their disrespect. They should at least mourn the loss of their residence! He'd wear black until the new wing was finished and he'd moved back in. Then he'd probably find another excuse. He liked black. It seemed more formal and majestic than the bright jewel tones the others wore.

Gratefully, he turned back toward the sanctuary of his office and almost ran down Guilliam.

"I've told you not to hover so closely!" Then Gregor saw Jake behind Guilliam. Jake without Sissy. Heat and life drained out of him.

Only something dire would separate that man from his charge.

"My Laudae is safely settled in the small Temple that serves Lord Chauncey's factories," Jake said. He looked gaunt with weariness. Dark-blond stubble stained his face. New worry lines radiated out from his eyes. And his hands twitched around the hilts of several weapons. "That is privileged information. For her safety we made the move in darkness, before dawn. I don't fear the people. I fear the people who can afford their own televisions and watch the news. The ones with access to vehicles and licenses to buy gasoline. The ones with the knowledge to create gunpowder and requisition the ingredients through your kitchen, My Laud."

"Laudae Sissy has agreed to allow Temple life and ritual to continue," Guilliam said. He looked nearly as weary and worried as the bodyguard.

"For now," Jake spat out. He'd lost the tiny bit of deference he'd once maintained in his posture.

"My office, now," Gregor barked. He stalked into the administrative wing that bordered the old palace and ceremonial centers of the Crystal Temple.

Jake took the lead, warily checking every cross corridor and shadowy alcove along the way as if he expected assassins to leap out at them at every turn.

Not good.

"What?" Gregor asked as he settled in his chair. He gestured magnanimously for the two men to seat themselves.

Guilliam took the straight visitor's chair, grumphing and growling rather than speaking.

Jake prowled, touching this, peering at that, removing a book and replacing it neatly back where he'd found it.

The man made Gregor nervous, and not just from his readiness to draw a weapon.

"Stop that!" Gregor finally shouted at Jake. "I don't have to put up with you. I can have you sent back to your unit."

"I'm afraid you can't," Guilliam said.

Jake grinned like a wild animal catching a glimpse of his long sought after prey.

"Why not? I am High Priest here."

"But Laudae Sissy is High Priestess." Guilliam's words were so quiet Gregor had to strain to hear them. "She has appointed Lieutenant Jake as her special investigator in the matter of the arson, the 'no bones' cult, and the concussion grenade in the park. She orders us to cooperate fully with him, or she will close all Temple activities."

"She can't do that!"

"She can and she will," Jake said. He leaned on Gregor's desk, face so close Gregor could smell the soap he'd bathed with. He'd moved as quickly as a cat on a mouse. And that feral grin was back. "The people love her. Hover cams follow her everywhere when she steps outside her sanctuary. One word—and she breaks your government and your entire culture. She leaves you vulnerable to riot from within and invasion from without."

Gregor closed his eyes. He saw in his mind's eye the communiqué from the CSS offering peace.

Was this what it was all about? Had the CSS planted a spy to manipulate events to lead him to this choice? He'd be damned if he allowed aliens in to taint the Covenant. He'd find that spy if it was the last thing he did. The communications officer, perhaps?

"I shall order my people to answer all of your questions, fully and honestly," Gregor said quietly. He had no choice at the moment.

"Starting with you. Now Guilliam has told me that Penelope is your daughter and Marilee was her mother. Penelope is high on my list of suspects. I need to know who else figures in this bloodline."

"I don't see what this . . ."

"Answer!" Jake's hand rested heavily on his sword hilt.

Gregor swallowed his pride and reluctantly gave over control of the situation to a lesser being.

✦   ✦   ✦

Mary accepted a written note from Ashel through the open window at the back of the Temple guest suite. The oldest of Sissy's acolytes had assumed a new maturity in accepting responsibility for clandestine communication between Sissy and the outside world.

"Laudae Shanet wishes to speak to you," Mary announced after she read the note, then set it afire from a ceremonial candle.

"I can't sit here any longer. All day we've been cornered inside. I need to feel Harmony beneath my feet, Empathy upon my back, and the wind in my face. We'll walk through the park on our way to meet Laudae Shanet," Sissy jumped up from the armchair her hosts insisted she use. The most comfortable place for their honored guest. It near swallowed her with its squishy cushions and deep seat. She had to tuck her feet under her or let them dangle awkwardly.

"Ashel," she called out the open window. "Join us."

"Marshie, too!" she piped back.

"Yes, bring your brother. He doesn't go out enough."

Marsh rarely spoke for himself. He tended to sit back and observe the world, big eyes noticing everything, his mouth firmly closed against any comments he might have. In a big, boisterous family, the quiet one often got overlooked. Sissy had done her best when she lived at home to include Marsh in family activities.

"But Jake said . . ."

"Mary, I don't care what Jake said. I cannot stay indoors one more minute and keep sane." Sissy herded her girls together and ushered them out the back door.

"Laudae Shanet is waiting for you at home," Ashel said, slipping her hand into Sissy's. "She says that no one at Crystal Temple is happy. And Jake is making a mess of things, scaring people."

"Jake can be very scary at times," Sissy agreed.

"I like him," Marsh whispered, taking her other hand. He had to elbow Suzie out of the way for that honored place.

The six acolytes ranged out around them, chins in the air as if they didn't care that they had been displaced by Worker children.

"Did you miss me when I was living at the Crystal Temple, Marsh?"

He nodded, reverting to his silent ways.

"We all missed you, Sissy," Ashel insisted. "Mama especially. She cried herself to sleep for weeks after you left."

"She was afraid," Marsh said, his voice so soft Sissy wasn't certain she heard him correctly.

Sissy let that one rest between them. She didn't want to let them know how frightened she had been when Laud Gregor so abruptly transformed her from a simple Worker to High Priestess of all Harmony.

"Stevie wandered all over the city at night looking for you. When he couldn't get in to see you, he started talking to you, but you weren't there. He just kept talking as if you were; even answering his questions."

Sissy gulped at that. "Stevie found me sometimes. He helped me read better."

"Will Jake come to supper?" Marsh asked.

Sissy's stomach growled to remind her that the dinner hour approached. Her entire family would be gathering to share a meal, to recount the day's highlights, to laugh together. She missed them all terribly.

Mostly she missed talking to Stevie, exploring ideas, planning the future, thinking up better ways to work at the factory.

"I like Jake, too," Ashel chimed in. "He's smart. He taught me how to tie my shoes." She pointed to the neat pink bows on top of her shoes.

"He taught me the alphabet and what sounds each letter makes," Marsh added.

"Yes. Jake is very smart." Jake might be the smartest person she knew. Smarter than Stevie. Laud Gregor knew about religion and politics. Jeoff and the other scientists knew their own fields. Pop knew how to work wood. Mama knew how to bake.

But Jake seemed to know about everything. He had a much better education than was allowed to a man born into the lower ranks of Military. Only those born to officer got more education than she had as a Worker. Jake knew too much. Including about the aliens who wanted to make contact and trade. Harmony had closed their borders long before Sissy was born. She had no idea if they'd had any prior contact with the rest of the galaxy.

So how did Jake know so much about them? No. He couldn't be . . . She refused to believe that. She trusted Jake with her life.

She loved him.

Sissy went cold with premonition. Her peripheral vision sparkled, just like the times when Harmony spoke through her.

Words remained trapped inside her. Maybe the cracks in her view had more to do with Empathy shining through fluttering leaves than prophecy.

$$\text{✦ ✦ ✦ ◇ ✦ ✦ ✦}$$

CHAPTER FIFTY-SIX

"**I SWEAR TO YOU THAT** Penelope did not set the fire," Gil stated for the fifth time.

"How do you know?" Jake demanded for the fifth time. He deliberately set their pace toward Sissy's refuge faster than Gil seemed capable of maintaining. The older man breathed hard. He had little energy left for lying.

Gil glared at him.

"Do I need to tell Laudae Sissy that you are not cooperating with me?"

"I've answered all your other questions," Gil panted. Still he kept up.

Jake gave him credit for that.

"Yes, you have answered my questions, and very well. I now know a lot more about the inner politics of both Temple and Noble. I know that Laudae Penelope is niece to Lady Marissa and that Lady Marissa's children have intermarried with both Temple and Noble. I know that Lady Marissa and Laudae Marilee were twins. That Lady Marissa has twin sons, both of whom assist her. I know that blood ties between the two castes mean a lot more than Temple admits. I know that a lot of Temple caste form permanent bonds with their mates and actually take a hand in raising their children. Both of those acts are seriously frowned upon by Laud Gregor. And if any of those relationships are exposed, he's likely to rotate the partners and their children to opposite ends of the empire."

"So you see why I am reluctant to admit a lasting bond with Laudae Penelope."

Ah, the spouse he'd admitted to in the tunnels. "How long is lasting? Longer than just the night of the fire, I'm guessing."

"Nearly eighteen years."

That stopped Jake in his tracks.

"Children?"

"Five."

"And all those jokes about rotating out to get away from Penelope were just smoke screens. You knew Gregor would never sign the order unless he knew about the relationship. You are both too valuable to him."

"Correct."

"Okay, I believe you. Penelope did not set the fire. What about the 'no bones' cult?"

"Absolutely not. She doesn't care about the past, our ancestors, how we bury the dead. Her world is focused on this day, this minute, and getting what she wants. In many ways she is no more mature than our middle children. Our eldest, who happens to be Shanet's acolyte Bethy, is more mature, readier to shoulder the responsibilities of ordination. My Penelope wants to be High Priestess for the glory and the honor, not to do the work. Plotting to eliminate a rival is frankly beyond her."

"And you still love her?"

"Yes." Gil's face glowed with the intensity of his emotion.

"I hope I'm as lucky as you someday in finding a woman I can love so completely." Trouble was, he had found her, but he couldn't be with her. He had to love Sissy from a distance and never have that love returned.

The Temple roof came into view through the trees at the center of a community park. An ugly squat building, only three stories high at the center. Built of dark stone, it spread out like a mutating multilimbed creature, with each wing a different height, length, and width.

As plain and ugly as any other building in the city. Except the Crystal Temple. It looked almost as if architects designed ugliness into the structures so they wouldn't compete in beauty with the Crystal Temple.

One more subtle reminder that Temple ruled everything. Including the HC. The original colonists had used solicited embryos from followers based on a personality file that looked for submission.

But even the most docile parents could spawn independent-thinking children. Look at Sissy. Gregor had hoped to control his new High Priestess and, through her, control the HC.

Sissy had surprised him. He couldn't control her once she found her feet and began thinking through each issue presented to her. And reading every memo that crossed her desk.

Had Gregor planned the attacks? Each one less remote and more desperate. First a concussion grenade to warn her. Then the "no bones" cult to make her death look like an accident with an out-of-control car. And most recently a fast-spreading fire that would have engulfed her and her acolytes if Jake hadn't been awake and smelled the smoke.

But wait . . . the first attack had come before Jake taught Sissy to read properly, before she'd begun to assert her independence. Before she started attending HC meetings. And the car in that incident had been Noble blue, not Temple black.

"Let's back up a moment, Gil," Jake mused out loud. He stopped in his tracks, needing every bit of his energy to think.

Guilliam turned as if to retrace their steps back to the Crystal Temple.

"Not literally. Figuratively." Jake grabbed his elbow and turned him so they faced each other. No masks, no lies, just two friends staring each other in the eye, trading ideas.

"We know that under normal circumstances Penelope would have followed in her mother's footsteps to become HPS," Jake continued. "But Gregor found Sissy instead. It all boils down to controlling the HC through the High Priestess. Who is in a position to do that if Penelope became HPS?"

"Laud Gregor . . ." Guilliam turned white with fear.

"I don't think so. Who has even more influence over her than him."

"Me." He shook his head violently.

"No. If you wanted that kind of power, you'd have accepted ordination years ago and begun maneuvering for the HP job. Who else has a great deal of influence over Penelope but not over Sissy?"

"Lady Marissa," Guilliam gasped.

"Precisely. With the added motive of revenge for the death of her sister Laudae Marilee."

"The night Marilee died, in her grief, Marissa threatened to take the job herself. But that was just grief talking, a need to revive her twin through her position as HPS," Gill insisted.

Jake let the silence between them stretch, giving Gil the time he needed to absorb these disturbing ideas.

"But Sissy didn't kill Marilee, the earthquake did," Gil protested.

"Sissy controlled the earthquake. But not before Marilee suffered mortal injury. In a mind twisted with grief, that makes Sissy responsible."

"I can't believe that Lady Marissa . . . She has been so kind to Laudae Sissy."

"Smoke and mirrors to keep anyone from looking to her as a suspect. She had to make it all seem an accident, or divert blame elsewhere. The insane are also very smart. But now she's getting desperate." Jake paused a moment. He didn't like the way his thoughts turned.

"Didn't you say they were twins? Twins that are closer than sisters, two halves of the same whole."

"Penelope and I have a set of twins, the youngest two. They think alike.

They think for each other. They get sick if we separate them for more than a few moments. Twins run in families . . . May all seven gods forgive me."

"Come. We have to get Sissy out of the factory Temple now."

The ground shook and threw them to the ground. Jake's ears rang from a subsonic boom. Flying debris rained down with burning embers.

✦   ✦   ✦

Like a strong hand on her back, an alien force shoved Sissy to the ground.

She fought to find Harmony in the chaos of her mind. She couldn't think. Discord clanged in her ears. Blackness crowded the edges of her vision while bright stars danced in front of her.

Flaming rubble poured down all around her. A glowing ember caught the sere leaves of a tree directly above her. After a long and dry summer, the woods provided ample fuel. In horror she watched as flames raced along a thick branch, catching leaves and twigs until the entire canopy exploded in flame.

"Ashel, Marsh!" she screamed. And couldn't hear her own voice.

Forcing a sense of calm, she swallowed deeply, sucking in smoky air. Dangerous. She coughed and coughed until her lungs threatened to turn inside out.

And still she couldn't hear anything above the clangor inside her own head.

Panic robbed her of all thought and movement.

"Mary, where are the girls?" she croaked the moment she caught enough breath to exhale. Frantically, she sought evidence of life among the debris.

Movement. A body.

Sissy focused. The blackness cleared a bit from the center of her vision. She could see to the sides now. Dazzle blindness receded.

One by one, she called to the children.

Inch by inch, she pulled herself to her knees, then upright.

A new trembling of the ground beneath her. She braced herself for yet another catastrophe.

Her back tingled and her fingers itched. "Jake!" Somehow she knew he ran toward her from behind. She spun and stepped toward him even as he grabbed her by the shoulders.

His mouth moved.

The words could not penetrate the noise in her head.

"Jake, what is happening?" she shouted so that he could hear her over the chaotic noise. "Jake, where are my girls, Ashel, and Marsh?"

He moved his mouth again.

Then, miraculously, her girls gathered round her, wrapped her in a hug. Ashel and Marsh squeezed beneath and between them to get even closer. Guilliam stood behind them, keeping a wary eye all around.

He and Jake flapped their mouths as rapidly as their arms, gesturing wildly.

"Speak up. Somebody say something. Why can't I hear you? Why can't I find the Harmonies?"

CHAPTER FIFTY-SEVEN

J AKE THRUST A HYSTERICAL SISSY into the arms of her girls. "Take care of her. The explosion hurt her ears." Though why the noise damaged Sissy and not the others, he couldn't say.

He had to slap the side of his head to clear a fullness in his own hearing. A weird buzzing sound persisted. He ignored it. He had to.

Others needed help. Already he heard the wail of sirens approaching. Crowds poured out of adjacent apartment complexes and the factory to watch the chaos. Hopefully, to help.

A pitiful few stumbled out of the damaged building.

Fires everywhere. Already people had organized bucket brigades. They'd done this before. They needed to know how to help themselves. The authorities weren't always there to help them. Firemen and equipment had to help the Temple, Nobles, and Professionals first. Workers and Poor last. Military and Spacers took care of their own.

In a blur of action he organized a "safe" zone for the injured. Set the watchers to sort out the minor injuries from the major. They knew how to calm the wailers and perform first aid.

He worked his way into the damaged building, hastening evacuees, lending a shoulder here, directions there.

Where the hell was Gil? He could use that man's organizational skills. Then Jake spotted him, covered in soot and sobbing quietly halfway up the first flight of stairs. "Bethy," he moaned. "My beautiful Bethy."

"Bethy?" Jake asked. Bethy. The eldest daughter, acolyte to Shanet.

"Discord!" he cursed as he hastened past Gil, taking the steps three at a time. Hoping against hope that someone, anyone on the top floor had survived.

Lady Marissa, in her desperation didn't care how many people she killed or crippled. Or did the malicious bitch know that in killing Sissy's entire family, and her beloved mentor and her girls, she had damaged the HPS far more than just robbing her of her life?

Two flights. Three. The stairs ended. A vast hole opened to the sky. Support beams, drywall, spouting water pipes, and hissing gas leaks blocked his way. He smelled the rotten egg odor of propane.

Above him, there was deathly silence. Not even the crackle of fire eating away at the building penetrated the thick air, though he could see the flickering redness against the inky blackness of smoke.

Defeat drained all strength from him. He collapsed on the last clear stair.

Only then did he notice blood streaming down his right leg and arm. To match the slice on his left arm. The back of his hand looked black with char and dried blood. His heart hurt so much he didn't feel the pain of his injuries.

"Shock," he told himself. He heaved himself down the steps, listening at every footfall for sounds of survivors trapped on the lower floors.

At the first landing another figure came into view. All that showed beneath the dirt and soot covering his face was his bright red square caste mark. Something about the shape of his nose and chin and the droop of resignation in his shoulders struck a chord with Jake.

"Morrie da Hawk?" he asked. He was about to ask why the Military man was here in a ruined Worker complex when the answer hit him.

The masked swordsman in the Temple corridor.

Lady Marissa couldn't have pulled off her assassination attempts on her own. She had to have help. Someone who knew how to kill. Someone who felt Harmony had deserted him. Someone with nothing left to lose.

Morrie da Hawk's wife and their chance to have children together had been stolen from him by a cruel and unjust system.

He had no pity for the man. Only the deep hurt of grief and fear.

Jake threw himself on his former friend with a flying tackle. "You murdering bastard!" He pummeled his face again and again. He gouged at the man's eyes. He kneed him in the groin.

Da Hawk lay there and let him.

"Fight back, damn it!" Jake screeched.

"Kill me. Just tell my spouse I love her, please."

"No way. You are going to tell the empire what you did, why you did it, and who paid you."

✦   ✦   ✦

"She won't see you. She's performing grief blessings," Jake told Laud Gregor several hours later.

The High Priest had arrived in a big black car with six acolytes and a squad of Law Enforcement Military. High Priest Gregor meant business.

Jake sat outside the sanctuary of the factory Temple with his leg propped up on a second chair plus a pillow and his arm in a sling. His dagger rested in his lap, ready to grab with his left hand at the first sign of trouble. He did not stand, did not salute, and gave the High Priest no sign of deference. Pammy would not be pleased. But then Jake wasn't in the mood to please anyone right now.

The squad, led by a lowly corporal, shifted uneasily at Jake's blatant disrespect. He scanned faces and spotted several familiar ones, from his own squad and da Hawk's. Cameron da Chester wore sergeant's stripes hastily glued to his sleeve.

Their other sergeant was missing because Morrie da Hawk was under arrest for a number of charges against the state, including the mass murder of almost five hundred Workers on the top three floors of Lord Chauncey's apartment complex. The squad needed to prove themselves and their loyalty. Not a good sign.

Could Jake bluff them into obedience as their officer? He'd had a very long day and he hurt. He was tired and didn't want to play mind games with Laud Gregor.

He saluted the squad without standing, waving at his heavily bandaged thigh by way of explanation. They snapped to full attention and saluted back.

Good. They acknowledged him as their superior. One of their own. With luck, they'd look to him first and Gregor second, despite the fact that Gregor outranked everyone in the empire except for Sissy.

"It's not Laudae Sissy I've come to see." Gregor looked totally blank, not giving away any of his emotions or motives. But he had referred to Sissy by her real name, not the made-up one he preferred.

One of his younger acolytes stood close upon Gregor's heels. The others kept a respectful distance, almost out of earshot.

Strange to see anyone but Guilliam at Gregor's elbow. But that good man and Penelope had gone into seclusion to mourn the death of their daughter.

"You've seen me. Now go away."

"Do you know how much trouble you have caused?" Gregor spoke softly enough so his words didn't carry to the acolytes or the squad.

"Yes. I've come close to bringing down the entire government and the Temple," Jake said blandly. "That's what happens when you build an oligarchy upon a false premise like the superiority of castes."

Now Gregor looked ready to explode.

The young acolyte handed him a pill from a belt pouch. "My Laud, your blood pressure," he cautioned quietly.

"Where is Guilliam?" Gregor snapped.

"With his spouse, mourning the death of their eldest daughter," Jake returned. "Something you can't understand because you don't love anyone but yourself."

"I told him to find Penelope a young lover to keep an eye on her. I never dreamed he'd do it himself."

"He didn't need anyone to keep an eye on her. He's the only one who has been sleeping with her for eighteen years, since before the birth of Bethy, their daughter who died today. Didn't you even notice that Penelope kept her five children close to her? Didn't put them in the nursery."

Gregor replied with a withering glance. "Temple caste do not marry. We have no need of the false familiarity of family." He swallowed the pill dry, took three deep breaths, and looked Jake square in the eye. "Who are you really, Jacob da Jacob pa Law Enforcement HQ H Prime?"

"I am bodyguard to My Laudae Sissy," Jake said, loudly enough for all to hear. "I take my orders from her and her alone." That meant that if the squad looked to Jake as their officer in charge they'd bypass Gregor and go directly to Sissy as their superior.

"You are more than just a bodyguard. You should not know anything about politics unless you are much better educated than your rank and your resumé suggest."

Jake went cold. He wasn't ready to be unmasked. A couple more days. All he needed was a couple more days to push Sissy in the direction of responding to the CSS offer of peace and trade. Troops and ships to protect their borders in exchange for Badger Metal. Then he could order a fast extraction from Pammy. Only then.

"You are General Armstrong da Beaure's top aide sent to spy on us, aren't you?" Gregor let his voice carry.

"Believe what you want." Jake hid his sigh of relief. Then he shrugged at the corporal. The HP didn't understand the chain of command among the Military. He'd just ensured that the squad would obey Jake and not Gregor.

"I found the man responsible for the attacks on the HPS. I delivered him to Law Enforcement HQ H Prime, as I was directed. Not my fault if he's telling everyone why he did it, who paid him, and how much."

"But you did it with hover cams following you and Sergeant Morrie da Hawk pa Capital Law Enforcement HQ H Prime talking all the way. Everyone in the empire now believes Lady Marissa responsible."

"She is responsible and should answer to the law, just like everyone else."

That made the squad a little uneasy. They whispered among themselves.

"But Lady Marissa is above the law. She is Noble and a member of the HC. Such people . . ."

"That's just it, she's a person, no better, no worse than any other person in the empire. She should be subject to the law and made to pay the penalty for murder just like a Worker, or a Spacer, or Military, or even Professional." The Poor didn't count. They got blamed for everything and tromped on by the law all over the galaxy.

"That is blasphemy and treason. Arrest this man!"

"Show me where it is blasphemy. Show me in the Covenant," Jake said in his most commanding voice. He gave a silent hand signal for the corporal to keep his men where they were. He almost stood. He wanted to lay the sharp Badger Metal blade across Gregor's throat, show the man that he was as vulnerable to bleeding as any *person* in the empire. The sharp pain running from his hip to his ankle kept him in place.

Upon reflection, staying seated was the better option, show the arrogant bastard a bit of disrespect.

"Your services as bodyguard are no longer necessary," Gregor sneered. "Get back to your unit. These men will escort you."

"Is Lady Marissa out of the equation?"

"We know what she did and why she did it. She won't try again."

"Yes, she will. She answers to no one but her own twisted grief that justifies any action in her mind. I'm not leaving until Laudae Sissy dismisses me." He dropped his voice to a whisper. "She's not likely to do that unless and until her hearing returns."

"Hearing? What is this? I was told she was unharmed." Gregor kept his voice equally quiet.

"On the outside. The physicians tell me it's probably temporary. She's so tuned into the vibrations of Harmony that the explosion disrupted her hearing. Might be temporary. Might not."

"Then how is she conducting grief blessings? That ritual requires a near constant blend of harmonies from the crystals."

"Vibrations. She might not be able to hear the crystals, but she can feel them. She and her girls *know* what vibrations blend and which ones repel each other. That's how she tells when someone lies."

"I'm going to tell her who you really are. She'll never trust you again." Gregor made to enter the little Temple.

"She can't hear you." Jake stuck out his arm to block the way. "So you'll have to write it down. Considering how many lies you've told her, what makes you think she'll believe your written word?" Jake cocked an eyebrow. He should be enjoying this. But he wasn't. He hurt too much physically and mentally. The cancer of this society made him sick to his stomach. He'd call Pammy for an immediate abort if it weren't for Sissy.

He could no more desert her now than he could cut out his own tongue.

"What will it take to remove your irritating presence from the Crystal Temple?"

"Bring Lady Marissa to justice."

"You know there is no way . . ."

"Then make a way. Bring the empire back to the true path of Harmony." Not that they'd been on that path since they'd slaughtered the original inhabitants.

"I am High Priest. I think I know the true path better than you." Gregor insisted.

Again that uneasy shifting among the squad. They weren't used to thinking.

"Open the High Altar and prove it. Show all of Harmony the original Covenant."

A long silence that stretched until the constant mournful chiming in the background suddenly ceased. It had been so incessant Jake had forgotten it.

"You only think you know better. You've deluded yourself into thinking that what is best for Gregor has to be best for Harmony. Time to open your eyes, My Laud. And your heart."

The doors behind Jake flung open. He turned his head, even as his hand tightened on his dagger.

Sissy stood there in borrowed black robes and headdress. Her six remaining girls and her youngest brother and sister ranged behind her. She checked to make sure the hover cam at the corner of the building caught her every movement and word. Then she removed the crystal veil.

The squad all bowed deeply from the waist. Jake ducked his head.

"My Laud Gregor," she said in a curiously flat voice. Over loud, as if she might hear herself if she shouted. "I am going back to the burial caves. I hereby close all Temples throughout Harmony and her empire to all rituals except funerals and grief blessings. I hereby close the High Council." She retreated two steps and slammed the doors closed again.

Half a heartbeat later she reopened them. "You." She pointed to the corporal. "Take your men and seal the High Council Chamber. Do as you and your commander see fit to make sure no one enters. No business. Until I say otherwise."

The squad bowed deeply again and took off at a jog trot.

Sissy disappeared, slamming the doors once more.

"You can't disrupt the lives of everyone in the empire like that!" Gregor shouted.

"Guess I'd better start packing. Not that I have anything to pack after the fire." Jake yawned and stretched. "My Laud Gregor, think about what will convince Laudae Sissy, High Priestess of Harmony to reopen the government and the religion it revolves around."

CHAPTER FIFTY-EIGHT

IT'S ALL YOUR FAULT!" Lady Marissa screeched outside the HC Chamber. "It's all gone wrong because of you, Laud Gregor." She pounded her fists on the chair arms where she slouched like a rag doll that had been left in the rain and faded in sunshine. Her white hair looked thin, unwashed, and stood out from her face in an untidy fuzz. And her eyes darted from shadow to shadow, never truly focusing on the here and now.

For the first time in months Penelope did not stand at her right shoulder. That place belonged to her two sons now. Both of them stood five respectful—and very separate—paces behind her.

Why had Gregor never before noticed the dark circles under Marissa's eyes, the hollowness of her cheeks, and the twitching in her posture?

Gregor turned his attention back to the Professional caste woman who worked swiftly and efficiently installing locks on all the doors of the HC Chamber. Two well-armed men stood between him and the locksmith. They made Jake look naked of weapons in comparison.

And they carried Spacer issue energy weapons.

He shuddered at the breakdown of civilization caused by one willful little girl.

Sissy.

"This action is totally uncalled for," Gregor said in as reasonable a tone as he could muster.

"My orders come directly from My Laudae Sissy," the locksmith muttered. "So do theirs." She jerked her head to indicate the Military men and women who stood at every door and window of the chamber.

"As High Priest of Harmony and Chairman of the High Council, I hereby override the Laudae's orders." He puffed out his chest and fixed a malevolent gaze upon them all.

"Sorry, My Laud, the Covenant says our HPS tops you on the HC and in the Temple," the sergeant with the big gun said. His face remained tight and blank. He refused to look Gregor in the eye.

The guards changed every two hours. New men every shift. No chance of one of them developing a trusting relationship with a Temple or Noble who might take advantage of them.

The locksmith dusted sawdust from around the shiny new lock. She handed the key to the sergeant. "That opens all five locks. It goes to your colonel. No one of lesser rank. There are no duplicates." She returned her tools to her belt pack.

Then she turned her attention to Gregor. "That will be fifty credits. Cash. No banks are open to take a check." She held out her hand.

"I don't carry cash," Gregor sniffed, affronted. "I did not authorize this work. Nor do I approve it. Go to Laudae Sissy and her pet lieutenant if you want payment." He turned his back on her.

"Then I'll take the key directly to the colonel myself. He'll probably double the guard and make a dead zone one hundred yards wide that no one can cross. I understand he's also taken control of three electronic listening posts within the Crystal Temple."

Gregor heard her chuckle as her steps retreated.

"All your fault, Gregor," Marissa repeated. "You killed my sister. You raised a Lood to replace her. Now everything is chaos. No government. No Temple. Nothing. Riots in the streets. No one has authority to quell them. Looting, burning, murders, rape! All your fault."

The conditions in the streets weren't quite that bad. One young man had thrown rocks at the Military squads still patrolling. He'd been arrested on the spot. Three cases of crowds breaking into a store and stealing expensive electronics. The store owner had stabbed a Worker in self-defense. Another crowd besieged a power plant demanding an end to electrical rationing.

The "rape" had been a middle-aged couple, each married to a different person, caught nude in the park after dark. The act became rape because she was Military and he Professional.

Bad enough. Harmony had been peaceful until this year. Harmonious. The people and the planet at one with each other.

"This never would have happened if Marilee had lived. We had no problems while she was Harmony's Avatar," Marissa pouted.

"We had the same problems. The same crimes. Every day. But the media didn't have hover cams everywhere, recording every incident, broadcasting them live without Temple editing and approval," Gregor replied. "They've been acting like a separate caste for years. Now they are more blatant about it."

He drew breath and continued. "Marilee was a mindless twit. She couldn't make a decision if her life depended upon it. In fact that is what cost her her life. She stood beside a rocking pillar in the forecourt. She could not decide if she should run inside or toward the High Altar. Either course would have been safer. No, she had to stand there and let that pillar collapse onto her."

"That is why she made such a good High Priestess. She let you and me make her decisions for her. Penelope will be just as effective for us. All we have to do is get rid of that Lood troublemaker." Marissa's eyes took on a cunning look. The same look she assumed just before she tried to manipulate the HC into something beneficial to her, no matter how many people it hurt.

Like the time she wanted the HC to reimburse her from tax revenues for a statue of herself she'd erected at each of her factories. Or the time she ordered her fleet of ships to cease trade with the Southern Continent until the HC lifted port duties on cargoes of household appliances. She had a monopoly on that trade as well.

"Believe it or not, Marissa, Sissy is the best HPS we've had in three generations. The natural disasters have lessened considerably since her ordination. No other HPS has been able to do that."

"I know precisely how to eliminate her," Marissa continued. She either hadn't heard him, or had chosen not to hear him.

"I intend to put an end to this. Guilliam!" he shouted for his assistant. "Guilliam, get back to work. You've sulked long enough."

✦   ✦   ✦

Sissy sat cross-legged on the floor of the mural cavern. Two dozen candles burned straight and steady. Not a whisper of a breeze to disturb them.

She had no idea of the time. Midnight and noon made no difference this deep inside Harmony's womb. She felt as if the world held its breath, waiting to see if Empathy would rise again in the morning.

No one entered this cave without her permission now. If anyone watched over her, they did it from a distance. Even Jake.

He seemed strange and altered lately. Distant and grim.

Maybe she was the one who was altered. She found no solace from her grief. Here, at least, she felt close to her dead family, as if someday she could reunite with them when she, too, was nothing but planetary dust.

The colors on the mural alternately faded and jumped into focus and she allowed her eyes to wander randomly over the scattered images. Big here, little there. Very important and filler information, she decided.

"Speak to me, Harmony. Tell me what I need to know," she whispered. Or shouted. She couldn't tell anymore.

Even the cave winds were silent.

Then a wisp of air stirred around her. The walls seemed to vibrate in a disturbing counterpoint to the clanging in her head. Her head was out of tune and out of rhythm with Harmony. The constant ringing behind her ears clashed with her perceptions. It pulsed, but not with her heartbeat.

She closed her eyes, trying desperately to understand this odd silence that was so loud.

Three deep breaths. She listened to her head until she could almost hear the whispers of many long-dead voices.

Then she opened her eyes. The center of the mural jumped out at her, the other images around it receded in a tight spiral.

Sissy stood and touched the picture of Harmony standing with her winglike sleeves stretched away from her body, as if gathering her people to her. Dozens of birds flew around her. But they weren't birds. They were people with wings. Marils.

This was the beginning of the mural's story.

Then Sissy followed the narrative around the spiral. When she came to the final group of figures in the far corner, the one that had been altered, she wept.

"I am so sorry, Harmony. How could we do this to ourselves. How could we do this to them, and to you?"

Jake followed Sissy's finger as she pointed out the path of the unreadable mural. "I knew you'd figure it out."

If she understood the mural, then she undoubtedly had grasped more of human history on Harmony than most of Her residents.

He didn't need to examine the images closely. He knew the story. The great grief of Harmony as her people and the newcomers lost understanding of each other's religion, grew suspicious of each other, blamed each other for the cyclic instability of the planet.

"When did the caste system begin?" Sissy asked in her flat voice. She looked directly at him, demanding.

Jake shrugged, knowing the explanation was too long and complex for writing on the tablet he carried with him.

She continued to stare, unflinching.

Nothing for it. He had to try. No chance of taking her back to the Crystal Temple archives and letting her read that very disturbing journal.

He picked a group of images near the end. "Here."

"Long after humans came to Harmony." She filled in the pieces he didn't know how to explain to her.

"Two hundred years," he said as he wrote the figure on the tablet. He always spoke, hoping against hope that her hearing would return unexpectedly.

If she caught any of his words, she never gave any indication.

"After we killed all the Marils: holy people who sought understanding of the universe in prayer and meditation," she stated.

Jake nodded and erased the tablet with a soft cloth, waiting for her next question.

"Why?"

Good one. He pointed to the next group of images showing a funeral procession of humans carrying humans. "Too many dead. Need more people." Ten thousand settlers reduced to less than one thousand. They'd endured disasters, famine, the resulting plagues. Those that remained were weak and disheartened.

They barely had enough people left to do the work of continued survival. Many generations would have to pass before they could resume something akin to the industrialized civilization they aspired to.

She tapped her foot impatiently. "How?"

He hoped she'd understand the science. "Frozen embryos on mother ship. Livestock and people." They'd also cannibalized the mother ship for building materials, and equipment, crashing it into the desert for easier retrieval.

Sissy started pacing. As restlessly as he usually did. All he could do was stand and wait.

"The survivors became Temple and Noble," she said.

Jake nodded. A ruling elite over the lesser mortals they created.

She stopped short in her circles of the room. "Mothers? How did they make the babies?"

"Artificial wombs," he wrote and said.

A look of disgust crossed Sissy's face. She touched a skeleton reverently. "Unnatural."

Jake nodded. He didn't need to fake his own disgust. With improvements in hyperspace drives and faster travel, new settlement ships had forsaken generation ships and human embryos. However, they still used them for livestock as animals didn't travel well.

Most of the CSS had outlawed the practice of artificial wombs.

"The caste system is unnatural." Sissy's head reared up and her eyes grew wide. "The survivors manipulated the embryos!"

A controlled environment where they could introduce the caste marks by manipulating the gills present in every fetus in the earliest days of development.

She turned abruptly and marched out of the cave.

Jake's heart wrenched. He needed to go with her, help her understand and come to terms with this information.

Three seconds later she returned, eyes narrowed in suspicion. "How do you know this?"

For once he had a logical explanation. "Guilliam gave me an old document to read."

"Get it. I want to read it."

No, you don't! The arrogance of the diarist, the cold-blooded contempt for the people who came out of those embryos, would destroy her.

"I will ask Guilliam," he said instead, hating the lie because he would never ask.

"Tell him I order it." She stalked away again, head high, determination firming her chin.

"For once I think I need to outstubborn you, Sissy. Though it hurts me not to give you everything you want."

CHAPTER FIFTY-NINE

SISSY FLICKED HER GAZE toward the entrance tunnel of the caves without moving her head. She detected footsteps marching toward her.

Some of her hearing had returned after she'd interpreted the mural— almost like a reward for a lesson well done. No sense in letting the world know about her recovery. Even if it was only partial and Harmony still clanged inside her head, discordant and annoying, telling her things she couldn't translate or understand.

She'd spent the last week studying all of the murals, taking notes, look- ing for patterns, seeking more understanding in the symbolism.

She compared skeletons and drew conclusions that shattered her faith and her trust.

The scientists left her alone. She heard them mumbling and grum- bling behind her back. They thought she should grieve. They thought she should react. They acted like they were family.

NO!

She firmly closed her thoughts on that subject and drew a thick black curtain across her mind. If she thought about family, she'd remember.

Jake left her alone with a kind of reverent fear. They both knew too much and couldn't talk about it.

Concentrate. Look for patterns. Follow the symbols. Learn new things.

Only deep within the womb of Harmony did the noise in her ears calm down. With profound concentration and the absence of interruption, she began to understand many things no one taught in school. Complex things that Laud Gregor, in his arrogance, had forgotten. Or hidden.

Slowly, she began to rebuild her faith in Harmony. But on a different level of partnership. Her ancestors had done horrible things. But they had sought out Harmony *here* for many of the same reasons the Marils had.

For her and for them, Harmony was the center of the universe. True understanding of life began here, in the womb of the Mother.

Eventually, she'd have to return to Harmony City and reopen the Temples. Revise the rituals. Change the lessons. But not yet.

Eventually, she'd have to think about her family.

Not yet. Never. Never. Never.

Jake approached her cautiously. He waited at her shoulder, hesitant to touch her to gain her attention.

She watched him from beneath lowered lids, pretending not to hear him. She let her fingertip trace a shower of stars descending upon Harmony.

Only they weren't stars.

Finally she looked at him. "What?"

He held up a tablet of paper with a message hastily scrawled across the top sheet. "Guilliam is here."

She removed the dust mask from her mouth and nose.

"Did he bring the document?"

"No. Something else brought him."

"Tell him to go away."

Jake shook his head. Then he scrawled another word. "Important."

Sissy scraped her filthy hands across her brown coveralls. Then she looked at them. Not much cleaner. Her clothing was as filthy as the rest of her from kicking up the dust of the ages. Her mask was close to clogging. She needed to change it and get back to the story the murals told her.

"I will see him after I clean up." Slowly she retreated to the outside world, Jake trailing behind her.

She should send him away. He didn't belong here.

She still needed him.

A decision best postponed.

Like her grief.

"You are angry with me," she said at the entrance. A momentary pause to allow the dazzle blindness to pass while her eyes adjusted from cave darkness to autumnal sunshine. She took the time to breathe deeply, like a baby taking its first gulp of air after the protection of its mother's womb.

A pause seemed to stretch forever while he stood too close.

And yet never close enough.

He scribbled on the tablet then held it up to her. "Upset. Worried." He wrote some more. Stopped abruptly and grabbed her shoulders, turning her to face him. "Never angry." He said slowly, mouthing each word carefully so that she could read his lips.

She didn't need to.

"Why?" Why upset and worried or why not angry? She didn't know which she asked. Only that she had to.

He ducked his head and shook it. With a gentle prod he urged her to descend the long and twisted path to the Temple.

Sissy lingered in the shower, reveling in the hot water and how much lighter and freer cleanliness made her feel.

Finally, she could hide no longer. She emerged into her reception room in the guest suite wearing black slacks and tunic top with a black shawl for warmth. Even with a fire in the hearth the seasonal chill penetrated the stone walls far sooner and deeper than in the city. She'd resorted to wearing thick socks and soft furry slippers—also black—to keep the cold at bay.

If she thought about it, she hadn't been truly warm since that day . . .

"Don't think about it," she told herself and put on a calm face to greet Guilliam.

She walked resolutely toward him, ignoring the woman who sat beside him on the double armchair. They were squeezed together intimately, and quite comfortable that way.

"My condolences, Guilliam, on the loss of your daughter. Have you had the benefit of a grief blessing?"

"We have, Laudae," Guilliam said. He and Penelope rose together and bowed to her. They wore the full black of deep mourning.

Sissy returned the greeting with a lesser bow and took the chair opposite them.

"All very polite and cordial. And utterly meaningless," Jake muttered from his post by the window, where he could observe the entire room including both entrances.

Sissy heard him but pretended not to. His overt cynicism shocked her. When had he become so bitter?

She knew when. She just would not think on it.

"What brings you here?" Sissy asked.

"Laud Gregor sent me," Guilliam said and wrote the same on another tablet.

Sissy raised her eyebrows at Penelope.

"I no longer travel without my spouse," Guilliam wrote on a tablet and held it up for Sissy.

"Spouse? Temple do not marry."

"Some do. We just don't allow Laud Gregor to know." He wrote neatly for all his haste.

Penelope produced a sheaf of papers that she had stuffed between herself and the arm of the chair. She looked at them long and hard, then handed them to Sissy. "Please read," she said, mouthing the words carefully.

Sissy looked from the pages to Penelope's face. A lot of the hardness had left her eyes, replaced with lines of sadness. A new sincerity radiated out from her.

Sissy read.

"Forgive me, please." A large and flamboyant hand. Yet Sissy sensed many more of the curlicues and flourishes had fallen away in the act of writing.

A quick glance at Penelope showed quiet tears slipping down her face.

Sissy read on.

"I was shallow and played mean tricks on you; seeing you only as an outsider with no right to the position promised to me from birth.

"While Marilee lived, we saw her only in moments of glorious pageantry and honor. To this day I do not know if she did any of the work of managing the government and the Temple caste that should have fallen upon her shoulders. My own work overseeing the Temple schools and the religious curriculum for the other castes seemed trivial in comparison."

Sissy took a deep breath. Penelope suddenly became a real person to her. More than a shallow troublemaker.

"Now that I have studied you—granted, for the purpose of pushing you to abandon the position of HPS—I see that you are the best person for the job. Possibly the only person alive for the job. My beloved spouse has shown me the cracks in our culture that need repair. As our children have grown toward their own priestly roles, I see more depth in our responsibilities than I thought possible.

"Again I beg you to forgive me and make use of me as you will in the hard tasks ahead of us. We fear change. Yet we have changed without realizing it. Now we must change again to come back to the path of Harmony we have ignored and obscured. Yours in Harmony, Laudae Penelope du Marilee pu Crystal Temple."

Moisture gathered in Sissy's eyes. She read the pages again.

Guilliam thrust another sheet of paper at Sissy. She took it, not trusting herself to speak without dissolving in tears. This one was written in Guilliam's neat hand. "With the loss of our daughter, we can only begin to touch on the grief you must feel. We understand. We share it with you. Allow us to perform a grief blessing with you. Please."

"I . . . do . . . not . . . need . . ." She couldn't continue. A large lump formed in her throat. She tried to swallow it. Couldn't.

Jake's hand squeezed her shoulder.

Penelope knelt at her feet.

The papers crumpled in her hands.

Something hard and twisted broke inside Sissy's chest. All of the pain and emptiness assailed her. Her family brutally murdered. Neighbors maimed. Shanet and her girls. Jilly. All innocent. All unknowing.

The madness of the original survivors had been perpetuated down the generations and grew among them like a cancer.

And Sissy was alone as she had never been alone, even in those first horrible days of separation when she went to Temple.

Alone.

The tears came in great shuddering sobs; racking her body; twisting her heart and her mind. She felt as if her heart was being ripped out.

The mountain sighed and sobbed with her.

CHAPTER SIXTY

JAKE GRABBED SISSY AS SHE doubled over, gasping for breath. The sobs overwhelmed her body. He reached for the ever-present inhaler.

Guilliam stayed his hand. "The drugs will not help her. She needs to complete the process."

"How can you be so calm? She's tearing herself apart!" He cradled her head against his shoulder. His cheek rested against her hair.

And still she choked out her sorrow.

"Have you ever lost a dear one?" Penelope asked. She busied herself pouring a glass of water from a pitcher on the side table.

"Yes," Jake muttered. He had to remember that his Harmonite persona had parents and a sibling back on H6 and not blurt out his continual pain at the loss of both his parents and brother.

His throat tightened.

Let them think he grieved for the out-of-caste lover. Let them think what they wanted.

He wanted to choke on the gaping hole in his soul where his family had been before the Marils bombed their home and sucked all the atmosphere off the planet.

Revenge for a genocidal crime centuries ago. A crime that no one living was responsible for.

He hugged Sissy all the more tightly, burying his face in her dark hair.

They held each other for a long time. At last her body quieted, and she relaxed her clenching fingers across his back. He eased away from her.

Penelope was right there with a tumbler of water, urging Sissy to sip. "Just a little at a time. Don't want you choking."

"Now it is time for your own grief blessing, My Laudae," Guilliam said. "Please allow Penelope and me to share it with you."

"Will you preside for me?" Sissy whispered looking to Penelope.

The older woman nodded. "I'd be honored. You must come, too, Jake. As odd as it seems to bring in one of another caste, you are part of this family. You need the grief blessing as much as we do. Bring in her acolytes and her siblings. We all need to share this." She offered her hand to Jake.

He took it, not trusting himself to speak.

They sat on the floor of the chapel, bringing the children into their circle. Penelope drew a series of palm-sized crystals of varying thicknesses and colors out of her pocket and set the array before her crossed legs.

Jake stared long and hard at the center piece, a tall black obelisk that shimmered in the soft lighting as if glowing from within.

He'd seen a similar one on the altar here, once, just after a funeral. Mostly all the altar crystals remained behind a locked cabinet in the altar. He'd been too busy chasing after rambunctious children to notice how different it was from the others, not just in color, but in . . . in majesty?

Then he realized the crystal had grown in a special matrix with Badger Metal.

He'd heard the wishful thinking of such a rarity. Pammy had told him to watch for one. If it could be grown, in theory, it should provide near instant communication across the galaxy, making the current ansibles obsolete. It would also lock on to any other similar unit like a homing beacon and reduce the chances of getting lost in hyperspace tenfold.

With smaller ones in nav units, maybe, just maybe, ships could communicate instantaneously, fly with avian precision. Avoid taking hits in battle.

Fifty times more valuable than Badger Metal alone.

Taking one back to the CSS wasn't enough. He needed the process. Better yet, Harmony needed to let the CSS know they had such a marvel. This was their ticket to writing a peace treaty on their own terms.

Harmony and the CSS allied with these crystals guiding their fleets would keep the Marils within their own borders long enough to open a dialogue with them. If they'd listen. After so many centuries surely they needed to end this war as much as humans did.

For the first time in weeks he allowed himself to smile. His future, all their futures, looked a little bit brighter. He just might succeed here after all.

With his own mission, not Pammy's, as his guiding light.

Penelope tapped the black piece lightly. A clear, sweet tone swelled up from it, caressing the ear and the soul with comfort. It enveloped all of them in the special warmth of uniting their grief, shaping it into a tangible thing that could be molded and tucked behind the heart for storage. The emotion and the music became a necessary and manageable part of them rather than a dominant force eating away at their minds and their souls.

Jake wished that Sissy could hear this.

She sat with her face upturned and a faint smile on her face.

"You fraud!" he mouthed. "You can hear."

She looked at him and cocked one eyebrow as if she had heard his silent words.

Did he expect anything less from his Laudae Sissy?

Damn he didn't want to leave her.

✦   ✦   ✦

Gregor stared at the pink pills the physicians had given him. Chew two when the acid in his stomach churned and boiled and threatened to burn holes in his throat.

He chomped through four of them. They helped. Some. Getting Sissy back into the Crystal Temple and reopening the HC would help more.

Her actions were unprecedented. And yet well within her rights as spelled out in the copy of the Covenant that sat in the middle of his desk. It was the only document on his desk. Eighteen pieces of old and crumbling paper. The oldest copy he and the archivist had been able to find. The closest to the original.

Strange, the archivist had known right where to find it when asked. "About time you read this, boy," he'd said as he handed it over.

Gregor fumed.

Sissy had been right. Every copy of the Covenant made a few corrections. Not many. Not serious changes. Accumulated over time, they added up. The most recent copy, made by his predecessor introduced the cutoff from contact with the rest of the galaxy. The one before that introduced the asylums to remove "Loods" from mainstream society. Prior to that, mutations in the caste marks were almost unknown. Now they happened in one in ten births.

Life changed with or without active human intervention.

He'd used the latest Military issue machine to make an exact copy of the newest version and sent them with Guilliam and Penelope. He hoped they would tempt Sissy back home.

Guilliam and Penelope. The thought of them together—*for eighteen years*—puzzled him more than the archaic language in the Covenant. From the beginning, the function and the duties of each caste were spelled out. Always Temple and Noble had been above the law, separate from the others. Their need for family alliances and life mating secondary to their need to govern and lead the people morally, ethically, spiritually, and governmentally.

No sense separating Guilliam from Penelope now. Though he'd like to find a way to do it just to spite the man he'd trusted so completely for decades.

What contribution to the Covenant had Gregor made? None. Nothing. He couldn't even control the mating of his most trusted acolyte and his priestess.

Was Gregor's destiny to take Harmony back to the original Covenant? Possibly. That might be too shocking to explain to the masses all at once.

He knew of one change he could make. A change more radical than all the others combined. A change that would bring Sissy home.

He could bring Lady Marissa to trial. Have her executed. The thought of the robotic arm swinging its merciless Badger Metal sword to sever her neck sent chills all the way to his bones and upset his stomach again. To die alone, at the whim of a machine, no chance to fight back. The most hideous way to die imaginable.

Alone. No last death ritual. No funerary rights. Ashes scattered on the open sea.

A true deterrent to most criminals. But Temple and Noble were above the law.

He could not order it. That would undermine everything Harmony and the Covenant stood for. A ruling elite above the law, guided by and overseen by Temple.

That was how the High Priestess earned full veto power over the HC.

Time had proved that people were happier when they didn't have to deal with politics and government. They liked knowing their destiny and the meaning of their lives without having to become philosophers and scholars. They just wanted to lead their lives with minimal interference. The Noble caste governed more effectively and efficiently if they did not have to answer to anyone but themselves.

There had to be another way to bring Sissy home.

He bent to study the Covenant more closely. Surely hidden in the obscure language and poetic subtleties he'd find something.

✦　✦　✦

"How long have you had your hearing back?"

Sissy kept her eyes lowered to the copy of the Covenant Guilliam and Penelope had brought her.

"You can hear me," Jake said. He loomed over her, standing between her reading and the light.

She finally looked up. "Did you need something?" She tried to keep her face bland and innocent.

"I asked how long have you had your hearing back?" His voice sounded stern, as if he were addressing an enlisted man caught with a dirty uniform. "No use pretending otherwise. I *know* you heard the black crystal chime. I saw it in your face."

"The black crystal is felt more than heard."

"Aha! You did hear me." He gloated.

"Some," she hedged.

"How much do you hear?"

Almost everything. No sense in lying to him. He had a way of knowing more about her than she did herself.

"Some," she replied. "The chiming in my head drowns out a lot."

"So why keep it a secret? This should be a joyful thing." He crouched down so that his face was level with hers.

"I find it useful." She tapped the pages of the Covenant.

"A continued excuse to stay away from Harmony City. Laud Gregor must be getting frantic. The empire is grinding to a halt."

"Exactly." She tapped the pages again. "I want copies of this Covenant published, released to the media. I want all of Harmony and her empire to know how far from the path we have strayed. Can I trust you to do that for me?"

"You can trust me with your life, My Laudae."

"I know that. But can I trust you with the fate of the empire?"

"What is that supposed to mean?"

She ducked her head, pretending not to hear or understand him. Not yet ready to expose the dark thoughts that crowded around her at night when all was silent, except the constant ringing in her head.

"You heard me." He lifted her chin, forcing her to look him in the eye. "Why wouldn't you trust me with the fate of the empire? You are the empire. Your life is more important than the Covenant, or the government, or even the CSS offer of peace."

"The CSS offer of peace. You always come back to that."

"I think it is key to maintaining the Covenant."

"Is that all?"

"Of course."

But he was lying. She wanted to weep again in a kind of grief as deep as she felt for the loss of her family.

Only this kind of grief could not be soothed by a ritual.

CHAPTER SIXTY-ONE

GREGOR FORCED HIMSELF TO bow to Sissy. His stomach roiled and his blood pressure boiled that he, High Priest of all Harmony, was reduced to bowing to the woman he had raised to become his equal.

She had the audacity to remain seated in an overstuffed chair set at an angle to the hearth. The Covenant forbade a single monarch. No one person had total power over Harmony.

Except this woman, this Lood, had brought an Empire to its knees in less than a year.

Nothing worked. Garbage piled in the streets. Banks closed. The marketplace had reverted to barter. Factories closed because Noble owners ran low on cash to pay their Workers. The Military still patrolled but arrested no one for theft or speaking their mind at the parks and community centers. They only did their jobs in cases of violence.

And now the Spacers reported shooting down five different spy ships with Maril markings. The CSS had sweetened the offer of peace with major trade concessions as well as immediate alliance against the Marils.

He had to get Sissy back to the capital and the government working again. No matter the cost to his pride.

If she'd just get rid of the damned cat in her lap that seemed to occupy all of her attention. Another monarchical trait; pampering useless animals and making them more important than the Nobles and priests who ran her government for her.

"Laudae Sissy," he said. Oh, how that common, unsophisticated name grated on him. But he had to use it or have her turn her back on him once more.

He didn't bother to include Jake in his greeting. The bodyguard slouched insolently against the wall between Gregor and Sissy. Gregor had no doubt he could stop any threat to Sissy, despite his seemingly lazy posture.

"Laud Gregor." Sissy spoke in that curiously flat voice. By all reports her hearing had not returned. Might never return. Could she function as HPS if she could not hear the crystals chiming during ritual?

If he could persuade her to retire due to ill health—he, or rather Guilliam, had found precedent for that—he could elevate Penelope and get life back to normal. Sissy seemed happy here mucking about with the bones in the caves. This might be her destiny.

"I have brought you an acolyte to replace Jilly," he said, being careful to speak each word slowly and loudly.

She tilted her head in a curious expression. Clearly she did not understand him.

Jake handed him an erasable tablet and a bold marker. "You have to write it down for her."

Grimacing at each stroke of the pen, Gregor wrote his words, big and black in a squarish printing, no room for misunderstanding.

"No. No one can replace Jilly."

"But the numbers." He hated the delay required for writing his answers.

"The numbers are right. Harmony and her six consort gods. A total of seven. Harmony Prime and her six colonies. A total of seven. Each priest and priestess must have six acolytes. A total of seven."

"We can't suddenly fire one acolyte from every P and PS in the empire."

"Natural attrition. Do not replace those who take ordination or reassign to other positions."

Gregor glared at her for several long moments. "As you wish," he finally acceded. That gave him an excuse to get rid of Guilliam for his disobedience in forming a permanent mating with Penelope.

"What else?" Sissy asked, almost bored.

"I come to beg you to return to the city,"

"Why should I?" Sissy replied after only a brief glance at the tablet. Her reading skills had improved tremendously.

"I plan to open the High Altar. I need you to preside over the ritual," he said and wrote at the same time.

"Good." She continued to look at him expectantly.

"What? What more do you want?"

"Is Lady Marissa still free and part of the government?" Jake asked for her. He made some curious signs with his hands, as if speaking to her in code.

Sissy nodded her acceptance of that condition.

"I have asked Lady Marissa to resign from the HC." Gregor wrote the words. His head throbbed with the lie. He hadn't asked. But he would demand it if that would bring Sissy home.

"Not enough." Sissy turned away from him contemplating the fire.

"That is all I can give you. To do other would break the caste system." She continued to stare at him expectantly.

Gregor turned on his heel and stomped back to his helicopter. He had only one choice remaining if he wanted to keep the entire empire from falling apart and becoming prey to both the Marils and the CSS.

✦　　✦　　✦

"Laudae." Gil bowed to Sissy. He seemed to spend more time here in the mountains with her, than doing his job back at Crystal Temple. He'd take ordination if he could stay here with Penelope and the children. Not that Penelope would agree to such a change.

"I understand your need for justice. Lady Marissa caused me and my family much grief." He ran his hands through his hair, wishing he could find better words, a better solution. "But bringing Lady Marissa to trial is too much too soon. You cannot break the caste system all at once."

"Why not? It is an artificial system." Her voice had gained a little inflection. She still spoke overloud and relied on written words to help.

"But it has worked well for centuries."

Guilliam had trouble keeping his pen strokes logical and ordered. His mind raced ahead and back again, losing its linear track.

"If the caste system worked so well, why did you show Jake the damning documents?"

"She's got you there, Gil. Why did you show me? Why not leave the bones and murals a total mystery."

Gil noted that Jake didn't bother writing anything anymore. Sissy seemed to understand him perfectly without aids.

"Because I knew she would figure out the murals."

Sissy rose from her place by the fire. "Show me." Without waiting to see if he followed, she pulled on outdoor shoes and a coat.

Jake shrugged and found his own sturdy boots.

They kept an almost comfortable silence on the trek up to the caves. Just inside the entrance, Sissy paused and drew in a deep breath, as if replenishing herself with Harmony's bounty. Gil did the same. The close stone walls welcomed him, promised him sanctuary and peace. The wind blowing from an opening higher up the mountain, down to this narrow entrance blew away a lot of the clutter in his mind.

"I grew up in caves very like this in the Central Mountains," he said quietly. "This feels like home."

"Are there murals like these elsewhere?" Jake asked. He struck a light to a torch. The smoke drifted behind them as they negotiated the long passage to the altar cavern.

"I have found similar ones throughout the Northern and Southern Continents," Gil said.

"When did you figure them out?" Sissy asked. She led them unerringly through the maze to the old cavern. The air was quieter here, below the main entrance.

"I never did completely. But when I found the diary in the archives, I remembered the murals and guessed much of the symbolism. I knew that you, with your deep connection to Harmony, would understand. I wanted Jake to know the truth, to guide you if you stumbled."

"I needed to know the truth. All of Harmony—the entire empire— needs to know," Sissy said.

"In time." Gil had to press his agenda. "The caste system worked be- cause people believe in Harmony's path and seek an order to their exis- tence, to the universe."

"The frozen embryos that became the first generation with castes had no choice," Sissy spat.

"The people who donated the embryos believed. They could not leave their old home, so they sent their unborn children in their place. Because they believed the teachings of the first settlers."

Sissy grunted something. They said nothing more until they entered the side cavern. The mural opened before them, colors more brilliant than he expected. He gasped in wonder.

"Never have I seen anything more magnificent. All the others are smaller, damaged by time and damp. Less complete."

"The cave system is dry. This room was sealed, possibly by the Marils," Jake said. "No one to damage it. Only time. Except for the modification in the corner. We still don't know who did that or why."

Gil glanced briefly at the small picture of Discord at Harmony's feet. "Whoever did that, didn't understand the rest of the story. Wasn't even very good at drawing." He dismissed the crude figure.

"Do you know how to read this?" Sissy asked. Her fingers caressed the center reverently.

"I know to start there in the middle and end in the right-hand corner. The exact sequence, though . . ." he shrugged.

"A spiral. In a wide oval that follows blessed Empathy's path across the sky. Like a bird of prey gliding on an updraft," Sissy whispered.

"The Marils may have been the victims here on Harmony. But they are far from innocent themselves. They are birds of prey at heart. Very violent and dangerous," Jake said. He remained by the room's entrance holding the torch. "We believe that they feast on carrion."

Sissy questioned that word.

"The rotting bodies of those they kill in battle."

She looked like she wanted to gag.

"For that reason alone, Harmony must remain united and functioning a while longer," Gil returned to the original purpose of his visit, pressing the advantage of her disgust.' "If you break the caste system all at once, we face chaos."

"We'll be vulnerable to invasion. We'll be lucky if it's the CSS. We'd all better pray it won't be the Marils," Jake added. He looked very uncomfortable with this conversation.

"And if we deserve invasion and death?" Sissy asked. She'd set her chin.

Gil couldn't allow her to win.

"Perhaps our ancestors deserved it. We don't."

"But . . ."

"Change we need. Breaking we don't, Laudae," Jake said. "We need to start looking outward."

"Gradual change," Gil coaxed. "Begin with the schools. Penelope wants to help with that. Bring gifted Worker and Military children into Professional schools. Bring the Poor in any way we can. Upgrade Worker schools with more teachers and textbooks. Begin building new schools that merge several castes," Gil explained the outline Penelope had given him.

"Let the children get used to dealing with other castes. As they grow familiar with each other, prejudice will dissolve," Sissy mused.

"Now, will you please return to Crystal Temple?" Gil pleaded.

"What about the . . . the ones born with altered caste marks?"

Gil noted that she never could say "Lood."

"I have it on good authority that the Spacers fix their Loods," Jake said. A look of hope crossed his face, as if he knew Sissy moved away from her extreme position.

"How?" Sissy asked, suspicion clouding her eyes. "The children cannot be manipulated in artificial wombs like the original settlers did."

"An easy process," Gil jumped in. "Much like when Jake had his caste mark upgraded to officer and Lauded to serve the temple. The same way I added sparkle to your caste mark when you were in hospital." He had to hang his head in guilt over that, but he watched her through lowered lashes.

"That was you?" Sissy laughed.

"I knew that doubters would respect the sparkle and acknowledge your authority. You see that the caste system is too ingrained to dissolve all at once. Give it time while we secure our borders through alliance and trade."

Sissy flashed Jake a stern glance.

He shrugged and put on a mask of innocence. He must have been pushing the same idea.

"We will tear down the asylums," Sissy insisted.

"The buildings are large and useful," Gil protested, seeing them as housing, schools, and hospitals for the Poor.

"Tear them down."

"Yes, My Laudae." No reminders of the horrors the asylums represented.

"Now will you return to Crystal Temple?"

"When something is done about Lady Marissa." Sissy left the room abruptly.

Jake followed, leaving Gil to find his own way out through the darkness.

A darkness that was easier to negotiate than the mess at Crystal Temple.

CHAPTER SIXTY-TWO

"I'M JUST A SNEAK THIEF," Jake told himself. "Pammy, you have a lot to answer for." Unfortunately, he'd have to answer to Pammy all too soon.

His time on Harmony drew to a close. Sissy wouldn't need him much longer. She moved Harmony toward the position Jake needed them in for his plans to work.

But first he had something important to steal.

He pressed himself into the deep shadows of the chapel. A vigil lamp burned on the altar. The permanent array of crystals there absorbed the faint gleams and glowed within as if alive. Maybe they were. On this crazy planet he'd almost believe that.

A huge black crystal stood at the center; an artifact worth several fortunes in the CSS.

Funerals and grief blessings dominated the rituals here. The crystal was essential for those. Strange he'd never noticed it before. But then, he couldn't remember coming into the chapel before. Sissy only came here on Holy Days, preferring to perform her rituals in the caves. Jake stayed outside, observing the comings and goings of the scientists on Holy Days.

After hearing and feeling the black crystal reach down into his soul and enfold him in love and comfort, he'd grown beyond *almost* believing in the path of Harmony.

That scared him more than facing Pammy with failure.

At this point failure was not an option.

Jake felt his way forward, keeping to the walls, away from any chairs or other things left surrounding the altar in the middle of the largest room in the complex.

The black seemed to swell as he approached the altar. The reddish lights within it concentrated at whatever point he fixed his gaze. He imagined a big accusing eye following him.

"Don't worry, you are safe from me," he told the crystal, with his mind as well as his whispers. As much as he coveted that crystal, he had to leave it behind. It was too big. It would slow him down.

He sought the dressing and storage room on the opposite end of the chapel from the entrance. He'd checked out any number of those dressing rooms—vestries they called them back home—while guarding Sissy. He knew the layout. Getting in and out should be simple.

Except his own guilt made his feet heavy and his steps slow. "It's for your own good," he told all of Harmony as well as himself. "You'll thank me when this is all over." If it would ever be all over.

It had to be. Everything was in position. All he had to do now was wait, and keep nudging Sissy in the direction the galaxy needed her to go.

"I could use a little help with that, Lady Harmony."

No answer.

Of course the planet didn't speak to him, an alien, as it did to Sissy. Lately, Sissy had had precious few conversations with the planet. He couldn't recall a single prophecy since . . . since Jilly died.

Oh, Sissy had faked a few.

But he could tell when she did that. He didn't even have to look in her eyes anymore. She gave off subtle signals with her posture and the timbre of her voice.

He didn't think anyone else knew her well enough to detect those signals.

Jake never got tired of observing and analyzing Sissy. He needed to know every nuance of her. He needed details to cherish when he had to betray and abandon her.

Enough wallowing. He had a job to do. By the light of a tiny portable torch he rummaged through the closet, drawers, and the enclosed cabinet designed to hold nothing but the elaborate headdresses, and special compartments for replacement crystals and the tools to repair the veils.

Finally he looked on the shelves that ran around the walls above everything else. Three black boxes crafted from finely grained wood with shell-and-bone embellishments. The portable kits the priests and priestesses took with them to minister elsewhere. Like the time he'd taken Sissy to ritually cleanse and bless the asylum.

Why hadn't she used a black for the blessing?

Because that ritual was for hope and new beginnings, not death and endings.

He pulled out a step stool with his toe, climbed the two treads, and reached as high as he could. His fingertips brushed one of the kits, edging it backward. With a curse, he held the torch in his mouth and reached with both hands, edging his elusive prize forward until it tipped on the edge.

With a sigh of relief he grasped it gingerly and lowered it until he could cradle it against his chest and get a firmer grip.

The overhead light flashed on, nearly blinding him.

He stumbled backward, terrified he'd drop the box.

"What are you doing?" Sissy asked.

Her voice sounded as black and cold as the depths of vacuum between the stars.

✦   ✦   ✦

Gregor waited until midnight to make his way to the garage. The little black car reserved for senior assistants sat waiting, fully fueled. It started with a touch, as it should. Mechanics assigned to Temple prided themselves on keeping all the vehicles ready at a moment's notice.

He drove along deserted back streets. As all roads were supposed to be this time of night. In the more populous areas of the city people still milled about, drinking, yelling complaints, burning garbage in the middle of the street, and making nuisances of themselves. No one had enforced the curfew since Sissy closed the government.

He imagined the Professionals and Nobles cowering behind closed doors, waiting for the riots to spill into their exclusive enclaves.

At least a third of the streetlights needed replacing.

He cursed the entire distance to his destination at the reduced visibility. The shrouding dimness might protect him, but only if he avoided crashing into something because he couldn't see it.

At last he found the long drive he sought. Parking the car in the blackness beneath a tree beside a burned-out streetlight, he prepared himself for a long walk. No one at the house must know he'd been there. No chance passerby must suspect he drove the hidden car.

Six deep breaths and his lungs felt almost fully inflated.

Another six didn't improve his breathing. Nothing for it. He had to do it now or lose his nerve and everything else he valued in life.

He found the gate across the drive firmly locked; the space between the gateposts and the shrubbery was too small for him to squeeze through.

Cursing with the fluency of a lifetime of having seen and heard the best and worst of life, he crawled along the base of the hedge looking for the inevitable. At last he found an opening between two shrubs wider than most. An ancient plant had died and the two adjacent ones grew to fill the gap with branches, but not the roots.

Long spiky branches grabbed his jacket. Dead spiky leaves pierced his palms. Thick spiky trunks pressed against his sides. He flattened himself against the ground and wiggled and shoved himself through the eight feet of hedge until he was clear.

Brushing himself off, he started walking through the extensive grounds that surrounded Lady Marissa's town house. Her primary home. Two miles to the palace. At least.

His breath came sharp and heavy by the time the glimmer of lights in the windows pierced the gloom.

Boldly he walked up the front steps and pushed open the door. He'd made certain it would respond to his touch.

"About time you arrived. I've been waiting for over an hour," Lady Marissa said. She sounded petulant and tired.

She sat with her back to him on one of the deeply cushioned lounges in the room to the right of the entrance hall. A small lamp on a table gave her enough light to read by. The cloying scent of her perfume caught in his throat.

"So what is your plan to end this madness and elevate Penelope to HPS?" Lady Marissa remained reclining, a notebook filled with government memos in one hand, her reading spectacles in the other.

"I have no plan to do that," Gregor said blandly. "I need to keep Sissy in place a while longer."

"Then what are you going to do?" Lady Marissa began pushing herself up with her elbows.

Gregor eased her back down with a touch to her shoulder. With his free hand he grabbed one of the many squishy pillows she had shoved beneath and beside her to support her back, knees, and head.

"I plan to remove you from the situation so that life can return to normal," he said, pressing the pillow across her face. "I can't let you murder any more people."

She thrashed and kicked.

He pressed harder.

She clawed at his hands.

He ignored the pain.

Her flailing grew weaker.

He held the pillow down.

She grew still. The rancid odor of her loosed bowels gagged him.

Still he held the pillow down.

After, he counted to one hundred slowly, then again, he finally lifted the pillow free.

Lady Marissa lay limp and unmoving. Her jaw hung slack. Blue tinged her lips. Her sightless eyes stared into the afterlife.

He stuffed the pillow back under her knees and left the same way he came.

CHAPTER SIXTY-THREE

"**D**ON'T STOP AND THINK about what you will say, Jake. Just tell me why you are sneaking around in the middle of the night pilfering Temple supplies," Sissy demanded. Her heart ached as she ran possible answers through her head. None of them sounded good.

Most of them sounded like betrayal.

He kept his eyes lowered as his hands fussed with the black kit box. "Jake?"

"What I do tonight, everything I have done since before I met you, has been for the good of Harmony and the empire. It may not look like it on the surface, but it is." Finally, he raised his eyes to meet hers.

It was like looking into a deep well of hurt. As deep as her grief at the loss of her family. All of them gone. Gone in a single flash.

All of them innocent.

The pain threatened to choke her again. She swallowed it. Ignored it.

The hurt of Jake betraying her pained her almost as much.

"There was a time when I would have believed you," she said quietly.

"Why don't you now?" His hands continued to fidget.

She grabbed the box away from him, checked to make sure the latch was secure and placed it on top of the headdress cabinet.

"Why don't you believe me, Laudae?"

"Because you are not who you say you are."

A long silence lay between them. A hurtful silence.

Sissy couldn't look at him.

"No, I am not who I pretend to be. In more ways than the obvious." He muttered the second sentence so softly she almost didn't hear him.

"Then tell me the truth." Even though the truth might hurt more than the lies.

He took a deep breath. "I am a spy for the Confederated Star Systems. My mission was to steal the formula for Badger Metal. But I have changed my mission. Now I see the best way for the CSS to get access to Badger Metal is to develop peaceful trade with Harmony. The best way for Harmony to maintain Her culture and have peace within as well as without is for a controlled alliance with the CSS."

"No!" Sissy grew cold at the thought of aliens polluting Harmony. She needed time to make changes. Time for the people to get used to the idea. Time. She couldn't break things all at once. He'd convinced her of that.

So why was he now pressing for the biggest change of all? Aliens.

"Think about it, My Laudae. Think long and hard. There are many things wrong within Harmony . . ."

"And we need to correct them from within, not change them according to outside influences. I'm working on that."

"You can't hold off the Marils indefinitely. Or the CSS. If they can't get Badger Metal through negotiation and trade, they will take it forcefully. Can you fight off one or both of your enemies while you battle Lady Marissa and Laud Gregor and the problem of the Loods and the breakdown of law and order?"

"I think you had better go."

"I report back to my unit in the morning."

"No. Go. Go back to your precious CSS. I owe you my life. I will not take yours. But I can no longer trust you at my side. Be gone by dawn, and I will not alert the Spacers and the Military. Disappear back to the stars quickly before I change my mind."

With tears clogging her eyes and her throat, she held the door open for him.

"Remember Jilly," he said quietly as he passed by her.

He slipped away into the darkness as silently and completely as a dream. Only the fractured memory of him remained.

"The answers are out there, among the stars," Jilly's voice whispered to her from the darkness.

✦   ✦   ✦

How to get off this bloody mountain? Jake wended his way downslope from the Temple complex. He'd paused only long enough to grab a coat and a bottle of water from his kit. No time to search for the enhanced goggles. He knew Sissy. She'd follow through with her threat. He had until dawn to find a spot safe enough to summon extraction.

Pammy had kept the details to herself. Jake only knew that when he pressed a special implant in his inner wrist a two-person fast shuttle would arrive within twenty minutes. He presumed the pilot would take him to a rendezvous with a cloaked vessel, probably empty. A crewed vessel would have trouble keeping quiet enough to avoid detection. Life-support power signatures alone would leave a trail even primitive sensors could find. But a small dead ship could drift for many long months, years even.

"That's far enough, Lieutenant." A woman's voice came from somewhere to his left. "I place you under arrest for High Treason against the HC and Blasphemy against Temple personnel."

"Crap." Jake reached to draw his sword. The muzzle of a highly illegal energy weapon pressed against his side.

Only a Spacer would have that weapon. She probably had night vision goggles, too.

Starlight and a sliver of a waning moon revealed only a deeper blackness against the black of night in a remote mountain glen without a lot of electric lights in the background.

Only one female Spacer scientist remained in the funerary complex. Lieutenant Commander Barba du Annalyse pu Science Fleet. The woman who had "found" the altered mural.

"Who gives you the authority to make an arrest?" Jake asked, stalling for time. He kept his hands raised and away from his body. A flick of his right wrist and he'd have a long stiletto at the ready. He just had to stay close enough to Barba to knock the blaster aside and stab her.

Gods, he didn't want to murder another person. He'd never get used to the *intimacy* of killing another sentient being with such a weapon. A blaster, on the other hand, gave Barba a sense of distance and detachment. Even if she'd never killed in close combat, she could pull the trigger with ease.

"Laud Gregor has authorized me to do what is necessary to remove your influence from Laudae Sissy." She sounded uncertain. Barba withdrew the weapon from direct contact, but she didn't retreat very far.

"You aren't Military, Barba. Laud Gregor can't give you the authority to do anything but turn me over to Military."

"Who says I have to leave you alive to ask questions? You aren't Professional, so you can't quote law or precedent."

Jake had a sense of distance and direction on her.

"Have you ever killed before, Barba?" he asked mildly. He spoke loudly, using his voice to cover the sound of his edging around to face her.

"Back off, Lieutenant."

"That illegal weapon makes you brave, heh?"

"Stop talking." She lost some of her assurance.

"You must be the one Laud Gregor bribed into forging the mural of Discord," he mused. "Did he tell you he planned to subvert the Covenant with that little bit of skullduggery?"

"Laud Gregor is the Covenant," she insisted. "We have to obey him, no matter what we think. Our caste doesn't have to think, we only have to obey."

"That's a load of crap. As a scientist, you think all the time. Think about this: Laudae Sissy, High Priestess and Avatar of Harmony is the Covenant. Laud Gregor is only her adviser." He edged a micron closer. Almost. Almost close enough.

"I said back off!" she nearly screeched.

"No, you back off." Jake struck out with his left hand, pushing the blaster aside as he lunged with his stiletto.

An energy whine whizzed past his ear. Then the thunk of rock shattering.

His blade bounced off gel armor. Damn.

She righted her aim.

Then she crumpled, the blaster shooting wildly

Jake dropped to the ground, desperate to avoid a killing bolt.

"Are you hurt?" Colonel Jeoff da George pa Law Enforcement HQ H Prime crouched over Jake, feeling arms and legs for trace of injury.

"Just my pride." He wiped dust off his face. "What'd you hit her with?"

"The hilt of my dagger to the back of the skull. Just like in training." Jeoff looked at the heavy knob of his weapon with surprise.

"First time outside of training you've engaged in combat?" Jake jerked himself back to standing. He scanned the campsite. Shadows moved all around him. The blaster noise had roused all the scientists.

"I'm a forensic scientist." Jeoff continued to shift his stare from his dagger to Barba.

"Thanks for the assist, Jeoff. But I've got to get out of here. Fast."

"I know. We Military have to stick together. Whichever Military you serve."

"Keep them occupied. You heard enough to arrest her for altering the mural. That should be enough to bring Temple authorities down on her hard."

"But Laud Gregor will . . ."

Jake didn't wait to hear the rest of Jeoff's protest. He didn't want to know the awful punishment Gregor would dish out for failure. A worse crime in the eyes of the HP than blasphemy—if the blasphemy helped him.

He grabbed the night vision goggles off Barba's face and ran downhill. Anywhere downhill and away from the prying eyes of the bone teams.

And Sissy.

He knew he could never outrun Sissy.

CHAPTER SIXTY-FOUR

SISSY RAN HER HANDS OVER the black kit box. "What in Harmony's name did Jake want with this?"

Her finger caught on the latch. Not quite closed.

She paused before refastening it. A lump of fear grew in her throat. Hastily she flipped open the lid.

The black velvet altar cloth lay askew, its folds uneven and corners turned back.

She drew it out, refolding it carefully as she mentally counted off the items that should nestle into assigned compartments. Candles, incense, blessed ritual water. A leaflet of prayers printed out for the bereaved. A crystal wand. Seven crystals of varying colors and sizes.

The fourth crystal compartment, the one reserved for a grief blessing, gaped empty.

"Why would he need that crystal?" Her heart swelled a moment. Would he miss her so much that he needed the black crystal tones to ease his grief at leaving?

A flash of memory near blinded her. With the clarity of a Harmony vision, she was back in Lord Chauncey's factory, watching the spinning nav unit. Waiting for the precise moment to drop in a tiny shard of a black crystal at the core.

A crystal grown in the same Badger Metal/crystal matrix as the one Jake had stolen. The crystal that sped communications through the depths of space.

The crystal that locked onto a beacon on Harmony Prime so that no spaceship would ever get lost in hyperspace.

The Lost Colony could not have gotten lost.

If not lost, where were they?

All thoughts of Jake fled.

A new flash of insight made her sick to her stomach. The Lost Colony had cut themselves off from Harmony. They sought a different way of life, away from the strict caste system of their mother planet.

They had done for themselves what Sissy could not do for all of Harmony.

Laud Gregor knew this and lied about them so that no one else followed their example into rebellion. He wanted the realignment of Workers and Professionals to free up Spacers and Military to bring the Lost Colony back to Harmony.

Or slaughter them.

As their ancestors had slaughtered the original inhabitants of Harmony.

She had to sit down.

Jake was right.

"Jake! Oh Harmony, why did I send him away?"

✦   ✦   ✦

"It is with a sad heart that we must inform Harmony of the death of Lady Marissa," Guilliam intoned with just the right amount of droop to his posture and his voice. "She suffered a massive heart attack last night. Her son, Lord Lukan found her this morning."

Gregor kept one eye on the television where Guilliam read the official Temple and HC statement of grief over the death of Lady Marissa.

With the other eye he watched the reaction of Admiral Nentares da Andromeda pa HQ H Prime and General Armstrong da Beaure pa HQ H Prime. Both of them heaved sighs of relief as they watched with him.

"Maybe now we can get something done," Nentares said. "The last two Maril incursions got away. We fear they took valuable fleet observations with them."

"I have sent Laudae Penelope to fetch Laudae Sissy from her mountain retreat." A little lesson in humility to both of them. He'd not go begging again.

"I have a report that her hearing has partially returned." Gregor made a show of shuffling papers on his desk and reading one aloud. The physicians told him that if her hearing would return the process would have begun by now. He needed no more reassurance. Sissy would return and reopen the government and Temple whether she wanted to or not.

"Have the Military forensics people confirmed the diagnosis of heart attack for Lady Marissa?" Armstrong asked.

"Her personal physician said there was no need for an autopsy," Gregor said. "He found no evidence of suspicious circumstances." And he wouldn't. A hefty bribe of two weeks' vacation at a private retreat on an exotic tropical beach guaranteed that.

Easy enough to arrange an accident so that he never returned.

"The task of informing the public falls to the Temple because Lady Marissa was born to our caste and chose to marry a Noble," Guilliam read from a prepared statement. "Upon the death of her spouse she assumed his place with the High Council. Her sister, the late High Priestess Laudae Marilee, remained in Temple. A state funeral for this remarkable lady will be held tomorrow at noon, here in the Crystal Temple forecourt at the High Altar. After the ritual, High Priestess Laudae Sissy and High Priest Laud Gregor will open the High Altar and reveal for the first time this century the tablets containing the original Covenant with Harmony."

Both the Military and Spacer officials raised eyebrows at the last.

"We hope this distraction of opening the High Altar will not keep Laudae Sissy from authorizing the shift of troops and ships to the frontier," Nentares said.

"I assure you, Laudae Sissy will sign the orders to arm merchant vessels and shift Workers and Professionals into noncombative roles. She will also cosign the necessary arrangements to reassign Military to defend the outer colonies on the ground, freeing your caste to take to the stars." Along the way to the frontier, all those extra troops would also stop off to subdue and reabsorb the Lost Colony. Gregor had the paperwork already prepared. He'd forge Sissy's signature if necessary.

"Lord Lukan, eldest son of Lady Marissa will assume her place on the High Council," Guilliam continued. "He and his twin brother Bevan have been managing her estates and businesses for the last three years to relieve their mother of some of her burdens. They chose not to inform the public of her history of heart failure and were prepared for this transition."

The statement would run another two pages. Gregor ceased to listen. He knew the words by heart. He'd written them. He'd made certain to keep out any mention of rumors that named Lady Marissa as the instigator of the bomb and the fire and the other assassination attempts on their beloved Laudae Sissy.

Gregor's face grew hot, and his stomach churned. he groped for his pills. His hands came up empty. Desperate to control his errant body before the heads of Spacer and Military noticed anything amiss, he slapped a button that would summon an acolyte.

Caleb poked his head through the door to the outer office. He took one look at Gregor and hastened to the credenza behind him. In seconds he slipped two of the pink digestion tablets and one of the blood pressure pills into Gregor's hand before bowing and retreating.

"Are you ailing?" Armstrong asked. He bounced out of his chair and poured a glass of water for Gregor from the pitcher on the credenza. While he was at it, he undoubtedly read the labels on the pill bottles Caleb had left in plain sight and easy reach.

"I will be fine as soon as Laudae Sissy returns and we return Lady Marissa to Harmony's womb."

"We cannot wait for her return to address the offer of peace and alliance with the CSS," Nentares said. "Their fleet waits just beyond the frontier. A word from you and they will assist against any further incursions by the Marils."

"I cannot authorize that without full agreement from the HC. Laudae Sissy still has veto power over such drastic action."

"Is Lord Lukan more agreeable than his mother?" Armstrong asked.

"Yes." He'd better be.

"Then start persuading Laudae Sissy. We can't wait beyond the end of tomorrow to send the message. Tonight would be better," Nentares said.

✦   ✦   ✦

Jake burst out of hyperspace blasting identity codes on all Harmony frequencies as well as CSS modulations. His anonymous little solo merchant craft bucked and shuddered hard enough to rattle his teeth.

"I don't like these transitions any better than you do, brat," he coaxed the vessel.

He fought off the last hyperspace disorientation and sleepy drugs as he scanned the spacescape for signs of someone friendly. He'd used the drugs because he couldn't risk a visitation from the ghosts of all the people he'd killed on Harmony. He had to sleep through hyperspace, no matter how dangerous that was on a solo mission.

Staying awake was more dangerous to his sanity.

"Confirm identity," a bored female voice blasted back at him. At least she spoke in the familiar accent of a native-born Earther.

Jake breathed a sigh of relief and re-sent the codes Pammy had given him oh those many months ago when he left SB3 and civilization. Right at the edge of sensor range he caught a blip that resolved into a massive battle wagon bristling with weaponry.

"Those codes are six months out of date," the female said with a little more interest.

"Warning. CSS Battleship Nobotov has locked on automatic targeting system. Warning," the sensor display blinked at him with ominous red letters.

"Nobotov, please back off on the weapons display. All I've got is a little asteroid blaster on my bow," Jake requested. He wanted to scream in frustration. Little Miss Bored and Anonymous in communications might take that as a threat and decide to liven up her day a bit.

"What else you got hidden inside?" a male voice asked. Probably a weapons officer.

"Nothing but a Badger Metal sword, dagger, two boot knives, and a brace of wrist stilettos," Jake replied. He didn't mention the nasty little serrated throwing stars at the small of his back or the black crystal in his pocket. He might need a few surprises.

"Where you been, Harmony?" the weapons officer chuckled.

Jake could picture the guy running deeper sensor scans looking for signs of anything more lethal. All the while the two spacecraft crept toward each other at ten thousand klicks a second.

"Run my codes past Pamela Marella," Jake said. Time to stop dancing around each other and start seriously negotiating getting Jake aboard that vessel. Alive.

"Admiral Marella is not available," Communications replied again.

"Admiral?" Jake put aside his amusement that Pammy would actually have a normal identity to cover her existence as the spymaster. She'd always insisted, to him at least, that she was civilian through and through. Somewhere in his foggy brain he had to have an emergency code.

Something about spring flowers. No an older quote. Something so archaic it came back into fashion least once a generation.

"A rose by any other name looks like a daisy." No that wasn't it. Ah, "A rose by any other name is still a rose." And Lieutenant Colonel Jeremiah Devlin was at heart Major Jake Hannigan. Or was he Jacob da Jacob pa Crystal Temple HPS Bodyguard?

He wasn't sure anymore who he was. Only that he was alone and missing Sissy.

"Admiral Marella sends her greetings. Opening docking bay five for you Lieutenant Colonel. Please remain inside your craft for decontamination and await escort to the captain's ready room."

"I need to debrief. Got anyone aboard with a security clearance alpha alpha alpha?"

The female whistled. A long pause. "Captain says you'll have to wait for Admiral Marella to arrive. About twelve hours."

"Good. I need to clean up and get some sleep." And have a medic remove his caste mark and Pammy's nanobots. He was tired of looking like a Nordic god. He wanted to be plain Jake again. Though his face would look mighty naked without the red square encircled with purple.

Briefly he wondered how he would identify people without caste marks? Should he salute or bow to a superior?

Did any of it matter if he never got to see Sissy again?

CHAPTER SIXTY-FIVE

"**T**ELL LAUD GREGOR THAT I refuse to preside at the funeral of Lady Marissa," Sissy told Penelope. She returned her attention to the alien skeleton laid out upon the altar inside the burial cave.

Interesting that the aliens placed their dead in a fetal position, as if truly returning to the womb. Humans laid their dead straight, as if they merely slept.

She'd learned a lot about bones these past months. With a little time to think, she could assemble one from scattered fragments, and had done so several times.

But this alien puzzled her. It didn't fit the pattern of either the humans or the other aliens she'd encountered.

"The people are expecting you, Sissy. The media have already reported your return to the city," Penelope replied. She kept her hands close to her sides and her eyes carefully averted from the bones.

"You look pale, Penelope. Are you all right?" Sissy reach a concerned hand to the woman's arm.

Penelope shied away from her touch. "How can you . . . how can you abide to touch those things?" She shuddered and backed up three steps toward the entrance.

"I have learned to revere them."

"I . . . I'm not supposed to leave without you," Penelope said, looking over her shoulder longingly toward the exit.

"I cannot preside at the funeral of the woman who tried to kill me. She slaughtered my entire family, wiped them out except for the two youngest. She murdered my friend Shanet and *your* daughter as well. I cannot forgive her, even in death. She deserved execution, alone and unloved at the mercy of a machine, not a peaceful heart attack at home within the bosom of *her* family."

Penelope hung her head. "She was good to me when I was a child and my mother ignored me, like a proper Temple."

"She murdered your daughter."

"You are right. She does not deserve a state funeral, but Laud Gregor has ordered it. We must obey."

"I refuse. And I urge all other Temple caste to refuse as well. Let him preside by himself. I will return afterward for the opening of the High Altar. Not before. Not in time for his display of pomp and circumstance." Sissy loved that phrase. Jake had taught her that one. It described Gregor so well. "After the funeral, I will convene the HC. We must address the matter of possible invasion and the CSS offer of peace."

"I will convey your message. I think that since I am ordered not to return without you that I, too, must delay until after the funeral." Penelope flashed Sissy a conspiratorial grin. "But I cannot remain in this cave a moment longer."

Sissy let her go. The welcoming silence enfolded her. External silence while she tried again to decode the whispering bells in her head. She knew the sound akin to the murmurs a baby heard while still in its mother's womb. Surely Mother Harmony was trying to communicate with her here in the womb of all life.

If only Harmony would give her a vision, a prophecy, something to explain or enlighten. But there were only the constant annoying half-heard conversations in her head.

✦   ✦   ✦

Gregor counted the ten hover cams scattered around the forecourt. All precisely as he had ordered them placed. They each had a good, but not complete view of the back of the altar. Only he and Sissy would know how to operate the hidden mechanism.

He had the archivist to thank for finding the ritual to open the altar. But he'd had to put up with more admonitions about being slackard in waiting so long.

Temple and Noble caste marks filled the first rank of observers. Beyond them Professionals and Military crowded close, pushing and shoving for a better view.

The respectful murmurs of the crowd had risen to a crescendo of impatience. And now it verged on angry.

He'd had enough of angry crowds these past few weeks. If they only knew what he'd done to end this crisis, they'd bow down and worship him.

Didn't they know how much pride he'd sacrificed in getting Sissy to come back to the capital? Then she'd had the audacity to humiliate him further by refusing to show up for the state funeral! Now she made him wait again, until the last vestiges of funeral music had died away, the casket was carted off to the crematorium, and the remnants of black ribbons cleaned up, and the black crystal removed from the altar before she graced the audience with her presence.

"Enough," Gregor said. He signaled the cameras to begin recording, took his wand from his sleeve and tapped out a rapid sequence that demanded silence and attention from the crowd.

The noise faded as the chimes echoed around the courtyard swelling and circling. Shuffling feet calmed. Expectant eyes looked up to him, then shifted attention over his right shoulder.

Damn the woman! He knew without looking that Sissy had waited for this precise moment to emerge from the tunnel into the Temple forecourt.

A little gasp of awe rippled through the crowd at her resplendent purple and black robes and her full veil of black and purple crystals.

And bare feet.

She held up both hands in blessing as she almost floated to her place at his side.

"About time you showed up," he hissed out the side of his mouth.

"The HPS is never late. Whatever time she arrives is precisely the proper time," Penelope whispered back to him.

"Penelope?" Discord! What was she doing in Sissy's robes and veil.

"Laudae Sissy is in your office reading and comparing *every* copy of the Covenant. You only sent the latest version to her." As she spoke, Penelope took her own wand and tapped out the opening sequence required for every High Ritual.

The crystals chimed dully. She just didn't have Sissy's gift for making them sing in perfect harmony with the rest of the universe.

"You always insisted upon avoiding a cult of personality among the priesthood. I'm here as part of a normal rotation," Penelope said smugly.

Then she proceeded with the ritual with polished grace, but no flare, and not a single deviation from the plan, not even when the crystals seemed to demand a different sequence to sound truly magnificent.

Sissy would have pursued the magnificent.

That was one of the reasons the people loved her. She lived her relationship with Harmony and the crystals. Her spirituality was a natural mantle that she shared with everyone she met.

As a High Priestess should.

Heaving a sigh, Gregor concluded the ritual invoking the presence of all the gods and asking their blessing upon their actions, to renew the Covenant in a spirit of Harmony, banishing Discord, Uniting all the people of the empire in a good and trusting dependence upon each other, each caste fulfilling its place within the whole.

With a flourish Gregor placed each of the altar crystals in a designated place within the tile mosaic around the High Altar. He tried not to grunt with the effort of lifting the big ones. Sweat popped out on his brow and his face flushed. Thankfully his veil hid his discomfort. When each crystal nestled into the design, Penelope brought forth seven fat candles, each a different color and length, and placed them into recesses at specific intervals away from the crystals.

Acolytes brought them lighted tapers. Together, they set flame to wicks, jointly bringing the last and largest candle to life at the center.

Light sprang outward, bounced off the crystal support columns. Gregor and Penelope together awakened the largest crystal with their wands. The matrix within the columns began to vibrate, setting up a hum almost below hearing that filled Gregor's head with the sense of the gods whispering to him in code.

Could Sissy interpret those whispers?

Nonsense. Only his imagination borne of too little sleep and too many digestive tablets.

The light returned to the altar, bounced again. A new note was added to the hum, making it more like a chorus of murmurs. Half-heard whispers he needed to decode but couldn't, not quite . . .

Then the shafts of sparkles hit the standing crystals. More notes. More voices. The courtyard filled with a wondrous, heavenly sound.

The crowd opened their throats, mimicking the sounds in joy.

Another bounce of light on a new trajectory. This time the brightly colored individual shafts joined and focused on a single point at the base of the High Altar.

The crowd gasped at the wondrous display. They pressed closer, eager to be a part of the wonder.

Mechanisms groaned, set into motion after too many centuries of disuse.

The magnificent hymn of crystal light continued, building to a climax.

Tension mounted among the spectators.

Gregor held his breath.

A click of a lock, almost obscured by the singing crystals.

The High Altar glided forward three feet and stopped on the edge of the dais.

Absolute silence filled the courtyard.

But the beautiful music echoed inside Gregor's head, whispering to him, enticing him forward with promises of new delights hidden from mortal view for centuries.

He released the pent-up breath from his lungs.

Penelope slipped her hand into his. "Shall we explore together . . . Dad?"

A bubble popped inside Gregor. Penelope's tentative reaching out to him as a relative, a member of a family, jarred every principle he held. Temple caste didn't need blood relations.

He dropped her hand and strode forward, down the steps revealed beneath the altar. Penelope and two hover cams followed him. Each step lit up as he trod downward. Soft blue light that should have soothed him caught on the facets of his veil beads and shot searing arrows into his eyes.

The stairs wound down and down again. No railing to ease his sense of vertigo.

The susurrations of sound continued, demanding attention, distorting reality.

The smell of stale air clawed at his nose and throat. That suited his mood better. He felt the walls closing in on him. If Penelope and the hover cams weren't treading on his heels, he'd turn and bolt for fresh air and openness. He could always claim the cavern empty, the original Covenant lost.

He hesitated.

Penelope prodded his back sharply. "You can't turn back now, Dad. Not ever," she whispered.

His balance tilted and he felt his blood pressure rise. He had to shoot his arms sideways to center himself. Once his feet steadied, he removed the veil. Better. His eyes adjusted to the dimness and he continued downward, keeping his gaze upon his feet and not the depth of the well of darkness around him.

And abruptly there were no more steps. Seven stone tablets arrayed around the walls of a seven-sided room.

The first words engraved upon the tablet directly in front of him froze his blood and shriveled his sense of self.

CHAPTER SIXTY-SIX

SISSY STARED AT THE SEVEN stone tablets propped up around and behind the altar in the largest indoor chapel of Crystal Temple. Workers still dusted them off, carefully not looking at them too closely.

She, on the other hand, read each poetic phrase with avid curiosity. She checked the wording against later copies, adding things to a chart on a huge eraser board. She'd chronicled and graphed every change made to the Covenant over the last three hundred years, amazed at how close and yet how far the spirit of those changes had taken the people of Harmony.

All of the High Priests and High Priestesses who came before her had a lot to answer for.

In her heart she thanked Jake for teaching her how to recognize the patterns of words and phrases, sound them out and memorize them so that next time she read them she didn't stumble and question their meaning. She hoped he understood the depth of her gratitude to him for everything he'd done for her.

Perhaps it was for the best that she'd banished him so abruptly. She didn't want him caught up in the quake storm she was about to create. She would most likely have to forfeit her life for the sake of the Covenant. At least she could die with a peaceful heart knowing that she had brought the people of Harmony back into the true spirit of the Covenant.

A better death than chained to a bed in a filthy Asylum.

Artificial caste system aside, her faith and that of the founders provided a beautiful anchor and guide to everyday life.

But, oh, a few moments of Jake's insight into politics would help her immensely.

At last she took a deep breath and clapped her hands. Sarah and Bella popped up to answer her summons. "Open the doors and tell the High Council they may convene here."

The two girls bounced off on their important errand. Quickly, Sissy arrayed the remaining four girls between tablets and instructed them to point out specific phrases to the HC as she mentioned them.

Gregor stormed in. The scowl on his face seemed a permanent fixture. One by one, the five Nobles trailed in behind him, puzzled and cautious.

"Please take seats," Sissy instructed them. "We may be here a while."

"About time we got back to business, Laudae," Lord Chauncey wheezed. "Do you know how much money I lost with my factories shut down? A lot of work piled up while you went off in a pout." He plopped down in one of the hard chairs in the front row. A Worker hurried to stuff cushions behind and beneath him.

"You lost no more money than you gained illegally by requiring full shifts on Holy Days." She fixed him with a glare that sent him blustering nonsense until he finally looked away, embarrassed.

"I find it interesting that the very first article of the Covenant our predecessors chose to change was the one highlighted on Tablet Five," Sissy began, fixing Laud Gregor with a stern gaze.

Mary flashed a small portable torch on the words at the top of the tablet.

"The Temple and Noble castes are ordained to make and fulfill all the laws of Harmony. In no case should they consider themselves above those laws," she said angrily.

"That's not what it says," Lord Nathaniel objected.

"Get closer and read it directly for yourself, My Lord," Sissy ordered.

"I'm not well enough, bring it to me. Better yet make a fair copy on paper. More legible, easier to handle."

"That is how this whole mess started. Making copies, changing inconvenient phrases as we went along. No one has consulted the originals, only the most recent copy," Sissy snarled. "Hoist your lazy body out of that chair and read it. Out loud so that all of us have confirmation that you understand it."

Startled gasps from all of them.

"Laudae Sissy, you have no right . . ." Gregor admonished.

"I have every right. Tablet Two, paragraph three. 'The High Priestess presides over and commands the High Council. Her vote outweighs all of the other members so that the laws and governance of Harmony may stay on a true and spiritual path.' "

That shut them up for a moment.

"All of us, including our predecessors have forgotten that with great power comes great responsibility," she continued, cutting off the deep breaths they drew just before shouting arguments.

"Temple has always kept the needs of the people in the forefront," Gregor said. He preened in a self-righteous pose.

"Since we were among the first to break the Covenant, I don't think we have looked beyond our own wants very often," Sissy replied.

"How so?" Lord Lukan, the newest member asked. At least thirty years younger than any of the other Nobles, he seemed the only one interested in doing anything beyond protecting his perceived privileges.

"Tablet One in seven paragraphs, outlines the duties of each caste. Interesting that the seventh caste is the media, independent of all the others, and there is no mention of the poor, but that is another issue. At the end of the description of Temple responsibilities is the reminder that we must set a moral example for all of the castes, including loyalty and fidelity to our spouses. Each ordained member of the Temple caste is expected to marry and beget children only within that marriage. We should love and respect our spouses and teach our children by example." She glared at Gregor.

At the back of the chapel, Penelope and Guilliam joined hands. Gently he raised them to kiss the back of her wrist.

"About the only article of the Covenant we haven't ignored, changed, or destroyed is the separation of castes," Sissy continued. "And that is the one that should be reevaluated, given the prospect of invasion and the need to work together in our own defense." She wanted to shatter the system, grind it to dust, and make certain everyone forgot it.

Not yet.

"I knew we should never have allowed you to elevate this Lood, Gregor," Chauncey muttered. "You said you could control her."

"The matter of Loods is addressed in the much more recent copy of the Covenant," Sissy said. She nodded to Sharan. The little girl took a long pointer to the chart on the white board. "Prior to fifty years ago caste mark anomalies were rare and quickly corrected medically. But when they jumped to ten percent of all births, the people and the HC panicked. Rather than dealing with the problem they decided to hide it. Deride it. Taint it." Again words that Jake had taught her.

She owed him so much . . .

"Do you realize how much maintaining the asylums costs?" Lord Lukan asked quietly. "If we didn't have to feed, clothe, sedate, and confine one hundred thousand Loods in Harmony City alone, we could put a lot more money into building up the fleet, expanding our trade network, and improving rotting roads, bridges, sewer systems."

"We can't allow trade beyond the empire," Lord Nathaniel protested. "It's forbidden."

"No, it is not," Sissy said quietly.

The Nobles continued arguing among themselves, shouting down Lord Lukan's logic.

"Shut up!" Sissy shouted. "Do you even listen to yourselves?"

They stared back at her, shocked into silence.

"Tablet Seven, paragraph seven: In our need to separate ourselves to construct a more harmonious and organized society, we must never forget our roots in humanity on Earth." She choked on that one. "We have found the home of our gods and settle here to find union with them. It is our duty and privilege to invite our cousins to learn from us and earn Harmony by our example."

Absolute silence followed her reading.

"My Lords and My Ladies, My Lauds and My Laudaes, the time has come to send an ambassador to the Confederated Star Systems to negotiate peace and alliance," Laud Gregor broke the silence, his words hesitant and soft. "We need not join them. We need only talk to them. Admiral Nentares is standing by to send a message. It must be sent now. The enemy has broken through our defenses in massive numbers and speeds toward H6 as we speak."

CHAPTER SIXTY-SEVEN

"SEVENTY-SIX, SEVENTY-SEVEN, ELEVEN times seven." Jake counted chin-ups on the bar in the closet of the cabin Security had given him. Should he try for a set of twelve? Why not?

Not much else to do while he waited for Pammy to take her sweet time getting here. He'd paced out the four meters by three meters dimensions one hundred forty-seven times, twenty-one times seven. He tried snoozing on the narrow bunk. The whisker-thin mattress didn't fit his back any better than the length fit his body. He couldn't get comfortable with his feet and arms dangling and his back counting the webbing of the frame.

The hatch swung outward.

Finally.

Jake kept up his exercise, committed to the eighty-four chin-ups after ninety-one push-ups and ninety-eight jumping jacks.

Admiral Pamela Marella stomped into the cabin, homing in on the computer terminal built into the wall by the chair like a fully armed plasma missile. She'd trimmed down a bit to fit into the dark blue uniform resplendent with gold buttons and braid.

"Eighty-two, eighty-three," Jake continued, as if uninterested in Pammy's theatrics. Or her lush figure.

"Is this real, Jake?"

"Eighty-four." Should he go for ninety-one just to piss her off?

"Lieutenant Colonel Jeremiah Devlin, answer me. This is important." She held her hands on her hips and tapped her foot.

"Eighty-nine, ninety, ninety-one. Is what real?" He dropped down from the bar and looked at her rather than the terminal. Seven months on Harmony and he'd almost forgotten about easy access to data, news, and entertainment.

"This communiqué from Harmony." Pammy continued tapping her foot while she pointed to the screen.

"No 'Hello. Hi, how are you?' No 'Nice to see you, Jake?' No 'Glad you made it out alive, Jake?' " Impishly, he kissed her cheek and kept his eyes respectfully away from the screen.

"Cut that out, Jake. I haven't time for your nonsense. Read the damn letter from High Priestess Sissy. What kind of name is Sissy? Shouldn't a High Priestess have a more elegant name?"

"They tried that. Didn't work. Sissy is . . . Sissy. Quite a gal. You have a lot in common." Jake slouched into the chair and pulled it close to the wall terminal. A facsimile of Sissy's neat but blocky handwriting stared back at him.

He gulped with a sudden, intense longing to be at her side, see her face, hear her speak these words. After several minutes of staring at the words without reading them, he gulped and forced himself to comprehend each carefully chosen word. He had to hunt for the scroll button when he came to the end of the screen. A film of moisture seemed to have covered his eyes and blocked his vision.

"Well?"

"Let me reexamine it. The phrasing is right. So is the handwriting. But those can be imitated." At last he found the down command and touched it gently. The words scrolled past slowly, adding one new line to the bottom while the top ate previous text.

"Hurry up, Jake. The Marils broke through Harmony's perimeter ten hours ago. They are poised and ready to absorb Harmony Six. If we don't come to their aid within minutes, it will be too late. We'll lose them and the Badger Metal." Pammy paced now. Her face a series of worry lines.

Jake read the last line. An offer of peace and trade. So many tons of Badger Metal in return for assistance against the Marils. So many loads of fresh grain for mass energy systems. So many troops and ships if the Marils should attack the CSS. But at no point did the offer allow more contact than a single diplomatic delegation to meet with CSS diplomats at a neutral location.

He sat back to think about the offer. It had Sissy's sensibility written into it as well as Gregor's caution.

He fingered the black crystal still in his pocket. Slowly, reluctantly he handed it to Pammy.

"In the next round of negotiations, offer to double the fleet and armaments in return for enough of these to anchor the nav systems in our entire fleet. Laudae Sissy should be able to figure out a way for the crystals to talk to each other and . . . and give us some advantage in avoiding hits in combat—like the Maril avian communication."

Pammy whistled in amazement as she turned the crystal over and over, letting the blanket lighting in the ceiling catch the facets. "Is this what I think it is?"

"You bet your sweet titties it is."

"I think you just earned another promotion and a fat bonus, Jake."

The screen kept scrolling. He thought he'd read the last of it. The computer thought otherwise.

Then at the very bottom a single line of tiny letters. "Remember Milton and Godfrey. I remember Jilly." He read those words out loud.

"That makes no sense at all," Pammy said.

"Unless Laudae Sissy knew I'd be reading this," Jake laughed.

"Who are Milton and Godfrey? And what is a Jilly? We've run the names through every database we can think of and nowhere do they show up together related to Harmony."

"Except in Laudae Sissy's menagerie. Godfrey is . . . was an exotic lizard, maimed. She rescued it, nurtured it. It adored her and loved sitting in her lap." Settled for Jake's when he had to. "Milton is her pet weasel. I guess it's a weasel, something like a ferret native to Harmony and survived terraforming. Anyway, the two never got along, natural enemies, predator and prey, except in Sissy's company. She makes everyone get along just by being . . . Sissy."

"And Jilly?"

He couldn't answer that. Not without choking into uncontrollable sobs.

"A prophetess," he said simply.

"Then this is real?"

"Very real. And very important. Send your fleet to the rescue and name your diplomats to meet theirs. Just make sure I'm part of the entourage."

"You can bet on that, Jake, my boy. Get a shower, I'll meet you in the mess cabin to debrief you in twenty minutes."

"Don't you want a place more private than the mess of a battleship to hear my story?"

"No place more private than a crowded and noisy mess cabin. No one can overhear us and listening devices would be overloaded." She stomped out, no more gently than she'd arrived.

"Reminds me of a solar flare," Jake muttered. "Yeah, she and Sissy have a lot in common."

✦   ✦   ✦

"You do not have to go, Lord Lukan," Gregor said. He placed a fatherly hand upon the younger man's shoulder. "Your twin brother has equal rank and authority."

"Bevan has less liking for compromise than I do," Lukan smiled to himself. "He and you will be more comfortable with him sitting on the HC than me."

Gregor frowned, not wanting to admit that he agreed.

"My brother cannot bring himself to speak to our barefaced comrades of the CSS. They are all Loods to him, and beneath a right to exist."

"An attitude all too common among our people," Gregor admitted.

"Having Laudae Sissy read a few lines of the Covenant to the people every Holy Day will help." Lukan looked longingly over his shoulder toward the waiting Spacer shuttle craft. "We need to go."

Lord Bevan, his mirror image turned his back on the Spacer captain who signaled the craft was ready to take Lord Lukan and his entourage to the vessel waiting for them in orbit.

The large number of people who had assembled to see the historic mission launched shuffled about. Laudae Sissy stood beside Gregor, silent and disapproving as ever. She, like every other Temple, wore a full array of robes and headdresses. All anonymous even down to their bare feet. Gregor had only height and relative build to distinguish any of them. Padded shoulders and wide drapes camouflaged much. All of the women and most of the men clung to the funereal black of official mourning.

The time had long since passed when Sissy should have let go of her grief for her family. She'd had time. Her family had all had respectful funerals. She'd had a grief blessing. Gregor did not understand why she wanted to cling to the destructive emotion. They had work to do, keeping the people calm in the middle of tremendous change.

One change he refused to accept was marriage within Temple. For that reason he had chosen Penelope and her acolytes to accompany Lord Lukan.

Even now she and Guilliam stood apart from the rest, heads bent close, hands clasped desperately.

Disgusting.

Penelope, at least, wore shoes.

"My brother will help you ease the changes into our civilization slowly," Lukan said quietly, as if he'd read Gregor's mind. "Very slowly."

Another shuffling of people as Lukan's assistants and servants loaded luggage and themselves into the waiting shuttle.

Sissy's dogs hopped in and out of the vessel, racing from her to Penelope and back to the shuttle.

Then a surge of young people across the wide stretch of pavement as all of the acolytes pushed forward to help Penelope's six girls in. Her oldest had accepted ordination to fill the vacancy left by Shanet. Penelope had not replaced her, keeping the symmetry of seven.

Guilliam escorted Penelope to the gaping hatch and reluctantly let go of her hand.

Lastly, Lukan took his place. The doors closed. The engines roared and the shuttle lifted free of Harmony's gravity.

Sissy raised her hands to lead those left behind in a prayer of farewell.

Only Penelope's voice came from beneath the veil, not Sissy's.

Gregor started running. "Call them back!" he yelled at anyone and everyone. "We have to stop them."

"Too late, My Laud," Guilliam held him back. "This was her wish."

"She said there was nothing left on Harmony to hold her," Penelope added. "Harmony stopped speaking to her. She has to search to find a new connection to the Universe."

"Out there," Guilliam finished.

They both sounded so terribly smug and satisfied.

Gregor sank down, deflated and defeated. "She tricked me. You all tricked me."

"We did what we had to do, My Laud," Penelope said. "We did as Harmony's avatar commanded."

"We can't tell anyone. The people will rebel if they know she has deserted them."

"That knowledge, like the changes to our Covenant will come slowly, bit by bit," Guilliam mused. "We begin by abolishing the asylums and fixing those with broken caste marks. As Laudae Sissy commanded."

"Then we integrate the schools," Penelope added.

"We begin by putting the tablets back in their crypt," Gregor snarled. "Laudae Sissy is gone. I am in charge now. She can't override my decisions anymore."

"She may be gone, but she still has influence. And she will never be forgotten," Penelope and Guilliam reminded him, together, in one unified voice.

"Mama?" One of Penelope's acolytes tugged at her sleeve. "We don't feel right." She and another acolyte of the same size removed their headdresses. Twins. Mirror images of each other.

"What's wrong, sweetie?" Guilliam lifted the girl who had spoken into his arms.

Penelope crouched down and wrapped her arms about the other one.

Both girls grew rigid and still. Their eyes lost focus and turned silver. Oh, no! Not again.

"Harmony becomes elusive," Guilliam's charge said.

"Harmony changes paths," Penelope's continued in the same voice without pause. As if they spoke as one being.

"Harmony's path is no longer straight."

"It leads where we do not expect along twisted and obscure avenues."

The ground beneath them shook and quivered. The buildings around them began to sway.

The girls began to sing.

CHAPTER SIXTY-EIGHT

SISSY MADE THE ROUNDS OF sleeping children in her care, six acolytes plus her youngest brother and sister. She kissed each in turn and tucked light blankets around them. Then she checked their nul-g straps that would keep them in bed if the artificial gravity failed. All secure.

The animals twitched in their crates secured to the floor and the walls. Some of them slept. Some of them fought the sleepy drugs.

A soft chime, not much louder than the ringing in her ears, came through the spaceship's communication system. "Hyperspace in two minutes." A soft feminine voice followed the bell. "Please inject sleep inducers now for full effect before hyperspace."

Sissy had given the children their shots only moments before. They'd fallen asleep within seconds. Only an antidote would wake them in less than twenty-four hours.

She returned to her own cabin, adjacent to the children's room. A hard narrow bed that folded against the wall during waking time awaited her.

The warning bell came again, louder this time, as she pulled the nul-g strap diagonally across her chest. "Hyperspace in one minute. Inject sleep inducers now." The voice became imperative, almost strident.

Sissy put her hand in the stationary glove and poised her free hand over the plunger. A long moment of hesitation.

The sterile ship felt empty and inanimate, more so than any structure on Harmony. The Host of Seven infused life into the stones and timber of every building and object made from Harmony's raw materials. Even the metal cars and paved roads had come from Harmony and vibrated minutely in sympathy with Her.

Out here in the nothingness of space, Sissy's body and mind felt empty, devoid of tune. She needed to find a way to connect to the universe beyond Harmony, to make it as much a part of her as her home.

How could she do that if she was drugged to insensibility?

Gently she withdrew her hand from the injection glove and sat back in her bunk, legs folded beneath her, spine against the metal wall that separated her cabin from the children's.

Angry bells that jangled her nerves and hurt her ears sounded throughout the ship. "Warning, hyperspace in seven seconds. Six, five . . ."

Sissy forced herself to keep her eyes open through the countdown. "Two, one."

The lights blinked off for the length of a heartbeat. They came back on in a softer hue, more blue than yellow. Sparkling lines shot across Sissy's vision, fracturing reality.

The constant noise in her head, that she'd almost learned to ignore, ceased abruptly.

The absolute silence frightened her. The last vestige of Harmony deserted her.

Her mind and soul emptied.

The cracks in her vision widened, opening to new realms, new perceptions.

And out of that crack stepped her mother.

"Mama," Sissy gasped, amazed that she looked just as she had last seen her, dressed in her favorite brown dress sprigged with tiny yellow flowers, a grease-stained apron tied around her plump form, flour dusting her sleeves and her face.

"Oh, Mama, I've missed you." Sissy opened her arms and tried to run to her mother. The nul-g strap held her firmly in place.

She ripped at it frantically, needing to feel her mother in her arms one more time.

"And what do you think you are trying to prove this time?" Stevie asked from right behind Mama. He held Anna's hand. His spouse cradled one hand beneath her swelling belly, emphasizing the precious new life that had ended with her own in the explosion.

The explosion.

Her family showed no signs of the devastating blast that had torn them limb from limb and pierced their bodies with deadly flying debris.

Papa stepped into Sissy's reality behind Stevie, followed by grandparents, uncles, aunts, another brother and sister. Shanet with her full entourage of seven, and finally little Jilly trailed in, too. The tiny ship's cabin filled with the ghostly presences of all those Sissy had lost.

Lost, never to regain.

They weren't real. They were ghosts. Figments of her imagination.

Tears slipped down her cheeks.

"What are you trying to prove?" Stevie repeated the question on all of their lips.

"I don't know. I just know that I have to go."

"Go where?" Mama asked gently.

Sissy shrugged, unable to speak or think coherently.

"Go where?" they all asked.

"Away. Away from Harmony. There is no Harmony left in me. The Goddess has deserted me. I have to go away to find Her again." There, she'd said it out loud. The thing that had eaten away at her since the explosion. Since discovering the truth about the origins of her people. Since reading the Covenant and knowing how far from it her people had strayed.

"Harmony is only as far away as you let Her be," Mama reminded her.

"I've lost everything, everyone I care about."

"What about Jake?"

"I forced him to leave. I cannot care for him. We are out of caste. He is not one of us."

"And yet you love him as one of your own."

"If we ever come together, I can never go home. Not until the caste system goes away completely. Not until prejudice against outsiders is totally forgotten."

"That will take generations," Stevie said. "Can you wait a lifetime to love again?"

"I've lost everything. I've lost Jake as well as all of you."

"We are only as far away as your memories, little 'un," Papa said.

"We are a part of you. You came from us. Someday you will return to us. But not until you recognize Harmony within you again," Stevie said.

Jilly stepped forward. Her eyes glazed with starshine. She looked directly at Sissy, and through her at the same time. "Did Harmony abandon you? Or did you abandon Harmony? Listen to the universe. Listen to your heart. They are one and the same." She blinked her eyes and they cleared. Then she wrinkled her nose just like she always did before telling a joke.

She stepped back behind the adults and faded back into the crack.

"What's the joke, Jilly? Find something funny for me to grab hold of."

The softest of giggles floated through the air. "The entire universe is a joke."

Mama giggled, too, as she stepped back into that other reality beyond Sissy's perceptions. One by one, they all disappeared until only Stevie remained. "Remember us, Sissy. Love us. Love Jake. Love the universe as you love us and it will love you back."

Then he, too, was gone.

The loud warning bells clanged. "End of hyperspace in seven minutes. Antidotes automatically administered in four minutes."

CHAPTER SIXTY-NINE

COLONEL (FULL BIRD COLONEL, NOT just an LC) Jeremiah Devlin, CSS diplomatic liaison to the Harmony delegation, tried to take a deep calming breath. His brand-new class A uniform constricted his chest and his throat. The artificial air of the space station tasted stale, despite the slight citrus essence added to make it seem more palatable.

He'd grown too used to the real thing on Harmony.

At least he'd stopped itching from Pammy's antidote nanobots. His body and coloring had returned to his normal neutral status. He felt shrunken without the added muscles. Bland with dark blond, straight hair instead of the bright yellow curls.

But he'd persuaded her to leave the caste mark, complete with the officer slash and the purple Lauding. Diminished, he could handle. A naked face he couldn't.

"You may have a new job, but never forget that your ass still belongs to me," Admiral Pamela Marella whispered beside him.

Not any more, Pammy. Not any more. I belong to the universe. And to Sissy.

Was Pamela Marella still smarting that he hadn't come to her bed, despite several vague and then very obvious invitations? He didn't care. The ship from Harmony would dock within minutes. He dared not hope he'd see Sissy again. At best, he might hear her voice in a carefully worded and coded message.

Anything, any contact at all was better than the emptiness in his heart and his gut.

"Why meet them here on Labyrinthe Seven Space Station, Admiral Marella? These people are going to have enough trouble dealing with us barefaced humans. A station filled with aliens may just send them running."

"Neutral territory. The First Contact Café is privately owned." She gave the human nickname for the giant station poised at the intersection of a whole bunch of crossroads across this sector of space.

"And," she continued, "this is just a substation of the original. Only four different species allowed. They all have to keep to their own atmosphere specific wings. These seven arms of the station are leased indefinitely and jointly to the CSS and Harmony. Three for us, three for them, and one for meeting rooms and communications. No aliens allowed without invitation, not even the owner, or any of her alien children," she explained.

"We need our own planet for Headquarters. Not a tin can with spaghetti sticking out of its sides." That's what the station looked like from space. Each one of those strands of spaghetti was over three kilometers long and half that in width. Only a third of the arms were occupied at the moment, waiting for new expansion in this sector.

The entire rig rotated at tremendous speeds to generate gravity, heavier at the ends of the arms, nul-g at the center where the transport pods ran.

Somewhere in another wing, A'bner Labyrinthe, owner of the station—or one of her daughters, no one could tell the difference—controlled atmosphere and pressure to suit the different species. Little mingling among species at any of the seven First Contact Cafés. A'bner herself handled most cross-species and cross-language negotiations.

But not this one. This was Jake's party, even if he wasn't head of the delegation.

"We're looking for a home for the Confederation," Pammy reassured him. "But habitable planets in neutral territory that no one else already occupies are few and far between. Then once we find a place we have to build. Give us another year."

"By that time we'll have hammered out the details of an alliance with Harmony," Admiral (retired) Telvino, the new CSS ambassador to the Harmony Delegation said from Jake's other side. He didn't look any more comfortable in his civilian suit than Jake felt in his uniform.

"Always thought there was something fishy about your death, Jake," he continued, staring at the bay doors where the Harmonites would appear quite soon. "Pammy may have given you a new identity and promotions, but you are my liaison now, not her spy. You stay out of the spy business from now on."

Jake raised his eyebrows at Pammy. Who outranked whom in this case? He'd have to wait and see how things developed. Quite possibly, his loyalty would land firmly beside Sissy and no one else. She outranked everyone.

Even if she never came here, Sissy was Harmony, and Harmony was Sissy. And Harmony was the spiritual center of the universe.

An enlisted man with communications markings on his uniform collar hastened forward, saluting in the general direction of all three of them so that no one was slighted.

Telvino returned the salute and accepted the flimsy proffered by the man. "A list of the delegation. You recognize any of these names, Jake? They all look like gobbledygook to me." He passed the sheet to Jake, barely glancing at it.

Jake instantly separated out first names, parental names, and locators. "Lord Lukan, their ambassador, is the son of Lady Marissa. Last I heard, he had succeeded his mother to the High Council. That makes him more than an ambassador, close to most senior Noble in the empire. The next five names are his assistants. I haven't met any of them."

"How can you tell?" Pammy read over his shoulder.

"First name, then the da or du indicates son of or daughter of the next name. Pa and pu, also masculine and feminine indicate who they work for, or where they are assigned. The five assistants all have Lord Lukan's name at the end with the addition of Labyrinthe Space Station. They will be Noble caste. Any Worker caste they bring with them as servants have only his name as their locator."

"What about these names, almost a separate list," Pammy pointed to a second column, equal to but separate from the Noble entourage, and just as lengthy.

"Temple caste. They've sent a highly ranked priestess from the Crystal Temple to oversee the negotiations, make sure any compromises don't stray from the spirit of the Covenant with Goddess Harmony." Jake's heart sank to his stomach. Laudae Penelope du Marilee, pu Crystal Temple/Labyrinthe Delegation. Her six acolytes and a passel of Worker attendants.

Not Sissy.

She hadn't come. She couldn't separate herself from Harmony.

He knew they could never be together, not as he longed for them to be.

He could only adore her from afar.

Now he wouldn't ever see her again.

He was almost sick to his stomach with disappointment.

A series of announcements over the comm system announced the arrival and docking of the big commercial transport from Harmony.

Jake and Telvino watched the proceedings with professional assessment from a large screen set into the wall beside the bay doors.

"Whew, she's big," Telvino whispered through his teeth.

"Luxury cruise ship designed for transporting Nobles around the empire. No discomfort or cramping allowed," Jake managed to say around the lump in his throat.

"Good pilot, hit the docking rig dead on first try," Telvino said, admiration verging on awe coloring his voice.

"Spacer caste. Born and bred to do nothing else. Probably the son, grandson, and great grandson of expert pilots. They cut their teeth on this kind of work," Jake explained.

They waited endless minutes while the rig locked on to exterior hatches, bays pressurized and matched atmospheres. Gauges on the side of the screen showed the progress of the invisible processes.

At last a soft bell indicated the bay doors ready to open.

A Noble, probably in his forties, with hair graying at the temples, pale skin, and bright blue eyes that matched his diamond caste mark stepped through first. He wore a formal robe of blue, not terribly different from priestly garb, subtle differences in cut and padding, more formfitting, less anonymous. No headdress or veil. With hands clasped in front of him he bowed slightly.

Telvino withdrew his outstretched hand and mimicked the bow, no deeper, no shallower. An equal greeting an equal.

Good move, Jake thought.

They introduced each other. Lukan brought forth his chief assistant, Garrin da Lukan pa Lukan/Labyrinthe Delegation.

"His son," Jake hissed into Telvino's ear.

More bows. Telvino introduced Jake.

Pammy seemed to have faded into the bulkheads like a good spy, unnoticed but observing.

Then a slender woman in formal purple-and-gold brocade robes with a full headdress and veil of purple and sparkling crystal beads, with no shoes, made her way to the front of the pack, followed by six young girls in similar but lighter garb.

"Laudae Penelope," Telvino said, bowing more deeply to her than he had to Lord Lukan.

A monster of a black dog broke free from the air lock and dashed forward. He barked and jumped at Jake, begging for pets. A brown mongrel followed along with a white puffball and a small gray yapper. They all demanded immediate and glorious attention.

Jake's entire being smiled in relief. He raised his eyes from hugging all four dogs at once and captured the gaze of the woman. He'd know this priestess anywhere. He'd know Sissy by her posture, her lightness of step, by her scent, by a dozen different ways. She could never hide from him. He gave up questioning why she was here, why she used Penelope's identity and kept her own hidden.

"Jake!" a little boy and his sister screamed and hurled themselves into his arms.

"Marsh. Ashel," he crowed in delight, swinging them around. He held them tight, drinking in their warmth, their scent, the feel of their little bodies trusting and loving him.

That confirmed it. Only Sissy would bring her brother and sister along with six acolytes and four dogs and who knew what other kinds of critters that hadn't debarked yet. He nodded and winked to the little girls.

He thought his swelling heart would burst with joy.

The girls bowed formally to him, then erupted into their own version of hugs, telling him all about the journey in a hurried babble he could barely decipher.

Sissy looked around, the crystals in her veil swinging and catching the light, sending out wild rainbows. "This place has no soul. We need to perform rituals to give it one. We must forge a new Path of Harmony on a proper note."

EPILOGUE

"**J**AKE," **SISSY WHISPERED.** She held her hand over his mouth so that he would not make noise when he wakened.

He opened his eyes, focusing immediately on her face, and smiled.

She pulled her hand away, fully aware that she no longer had a right to such an intimate touch, or to have slipped into his bedroom while the space station slept.

"What do you need, My Laudae?" he asked, equally quiet. He slept alone, but Sissy had learned long ago others could listen from afar.

"I need to send a message to Harmony. Lord Lukan has forbidden it. He says I'm no longer High Priestess since I deserted our home and I . . . I don't have visions anymore." She hung her head in shame, half believing the Noble.

"Sounds like Laud Gregor has been talking to him." Jake swung his legs over the side of the narrow bed without a yawn or stretch, ready to do her bidding once more. "We both know that Laud Gregor sometimes confuses what is best for him and what is best for Harmony."

"Can you do this for me, Jake? I need to tell the people of Harmony that I have not deserted or betrayed them. I have to tell them that I seek a return to the true path. They need to trust me."

"I know some people on the communications deck."

"I knew you would. It is CSS shift. Your people do not have to obey Lord Lukan." She scuttled backward and rose to her feet, giving him room to stand. His quarters were more cramped here than they had been at Crystal Temple. Hers were small too, but much bigger than this.

"CSS shift means Harmony frequencies are locked down. We can't talk to them without someone from Lord Lukan's delegation supervising." He frowned.

"Will this help?" She drew a black crystal from her pocket.

Jake grinned at her. "That should override any locks." Then he looked her up and down.

"No formal robes or headdress?" he asked, shrugging into a uniform jacket. His arms nearly touched the sides of the cabin.

"I don't want to be recognized in the corridors." She hung her head so that her hair covered her cast marks, and slouched her shoulders, reducing her height. The baggy brown Worker coveralls masked her shape.

"Tell you a secret, Laudae Sissy, you forgot your shoes. No one in space goes barefoot, except you." He leaned over and grinned, almost close enough to kiss her cheek.

"Maybe I'll start a new fashion." She flung back her hair and stood up straighter.

"You sure did back on Harmony. Come on." He took her hand and led her into the passageway. Then he checked in both directions for observers before heading for the lift at the center of the station. "We'll have to send the message live, no delay, no chance for someone to edit it to their advantage. Maybe you should send it direct to Little Johnny. He'll make sure it's broadcast properly."

"Jake, what do I say?" she whispered as they entered the nul-g section. She liked floating here, drifting in the air currents, free of restraints and responsibilities.

"Speak from the heart, Sissy. Just tell the people what is in your heart."

"Is that enough?"

"There is nothing else."

"It's just that they are so angry and afraid."

"Someone very smart reminded me that Anger, Fear, and Greed are Harmony's bastard stepchildren who need to stay in their place. Unity and Nurture balance them under the tutelage of their parents Harmony and Empathy." He grinned again.

"Yes, I remember that lesson for Holy Day School." She returned his smile. "Will that be enough?"

"If it isn't, then remind the empire that they take themselves far too seriously. The entire universe is a joke."

Jilly's words.

"Jake, where did you hear that?"

He stepped into a transport pod.

"Jake?"